THE GREEK'S
SECRET HEIR

REBECCA WINTERS

THE MARINE
MAKES AMENDS

VICTORIA PADE

MILLS & BOON

First Published in Great Britain 2020
by Mills & Boon, an imprint of HarperCollinsPublishers,
1 London Bridge Street, London, SE1 9GF

The Greek's Secret Heir © 2020 Rebecca Winters
The Marine Makes Amends © 2020 Victoria Pade

ISBN: 978-0-263-29896-3

0121

MIX
Paper from
responsible sources
FSC
FSC C007454

THE GREEK'S
SECRET HEIR

REBECCA WINTERS

To my darling children. They're so supportive,
I'm the luckiest mum in the world!

PROLOGUE

"Monika? I'm so hot I'm going for a quick swim before I'm burned to a crisp."

Her sandy-haired friend didn't open her eyes. "I'll join you in a few minutes."

Alexa Remis, almost eighteen, got up from one of the rental loungers set out along the semicrowded Perea Beach outside Salonica, otherwise called Thessaloniki, Greece. The August temperature had climbed to the high eighties, perfect for her three-week vacation before school started again on Cyprus, nearly a thousand miles away. This was only her second day of freedom from books and tests, but it would go too fast and she wanted to make the most of it.

After wading into a surreal world of turquoise water, she kept going until she could immerse herself in the deepening cobalt blue beyond. Talk about paradise! On impulse she did a series of somersaults and ended up colliding with a hard, male body who gripped her arms to steady her.

"I'm sorry!" she cried after lifting her head. Once he let go, Alexa had to tread water to stay afloat.

"It was my fault, *despinis*." The sincere apology,

spoken in Greek, came from the gorgeous guy staring straight into her eyes. In the afternoon sun she couldn't tell if his eyes were black or brown between those black lashes. "I'm Nico Angelis."

"I'm... Mara Titos." She'd almost made her first mistake by telling him her real name. Her grandfather was the Greek ambassador in Nicosia in Cyprus. For security reasons he and her grandmother had made her promise never to reveal who she really was to anyone while on vacation. With so much political unrest there, they didn't want Alexa to be a target for enemies.

Meeting this Adonis out swimming had thrown her off-balance. "Where did you come from, Nico?"

He pointed to a sleek white cruiser in the distance, revealing his well-defined chest. "My friends and I have been racing each other."

"And I ruined it for you by being in your way."

His gaze wandered over her, making her feel a voluptuous warmth that was completely different from the effect of the sun. "I didn't watch where I was going, but believe me, I'm not complaining about running into a beautiful mermaid. I didn't know they came with long chestnut hair and sea-green eyes." She smiled as he asked, "Do you live here?"

"No." *Remember what you're supposed to tell people, Alexa.* "I live in France with my mom, but am on vacation until school starts."

"You're a long way from home. I've just turned nineteen and must join the Greek navy in three weeks to do my military service."

They swam around each other. "Are you looking forward to it?"

"Not particularly. I'd much rather stay right here."

The comment sounded so personal her heart picked up speed. "How long will you have to be gone?"

"Two years." He studied her features, lingering on her lips. "At the moment a year sounds like a lifetime."

"One more year in a strict French schoolroom before college sounds like a lifetime to me too." After he chuckled, she heard voices in the distance coming from the cruiser. "I think your friends are calling to you." But Alexa didn't want their conversation to end.

"That's okay. They can wait. I have more pressing matters here." His compelling mouth broke out into a smile, turning her body to liquid. "What about you?"

Remember for security reasons that Monika has a different name too. "My cousin Leia is sunbathing. I'm staying with her and the Vasilakis family during my vacation."

"How long are you here for?"

"Three weeks."

"That's perfect. It gives us time to make some plans."

He had a masterful way about him that made her breathless. There was no guy in Europe or anywhere else who acted or looked like Nico. The dark hair plastered to his head reminded her of a copy of a statue of a young Emperor Augustus in the Archaeological Museum of Salonica she'd seen yesterday.

Monika's parents, the Gatakis, who'd only recently begun working at the embassy with Alexa's grandfather, kept a house here. They'd insisted the girls have one day of intellectual pursuits before hitting the beach for the rest of their holiday.

As far as Alexa was concerned, Nico, with his chiseled features and firm jaw, could have been a model and was so handsome, she couldn't take her eyes off him.

"What did you have in mind?" She knew she was being picked up. Other guys had tried. Before now she'd never been tempted to break her grandparents' rules, but this guy was different. She decided to go with it and see what happened.

"Tell your cousin you're swimming to the cruiser with me. I know a place along the coast where we can buy food and eat on deck while we get to know each other better. I'll bring you back before it gets too late. Wherever I'm stationed in the military, I'd like a happy memory to take with me."

That worked both ways. "What about your friends?"

"I'll drop them at the pier."

So it was Nico's boat. Alexa made a snap decision. "I'll swim to shore and let her know."

His smile faded. "If you don't come back, I'll know this meeting wasn't meant to be after all and you really are a mermaid who'll disappear on me."

Alexa took off for the beach, haunted by what he'd just said. She reached the lounger dripping wet and told Monika what had happened. "He's going to take me for a boat ride."

Her friend jumped to her feet. "Are you crazy? Don't you know who that is?" She sounded almost angry.

"Should I?"

"Nico Angelis is the only son of the billionaire Estefen Angelis, the famous Angelis Shipping Lines owner in Salonica. I've told you about him before."

Alexa didn't remember.

"Over the last year he's been in the news—he gets

around." At least Monika knew of him. Alexa's grandparents couldn't object to that. "There've been times
when he's played volleyball here on the beach with some
of his highbrow friends, picking up girls. He's the last
guy on earth you should ever get mixed up with."

Whoa. How could Alexa have known something like
that while she'd been living in Cyprus for so many
years with her grandparents? "He's still out there waiting for me."

Monika laughed. "You really think so with a line
like the one he just fed you? A mermaid? How naive
can you get."

Alexa felt foolish. "Maybe I am. But all the same, I'm
swimming back out." She hurried into the water once
more, wondering, fearing that he'd disappeared. Somehow the idea of never seeing him again disturbed her.

"Mara?"

He was still there. Alexa had almost forgotten that
was the name she'd given him. She had her answer and
knew she was going to spend the next few hours with
him no matter what Monika said.

"Nico!"

CHAPTER ONE

Nineteen years later

ON A WARM Saturday evening in June, thirty-eight-year-old Nico Angelis drove up to the front of the Papadakis mansion in Salonica. Nico was still trying to get over the pain of losing Tio Papadakis six months ago.

They'd met in the military and became best friends. Later, they'd each served as the other's best man at their weddings. But a dinner out last December had ended in tragedy for his friend.

Tio had been driving the car that had killed him and had put his wife Irena in a wheelchair with a bruised spine. It had taken her a month to be able to walk again without help and she still used her wheelchair sometimes. Until then she'd had a health caregiver who looked after her and provided the therapy she needed.

Since the accident Nico had tried to look in on Irena and her two sons once a week. He'd lost his wife years earlier and knew the pain Irena had to be in. Nico suffered survivor's guilt over the part he'd played in his own wife's death that couldn't be erased. He didn't think it would ever go away. To be able to help Irena by talking to her about Tio made him feel like he was doing something worthwhile.

Eleven years earlier his wife Raisa and their unborn child had been killed in a plane crash. Like Tio, Nico had been at the controls when the accident occurred. For an inexplicable reason, Nico and his copilot had escaped death.

Since then, Nico had plunged into his work to deal with his pain and put away thoughts that he didn't have a child to cherish. He'd wanted their baby more than anything in this world and had been so excited for its impending birth. A son or daughter to love would have meant everything to him, but it hadn't happened.

At least Irena had her boys. Nico envied Irena that blessing and had learned to love her sons like his own. Raisa's death was something no one could fix, but he could give Irena and her boys his love and support.

Two months ago Nico's father had stepped down as head of the Angelis Shipping Lines, owing to heart trouble. Nico, one of three vice presidents at the time, had been voted in as CEO of the corporation.

Their headquarters maintained the largest cargo shipping company in the Balkan hinterland and South-eastern Europe. The Angelis conglomerate also owned several manufacturing companies and the *Halkidiki News*, a newspaper servicing Northern Greece.

It had been managed by his uncle—the brother-in-law of Nico's mother—for over a decade. But he'd caused a scandal in the family and their father had promoted Nico's thirty-six-year-old sister Giannina to executive status at the newspaper to keep him under control.

Their uncle, who'd been born a Hellenian before becoming a Greek citizen, resented a woman having that kind of power and hadn't been making it easy for her. Nico was proud of how Giannina handled their uncle as she worked her way up in administration at the newspaper.

It pleased him that their father saw her potential to be a tour de force. Now, with the responsibility of the Angelis Shipping Lines falling on his shoulders, Nico had little time for anything else besides looking after his parents and of course Irena and her boys.

These days Nico commuted to headquarters in Salonica by helicopter from his villa in Sarti eighty-seven miles away. Tonight he was running late. The housekeeper Melia let him in and told him he'd find Irena and Kristos in the salon. Apparently her younger son Yanni was over at a friend's house.

"Nico, at last!" Irena cried and held out her arms to him. He hugged her. She'd been a redheaded beauty who'd claimed Tio's heart in his teens.

Kristos got up from the couch to give him a hug. "I was afraid you might not come, Uncle Nico." Her boys had called him that for years. They'd never know how much they meant to him.

"Sorry I'm late. Already I'm learning why I rarely saw my father growing up."

"He's paid a price for it," Irena interjected. "Don't let hard work cut your life short, Nico." She stopped there, unlike Giannina who would have said she feared he didn't have any other life now. His sister worried that he hadn't found another woman and she wouldn't let it go. Nico had been involved with several women from time to time, but he'd had it with love and commitment.

"I'm not planning on it," he muttered, looking at Irena with concern. "Have you been brooding again?"

"Yes. I miss Tio more than usual tonight."

Nico could relate. "Why is that?"

"Because of me," Kristos broke in. The handsome nineteen-year-old had grown tall like his father. Nico would have given anything for a son like him, but fate had stepped in once again the way it had done when he himself was nineteen, robbing him of any happiness for a long, long time.

"Isn't college going well for you?"

"That's not it. Mama's upset because I've met a girl and want to get engaged now. We're thinking a wedding at the end of August. By then the apartment we've settled on near the university will be free."

She shook her head. "It's way too soon for you to be so involved. Your life is only beginning, darling. I'm sure her mother would say the same thing. You need to wait several years at least. Your father would be in total agreement with me."

"That's not true, Mama. I've done my military service and have an important job in the family business. I can support us, and both our college classes are going along fine. It's not too soon. We're in love and don't want to wait."

Irena's eyes met Nico's, pleading with him to do something about this. He knew Tio's stubborn father was behind Irena's hesitation. The older man hadn't approved of Tio's marriage and was now interfering in his grandson's love life.

"What's her name, Kristos?"

"Dimitra Remis."

"Tell me about her."

His warm gray eyes lit up. "She's eighteen, smart and gorgeous."

Nico grinned. "Of course she is."

"She's barely eighteen," a troubled Irena informed him.

"Dimitra goes to the University of Salonica too, Uncle Nico. I can't begin to describe how wonderful she is."

Kristos was definitely smitten. "Tell me about her mother and father."

"Her parents are Greek. They fell in love. However, through unavoidable circumstances, they lost touch with each other and he disappeared from her mother's life before she ever knew she was pregnant."

"That's very sad." Nico thought about the unborn child he'd lost when Raisa had died. "It's tragic the man never knew he had a daughter."

"Dimitra always wanted to know him. That ache will never go away for her."

"Of course not," Nico murmured. Certain aches always remained, as Nico knew so well. His yearning to have a family of his own would always be there, but it hadn't been meant to be.

"I'm thankful I had nineteen years with Papa," Kristos broke in on Nico's thoughts. "But Dimitra has still had a wonderful life. Until last August she and her mother lived with her great-grandparents in Canada. He was the Greek ambassador in Ottawa before his retirement. Since coming back to Greece, they have a home here and her mother teaches on the faculty at the University of Salonica in the language department."

"That sounds impressive."

"You and Mama will love Dimitra. I've bought her an engagement ring she doesn't know about yet. Naturally I want to announce our engagement right away, but Mama wants us to wait."

Irena moved the wheelchair closer. "That's right, darling. You need time to do a little more living before making a decision that will change your life."

Kristos looked to Nico for the answer he wanted. "What do *you* say?"

It was like déjà vu for Nico who understood what it was like to be painfully, excruciatingly in love at that age and want to get married. But no commitment like that should be pursued at their tender age, as he had learned the hard way.

After Mara Tito had sent back all the letters Nico had written to her nineteen years ago, *unopened*, he'd gotten the message and had learned a bitter truth. The true love he'd thought they'd shared after three weeks of nonstop enchantment had only been on his part. It hadn't lasted for her. The longing to marry her and have children with her had been *his* dream, not hers.

The second he'd left to do his military service, she'd never thought about him again. He'd been a fool to think otherwise. When he and Tio had returned home a year later, she was nowhere to be found and untraceable. The phone number at the Vasilakis residence had been disconnected.

All the considerable resources at his disposal as an Angelis to do searches both here and in France had turned up literally nothing. After three difficult years of trying to forget her, he'd met Raisa Nephus and in time had married her.

When Nico thought of how happy Kristos was right now, it worried him that this girl he loved might not prove to love him with the same depth of passion. A real broken heart took years to get over, if ever...

"Uncle Nico?" Kristos prodded him.

Nico realized Irena's son was waiting to hear his view on the situation. While his friend lay dying in the hospital he'd promised Tio to look after Kristos and Yanni. Nico's first instinct was to tell Kristos he couldn't give him his blessing. To get engaged this soon could ruin the rest of his life. No one knew that better than Nico.

In time he'd learned to love Raisa enough to marry her, but it hadn't been like his feelings for Mara. Raisa had deserved more, and after she'd died in the plane he'd been flying, his guilt had intensified because he hadn't been able to save her or their baby she was carrying...

But his past life had nothing to do with Kristos. Nico and Irena needed to make a concession to her son so he wouldn't feel that the entire world had conspired against him.

"Tell you what, Kristos. Your birthday is coming up soon. Invite her over for an informal meal. I'll drop by at some point after work and you can introduce me. What do you think, Irena?" He darted her a speaking glance.

"We could do that," she said in an unenthusiastic voice, obviously deciding to go along with Nico's idea.

"Thank you, Mama! I'll call her and we'll pick a date that's good for everyone. I promise you two will love her." Kristos kissed his mother and hugged Nico before leaving the room.

Nico got to his feet. "I'm afraid I've let you down, Irena."

"No. You haven't. It was the perfect thing to say, otherwise he would have declared he and Dimitra were going to run away and get married. You've at least bought us a little more time to convince him to think about it."

"We can hope."

Deep down Nico didn't believe Kristos could be made to see reason, not if he loved this Dimitra the way Nico had loved Mara.

In time Raisa had taught him that there were different kinds of love. Though he'd never felt the fire for her he'd felt for Mara, he'd married Raisa. The excitement of a baby coming had brought him a whole new world to look forward to. Until her death they'd been thrilled at the thought of a son or daughter to complete their lives.

As for Kristos, hopefully Nico could reason with him to the point he wouldn't jump into anything too fast, but he wasn't holding his breath.

Alexa had already gotten under the covers when her brunette daughter tiptoed into her bedroom, letting light in from the hall. "Mama? Are you asleep?"

She chuckled. "I was getting there."

"Can we talk for a second?"

"Sure. Come sit on the bed. What's so important it can't wait until tomorrow?"

"Kristos has a birthday coming up. His mother has invited us to dinner so we can all meet." That *was* news.

"I've never met her or his younger brother. It's on Saturday, a week from today. You can come, right?" Her light green eyes implored Alexa to agree.

To meet the mother meant things were getting more serious between her daughter and the young man Alexa had met at the university a few months ago. She'd been introduced to him when Dimitra had brought him to her faculty office. They'd talked for a few minutes and she'd learned, among other things, that his father had died in a car accident in December.

Alexa had to admit he was good-looking with a definite charm and intelligence. But after falling in love with Nico Angelis at seventeen, their brief time together in Salonica had ended in total disaster. When he'd left for the military three weeks later, he'd never gotten in touch with her again.

Four years passed before Alexa learned the true reason why he'd disappeared from her life. Because of those four years of suffering, Alexa didn't want her daughter to be thinking marriage with Kristos. Not yet. They were both very young. If anything went wrong and Kristos ended up hurting her, she didn't want Dimitra to go through that same kind of grief as Alexa at such a tender age.

"I'll have to check my schedule at the university in case there's a dinner conflict."

"Surely you can get out of it. This dinner is important to me."

She sighed. "When you're young, everything's important."

"I love Kristos."

"You'll probably love several men before you find the right one for you."

"Even if it didn't last, you fell in love with Papa when you were my age and had me."

Heaven help me. "You're right."

"Do you ever wonder where he is now or what he's doing?"

"I did in the beginning, but it's been years, honey." In truth Alexa knew exactly where Nico was and what his life was like married to an Athenian beauty. He was an Angelis and rising to the top. She'd done everything possible not to think about him over the years.

"I never stop wondering about him, Mama. What would it have been like if you'd been able to marry him. You can't deny you wanted to marry him. You told me *he* was the one for you no matter what. Right?"

Alexa moaned inwardly. "That's true, but it's also true that I was too young. Honey, you've got years to be thinking of getting married."

"I'm eighteen."

"Barely."

"I don't want to wait!" She was Alexa's daughter all right, at least the way Alexa used to be. "Please do this for me."

She patted her arm. "I'll think about it. Now go to bed. Morning will be here before we know it."

Her daughter didn't say anything else and slipped away, hurt by her mother's unenthusiastic response.

Alexa turned over and buried her wet face in the pillow. Tonight's conversation with Dimitra had brought back the past with swift, sharp pain. Only two weeks after Nico had left for military service, Alexa's grandfather Gavril had been made the Greek ambassador in Ottawa, Canada. It wasn't until they moved there from Nicosia on Cyprus that Alexa discovered she was pregnant.

As Alexa had found out, *once you started a partial truth, it lived with you forever.*

She'd wanted her daughter to grow up having a respectable background. But she was also desperate to cover her shame and embarrassment over her failed relationship at seventeen years of age with a playboy who'd never loved her. With a baby coming, the only thing she could say to people was that something unavoidable had happened that had kept her and Dimitra's father apart. They'd lost total touch with each other.

It was the same explanation she'd given her daughter when she was old enough to understand.

Alexa prayed it would stop Dimitra from asking too many questions about her father. She also hoped to avoid scandal involving Nico's prominent family, or scandal for her grandfather who held an important position in the government.

It wasn't until four years later that Monika Gataki, Alexa's teenage friend whom she hadn't heard from in several years, phoned Alexa out of the blue. She made an admission that changed Alexa's world forever. Monika admitted that she'd been so jealous of Alexa's relationship with Nico, she'd sent all his letters back unopened.

He'd honestly sent her the letters he'd promised?

The phone call sent her into shock. Alexa couldn't believe Monika had done something so horrible, so *immoral.* After four years of guilt, a repentant Monika—

who didn't expect to be forgiven—couldn't stay quiet any longer.

The devastating revelation meant Alexa and Dimitra could have had a wonderful life with Nico once he'd returned from the military. After getting off the phone, she told her grandparents everything and prayed that it wasn't too late to tell Nico the truth.

But when her grandfather made inquiries through his private sources to locate Nico, he learned that Nico had recently married a woman from an illustrious family in Athens and was now an executive at Angelis Shipping Lines.

The news that her beloved Nico had recently married changed everything. It made her wonder how long it had taken him to get over her and find another woman to love.

Alexa couldn't bring herself to tell him about their daughter. Obviously he'd moved on and had found love, something Alexa never expected to find again. It hurt to know that he'd met another woman he cared about enough to marry, but Alexa didn't want to ruin his chance for happiness. To take vows meant he had embraced a new life. Did she dare disturb the life he was living now?

Could his new marriage survive the fact that he had a daughter? How would he and his wife deal with it? Alexa couldn't do that to him or to the woman he'd married. As for Dimitra, she'd been a happy, contented child since birth, protected by love and from any hint of scandal or gossip.

Even if Nico were to be told and wanted to see Dimitra, how would her daughter react? Only being four years old, would she be frightened and upset? Or would she love Nico immediately and want to be around the daddy she'd always asked about no matter what?

How would her precious daughter handle visitation when they all lived thousands of miles apart? Her little girl's life would never be the same. Alexa's instinct was to protect Dimitra to the death. In the end she decided never to tell father or daughter the truth.

But she did give Dimitra the one little two-by-two photo Alexa had taken of a handsome Nico at nineteen so she'd have something to treasure. She'd also told her he'd gone by the nickname Dino and she'd met him in Greece on vacation before leaving for Canada with her grandparents.

Alexa claimed she'd found it on a shelf in the closet among some things she'd stored. Dimitra kept it like a sacred treasure, making Alexa realize how her daughter hungered for the daddy she'd never known. Dimitra had noticed he had dark hair like her own and that made her happy.

Alexa's grandparents believed she should seek out Nico and tell him everything. They said he had a right to know he was a father, but they also said it was her decision to make. They hoped she could live with her silence. She'd assured them she could now that she knew Nico was happily married. The knowledge had helped her put her pain and feelings on hold. Her grandparents accepted her decision.

For many years she'd been forced to deal with her guilt and fought not to let it consume her. But recently everything had changed. For one thing, Alexa's grandmother had died and her grandfather had moved them back to Salonica after retirement.

Once they were settled in the home he'd bought here, Alexa had been watching the news with him. Suddenly a breathtaking picture of a dark-haired Nico Angelis flashed on the screen. He'd just been named CEO of Angelis Shipping Lines and stood with a group of officials as he christened their latest tanker. After nineteen years, the first sight of a grown-up Nico brought Alexa close to a faint.

CHAPTER TWO

NOW THAT THE FAMILY was back in Greece, it was inevitable Alexa would see an important national figure like Nico Angelis on TV. Sure enough the other night the news had shown him among a group of foreign dignitaries discussing a new water route to the east on the Aegean.

He stood a little taller than the other men. With his broad shoulders, there was no man on earth to match him. The woman he'd married had to have thought the same thing. By now he probably had several children. They'd be Dimitra's half brothers or sisters...

He'd been dashing at nineteen. At thirty-eight years of age, he'd become the quintessential Greek male. Dimitra would be astounded to learn her birth father was someone so famous and outstanding. *And impossibly appealing.*

But if at this late stage Alexa decided to divulge the truth to him and Dimitra, it could bring chaos. What if he couldn't accept his daughter in the fullest sense? Alexa would never be forgiven by either of them no matter how much she'd believed she'd done the right thing at the time. Her relationship with her daughter could be permanently jeopardized. Alexa couldn't afford to risk that.

Dimitra was her life. Because she loved her so much, she decided to relent and agree to meet Kristos's mother to avoid hurting Dimitra. They'd never had a truly serious disagreement in their lives. Considering that her daughter was head over heels in love, Alexa needed to decide which battle to fight. This wasn't one of them. Dimitra, who'd only dated a little before meeting Kristos, was only asking her to meet his mother.

She slid out of bed and padded down the hall to her daughter's bedroom. Dimitra was just coming out of the bathroom. It looked like she'd been crying.

"Mama?"

"I couldn't let you go to bed until I told you I'd be happy to have dinner with Kristos and his mother."

Following a cry of joy, Dimitra hugged her so hard she almost knocked her over.

The night of the dinner, Alexa walked into her grandfather's den wearing a white silk dress with a small blue print. He could still get around, but his arthritis was worse and at night he'd get so tired, he used a wheelchair. "I promise we won't stay out late."

"Take as long as you want."

Her daughter hugged him. "Good night, Papoú. Please don't wear yourself out." *Papoú* was the Greek word for grandfather, but it worked for her great-grandfather too.

"Don't you worry about me. Good night, sweetheart. Have a wonderful time."

Before leaving the house, Alexa gave her grandfather a kiss, then thanked his caregiver Phyllis who lived with them.

The minute the two of them stepped outside into the soft June night air Alexa was overwhelmed by the summery fragrance unique to Salonica and it swept her back to other glorious nights here nineteen years ago.

After getting off work, Nico would come to the Gataki house to collect her and then she and Nico would go to the beach and end up in each other's arms.

Not for the first time did Alexa's daughter remind her of herself, getting ready to meet Nico for another rapture-filled night of being together. Dimitra's high spirits over the dinner ahead had brought a flush to her cheeks. But this private get-together had put Alexa on edge.

The conversation with Kristos's mother would inevitably bring up the subject of Dimitra's father. What kind of work had he been doing before they lost touch? How had they met? Alexa was ready with answers, but each time she had to explain to anyone now that they were back in Greece, it burned like a branding iron. After all these years, Alexa was back and geographically close to Nico. *Too* close.

Once in the car, she followed her daughter's directions to the Papadakis villa in the upper city. Dimitra had already told her about Kristos's mother who was still recovering after the accident that had killed her husband.

Kristos was the elder son of Tio Papadakis, who'd been one of the vice presidents of Papadakis Shipping Lines before his death six months earlier. In addition to his studies Kristos worked part-time in the family business under his CEO grandfather and hoped to rise in the business.

Alexa found it an amazing coincidence that Kristos, like Nico, had been born into a renowned Greek shipping family here in Salonica. No doubt his assured future and that of his younger brother boded well for a wonderful life.

She knew her daughter's one great wish was that both women would give their blessing for her and Kristos to be married soon. They were of legal age, but Dimitra wanted her mother to be happy about it. Of course she did.

"There it is!" her cry broke into Alexa's thoughts. "The gray-and-white mansion ahead with the statuary. Isn't it beautiful?"

"It certainly is."

"Kristos said to pull into the circular drive and park in front."

No sooner had Alexa pulled the car to a stop than a dark blond Kristos hurried out the front door and down the steps to greet them. He wore a light blue blazer over a button-down shirt and trousers. Dimitra had dressed in a yellow sundress. As Alexa had thought before when he'd come to her office at the university with her daughter, they made a good-looking couple.

He came around with Dimitra and helped Alexa out of the car. "Mama is looking forward to meeting you, Kyría Remis. We're eating outside."

She followed the two of them through the elegant mansion and out the doors to the back patio surrounded by a flowering garden. The lovely redheaded woman in a deep blue silk dress got up from her wheelchair to greet them. "I'm delighted the two of you have come, Kyría Remis."

"We're pleased to be here and meet you, Kyría Papadakis. Thank you for inviting us."

"Call me Irena. Let's talk at the table while my housekeeper Melia serves us, shall we? My son has been impatient for this night to come."

Irena had to be close to Alexa's age with a charm her son had inherited. "My daughter has been no different."

Like coconspirators, the two women smiled at each other in understanding before Kristos assisted his mother to the candlelit round table. She walked carefully while Alexa and Dimitra found places and the four of them sat. A fifth place had been set, no doubt for her younger son.

Soon their dinner arrived and they began to eat. "Kristos told me he met you at the university. What do you teach, Kyría Remis?"

"English to business students, and please call me Alexa."

Irena nodded with a smile. "How long did you live in Canada?"

"The whole of Dimitra's life. Once she went to first grade, I started a program to become a teacher while I attended the University of Ottawa. After my postgraduate studies, I started teaching Greek there."

"I'm very impressed."

"Don't be, but thank you, Irena." She drank some of her coffee. "When my grandmother passed away last year, my retired grandfather wanted to move back here. We came last August. Because of my experience living in an English-speaking country for so long, I joined the faculty here to teach English in a bilingual program."

"We're glad you did," Kristos interjected. "Otherwise we wouldn't have met." He couldn't take his eyes off Dimitra. Alexa had to acknowledge that like these two, she and Nico had been just as love struck and oblivious to everything except one another.

"What are you studying at the university, Dimitra?"

"She's terrific at math, Mama."

"My least favorite subject," Irena murmured.

Alexa nodded. "And mine."

Dimitra flashed Kristos's mother a smile. "Mama says I get it from my father."

"Lucky you."

Tell the truth when you can, Alexa.

"When I met Dimitra's father, he had plans to take engineering classes in college. We were both students and met on vacation," she said without naming a location, "but were unavoidably separated. In time we lost touch."

She eyed Irena, needing to change the subject. "I'm so sorry about your husband. How wonderful that you have two devoted sons."

Irena nodded. "I'd say both you and I are lucky in the children department."

"You're right about that."

Kristos looked at his mother. "I wish Papa were here to meet Dimitra. Why do you think Nico is so late?"

Nico? Alexa thought his brother's name was Yanni.

"Business, of course. Since becoming CEO, his life isn't his own anymore."

"But he said he'd come."

"He knows it's your birthday. I'm sure he'll phone if he can't make it. Forgive us, Alexa. We're talking about my husband's best friend, Nico Angelis."

"I call him Uncle Nico," Kristos volunteered.

"He's done everything for us since Tio passed away and said he'd drop by."

Irena kept on talking, but Alexa had gone into shock. *Nico Angelis had been the best friend of Irena's husband?*

He was coming here to this house *tonight*? Would his wife be with him? No. It wasn't possible. Her body went hot, then cold. She felt sick.

"Excuse me, Irena. Would you mind if I used your powder room for a moment? I'll be right back."

"Please. It's inside the doors on your left."

"Are you all right, Mama?"

"Yes, honey." Alexa got up from the table, praying her legs would support her before she fell into a dead faint in front of them.

Ready or not, your moment of truth has come, Alexa Remis. Pray the world doesn't come down on your head to bury you.

Nico got out of his car and only had to wait a moment before Melia answered the door. As he thanked her, Kristos came up behind her. "I was afraid you wouldn't be able to make it."

They hugged before he handed him a gift. "Happy Birthday. I would have been here earlier, but had to put out a fire at work first. You can open that later."

"Thanks. We're eating outside."

"Lead the way."

When they reached the patio, Nico walked around to kiss Irena's cheek, then glanced at the lovely young woman in the yellow dress seated at the table. Wavy brunette hair fell to her neck. With her coloring, she reminded him in a curious way of his sister Giannina. She was well-known for her beauty and could have been married long before now but for an unhappy love affair that had put her off men. He had to believe that would change in time.

"Uncle Nico? I'd like you to meet my girlfriend, Dimitra Remis."

He smiled at her. "It's my pleasure, Dimitra."

"How do you do, Kýrie Angelis."

Nico found his place and sat. "Your name happens to be a particular favorite of mine."

"My mother's too. She's always loved the Greek myths and named me for the goddess of the grain."

Once upon a time Nico remembered another beautiful young woman who'd also loved the myths, but that had been in another world when he'd been a different person. "I've heard you have a remarkable mother and was told she would be here with you."

"Kyría Remis excused herself for a few minutes," Irena explained.

Melia brought his dinner and he started to eat. Dimitra looked across the table at him. "Kristos told me the Papadakis family wouldn't have made it through the last six months without you, Kýrie Angelis." Between her expectant light green eyes and warm smile, he could understand why Kristos was so taken with her.

"He's the best friend we could ever have!" Kristos blurted before Nico could get a word out. Kristos had just opened the gift Nico had given him—a framed picture of Tio when they'd first gone in the military. Tio had been eighteen and looked a lot like Kristos at that age. He showed it to Dimitra. "I'll treasure this, Uncle Nico."

"I've long wanted you to have it."

Kristos passed it to his mother, but at this point Nico looked beyond Irena to a woman of medium height who'd come out on the patio. A blue-on-white print dress clung to her stunning figure. Light from the candles illuminated the gold strands in her shoulder-length chestnut hair.

Only one woman he'd ever known had hair that color, but it had cascaded down her back like a mermaid's. Maybe he was hallucinating. He got to his feet and found himself looking into the sea-green eyes of the Aegean enchantress who'd stolen his heart.

Thee mou! he cried inwardly as she sat. It was *Mara*!

She looked to be in her late twenties, not the thirty-six she must be now.

Dimitra was *her* daughter?

Nico's mind reeled. As he did the math, he felt a stabbing pain in his heart. She'd told him she'd come to Salonica on vacation from France to be with her cousin. She must have been with another guy during the hours when he'd been at work for his father. She would have had the time to meet someone else. He smothered a groan. So many lies…

That was why she'd sent back all Nico's letters without reading them. She'd fallen for the other guy and had ended up having his baby. How many guys had she played while on vacation?

"Uncle Nico? Please meet Alexa Remis, Dimitra's mother."

Alexa? Since when?

It amazed him that Mara Tito, who'd supposedly returned to France after her vacation was over, could look him straight in the eye without flinching...unless she'd developed a serious case of amnesia.

The last thing he wanted to do was ruin this evening for Kristos and the attractive young woman seated across the table from him. He would play Mara's game for now. After nineteen years, Nico could be patient until he got answers he'd assumed would never see the light of day in this lifetime. But soon there would be a reckoning.

"Kristos has been anxious for us to meet, Kyría Remis. He's told me you're teaching English at the university." His thoughts reeled while he stared at her. To think she was back here in Salonica. A professor. The mother of the young woman Kristos loved. Nico was incredulous.

"Yes. I'm on vacation now but will be starting a full load in the fall. Dimitra is taking classes this summer," she said in a quiet voice, at this point avoiding his eyes.

No doubt she was terrified he was going to expose her. He had every right to destroy her in front of all of them. The way she was trembling, he could tell she was waiting for him to unmask her.

What in the hell had happened to the supposedly guileless young woman he'd met years ago and instantly adored? How could he have been so wrong about her? "I've learned you've been living in Ottawa, Canada, since your daughter was born."

She nodded, still afraid to meet his gaze. So much for the fictional woman living in France. Canada was where she'd been all these years? Nico couldn't comprehend it, let alone the fact that he was seated a few feet from the woman he'd loved to distraction.

She was more gorgeous than she'd been at seventeen, and she'd given birth to another man's baby. But there was no ring on her finger. Had she not loved the father of her baby either? It was possible, given she'd made up the fiction that they'd been unavoidably separated. Nico couldn't fathom any of it, especially the letters she'd never opened. The fact that she had sent them back to him to make certain he got the message she wasn't interested had exhibited a cruelty he hadn't known her capable of.

He sat back, studying her through narrowed lids. "Our university is fortunate to have a teacher of your talents who's fluent in English and Greek."

"I'm the one who's fortunate, Kýrie Angelis."

Nico eyed Dimitra. "Are you going to follow in your mother's footsteps and become a foreign-language teacher too?"

She shook her head. "I'm looking at a degree in orthopedic engineering. It develops therapies to treat musculoskeletal disease."

"What would make you choose a field like that?"

"My *papoú* has arthritis, but he's also afflicted by the disorder. I'd love it if I could do something to help others like him one day."

"I told you Dimitra was intelligent," Kristos interjected. "Her math skills are off the charts."

Nico smiled. "I'm impressed, Dimitra." He was

touched by her love for the grandfather Nico had never known existed. But she had a long, hard road of studies ahead of her. To combine it with marriage at this stage wouldn't be easy. He flicked his glance to Mara. "You must be proud of your daughter."

"She's wonderful."

"Mama is wonderful too, Kýrie Angelis. I do wish I'd known my father, but I've been lucky to have my *papoú* all my life. He's brilliant and a sweetheart."

Nico got the feeling Dimitra was a sweetheart too. But he'd been fooled before and worried that one day Kristos could be hurt after falling under Dimitra's spell. "I understand your *papoú* became the ambassador for Greece in Ottawa a long time ago."

"All my life, actually. Mama and I lived with him and my great-grandmother Iris until she died. Then we moved back here."

"I guess there'd be no point in asking how you like living here in Salonica, Dimitra."

She blushed while Kristos chuckled.

Just then sixteen-year-old Yanni came out on the patio and kissed his mom. With Nico's emotions in total chaos, Yanni's appearance gave him the perfect excuse to leave. He needed to get out of there. "Take my place, Yanni."

"Hey, Uncle Nico."

"I'm sorry I have to cut this short. I've got to go back to the office to deal with a situation that will keep me there half the night."

"I wish you didn't have to go," Irena murmured, "but I understand."

No, she didn't. No one but Mara had any idea what he was feeling as he walked around to give Irena a kiss.

"Thank you for a delicious dinner. We'll talk later," he whispered before glancing at her guests. "It was a pleasure to meet you, Dimitra, *Alexa*. Kristos is a lucky man."

Dimitra beamed. "Thank you, Kýrie Angelis. I feel lucky too."

Mara avoided his gaze.

"I'll see you out, Uncle Nico."

Kristos walked him through the mansion to the car. "What do you think?" he asked before Nico got in the driver's seat. Kristos was painfully in love and Nico could see why. There'd be no talking him out of it.

"She's an intelligent, charming young woman. I find nothing wrong with her." It was the truth. That was the problem. Only time would reveal what wasn't visible right now.

Like mother, like daughter? Mara hadn't wasted any time finding another man to enamor within those three weeks. Or maybe she'd slept with the other guy after Nico had boarded the plane for military service. She hadn't been scheduled to return to France for at least three more days. That had been her story.

Who knew what had really happened though? How could he trust anything she'd told him? Seeing her tonight looking more beautiful than he could have thought possible brought it all back.

"Then will you tell Mama that?"

"I'm sure your mother feels like I do, but we'll finish this discussion when I don't have an emergency." Right now he couldn't think.

Kristos squeezed his shoulder. "I love the picture of Papa. Thanks for coming, for everything."

"Anytime. You know that." He wondered if Mara would be guilt ridden enough tonight to admit to the others that she'd known Nico a long time ago. It would be fascinating to find out how long it took her before she couldn't keep her secret from them any longer. Surely she had to know he wouldn't keep quiet forever about something so earthshaking.

Nico got behind the wheel and started the car. He pulled around the white BMW parked in front of him, which must be Mara's...or Alexa's...or whatever name she'd chosen to go by in her life.

His anger growing, he wasn't worried about her swimming away. Not this time. After nineteen years he knew where to go for the truth. It was time to be enlightened by the woman who'd once entranced him. Her disappearance had sent him to hell for a long, long time.

CHAPTER THREE

"Mama?"

"Come in."

Dimitra tiptoed into Alexa's bedroom and sat on the side of the bed. "I know you got sick tonight. You went so pale at the dinner table, I was frightened. And you were so quiet on the way home, I think you need to see a doctor."

Alexa *did* need a doctor, but not the kind her daughter was talking about. The bell had tolled for her tonight and there wasn't a physician on earth who could help her. Years ago, when her grandparents had asked her if she could handle her silence, she'd said yes, never dreaming she'd see Nico again. The flesh-and-blood reality of him had sent her into shock for a second time tonight.

"The sickness is passing, honey. I'm going to be okay, but it saddens me this happened while we were having such a good time."

"Kristos's mother was so kind and friendly. I really like her. What I hope is that his Uncle Nico liked me and approves of me. I know he's not really his uncle, but Kristos worships him and loves him almost as much as his own father."

"I'm sure he thought you were wonderful. Who wouldn't love you?"

"You say that because you're my mom. I happen to know his opinion will go a long way with Kristos."

Alexa's heart pounded. "What about you?" she ventured in a trembling voice. "Did *you* like Kýrie Angelis?" She had to know her daughter's instant reaction.

"Who wouldn't?" her daughter responded so fast, Alexa couldn't believe it. "He's awesome in every way, Mama. You know that little photo of my father you gave me years ago? It kind of reminds me of Kýrie Angelis. My father was dark and handsome too. I can see why you fell for him. I hope that doesn't bother you for me to talk about my father."

Oh, Dimitra. You have no idea what those words mean to me since you'll probably be meeting him again—knowing who he is this time—within the next twelve to twenty-four hours.

"Of course it doesn't, and I just wanted to say that Kristos comes from a lovely family, honey. I'll send his mother a thank-you note for inviting us."

"I will too, but I'm worried about you."

"I'll be all right." She patted her daughter's hand. But Alexa couldn't predict anything about the future. Tonight she'd seen a dangerous glint in Nico's midnight-brown eyes that let her know there'd be no avoiding him now. She hadn't seen the last of him.

At nineteen he'd been a man of integrity and it appeared he still was. During dinner tonight he hadn't disappointed her. Another man might have created an ugly scene she would never have been able to survive. Not Nico. After all these years of no news, to see her again and realize she'd had a daughter and had been living a different life, his anger would have reached its zenith.

But he'd been born a breed apart from other men. For the short time he'd been at the Papadakis mansion, he'd known how to expose some of her lies and sins of omission with such expertise, no one suspected anything. That explained one of the reasons why he'd been made the head of the Angelis empire.

"Can I get you anything, Mama?"

"No, thank you, honey. All I need is sleep. This stomachache will pass."

Dimitra got up from the bed. "I'll check on Papoú now."

"He'll like that if he's not already asleep."

Her daughter lingered for a moment longer. "Will you tell me one more thing?"

Alexa moaned inwardly. "I like Kristos and his mother very much." She knew it wasn't the full answer Dimitra wanted, but she didn't dare discuss things now. Tomorrow she would contact Nico. Very soon the world Dimitra had known was going to change.

Once her daughter learned that he was her father, there was no way to predict the outcome of anything, let alone a possible marriage.

"I'm sorry, but I'm tired, honey."

"I know."

"Can we talk tomorrow?"

"Of course. Good night, Mama." Her resigned daughter gave Alexa a kiss before leaving the bedroom.

Alexa turned out the light on the bedside table and lay there in the dark, dying inside over so many things, not the least of which was her visceral reaction to Nico.

When she'd seen him on the patio, she'd found herself as out of breath as that moment in the sea when they'd run into each other years ago. He still had the power to transform her world until nothing existed but him. Though she knew he was a married man, it made no difference. She was still attracted to him.

Right now she was terrified over what was to come once she'd phoned Irena Papadakis for Nico's phone number. Since Irena would learn the truth, if she hadn't already, Alexa would have to take the risk to ask for her help in getting in touch with Nico. She'd phone her first thing in the morning.

After five minutes her anxiety drove her out of bed and she got up to get a drink of water. While she was coming out of the bathroom she heard the ding on her phone. Someone had sent her a text, probably Michalis Androu, the divorced Cypriot also on the faculty.

Two months ago he'd invited her for drinks. A month later he'd asked her to go to the opera with him. She liked him, but shouldn't have accepted a dinner date for this coming Friday. It would be the last time.

She walked over to the bedside table to look at her phone and almost collapsed when she saw who'd sent it. How had he found her phone number? Her body trembled as she sank down on the side of the bed to read it.

This text shouldn't come as a surprise. We have to talk. I'll meet you at Ravaisi's on the beach at seven tomorrow evening. If you don't come, I'll drive to your house and wait for you for as long as it takes. Nico.

Alexa's eyes closed tightly. She fell back. *Ravaisi's.*

They'd eaten fresh seafood on its veranda on Perea Beach their last evening before he'd left for the military. It had been a night like tonight. The moon had looked like a pale yellow globe, lighting the calm water of the Aegean. Later they'd swum to his cruiser anchored a little way offshore.

She'd clung to Nico's hand as he helped her up the ladder. Once on board, he'd led her down the stairs to the lower deck. He'd planned a surprise for her on their last night together. All Alexa had to do was follow. She loved him with every fiber of her heart and soul and would follow him to the ends of the earth.

Nico had pulled her inside the bedroom and locked the door.

A cry of sheer delight escaped her lips at the sight that greeted her. The room had been filled with lighted candles, dispersing a fragrant scent of orange blossoms. Her gaze gravitated to an urn full of glorious blue hydrangeas placed on the bedside table. A few days earlier she'd happened to mention they were her favorite flower. He'd remembered everything.

Nico, she whispered in awe. *I feel like I'm in a dream.*

You look like one. When I first saw you in the water three weeks ago, I thought you were a mermaid coming out of the foam.

She clung to his hard body. His words would always have the power to make her blush. *Would you believe me if I told you I thought you looked like the statue of the young Emperor Augustus in the Salonica Archaeological Museum?*

Agape mou.

After calling her his love, he'd picked her up like a

bride and carried her to the bed. *Let me love you*, he'd said urgently. *The thought of not seeing you for another year is more than I can bear.* Nico pulled her on the bed and began to devour her. That was the first time they'd made love, the magical night Dimitra had been conceived.

Breathtaking memories of that night so long ago brought the tears gushing. There'd be no sleep for her tonight. Alexa got off the bed to wash her face. Somehow she had to get through tomorrow knowing what awaited her on that beach.

"You're still here, Kýrie Angelis?"

Nico looked up at the night watchman who'd worked for his father. It was ten after six in the evening. "Sunday's the best time to get things done. No one else is around."

"I never saw anyone work so hard."

"How else to try and fill my father's shoes?"

"You already do that, *kýrie.*"

"Don't I wish, but thank you, Gus. I'll be gone from here shortly. Have a good evening."

As soon as the older man left, Nico took his private elevator to the apartment above the office. After Raisa's death, he'd sold their villa in Salonica and had bought the one on Sarti, near the town of Sithonia that he now called home.

When he had to be in town, however, he stayed here for convenience since his father hadn't used it for several years. Last night after seeing Mara at dinner he'd flown to Sithonia to get some needed items, then he'd returned to the office apartment. Work was always waiting for him. Today he'd settled down to stay busy. It was the only panacea to keep him from climbing the walls while he waited for tonight to come.

Mara hadn't sent a message to let him know she'd received his text, let alone confirmed that she planned to meet him. He didn't have any expectations where she was concerned, but it didn't matter.

Nico couldn't get used to the idea that her real name was Alexa Remis, that she'd lived with her daughter and grandparents in Canada after leaving Salonica for good.

No wonder Nico had never been able to find her! To think of the hours, weeks and months he'd spent trying to track her down in Greece, then in France. Tio had helped him after his marriage to Irena, but there'd been no trace of Leia or the Vasilakis family either. Like Mara, they'd disappeared off the face of the earth.

For a long time he feared the worst—that she'd been kidnapped or killed—even though there'd been no news of any kind to support that theory. His parents, who'd tried to help him, tended to think the same thing. It haunted him until one day when Giannina said, *Have you ever thought she just doesn't want to be found? Maybe she met another guy after you left and didn't want to tell you. Maybe she felt trapped.*

He'd stared at his practical sister, so wise even though she was two years younger. *You really think that's the answer?*

I don't know. I like guys, but can't imagine being tied down to one until I'm at least twenty-five or twenty-six. Maybe not even then. But for you to spend your life looking for her when you could have any woman you wanted makes no sense.

If that's true, then she was a coward not to tell me goodbye.

Maybe not a coward, but a flirt who got in too deep and was too young and frightened to tell you the truth. I know it's easy for me to say, but I wouldn't waste another minute thinking about her.

After all these years, their conversation rang true as he headed for Perea Beach. Last night he'd learned for himself that his sister had been right. Mara *had* met another guy and had had his baby. She'd also given Nico a false name and background.

Had she operated that way with every guy she'd met back then? Maybe she'd been young like himself, but he still had a hard time imagining most girls that age were so deceitful.

He made his way to the beach. A white BMW sat in one of the parking spaces at the side of the restaurant. He recognized it from the night before and was glad to see she had the guts to face him and he wouldn't have to track her down.

Grabbing his knapsack, he got out of the car and walked inside. The hostess greeted him warmly. *"Kalispéra, kýrie."* She smiled at him. "I've seen you on television. Welcome to our restaurant."

"Efharisto."

"Where would you like to sit?"

"I'm meeting someone whom I think is already here, but I don't see her."

"Then she might be on the veranda. Feel free to go out and look for her."

He took a deep breath and walked through the restaurant to the door leading to the veranda. Nico and

Mara had eaten outside that last night he'd been in Salonica. When he saw her seated now at the same table as all those years before, his heart dropped to his feet. The possibility that she'd suffered amnesia could be stricken off his list.

He sat opposite her and put his knapsack on the chair next to him. The sun wouldn't set for another hour and a half. The rays brought out the fabulous coloring of her hair. "*Kalispéra*, Mara."

"*Kalispéra,*" she half whispered. Tears glazed her eyes, making them a deeper green, like the sea in front of them. In a simple pink top and white skirt, she looked so damn beautiful it destroyed any peace of mind he'd tried to achieve since last evening.

"I wondered if a day might come when we'd meet again by chance," Nico said.

"You're not the only one," she confessed.

Nico's brows furrowed. "The difference is, the Mara I fell in love with always knew where my parents lived and could have found me anytime to tell me she'd had a change of heart."

A distressed expression crossed over her features. "That's true, and no one deserves the truth more than you." But before she could say anything else, a waiter approached.

"I couldn't eat anything, Nico. Just coffee."

Food was the last thing on Nico's mind. "Two coffees," he told the waiter who came right back with them.

Once they'd been served, Nico reached inside his knapsack and handed her the bag he pulled out of it. "These belong to you. They've stayed in a storage closet for nineteen years. Once I had a dream that I'd find you and learn what terrible thing must have happened, like kidnapping or worse, that prevented you from answering them."

She sat motionless.

"I'd hoped to find you so we could read them together. But that day never came and I forgot about them until last night when I saw you walk out on the patio."

Her hand shook as she lowered her coffee mug and looked inside the bag. An audible gasp escaped her lips and she pulled out one of the unopened letters. She studied the address on the front of the envelope, then pulled out another one.

"There are dozens of letters here!" she cried, sounding incredulous.

Her acting was phenomenal. There'd been no kidnapping or worse. He knew she'd received them and had sent them back unopened. "That's right. All of them addressed to Mara Tito at the Vasilakis residence in Salonica." He drank more coffee. "You'll notice the Return to Sender handwritten on the side." She couldn't deny what she'd done. The proof was in her hands.

Alexa's head reared, causing her shimmery chestnut hair to settle against her shoulders. Tears poured down her white cheeks. Her breakdown of emotion surprised him.

He broke the silence. "For a long time I wanted an answer to the question why, but I don't need it now. Last night I met your daughter. Clearly you got involved with another man while you were in Greece and had his baby. For what it's worth, I would say you've done a wonderful job of raising her."

He put some euros on the table and stood. "Thank you for meeting me. *Andio*, Kyría Remis."

"No—wait, Nico!"

He ignored her cry and walked away. Never again.

It shouldn't have surprised Alexa that he'd said goodbye and left with an abruptness that took her breath away. His fear that something terrible had happened to her years ago crushed her with fresh guilt. Tonight he'd thought he'd learned the whole truth and was anxious to get home to his wife.

When she could get a grip on her emotions, she put the letters back in the bag he'd given her and left the restaurant on legs that barely supported her. During the drive home she trembled like a leaf. To her relief, Phyllis told her Dimitra had gone out with Kristos. Alexa's grandfather had fallen asleep watching a soccer match on TV.

Thankful to be alone, she grabbed a letter opener from his desk and hurried to the bedroom. She undressed and got ready for bed. Before her daughter came home, she wanted to read the letters Nico had written and kept all these years. How amazing that he hadn't thrown them away a long time ago.

Once under the covers, she emptied the contents of the bag. After a search she found the first letter he'd written to her in his unique penmanship. It was dated on the day he'd left Salonica.

Oh, Nico, darling... She drowned in tears. *You really did send them.*

The Return to Sender bore Monika's distinct hand. Even though Monika had confessed what she'd done fifteen years ago Alexa was hit with a wave of fresh hurt. How could she have done something so treacherous?

Using the opener, Alexa pulled out the one-page letter. A gold ring fell on the bedspread. Her heart pounded so hard, she thought she was going to be sick.

Mara—beloved
I have to write this fast. We're on a bus headed for the airport. I'll post this before I get on the plane.

Do you have any idea how I'm feeling right now? After spending last night in your arms, I'll never be the same. Saying goodbye to you felt like a part of me was being torn away.

Please wear this ring. I had it engraved for you. It's our engaged-to-be-engaged ring.

The sobs kept coming. Alexa could hardly read what had been engraved on the inside: *Gia Pánta*. It meant forever. She slid it on her ring finger.

You should get this tomorrow. I'll write you every night.

In three days you'll be going back to your mom in France. I look forward to meeting her after I get home.

We're going to have one wonderful wedding because you're going to become my wife. I can't wait.

Be sure that Leia forwards my letters the second she gets them. I won't be able to live until I start getting your letters and you send me your address in France. You can write to the address on the envelope and I'll get it no matter where I am.

S'agapo, Mara. I love you. You complete my
life. Don't let anything happen to you. I couldn't
live without you now.
Yours forever,
Nico

Convulsing, Alexa took a long time before her tears
ebbed and she was able to search for the second letter
he'd written. She tried to read it, but she began crying
anew and it was almost impossible.

Agapiménos—my beloved
Boot camp is everything you've ever heard about,
but I can handle it because I know I'll get a letter
from you at the end of every day, telling me everything you've been doing.
    When you're back in France, you better not fall
for one of those French guys.
    Good news. I'm bunking with a guy named Tio
Papadakis. Would you believe his family owns the
Papadakis Shipping Lines in Salonica? We have
so much in common, it's crazy.
    He's writing a redheaded girl in Salonica. Her
name is Irena and he's planning to marry her before our tour of duty is finished. They'll be going
to the University of Salonica too. We'll all be in
school together.

Having just met Irena, and being in Tio's home with
his children, Alexa could hardly go on reading. It was
too piercingly wonderful and painful at the same time.
Her tears made the ink run. Nico's love of life, his love

for her, all of it had been ripped away, depriving them of the joy of marriage, of being parents and raising their precious Dimitra together.

Suddenly she heard noise and realized her daughter had come home. Alexa hurriedly put all the letters back in the bag, and hid it on the floor at the side of the bed. Then she turned off the lamp and drew the covers over her. Tomorrow would come soon enough, changing their lives forever.

In the middle of the night she couldn't stand it any longer. After turning on the lamp, she spent the next five hours reading one love letter after the other. Finally she read the last one he'd sent at the end of December, four months after he'd left Salonica. It was so short, it devastated her.

Mara darling
After all this time I believe in my heart something unspeakable has happened to you. Something beyond your control. The woman I love and who loves me wouldn't do this to us without a reason.

I live for word from you or about you. My prayer is that somehow, some way, you'll read this letter and be able to get in touch with me by any means available.

I'll never give up. If this letter is returned to me and I'm still in the dark after my service is over, I'll come looking for you and never stop.
Love forever,
Nico

Alexa finally recovered enough to put all the letters back in the bag except the last one, then got out of bed. After a shower, she dressed for the day in jeans and a T-shirt. With his last letter tucked in her back pocket, she left the bedroom. Her watch said eight thirty. Her grandfather would be up. She'd talk to him until Dimitra awakened.

Carrying the bag, she found him in the kitchen eating the breakfast Phyllis had prepared. He looked up. "There you are! I thought you'd be up before now. You don't look well."

Alexa kissed his forehead. "I've been awake since three o'clock. These are the reason why." She showed him the bag with the letters.

He studied several, then squinted at her. "There's only one way you're in possession of them. You've seen Nico. So...the long silence has been broken."

She nodded. "It turns out Nico Angelis was the best friend of Tio Papadakis. Would you believe it? He showed up at the dinner Saturday night. When we got home later, I received a text to meet him at a restaurant on the beach last night. He came with these letters.

"To quote him, 'For a long time I wanted an answer to the question why, but I don't need it now. Last night I met your daughter. Clearly you got involved with another man while you were in Greece and had his baby. For what it's worth, I would say you've done a wonderful job of raising her.' Then he said goodbye before I could tell him anything."

Her grandfather looked sad. "So he's a gentleman to the end."

She nodded. "This morning I'm going to tell Dimitra."

"Tell me what?" Her daughter had just come into the kitchen. Alexa turned her head toward her. "That you don't want me to marry Kristos? Did the thought of my being too young make you so upset we had to leave the dinner early? Was that it?"

Alexa took a deep breath. "No, honey. What I have to tell you has nothing to do with you and Kristos. Please sit down and listen. I have news that's going to change your world."

"I don't understand."

"Of course you don't. The fact is, I told you a half-truth the first time you asked me about your daddy."

"What do you mean?"

This was it. "Your father and I *did* get unavoidably separated, but I could have contacted him through his parents. There are reasons why I didn't do that or why I didn't reveal his true name to you."

"Which is?"

"Nico Angelis."

Her daughter laughed. "Are you teasing me?"

Heaven help me. "Not at all."

Dimitra eyed her incredulously. "You don't mean *the* Nico Angelis who came to dinner the other night—"

"Yes, honey. You said Kýrie Angelis reminded you of the photo I gave you of your father. That's because it is him. It's a picture I took of him when I was seventeen while I was on vacation in Salonica. In a short three-week period Nico and I fell madly in love and planned to be married after he finished his military service. He'd promised to write to me, but he never did, and I never heard from him again."

Dimitra paled and finally sat on a chair.

"I discovered I was pregnant two months after he'd left Salonica and we'd moved to Canada. When you were old enough, I told you your daddy's name was Dino. That was done to protect your reputation, and the grandparents and Nico from gossip. The news would have brought scandal to his illustrious family and to your *papoú*."

Tears filled Dimitra's eyes. "Is this the truth, Pàpoú?"

"Yes, sweetheart."

Alexa sat by her. "To this day Nico still doesn't know he's your father."

"What?"

"I never told him. Though your *papoú* knew how to get in touch with Nico's parents and would have gotten word to him that he had a daughter, I'm the one who begged him to do nothing because I was convinced Nico had only been having fun with me and had lost interest after he'd left. Saturday night was the first time I've seen him in nineteen years."

"You're kidding! What happened? Why didn't you ever hear from him? How could he have been so horrible to you?"

Alexa loved Dimitra for coming to her defense. She took a deep breath. "He wasn't the one who was horrible. My friend Monika, the girl I was staying with, was jealous of our relationship. Once I returned to Nicosia, she sent back every letter he ever wrote. But it took four years before she confessed to me what she had done."

Her daughter shook her head, looking totally fragmented. "I don't believe it."

"They're in that bag right there, stamped and postmarked. Nico was my errand last night and he gave them to me. You're free to read them. You'll learn a lot about your wonderful father. I loved him heart and soul. There's no one like him." Alexa pulled his last letter out of her pocket and handed it to her. "When you read this, you'll see what a remarkable human being he really is. He never lost his faith in us."

Her daughter took it from her, then jumped up from the chair. "But this is outrageous! She actually intercepted your letters and sent them back to him unopened?"

"Yes."

"That's the most hideous thing I ever heard!" Dimitra cried. Tears gushed down her cheeks. "How could anyone do something that evil?"

"It was a very evil act, I agree. After her confession, I was beside myself and wanted Nico to know the truth, that he had a four-year-old daughter. But your *papoú* found out he'd just gotten married to a prominent woman from a family from Athens. It was the biggest society wedding of the year in Greece. He was also rising in his career and the media focus on him was growing."

Dimitra let out a wounded cry. "Was that more important than his finding out he had a daughter?" Her pain-filled words rang in the room.

"I couldn't bear the thought of risking his happiness when he'd found love again. Your *papoú* wanted me to tell him, but I was afraid of ruining his life, so I stayed quiet. After seeing him on Saturday night, I had no choice but to tell you the truth, knowing you'll never be able to forgive me."

She shook her head, still in disbelief. "He didn't act like he knew you…"

"No. He saved me the horror of having to confess to something you never knew about in front of everyone. There's no more honorable man alive than your father and he still has to be told you're his daughter. I would have told him last night, but he left the restaurant too fast because he was so upset to think I'd lied to him. I plan to tell him today.

"He should be at work. Of course I can't expect forgiveness from him either. Please don't tell Kristos any of this until I've had a chance to talk to Nico first. He needs to hear this from me."

The look of desolation in Dimitra's eyes would haunt her forever.

CHAPTER FOUR

NICO'S CALL TO the port authority in Izmir was the first item on his busy agenda. Once completed, his phone rang. It was his sister at the newspaper.

"I'm so glad you answered."

"How are things going?"

"They'd be a lot better if Uncle Ari didn't squelch my ideas and put me down in front of the others. Sometimes he's actually cruel to me."

Nico's brows furrowed. "I knew he wasn't happy about your promotion over him, but that's no excuse. Baba felt you deserved to become the managing editor. I've never known anyone who worked harder."

"Thanks for saying that, Nico. I'll have to find a way to get along with Ari. But on to a happier note, it's Mama's birthday on Friday night. Let's plan a surprise for her and Baba."

Since last night, Mara had been the only thing on his mind. He couldn't think of her as Alexa. Giannina's phone call had caught him off guard. "What sort of plans?"

"How about a small party with friends on the yacht?"

"Sounds good."

"Nico? You don't seem like yourself. What's going on?"

"Do you remember years ago when you told me my girlfriend had probably fallen for some other guy and that's why she shut me down?"

"That was a ghastly time for you. I didn't know if you'd ever recover."

His eyes shut tightly. "Saturday night I met her by accident and you were right. She did meet another guy that summer in Salonica and then she moved to Canada. Now she's back and she has an eighteen-year-old daughter."

"Whoa. If I recall, I told you she probably didn't want to get in too deep."

"Not with me anyway. The point is, your astute comments at the time gave me another perspective that helped me move on. Eventually I met Raisa."

"I'm glad if anything I said made a difference."

"It did, and I thought you'd like to know. Count me in for Friday and call me when you need help. We'll talk then about what's going on at your work and come up with an idea to ease the situation."

"You're on. Love you."

No sooner had he hung up than his phone rang again. Only a few people besides his family had his cell phone number. If it was Kristos or Irena, he might not get any work done.

He checked the caller ID. Alexa Remis.

Nico gripped the phone tighter, not wanting anything to do with her. Why was she calling? Last night he'd walked away for good. That chapter of his life was over. Again. Or so he'd thought. He'd have to speak to her now though, otherwise it would bother him so much he wouldn't be able to concentrate.

He answered. "Kyría Remis?" Nico still couldn't call her Alexa.

"Thank you for answering. I know you're busy and so I'll make this quick. I have information you need to be told about as soon as possible, but I can't tell you over the phone. I'll meet you in the garden at the Vlatadon Monastery any time you say. Come alone."

What information?

He gripped his phone tighter. If this had something serious to do with Kristos and her daughter, surely Irena would have called him instead. His brows met in a frown. Her words, plus her tone, told him she'd meant every word.

"I can meet you there in half an hour." He hadn't planned on taking a lunch break, but would make an exception this once. The sooner this was over, the better.

"Thank you. I'll see you there." She hung up.

After letting his secretary know he'd be out of the office for an hour, he left in his car and headed up to Ano Poli in the traditional area of Salonica. The Byzantine church she referred to had been built on the spot with a fabulous view of the sea. The Apostle Paul was said to have spoken to the Thessalonians from that vantage point. Nico and Mara had taken a picnic up there, enthralled with the place and each other.

He parked near her white car. A busload of tourists arrived as he walked around the side of the monastery to the garden. She sat on a bench at the far end beneath a tree where they'd once eaten their picnic. The second she saw him, she stood. Today she wore an attractive light green skirt and blouse. *Face it.* She'd always looked fantastic in anything.

"Thank you for coming." She acted frightened, which he found strange. "I wanted you to be alone because of what I have to say. Last night you walked away before I could tell you news that will not only change your life, but also that of your wife. You'll know better than anyone how to tell her if that's what you choose."

What in the hell was she talking about? "My wife died eleven years ago."

He heard a gasp before the color left her face. She couldn't have faked that reaction or the way she sank back down on the bench, close to a faint. Maybe a minute passed before she spoke. "I'm so sorry. I had no idea…" Her haunted eyes lifted to his in pleading. "Nico… Dimitra is *our* daughter."

He couldn't have heard her correctly. "What did you say?"

"I thought of course you'd figured it out at Irena's, but I know now from what you said that it didn't occur to you."

His body broke out in a cold sweat.

"*You* are her father. I told Dimitra you were called by the nickname Dino to protect her reputation after she was born to an underage woman who wasn't married."

It couldn't be true, could it? Nico thought he must be losing his mind.

"I know we took precautions, but she was conceived anyway. When she was born, I had your name written on her birth certificate. My grandparents watched me sign it. Here's the proof." She reached for her purse and pulled out the paper.

His mind reeled. Incredulous, he sat and took the

authentic-looking stamped and sealed document from her trembling hand and read it.

Certificate of Live Birth
Montfort Hospital, Ottawa, Ontario, Canada
Stamped and dated May 14
Mother of child: Alexa Soriano Remis
Father of child: Nicholas Timon Angelis
Full name of child: Dimitra Angelis Remis
Signature of attending doctor, M. Viret

When he lifted his head, those moist sea-green eyes stared into his. A calm seemed to have come over her. "This morning our daughter heard for the first time that you are her father. After leaving her in a shell-shocked condition with my grandfather, I came directly to you. There was a reason I lied to you from the moment we collided in the sea. But that's not the real story."

He stood and paced for a minute, rubbing the back of his neck while he tried to clear his mind. "I left you pregnant—"

Her chin trembled. "Yes, but neither of us could have known at the time."

The incredible news had rendered him speechless.

"Nico, you remember the myth we talked about where Hera almost caught Zeus with a mistress named Io? He turned Io into a heifer to deceive her. Hera wasn't fooled. Driven by jealousy, she placed Io where the giant would always watch her so Io and Zeus could never be together."

"Of course," he whispered. Nico remembered every minute of their time together, the things they'd said and told each other. You didn't forget things like that. To think that all these years Alexa had been raising *their* daughter. He couldn't comprehend it.

She got up from the bench. "That myth is *our* story, Nico."

"What do you mean?"

"My fictional cousin Leia Vasilakis was in reality a friend I met in Nicosia while I lived there. Her family worked with my grandfather who was the ambassador on Cyprus then. He made all of us take fictional names while on vacation because of political unrest, fearing the enemy might use me for a target."

Nico listened, but he had a hard time taking it all in.

"Last evening you told me you thought something horrible had happened to me. That was my grandfather's fear when I went on vacation, that an enemy might try to take me hostage to force my grandfather's hand in some insidious way. Thus the fake name. But I was never taken hostage. The person who carried out the treachery was my own friend, Monika Gataki. You knew her as Leia."

What she was saying now had the ring of truth, leaving Nico dumbstruck.

"Her family asked me to spend my three-week vacation with them in Salonica. The second day we arrived, I met you. From that first moment, Monika was so consumed by jealousy over my relationship with you, she found a way to hurt us and returned every letter you wrote to me at her parents' address. Her revenge was as total as Hera's, destroying your life and mine."

With each veil dashed from his eyes, Nico struggled for breath. "How could anyone have been that spiteful?"

"I asked myself that same question." She swallowed hard. "I didn't know what she'd done until four years later when she phoned me out of guilt and told me the truth. I almost died with that revelation, knowing it was too late for us."

"Too late?"

"Yes. My grandfather made inquiries about you and found out you were just recently married."

Nico wheeled around. Anger raged inside him. "It's never too late to learn you're a father! Married or not, why in the hell didn't you tell me we had a child? In fact, why didn't you get in touch with me the second you knew you were pregnant?"

She edged away from him. "I knew you'd ask me these questions. But the reasoning of a seventeen-year-old girl who was intimidated by what Monika had told me about your family won't make any sense to you. I've known from the beginning that neither Dimitra or you will ever forgive me. I'm leaving it up to the two of you to do what you want now that you both know the truth."

In the next instant she ran past him and the tourists toward the parking area while he stood there with the birth certificate—his *daughter's* birth certificate—still clutched in his hand.

Alexa had done the unpardonable to Nico. The second she returned to the house, a sobbing Dimitra met her in the living room. Her daughter had gotten dressed and had been waiting for her. She held up one of the letters.

"I've been reading everything. This is his first letter to you. He loved you, Mama. He really loved you! I don't know how Monika could have done that to you. But it's *your* lie I can't forgive. You could have gotten in touch with his family when you found out you were pregnant. They would have contacted him. He would have uncovered the mystery because he's that kind of man. All these years I could have had my father."

"Honey—"

"I'm leaving," she broke in. "Kristos phoned and is coming for me. My father has already told him what you confessed at the monastery. I don't know when I'll be back." She flew out the front door.

"Dimitra—"

"Let her go, Alexa. Give her time."

She turned to her grandfather. "I did it all wrong, Papoú."

"You did what you felt was best for everyone. But now you have another problem."

"I know. My penance will be to live with what I've done for the rest of my life."

"That too, but I just had a call from Kýrie Angelis. He's coming by for you in…" he checked his watch "…twenty minutes."

She panicked. "I don't believe it."

"Why? Dimitra needed to go off and talk everything over with Kristos. That leaves Nico. You dropped your bombshell, now he needs to talk everything over with you. He's one of the most important men in Greece, a man who has been used to taking charge all his life and doesn't hesitate. That's why he's so successful."

Alexa shuddered. "I've told him everything."

"In one hour? You think?" Her grandfather laughed.

"I'm afraid of his anger."

"I don't blame you, but now you've opened the door."

"Because I've been forced."

"Your grandmother Iris has to be cheering. She'd hoped for this day long before she passed away."

"So have you, Papoú," she said in a broken voice.

"When he gets here, I want him to come in so I can shake his hand. He never stopped trying to do the honorable thing where you were concerned. These letters prove it."

"I—I need to freshen up," she stammered and hurried to the bathroom.

Alexa looked and felt like death. The doorbell rang while she finished putting on lipstick. She still had to give her hair a brushing. When she walked back to the living room, Phyllis had already let Nico inside.

He'd changed out of his business suit and wore casual pants with a white crewneck cotton sweater. Her breath caught at his virile, masculine appeal.

Nico darted Alexa a glance. "It's an honor and privilege to meet your grandfather." She caught no hint of anger in his voice just now. "Gavril Filo has given remarkable service to our country, but even more, he has helped you raise our daughter. For that I'll be eternally grateful."

Moved by his kind words to her *papoú*, she walked over to the wheelchair and slid an arm around her grandfather's shoulders. "After my parents died, he and my grandmother raised me too. No one will ever know what they mean to me."

"I can only imagine."

Her grandfather lifted his head. "I can only imagine

how much you two need to talk, even if it should have happened nineteen years ago. You go on, honey. Phyllis is here." He patted Alexa's hand.

Tears slid down her cheeks. She hugged him hard. "There's no one like you. I'll be back soon."

She and Nico left the house. With a sense of déjà vu, he helped her into a new black Mercedes and walked around to get behind the wheel. "The only place we can talk without interruption is my cruiser. It's not the same one. After I returned from military service and couldn't find you, I traded it in for a new one. You're the only person who would understand why."

"I do," she whispered. "That was the most wonderful night of my entire life." He'd said the same thing in his letter.

"And our beautiful daughter was the result."

"Yes." Her voice throbbed.

He drove them toward the pier where he'd docked his boat in the past. "She has traits that remind me of my sister Giannina, but now that I think about it, her smile is all yours."

Alexa bowed her head. "Whenever I look at her, I see you." She struggled for breath. "How you must despise me." Her voice shook.

"To be sure, my anger over Monika Gataki's malicious actions is white-hot. As for my feelings of anger, frustration, hurt and disappointment where you're concerned, I'm trying to sort them out. But my first instinct after you left the monastery was to phone Kristos with the truth.

"He wants his mother's blessing and mine to marry Dimitra before long. That dinner at Irena's was meant for me to meet her and her mother. Now that I've learned she's our daughter, I felt it necessary that he know everything immediately."

"I'm glad you did. She loves him very much and will turn to him for comfort. I'll be lucky if she ever speaks to me again."

Nico's silence told her he agreed, causing her to shiver.

When they reached the pier, she got out and walked along the dock to a sleek blue thirty-foot cruiser. He helped her aboard and undid the ropes. After tossing her a life jacket, he started the engine and moved them out at wake speed. She sat across from him. In another minute they took off for open water.

Before long he shut off the engine and lowered the anchor. A hot sun shone down on them. Nico got up and walked over to one of the padded benches. "Come over here and help me put all this together."

She moved to the other bench opposite him. "It started with Monika."

"First off, tell me why she was so jealous. I'm still trying to get my head around it."

"Oh, Nico…" She made a sound. "You'd have to be a woman to understand."

"Try me." Wanting answers, he hadn't slept since the dinner at the Papadakis mansion.

"It began the day you and I met. When I swam back to the beach, I told her I'd met a guy named Nico Angelis, and that he wanted me to go on a boat ride with him. I didn't want her to worry while I was gone. It surprised me when she immediately flew into a rage about you."

"In what way?"

"She said she'd seen you on the beach before and wondered that I hadn't remembered what she'd said about you, your prestigious background and elite friends. She said you came from one of the most powerful, influential families in Greece. Monika warned me you were a playboy with movie-star looks and told me I was a fool to fall for your ridiculous line about my looking like a mermaid."

He sucked in his breath. "That was no act. You looked and swam exactly like one."

"Unbeknownst to me, the fact that you'd asked me to go on your cruiser did a lot of damage. I realize now it was jealousy because you'd never sought her out. Even though she was attractive, you hadn't noticed her, but you'd shown interest in me. She'd been so sure you were just playing with me.

"When you kept coming around for the next three weeks, it was too much for her. She taunted me endlessly, but I was so crazy in love with you, I didn't let it bother me or realize what was happening to her."

He grimaced and sat forward with hands clasped between his powerful legs. "You never said a word of this to me."

"At the time I didn't worry that she was so upset. That realization came later. It wouldn't have occurred to me to tell you. It would have sounded like I was bragging, that you preferred me to her. The last thing I would have wanted was for you to think me petty, or that I found pleasure in hurting her.

"To my horror, I underestimated the depth of a dangerous jealousy that would drive her to destroy us. I'm afraid I was too naive and insecure to realize what was going on."

Nico got up, trying to contain his rage over what Monika had done. "I'd met her several times at the house when I'd gone to pick you up. I hadn't realized the depth of her bitter jealousy. She'd seemed nice enough. What in heaven's name made her admit to her evil?"

"Her parents noticed that she and I had stopped writing to each other. They were concerned and wanted to know why. For a long time she refused to tell them, and they knew something was terribly wrong. One day they broke her down and she confessed to returning the letters.

"They were horrified and called me to apologize. I'd always liked the Gataki family. They'd been kind to me and my grandparents. Monika got on the phone and cried. She said she knew I could never forgive her. I told her that was up to God."

Mara's character hadn't changed after all. His eyes played over her. "Did she know about Dimitra?"

"No. I never told her or her parents in the first place because I didn't learn I was pregnant until after we'd moved to Canada. Before her attack of conscience, if she'd known I was carrying your child, she likely would have gloated over my pain at being dumped, as she called it. I could imagine her calling me an idiot for believing that you loved me. I couldn't have withstood her mockery. That phone call from her and her family made me realize she did have a conscience, but she found it too late for us."

"I had no idea she would go that far," he ground out.

"No one did. After she confessed, I was afraid to

call you with the news, knowing you'd recently been married to one of the most prominent women in Athens and had risen in the company."

Nico groaned aloud. "But letting me know I was a father the second you knew you were pregnant should have superseded every consideration!"

She shuddered. "You're right. It should have, which proves I was a flawed human being not to get word to you from that first moment. And there's no excuse for not telling you the truth once I heard what Monika had done. My only defense is that I felt it would have been so cruel to tell you and your wife about Dimitra. It terrified me it could do real damage to your happiness.

"I tried putting myself in your place, Nico. Thinking about being newly married, how hard it would have been to suddenly hear you had a four-year-old daughter on the other side of the world. No bride would want to be told news like that. Not when she loved you and wanted to make a home and life with you, give you children."

Nico shook his head. Raisa had known how deeply in love he'd been with Mara. He agreed that to find out his former lover was alive and taking care of their four-year-old daughter so soon after his marriage to Raisa would have caused tremendous turmoil.

Though he imagined they would have stayed married, how did he know if Raisa could have handled his having a daughter from the woman he'd loved so desperately? The woman who was alive and had never married?

Again his lingering guilt over not loving Raisa as deeply as he'd loved Mara merged with his guilt that he hadn't been able to save her or their unborn child in that crash. That guilt would always torment him.

"You have to understand, Nico," she continued, unaware of his torment. "I didn't know if you would have welcomed a relationship with Dimitra at any age. The last time I saw you, you had to go off to do your military duty. You took my very soul with you. On our last night together you crushed me in your arms, promising to write me the second you could.

"But no letters had come by the time I'd returned to Nicosia with Leia's family four days later. After a week of being with my grandparents again, there still weren't any letters from you sent to me at her parents' house. You never phoned." Tears poured down her cheeks.

He grimaced. "Because I was in the military, the rules forbade me to make any phone calls. To think Leia intercepted all my letters and sent them back to me unopened... The pain she caused both of us was beyond cruelty."

Alexa nodded. "Her jealousy destroyed our dreams, knowing we were wildly in love. I remember waiting for Monika to call me and tell me the mail had come. My plan was to go over to her house and pick up all the letters I knew you would have sent me and forwarded."

Nico paced the deck. "How could that Monika have done such a thing?"

"It's beyond my comprehension. I waited and waited. There was so much I had to tell you, and I'd taken all those pictures I'd promised to send you. But in the middle of that nightmare, my grandfather received news that he'd been made the Greek ambassador to Canada. We were forced to leave immediately for his new post."

Another groan came out of Nico. "I can't believe you ended up in Canada."

"I about died having to fly so far away from you. Once we made the flight and had gotten settled in Ottawa, there were still no letters from you forwarded by Monika. At first I was convinced you'd been injured on maneuvers and couldn't write. After a month with no word, I knew something horrible must have happened to you. But if you'd died, it would have been all over the news. My grandfather assured me of that. Not hearing from you caused me the most excruciating pain I've ever known in my life."

"All because of Monika," he bit out.

"Yes. In time I finally had to accept the fact that Monika had been right. You'd played me, nothing more. It didn't seem possible, not after we'd planned to be married once you returned from military service. We'd dreamed of a whole life together and talked about children, but I decided you really hadn't meant it."

Nico looked out over the water, turned inside out by what she was telling him. "My letters proved otherwise."

"They did, but back then I had no knowledge of anything, and my agony increased when I discovered I was pregnant. I'd been nauseated at school and the doctor ran tests. I was so thrilled to be having your baby, but the unexpected news changed my entire world."

"It would have changed mine if you'd gotten word to my parents."

"I realize that now. My grandfather said he would track you down through your family so you could know you were a father. But I begged him not to do anything.

"I remembered you telling me your family had been forced to live down a scandal to do with your uncle Ari. I couldn't remember details, but you said it had affected your aunt in a terrible way and she'd never been the same. I didn't want to add to that misery with another scandal. And I felt such shame that my time with you had been nothing more than a summer fling, the kind Monika had alluded to."

Nico let loose a curse.

"My only excuse was that I was a witless teenager who'd ignored my grandparents' advice and had gotten into trouble like so many other girls. I definitely didn't tell Monika I was expecting. She would have derided me for being the gullible fool who would now pay the price forever. I chose to say nothing to avoid her merciless ridicule."

He lifted his head to look at her. "What's happened to Monika?"

"Over time we stopped writing letters. She never had faith in your love for me. I no longer considered her a friend by the time she told me the truth. The last contact with her was that phone call. It altered my view of life."

"Tell me about it," he said in a withering tone.

"I've gone over that moment for nineteen years. What if I'd told Monika I was pregnant the moment I knew? Would she have felt shame and admitted to me what she'd done to sabotage our love? Would she have confessed that she'd returned every letter? Or would she have laughed and stayed silent?"

"That was a missed opportunity."

"It was, Nico, and I'll suffer for it for the rest of my

life. Last month I saw you on TV and it made it worse to know you were so close."

"You saw me on the news?"

"I've seen you several times, and it has haunted me. I reasoned that Dimitra was an adult now and could make up her own mind if she wanted to get to know you. Her age and distance were no longer a problem for visits.

"But I worried about you. Would you welcome a relationship with your grown-up daughter at this stage of life? How would it affect you and your wife and children? I was tortured by endless questions with no satisfactory answers. Then I saw you at Irena's…"

"You handled your shock well enough," he muttered.

"Thank you for not exposing me in front of the others. Dimitra will always blame me for keeping her apart from you. I know she'll never forgive me. I don't deserve forgiveness and will never know the answer to certain questions if I'd just come forward with the truth.

"Naturally you would have had no choice but to think the worst about the girl who'd promised to write you back faithfully every day until your military duty came to an end."

Nico couldn't take much more of this.

"I was blessed to be able to turn to my patient, loving grandparents who listened to my heartfelt plea to stay quiet and honored my wishes. They agreed to help me raise my love child. It wasn't fair to them, Nico. They raised me from the age of five when my parents were killed in a train accident. My grandparents were and are saints."

"I agree."

"As you can imagine, Dimitra has turned out to be the great joy of my grandparents' lives. She's also my darling daughter who became my raison d'être."

CHAPTER FIVE

ALEXA WALKED AROUND the deck for a minute, then drew closer to Nico. "Would you tell me a bit about your wife? Were you happy with her, Nico? Tell me you were."

"Yes." It was the truth.

"I'm so glad. It means you recovered from what happened with us and wanted love in your life again."

He gripped the side of the boat. This conversation about Raisa needed to end. "Didn't you?" he riposted. "I can't imagine your not finding someone else."

"There were two men I cared about in Canada, but I could never be sure how Dimitra would be able to accept one into our lives."

"Then you did entertain the idea."

"Yes, but I could never commit. Dimitra has always been my priority. Close as I came to marriage in the past, I was afraid to go through with it in case it didn't work out and she was unhappy. I'd rather have seen her future settled first, whenever that time came.

"Then she met Kristos. I know her love for him is real, but they're still so young. I'd rather they waited another year at least. As you and I have learned, you never know how long love will last, no matter the reason for it getting cut off by unforeseen circumstances."

Nico had been the victim of unforeseen circumstances twice in his life. "It's Irena's fear too." He looked out over the water, still incredulous over what he'd learned.

"Do you mind if I ask how you met your wife? Unless it's too painful."

"Not at all." He turned so he could look at her. "I learned to fly in the military, but that was after I stopped sending you letters. When I returned home I bought a small plane. I soon started flying everywhere when I had to go to meetings outside of Salonica. One evening I flew to Athens and met Raisa at a party for a friend.

"We started talking and one thing led to another. It felt good to connect with someone again and we began seeing each other on a regular basis. I thought it would put her off when I told her about you and me. She knew I was still looking for you, but she was patient and never gave up. The day came when I realized my search was futile. That's when I asked her to marry me.

"One morning I took her on a flight with me and a coworker. She'd just found out we were expecting. It was a beautiful clear day with a nice tailwind. But then, suddenly, our flight from Chios where we'd celebrated our exciting news took on a different dimension.

"I had to struggle to keep us straight and level. In a flash, up became down. It was wind shear. Our seat belts barely restrained us. We crashed. I and my coworker survived, but Raisa didn't make it. I haven't taken control of a plane since."

Alexa moved closer. "You lost your wife and unborn

child. Oh, Nico. I'm so heartsick for you, I don't know what to say." The compassion in her voice sounded like the old Mara, calling up memories.

"That was eleven years ago. Since then I've immersed myself in work. To learn I have a daughter is a miracle I never expected. I don't know if she'll want a relationship with me, but I plan to find out."

"More than anything in this world I want the two of you to have one."

His breath caught. *Why? To placate your guilt?* Nico had listened to her reasons for keeping silent. On an intellectual level, he understood. But it didn't erase the pain. He couldn't talk about this any longer. "I'll take you back home before your grandfather starts to worry."

They went back to the pier and he drove her home in silence. En route she turned to him. "Nico? I promise you that our daughter has wanted her father all her life. I gave her a small photo of you when she was around five which she has treasured. It was your profile. When we got home from Irena's, she said you reminded her of the picture I gave her. She also said you were awesome. Now that she knows you are her father, her world has been transformed."

"You can't know that when she's only just learned the truth," he bit out.

"But I do. Not only does she adore Kristos who adores you, Dimitra read your letters after I left for the monastery. She's already your champion. When I returned, she said, 'He really loved you, Mama. I don't know how Monika could have done that to you, but it's *your* lie I can't forgive. *You* could have gotten in touch with his family as soon as you found out you were pregnant. They would have contacted him and he would have uncovered the mystery because he's that kind of wonderful man.'"

Though Alexa's words about Dimitra worked like a balm on Nico's tormented soul, they didn't take away the remembered pain of those dreadful first years. Being with Mara, talking with her like this, had opened a deep wound.

Every explanation she'd given him for her silence had expressed fear of hurting him or bringing shame to him and their families. The sweetness he'd found in her from the start was still an inherent part of her nature. He could never blame her for wanting to avoid causing his family pain.

After hearing her explanations, he could see how difficult everything had been for her. But he couldn't help thinking that one phone call nineteen years ago, after she discovered she was pregnant, would have made their lives so different.

When they reached the house, she got out. "I'll run inside. In case Dimitra is there, shall I send her out?"

"I don't want to force something on her she's not ready for. I'd prefer to phone her and we'll go from there."

"All right."

"Alexa?" He couldn't believe he had to call her that now.

"Yes?"

He paused for a moment, but he was too full of emotions to say anything more right now. "Nothing. It'll keep."

She whispered good-night and hurried into the house.

With a groan, he phoned Irena.

"Nico?"

"Sorry to call this late. Is Kristos home by any chance?"

"No. He's still out with Dimitra. I thought I'd better let you know her mother called to ask me for your phone number. I admit I was surprised."

Nico sucked in his breath. "I'll tell you why after I speak with him tomorrow." He couldn't go into it now.

"You don't sound yourself."

His hands tightened on the steering wheel. "I'm not. I'll explain later. *Kalinikta*, Irena."

After hanging up, he left for headquarters and sent Kristos a text.

Call me before you go to bed. I don't care how late.

He'd barely entered his office when his phone rang and he answered immediately. It was Kristos. "Thanks for calling me."

"I would have phoned you without your text, Uncle Nico. Dimitra is still with me and wants to talk to you, but she doesn't know how you feel now that you've been told the truth."

His throat swelled with emotion. "I'm overjoyed to learn I have a daughter." As he'd told Alexa, Dimitra was a miracle.

"I knew it! And that's exactly how she feels about you. Where are you?"

"At my office."

"Can we come over? She doesn't want to wait any longer to talk to you."

Neither did Nico, who was only now beginning to

unthaw and realize he had a daughter. "I'll tell Gus to let you in."

"We'll be there in five minutes."

It was the longest five minutes Nico had ever lived through and he stood by the elevator, waiting anxiously. When the doors opened, Dimitra emerged. She'd come up alone with a tearstained face.

"All my life I've wished I could meet my father. To think we've already had dinner together and you've always been here. I just didn't know it." Her voice trembled. "Do you mind if I call you Baba?"

"I'd be crushed if you didn't." Nico held out his arms and she ran into them. *I kóri mou. My daughter.* He was holding the child he and Alexa had created. It didn't seem possible. He rocked her for a long time, overwhelmed that this blessing had come into his life…a life he'd thought had lost its flavor forever.

This loving young woman had been the product of a great love. Raw anger rose inside him for the years he'd missed being a father to her.

He knew and understood why Alexa had done this to them, but it still hurt to the core of his being.

The next Friday night after dinner with Michalis Androu—whom she'd politely told she wasn't ready to explore a relationship—Alexa went in the house, torn apart by all that was happening. The last time she'd been with Nico, the solemn side of him was so different from the man Alexa had fallen in love with, she found herself mourning for the old dynamic Nico. He'd been a man full of life and had made her thankful to be alive.

She kissed her grandfather good-night and went to

bed. Since the night her daughter had gone off with Kristos, Dimitra had treated her like a stranger. For the last five days Kristos had picked her up and brought her home from the university before he went to work but Alexa hadn't seen or talked to either of them.

On Saturday morning Alexa awakened early, put on her headphones and left to go for a run around the neighborhood while Dimitra was still asleep. The only thing that helped relieve stress for Alexa was to get out of the house and run for a half hour every morning. She'd been doing it for years.

It wasn't until she got home and removed the headphones that she saw she'd received a text.

Nico.

Would the day ever come when her heart didn't jump at the sight or sound of him?

She sank down on the bed to read it.

Can you come to my office ASAP? I'll inform the front desk to send you up in the private elevator. This is important.

Alexa put a hand to her throat. Naturally it was important where their daughter was concerned. In a week his whole life had been turned upside down. So had hers. She answered him.

I'll be there in an hour.

After a quick shower, she dressed and told her grandfather she'd be back soon. Dimitra still hadn't come out of her bedroom when Alexa left for Angelis headquarters.

* * *

The fact that Nico was now CEO of a huge conglomerate hadn't escaped her. But at seventeen she hadn't truly realized what his destiny would be. She pulled into the guest parking and walked inside. After introducing herself, the male receptionist escorted her to a private elevator and pressed the button that sent her skyward.

Once the doors opened, Nico stood there wearing white cargo pants and a dark blue polo shirt. He'd always loved casual clothes and had staggering appeal no matter what he wore. Their eyes fused for a moment, taking her back in time to that first moment in the Aegean. She'd thought him drop-dead gorgeous at nineteen. He'd only grown more attractive over the years. Nico had exceeded the promise of the breathtaking man in the teenager.

"Thanks for coming."

"I'm glad you texted me. Our daughter isn't speaking to me, but I know she's been with you this week. I hope you can tell me how she's handling things." She followed him into his large, impressive office that matched a man of his stature and importance.

He indicated the couch for her to sit, then found himself a chair. "I thought you should know that last evening I took her to meet her aunt and grandparents. It was Mama's birthday and we had a party on the yacht. Giannina arranged everything. Dimitra has brought them the greatest happiness they've ever known."

"You've done the same thing for her, Nico." Despite the anger he had to feel for what Alexa had done, he'd embraced their daughter and had welcomed her into his family. Alexa had loved him heart and soul years ago. Now she loved and adored him more for the loving father he'd become just knowing of their daughter's existence.

"It's especially touching for them since she's their only living grandchild. I wanted you to know they've welcomed her with open arms."

Marvelous as the news was, Alexa jumped up, too anxiety ridden over her own guilt to sit still. She hugged her arms to her waist. "Dimitra has to be overjoyed to find the missing piece of her life and be accepted so completely. But I can only imagine what they think of me."

"They know everything." He stood. "When you went missing, they tried to help me find you."

Alexa hadn't known that. Her silence had touched his family too. Her heart hung heavy for Nico. If his wife hadn't died, there would be two grandchildren for his parents to love.

"I'm touched that they tried to help you. It's all the more reason why they must despise me for what I've done to you and Dimitra."

"For now they're reserving judgment because they're too happy. But there's something you need to know. A press release will be coming out in the media. I didn't want you to find that out before I told you. It's going to affect all of us and the people we associate with, including Raisa's parents and siblings."

Alexa's hand went to her mouth. "The news is going to be so hurtful for them."

"They knew about you."

"But not our daughter, who might never get past what I've done."

His piercing dark gaze found hers. "One thing I've learned since the dinner at Irena's. Don't ever say never."

She took a deep breath. "You're right. I never thought I'd see you again and here we are."

He grimaced. "It was like that moment when you swam back to me at Perea Beach. I feared you were a mermaid who'd disappeared on me and was gone forever until you cried my name. Nineteen years later you appeared once more, this time on Irena's patio."

She took a deep breath. "Fate had a way of uniting you with Dimitra. I'm reminded of the Greek myth about the three Fate goddesses who assigned individual destinies to mortals at birth.

"Lachesis, the Alloter, kept all knowledge of Dimitra from you. Yet even Lachesis's power couldn't prevent you and Dimitra from meeting." She cleared her throat. "We have Kristos to thank for that. Maybe it *is* true love between them, and it's so powerful it broke the spell."

"Maybe," he murmured, putting a hand on her arm. His touch sent darts of awareness through her body. "Your knowledge of the myths is remarkable."

Little did he know Alexa had made them a lifelong study. She lifted her head. They were so close, she could imagine him kissing her and wanted it so badly she could taste it.

"Nico, thank you for telling me about the party. For Dimitra to be accepted and loved by you and your family will have made her feel reborn. As for being forewarned that there'll be a media explosion, I'm now forearmed. I can't thank you enough. Now I have to get back to my grandfather and will let myself out."

For self-preservation she had to get out of there. Being with him like this was the hardest thing on earth to handle. He ran a hand up her arm before letting her go. The old Nico wouldn't have let her walk out of there.

As she rode the elevator to the lobby, she had to admit that all these years apart hadn't changed her feelings for Nico. If anything, they'd grown stronger. Just now she'd wanted to throw herself in his arms the way she'd done years ago while they'd kissed each other senseless.

But the myth about Hera and her jealousy of Io had done its damage, and Alexa had made it worse by keeping quiet. The result had caused her to lose Nico as she'd known it would if he ever learned the truth. If there'd been a glimmer of hope that deep down he still wanted to be with her, he would have pulled her back so she couldn't leave his office.

As she walked to her car, she was left with one heart-wrenching, undeniable truth. *You'll always be in love with him*.

Nico watched the elevator doors close.

A primordial urge to go after her shook him to the core. The desire for her that had burned nineteen years ago blazed hotter than ever. All the pain he'd lived through hadn't extinguished it. Knowing what she'd done to keep the knowledge of their child from him, hearing her reasons why, still hadn't killed his longing to be with her. How was that even possible?

Yet she'd left his office as soon as he'd told her about the family party and how the news he had a daughter would get out and impact all their lives. The Mara he'd loved would have stayed and ended up in his arms. But he had to get it in his head that she'd grown up and changed. There was no Mara. She'd turned into Alexa.

This was one time when he needed Tio—the one person who'd been there at the height of Nico's pain and could understand what seeing Alexa again, now, meant to him. Only his best friend could know what Nico was going through right now and would tell him this insanity would pass. But would it?

Dimitra was a constant reminder of her mother. The thought that he'd never be free of his memories was so terrifying, he rushed over to the desk and buzzed his secretary to tell him that he was leaving. Irena had become his best friend. He'd drive over and talk to her about how he could have a relationship with his daughter that didn't include Alexa.

But a half hour later, his talk with Irena on the patio brought no relief.

"Kristos has told me how much Dimitra already loves you, Nico. But she also adores her mother, even if she's in turmoil right now. You and Alexa are her parents, and you're both going to be included in her life from now on. The sooner you can handle that the better because... I have news. I would have called you if you hadn't come over."

Nico didn't like the sound of more news and got to his feet.

Irena eyed him with compassion. "Kristos gave her a ring last night."

He stopped pacing. "Somehow that doesn't surprise me. He loves her. Now that her circumstances have changed, he wants to protect the woman he loves."

"I agree. So it's up to you and me how we accept the news, even if we still believe it's too soon. My father-in-law will erupt when he hears."

"If I know your son, he won't care and wants to shout it to the world." Nico had felt the same way about Mara.

She nodded. "He already asked me if we could have an engagement party here, but I told him nothing could be done without her mother being involved."

Nico rubbed his lower lip with his thumb. "I was with Alexa at my office earlier. She doesn't think Dimitra will forgive her for what she did. But what you've just told me has given me an idea. Do you know Kristos's schedule for today?"

"Only that he was picking up Dimitra and probably wouldn't be home until late."

"Good. That might give me time to tell Alexa the latest news and plan a strategy that will help mother and daughter work through their pain."

"If anyone can bring that about, it's you, Nico. But what about *your* pain?"

"Like you said, the sooner I can handle the fact that Alexa and I are both inextricably involved in our daughter's life, the better. Thanks for talking to me, Irena. You've been a big help. Now I've got a phone call to make and will tell you the outcome later."

He kissed her cheek and let himself out to make the call. Maybe Alexa didn't want to hear from him so soon, but a part of him rejoiced that he had a vital reason to talk to her before the day was out. What was wrong with him? Where was his loyalty to Raisa to even be thinking this way?

After picking up some groceries, Alexa drove home filled with anxiety. Dimitra still wasn't speaking to her, and she couldn't bear it. After seeing Nico and hearing about his family party, she wanted to connect with her daughter and know how she was feeling about her new family. So far, Nico had been Alexa's only conduit for information.

Once in the house, she realized no one was home. Phyllis had probably taken her grandfather out on this beautiful day. Dimitra had to be off with Kristos. Alexa put the groceries away, remembering those moments in Nico's office when she would have given anything for him to pull her into his arms. How insane was that? As if her thoughts had conjured him, her phone rang and she saw the caller ID.

Her heart leaped to her throat before she answered it, struggling to sound normal. "Nico?"

"Have you heard the news?" he asked without preamble.

She trembled. "I don't know what you mean."

"That's good. Do you have plans for the rest of the day?"

"Nico...don't keep me in suspense."

"We have to talk, but not on the phone."

This had something to do with Dimitra she wasn't going to like. Maybe she was planning to move out because she couldn't stand to be around her mother anymore. "I'll meet you wherever you say." She felt desperate.

"Why don't I come by for you? How soon can you be ready?"

Her eyes closed tightly. This was serious. "Right now." It was close to four o'clock.

"Then I'll be there in ten minutes."

She clicked off and freshened up in the bathroom. Makeup would help put some color in her cheeks. With a coat of coral lipstick and a quick brushing of her hair, she felt a little more presentable. Not that Nico would notice. What an irony that the man she'd turned into an enemy was turning out to be the only person she could appeal to for help. Nothing was making sense right now.

CHAPTER SIX

AFTER LEAVING A NOTE on the fridge saying that Alexa was with Nico and would be back later, she walked out to the curb in front to wait for him. The sight of the black car and striking male driving it shouldn't have excited her. The way she was feeling, she could be seventeen again. Once the car came to a stop, she got in before he could walk around and open her door for her.

Their gazes collided. "If the news is bad, please drive us somewhere away from the house. I don't want Dimitra or my grandfather to come home and see me too upset to face them."

He started the car and they took off. "I thought we'd drive to Pella and enjoy the Roditis wine you used to love."

She panicked. "You think I'm going to need it?" He'd taken her there one glorious day long ago. They'd been delirious with love while they sampled the pink wine from a vineyard under a hot sun.

"I think we both do."

Alexa fastened her seat belt, not knowing how to deal with that remark. "Why didn't you just tell me what this is about before I left you earlier?"

Nico drove with a mastery that was reflected in everything he did. "I left the office right after you did, but I didn't hear the news until I dropped by Irena's. Kristos and our daughter got engaged last night."

The news wasn't what Alexa had expected. She was so surprised, she didn't say anything at first.

"What's made you go quiet?"

She bit her lip. "I thought you were going to tell me that Dimitra was moving out. That's been my greatest fear." Her voice had started to wobble. "I thought she despised me so much she couldn't stand to live with me anymore. I wouldn't have blamed her. In fact I've had nightmares about it since I saw you at Irena's."

He reached out to cover her hand. His warmth enveloped her whole body. Nico could have no idea how much she craved his touch. "If you'd heard the marvelous things she'd said about you to my parents and Giannina, you'd know the thought has never crossed her mind."

Nico's words broke Alexa down and she sobbed. He held her hand a little tighter before letting it go.

"Thank you for being so kind to me, Nico." She wiped her eyes. "I don't deserve it after what I've done to you. In truth I don't know how you can stand to be around me."

She heard his sharp intake of breath. "This afternoon Irena reminded me that you and I will always be involved in our daughter's life. It will help all of us if we get along and do what's best for her. That's why I wanted you to come with me. Sharing Dimitra is a new experience for both of us. I'm trying to tread carefully."

"And doing a beautiful job of it!" she declared, lifting

her head to look at him through tear-drenched eyes. "I mean it, Nico. Besides everything else, you really are an exceptional human being. Our daughter has already figured that out."

"Then let's decide what to do next. I believe you and I and Irena are all in agreement about Kristos and Dimitra moving too fast. But that ring on her finger has made it a fait accompli. It's my opinion that if the first thing we do as her parents is fight them on this engagement, then—"

"Then it would be the worst thing we could do," she broke in. "I couldn't agree with you more."

By now they'd reached the vineyard outside Pella. Nico slowed down and drove along the road to the winery. A few tourists came out the door. "What do you say we go in and plot."

For a moment he sounded just like the old Nico, filling her with thrill after thrill. She laughed all the way inside the winery's front door. It astonished her she could do that when she'd been sobbing so hard before. He found them a table and ordered the same wine they'd once enjoyed. "This is like a window in time for me," she said.

Over the rim of the wineglass his dark eyes stared at her with an intensity that made her quiver. "For me too. I haven't been back here since." His deep voice pierced her insides.

She sipped her wine, unable to believe they were together like this again. But it was dangerous to go down that road of the past. To break the spell he'd been casting on her since they'd been in the car, she changed the subject.

"I'm thinking something should be done to celebrate their engagement. If I show Dimitra I support her, maybe it would help our relationship."

He nodded. "You took the words out of my mouth. Since I'm a friend of the Papadakis family and would do this for Kristos and his mother no matter what, you and I could host an engagement party for them at my villa on Sarti. We'd let them make up the guest list."

Was there ever a more wonderful man born? Her eyes filled. "That's very generous of you, Nico."

"We're only talking an engagement party. Being the mother of the bride, you'll be the one to plan the wedding when the time comes. That is if they make it that far." When her face fell, he laughed.

"You're still a big tease." She was loving this time with him so much it frightened her. "Sometimes in the past you were so exasperating, I wanted to run away from you."

"But you didn't," he said in his deep voice, capturing her gaze. "Even if you'd tried, you know you wouldn't have gotten very far."

"You're right. I fell for you so hard, I would have turned around and flung myself at you. I was pathetic."

His devilish grin set her on fire. When they'd been on his cruiser together talking about everything, he'd been upset and morose. Today she saw no sign of that side of him, thank heaven. She couldn't bear it if he wasn't the same wonderful Nico she would always adore.

Nico's dark eyes played over her in the old familiar way that sent her heart thudding. "I'm glad to see a smile on your face." That was only possible because being with him again had brought her to life. He provided the magic. "If you're ready, we'll drive back to Salonica. When I take you home, we might run into the happy couple and can tell them what we'd like to do for them, if they're amenable."

"They'll be overjoyed and you know it. I could never deny you anything. Our daughter is no different."

"But you did deny me," he came back, surprising her.

"What do you mean?"

A mysterious look crossed over his handsome face. "Have you forgotten I asked you to run away with me after we finished our wine here years ago?"

She laughed. "But you weren't being serious."

"Oh, I was deadly serious. Remember that hot-air-balloon concession we passed that day? I'd planned for the person taking us up to head for Hellenia where my uncle's family lived. We could have hidden out there with no one the wiser and waited until you'd turned eighteen. Then we could have gotten married and started a new life."

"Nico—I don't believe it!"

"At the last minute I changed my mind because an even better plan came to me that wouldn't involve my uncle. But it would take a lot more planning."

She flashed him a wide smile. "Am I going to hear about that one?"

"One of these days when we're not pressed with helping our daughter, I'll share it all."

"I don't know if I want to hear it."

"Why not?"

"Because I'll wish you'd carried it out."

That deep, rich laughter burst out of him, filling her

with joy. On the way back they talked about possible dates for the engagement party. When he pulled in the driveway, they didn't see Kristos's car.

"I imagine Dimitra is still out with Kristos." She opened the door, afraid to remain any longer and realize she'd rather stay right where she was and never leave. Before getting out she turned to him.

"No matter how this goes with our daughter, I'll never be able to thank you enough for everything you've done to make this easier. You never deserved what I did to you."

"We didn't deserve what Monika did. Why don't we agree not to talk about that anymore. That portion of our lives is over."

"You honestly mean it?"

"How could I not when I've been united with our daughter. It's a time to rejoice, not wallow in pain."

This sounded like the Nico she'd once loved. "All right. We won't go over that ground anymore. Thank you for today. *Kalinikta*, Nico."

She dashed toward the house and hurried inside, surprising her daughter and grandfather who sat talking in the living room. She was back after all!

Their *papoú* smiled. "We're glad you're home, Alexa."

Her daughter avoided acknowledging her.

"I couldn't get here soon enough." She moved closer. "I've just heard you're engaged to Kristos."

Dimitra jumped up looking shocked. "You already know?"

"Yes. Irena told your father and he just told me."

"If you're going to tell me we're too young to—"

"I'm not," Alexa interrupted her. This was the first time her daughter had said a word to her in days. "We both think you and Kristos are perfect for each other."

Her eyes lit up. "You mean it?" she cried.

"With all my heart."

"My father thinks so too?"

"Yes. He thinks *you're* perfect and will make Kristos a wonderful wife. So do I. As you reminded me a week ago, I told you I met the one at seventeen. Now it's your turn, and you're *eighteen*."

"Mama—" Her daughter reached for her and they hugged. Alexa's grandfather had tears in his eyes, smiling his approval.

"Your father has offered his villa on Sarti to announce your engagement. He's asked me to help him. But only if it's what the two of you want."

A cry of pure joy came out of her. "We couldn't want anything more! All my dreams are coming true!" She hugged her *papoú* hard, then turned to Alexa and hugged her again. "I've got to phone Kristos and tell him what's happened."

After she disappeared, Alexa's grandfather shared a long glance with her. "You made a very wise decision just now."

"Don't give me too much credit. That's Nico's influence. He knows more about parenting than I do."

"I disagree. You've been a wonderful mother, otherwise Dimitra wouldn't be making this kind of progress so fast."

"You're the wise one and I'll love you forever." She reached out and put her arms around him. Alexa wasn't naive enough to think everything was perfect, but at least the three of them were functioning enough to get through this first stage. For that blessing she was beyond thankful.

Two weeks later, after college classes were over on Friday, Nico drove Alexa, Dimitra and their *papoú* to Sarti. He could have arranged for them to fly to Sithonia and then go on to Sarti, but the scenery was worth the drive. His daughter sat up front with him. Alexa got in the back to help her grandfather during the eighty-plus mile ride. They would stay at his villa for the weekend.

Kristos was coming by helicopter. The party would take place on Saturday afternoon. All the guests, including Irena and her family, would fly in on Saturday beforehand.

Nico still couldn't get over the fact that three weeks ago he'd gone to Irena's as a single man, and this afternoon he was bringing his former lover and beautiful daughter to his home. Things like this just didn't happen in normal life.

"Baba? Where are we exactly?"

He smiled. "We're on Sithonia, one of the three legs jutting into the Aegean from Salonica. I've been driving us along the coast of the Chalkidiki Peninsula." The road wound through the base of the green mountains, making a contrast to the turquoise waters of the Aegean. Nico always found it a breathtaking sight.

"It's so beautiful, but I thought I saw lightning above the mountains."

"We get it in summer, but it won't stop us from enjoying Sarti Beach tomorrow."

"Where's your villa?"

He could see Alexa through the rearview mirror. She was eyeing scenery she'd never viewed. By the look on her beautiful face, she was entranced.

"On the mountain overlooking the beach. You'll love the purity of the sand and water. It's not too deep."

Perfect for a mermaid with chestnut hair who loved to play in the water for hours. The vision of a young Alexa who'd enthralled him from day one flashed into his mind. They were occurring more often, disturbing him whether awake or asleep.

One more curve on the road and a view of Mount Athos opened up in the distance. The sight brought exclamations from everyone. "Ooh, I'd love to climb that with Kristos!" Dimitra exclaimed.

Nico chuckled. "I'm afraid you can't."

"Why not?"

"No women are allowed," her grandfather interjected. "It's forbidden."

"That's the most absurd thing I ever heard! What goes on there, Papoú?"

Nico's eyes met Alexa's through the mirror. Hers were smiling. Their daughter was a delight to both of them.

"You'd be surprised. It's the center of Eastern Orthodox monasticism. There are over twenty monasteries under the direct jurisdiction of the Ecumenical Patriarch of Constantinople. Not even female animals are allowed."

"Are you serious? That's incredible. I didn't realize. You always know everything."

"Not everything, but close."

Nico liked the older man very much. At Gavril's remark he burst into laughter along with Alexa, unable to remember the last time he'd enjoyed himself this much. Years in fact.

Being with Alexa had everything to do with this change in him. When he'd taken her to the vineyard recently, he'd meant what he'd said to her about forgetting the past. It *was* over. Inexplicably his anger seemed to have dissipated and his life had taken on a whole new meaning.

"We're almost home." He took a private road that wound up the mountainside to his white villa.

"You've got to be kidding me," Dimitra murmured after they arrived. "This is the most fabulous place I've ever seen in my life!" She undid her seat belt and turned to him. "I love it, Baba. I love you." In the next breath she threw her arms around him.

Nico's throat swelled with emotion as he kissed her cheek. "When I bought this place, I never imagined the day would come when my very own daughter would be here with me. I love you too," he said in a thick tone. "What do you say we get out so I can help your grandfather? He's had to sit for a long time."

"You're right. Since the moment I knew you were my father, my head's been spinning. I don't know what I'm doing and have only been thinking of my own happiness." Nico adored his daughter and felt the same way.

Just then they heard the whir of rotor blades. A helicopter was landing at the rear of the villa. "That'll be your fiancé."

She turned to get out. "I feel like I'm in a dream."

Nico could relate.

Within seconds Kristos came running. The two lovebirds threw their arms around each other. Nico glanced at Alexa who was getting out of her side of the car. He took her grandfather's wheelchair from the trunk.

"Here you go, Gavril. I'll have you comfortable in a hurry." The older man deserved anything Nico could do for him after he'd sacrificed his life helping raise their daughter all these years.

"I'm fine, Nico."

Thanos and Anna, the married couple who looked after his place and served in many capacities, came out to carry the luggage inside.

Alexa stayed by her grandfather as Nico wheeled him through the sprawling, one-story villa to a guest room. Together they helped him get settled. "Anna will bring you a tray of food. Alexa's room is next door to you."

Gavril caught his arm. "You treat me like a king. Now you go on and help the others."

"I'll be right back and we'll eat together," Alexa assured him. After giving him a kiss, she followed Nico to the next guest room.

"Dimitra's room is at the end of the hall."

She walked to the window that overlooked the beach. "This spacious, airy villa is incredible, Nico. There's still a view since the light hasn't disappeared yet. You and your wife must have been beyond happy here."

The mention of Raisa jolted him because he hadn't been thinking about her at all. What was wrong with him? "We lived in a villa in Salonica. After she died, I sold it and bought this one."

Alexa looked over at him. "I'm sorry. I spoke without thinking."

"You have nothing to apologize for. Say whatever you want. When I'm in town and have to stay over, I use the apartment above the office. If you'd like to freshen up, I'll see to settling Dimitra and have food sent to you and Gavril."

Her eyes filled. "Thank you for being this wonderful to us."

"I can't do enough for our daughter." In truth he couldn't do enough for Alexa at this point. She'd handled the responsibility of raising their daughter alone, without him. He suffered over those missing years when he'd had no part in loving her and raising Dimitra from babyhood to the age she was now. The three of them had been cheated of that time together.

If he closed his eyes, nothing seemed to have changed. Her words and the way she said them made him believe they'd gone back in time to those three weeks when he'd lost his heart.

But there was a problem because when he opened them, his mermaid had grown into a stunning, sophisticated woman, a mother who had a career and responsibilities. Did she long for those days when they were so much in love, nothing else mattered?

Raisa had been very much aware of Nico's feelings for Mara. Now that she was gone, did he have the right to be thinking about Mara all over again? Did he deserve a second chance at happiness with her? Before this weekend was out, he wanted to take her out on the beach and spend time alone with her. But did he dare? Would she want to be with him again like that?

Riddled with questions and guilt, he left the room.

* * *

The Saturday announcement party with family and a few close friends had put permanent smiles on the faces of the engaged couple. Most everyone had enjoyed the swimming pool. Alexa had preferred to walk around taking pictures with her phone, many of them of Nico.

All the fabulous catered food and music had made it an unforgettable day followed by professional picture taking to preserve memories. Though Nico's parents and sister couldn't have been nicer to Alexa and her grandfather, the two of them stayed close to Irena and her son Yanni.

Before all the guests had to leave, Alexa took Irena to her bedroom. It was there she shared the second letter Nico had sent her. As Irena read it, tears trickled down her cheeks.

"This gives me chills, Alexa."

"It did the same thing to me the first time I read it. I'd just been in your home with you the day before. Everything Nico wrote about Tio and you was true, down to your beautiful red hair."

She stared at Alexa. "It's unbelievable that my son met your daughter. What were the chances?"

"I know. He's the best!"

"So is she. I'm crazy about her. But I'm talking about Nico."

Alexa blinked. "What do you mean?"

"When he couldn't find you, he changed and was never the same again. I know because Tio and I helped him search for you. He was so in love and so heartbroken when he couldn't find you, it really wasted him for a long, long time. Now suddenly you've reappeared in his life, with *his* daughter no less. The change in him is more dramatic than you can imagine."

"But he got married!"

"Yes." Irena put a hand on her arm. "He realized he couldn't live on hope forever and she was a lovely person who adored him. But she knew you'd been the love of his life. If she'd lived and they'd had a baby to love, I have no doubts it would have helped him to be happier."

Alexa shook her head. "Her death was so terrible."

"Agreed, but he's handled it surprisingly well. What he's never gotten over is the loss of you. Not really. That's why I can tell you that your presence has brought about a miraculous healing. The sorrow he's worn like a burden since the first time I met him, is gone. Today he's a new man and that's all to do with you."

Irena's confession thrilled her. "Thank you for telling me this, but the fact remains, I did a terrible thing not to let him know I was pregnant at the very beginning. If I disgust you for what I held back, you're being very kind to me. It means more to me than you know."

"Alexa...if I'd been in your situation at that age, when Nico's parents were so prominent and your grandfather's career was at stake, I know I wouldn't have told Tio."

She wiped her eyes. "You're just saying that because you're such a good person."

"No. I'm telling you the truth. Tio's parents didn't approve of his relationship with me. I didn't come from a family of privilege. They did everything in their power to dissuade him from being with me. We eloped so they couldn't stop us, while he was still training in the military."

Alexa blinked in disbelief. "I didn't know that."

"It's taken a long time to win them over. I'm still not there yet in their eyes. Thank you for showing me this." Her voice caught. "It's another proof that Tio really did love me."

She started to give the letter back, but Alexa refused it. "Nico's letters provided me the same proof. You keep it and read it whenever you want. Now give me a minute to change into my bathing suit. It's a beautiful night and I feel like a swim before going to bed. You stay in here. When I'm ready, I'll walk you out to say goodbye."

Irena nodded, already reading the letter again.

Alexa left her to go in the bathroom to change. After putting on her beach robe she grabbed a big towel to take with her.

The two women hugged hard before they left the bedroom. Irena was quickly becoming a close friend. Alexa walked her out of the villa to the helicopter pad to see her off. Nico had gone to find Yanni. All the other guests had left.

While Dimitra and Kristos talked and ate on the patio with her grandfather, Alexa told them she was going to walk down the road to the beach. The sun hadn't set yet. It was a sight she wanted to see and told them she'd be back before long to help her grandfather get to bed.

Irena had given Alexa a lot to think about and she needed to be alone with her thoughts as she made her way toward the sea below. Nico couldn't have found a more enchanting spot on earth to live. She hoped she could be forgiven for being happy he hadn't lived here with his wife.

When she reached the beach, she slipped off her beach robe and put it on top of the towel before walking into the gentle sea. At any second the sun would drop below the horizon.

Getting in the water with Nico had been one of their greatest pleasures during those three weeks years ago. But to want to be alone with him now would be asking too much, even if she wanted to believe Irena. Alexa didn't doubt Nico was happy to finally know the truth about everything, but that didn't mean the sight of her made him want to go back to where they'd left off.

The other day in his office, he hadn't followed through and kissed her senseless the way he'd once done. He'd held back, which told Alexa she didn't dare imagine all had been forgiven.

For another thing, Nico couldn't have been celibate all this time since his wife's death. There had to be a woman he was seeing right now. This weekend Nico had been the ultimate host, but once they were all back in Salonica tomorrow, he'd be free to see any woman he wanted. To imagine that Alexa could be an intimate part of his life again sounded almost beyond the realm of possibility.

How would he feel to know Alexa was longing to get back in his arms and stay there? While she'd been at his villa, she'd been able to handle being around him because other people had provided a buffer. Giannina, among others, had pulled her aside.

She'd said she'd like to go to lunch with her next week so they could talk. Apparently she'd forgiven

Alexa enough for what she'd done to her brother to extend the olive branch. Alexa liked her and had agreed to meet her.

But now that everyone had gone, Alexa was prey to her emotions. Needing to rid herself of doubts and unassuaged longings, she swam hard until she'd worn herself out. As she swam toward the beach, she realized she wasn't alone.

CHAPTER SEVEN

"*NICO*—"

He looked like a Greek god as he walked into the water wearing his black trunks. "The family told me you were down here. I decided to join you."

Her heart was beating way too fast to be healthy. She started treading water. "I couldn't resist. Thanks to you, the party was a huge success, and this place is paradise."

Nico swam around her, reminding her of those magical nights in the sea years ago. "Our daughter just told me she's never been so happy in her life."

"I believe it."

His gaze pierced her. "What about you, Alexa? Are *you* happy?"

Being with Nico again had brought her an out-of-this-world kind of happiness. "You have no idea. Our daughter is finally getting to know her long-lost father, and she's engaged to be married to a very remarkable man I'm already crazy about." She smiled. "I'll ask you the same question."

He came closer. "You want to know if I'm happy?"

She had trouble swallowing. Her desire for him was so great, she thought she'd go crazy if he didn't reach for her. "Yes. Less than a month ago you had no idea what was going to happen and how it would affect your entire universe."

"That's the perfect way to describe it. When I kept getting those unopened letters and couldn't find you after I returned home, I knew my universe would never be the same again. Yet here you are tonight, bringing me more happiness than I deserve."

His answer thrilled her, but it puzzled her too. "What do you mean, deserve?"

"I'm not the person I once was."

His words haunted her. "I could say the same thing about myself. Time changes all of us."

It hurt that the fun-loving man she worshipped had all of a sudden reverted to his more solemn self once more. Something troubling had to be going on inside him. She didn't know what to say and started swimming toward the beach. He followed her out of the water. Alexa reached for the towel to dry herself off.

Nico did the same thing. "If you've had enough, I'll drive you up to the villa."

"Thank you."

He didn't even want to walk in the sand with her for a few minutes? That was so unlike the Nico of the past. But what could she expect if he didn't love her the way he once had? Irena said he'd changed, but something prevented Nico from reaching for her physically.

She slipped on her beach robe and they made their way to the estate car parked where the private road ended. Her attraction to him had never been stronger, but she couldn't forget he'd found love with Raisa and had married her. Maybe her memory was holding him back. Nor could she deny the fact that she'd caused pain to the two people she loved most. To expect feelings or attraction from Nico at this point wasn't realistic.

It only took a minute to reach the villa. "Thank you so much for this fabulous party, Nico. Dimitra has been glowing. So has Kristos. Irena loves you for being so devoted to her and her family. Everything good has happened because of you."

She got out of the car without his help and hurried to the patio. Nico followed. "Come on, Grandpa. I don't know about you, but I'm exhausted," Alexa said.

"We appreciate all you've done, Nico," her grandfather assured him, then looked at Dimitra and Kristos. "You two need some time alone. I'm ready."

Dimitra got up. "Good night, Papoú, Mama. See you both in the morning. Thank you for everything." She kissed both of them and turned to her father. "Oh, Baba, this party has been so perfect. Thank you with all my heart."

Alexa watched father and daughter embrace and then pushed the wheelchair inside and through the house to her grandfather's bedroom. She helped him undress and get into bed.

"Looks like you and Dimitra are on a normal footing again."

She glanced at him. "We're getting there, with Nico's help." Alexa wished she could say the same about herself and Nico. "He has turned my nightmare into something we can all live with. He'll never know how grateful I am. Now I'm going to say good-night and see you in the morning. You've got your phone. If you need anything, call me and I'll come running. Good night."

* * *

Nico went to work the next week, but by the time the board of directors meeting ended on Friday, he realized he'd been worthless. He was no longer the same man who'd been running the Angelis empire. In the last four weeks his world had undergone an upheaval of biblical proportions.

After all these years he finally had answers to the questions that had tortured him. Alexa was alive and living in Salonica, not France. Dimitra was proving to be the most enchanting daughter any father could imagine having. To find out he'd had a child of his body with the woman he'd loved beyond all else had completely changed his vision of life.

By now the news had gone out through the media. Years ago the plane crash that had killed Nico's wife and unborn child had been sensationalized. Now came even more sensational news surrounding him. The recently appointed CEO of the Angelis Corporation had an eighteen-year-old daughter, but his deceased wife hadn't been the mother. Furthermore, the mother proved to be the granddaughter of the former Greek ambassador to Cyprus and Canada.

Kristos hadn't been spared either. His plan to marry the daughter of Nico Angelis in the near future had been spread all over the media. Sadly the horror of the car crash that had killed his father, a vice president in the Papadakis Shipping Lines, had also been brought to the surface once more.

Nico had known it would all come out.

Much as he wished the news hadn't hurt their families, he'd been too overjoyed with his daughter to let it affect him. But he worried for Alexa and the impact it had made on her. By the time the board meeting had ended late Friday afternoon, his concern drove him to phone her. He was glad for the excuse.

All week he'd resisted the temptation to call her. After Nico had driven them back to Salonica on Sunday and helped her grandfather inside, he'd been forced to face the truth. He hadn't wanted to leave her. If it had been possible, he would have asked her to stay at the villa for a week or longer.

That moment in the water with Alexa had changed him. When the family had told him she'd gone down for a swim, he couldn't join her fast enough, and there she was. He kept looking at her gorgeous face and hair. It was then he realized he wasn't angry. Not anymore. He found himself wanting to be with her again in every sense of the word. He wanted her in his arms and his bed.

Being around Alexa for the weekend hadn't been nearly long enough. To have to say goodbye Sunday afternoon had been difficult, yet she'd shown no regret that he was leaving. He couldn't stand the separation any longer.

With determination he reached for his cell and made the call. She answered on the third ring.

"Nico?" She sounded surprised. Her reaction deflated him. What had he expected? That she would sound breathless the way she once did waiting to hear from him?

There was a lot he wanted to discuss with her, but not over the phone. "I'll make this quick. Do you have plans for this evening?"

"Only to watch a soccer match with my grandfather. We're eating dinner right now."

That ruled out his first suggestion. "Would you mind if I came by to pick you up? We could go for a ride. It won't take long. I need your advice about Dimitra."

"Is everything all right?" Alarm had tinged her voice. "I know you've been with her several times this week."

"We're fine, but I'm a new father and would like your input."

"I'm not sure how much help I can be. How soon do you want to come?"

"Shall we say half an hour, or do you need more time?"

"No, no. I'll be ready. See you soon."

He hung up, relieved she hadn't turned him down. Once he'd showered and changed out of his suit, he took off for the Filo home. She met him at the door bringing a faint floral fragrance with her that was new. In those pleated white pants and fitted khaki-colored top, Nico had a hard time not staring at the feminine mold of her body.

After he helped her in the car, he drove them down to the beach and parked near the water.

"We've been here before," she murmured.

He shut off the engine and turned to her, studying her stunning profile. The sun would be going down soon and the golden-hour light brought out the gold highlights of her hair. How many times had he kissed her and played with it, never wanting to stop. "The beach was our home. It seems natural to come here. Let's walk."

Alexa removed her shoes and got out. After stepping on the sand she looked at him with a hint of anxiety. "What did you want to ask me about Dimitra?"

Damn. She was feeling uncomfortable with him. They'd never had that trouble in their past life together. "I'll get to that in a minute. First, I've been worried about the coverage in the news the other night. How are you and Gavril handling it?"

"We're fine. He's no longer working for the government, and I won't be working at the university until the end of August. Neither of us is in the limelight."

"What about Dimitra?"

"If it bothered her, she hasn't said. I know it's because she's so involved with Kristos. None of us has to face people the way *you* do on a daily basis. Before long the news will die down for us. Let's hope for you too since you didn't ask for any of this." The tremor in her voice tugged on his emotions.

"Don't worry about me."

She finally turned to him. "How can you say that? This whole situation hasn't been fair to you or your family." Her eyes, like precious green gems, filmed over. "If I'd done the right thing the moment I knew I was pregnant, this would nev—"

"Stop," he broke in on her. "We promised not to go there again. You did what you felt had to be done at the time. It's over. I realized that while we were at the villa last weekend and I saw you in the water. It reminded me of our past. Not only were you young, you weren't my wife when we made love. I fought it until that last night. The blame falls on me."

She made a strange sound. "Don't forget I was the

most willing participant on earth, Nico. I had no shame. You were my whole life."

And mine. "Love hit us hard, but make no mistake. I'm the reason for your pregnancy and take full responsibility, even if it is nineteen years too late. I should have known better than to act on my desires before our marriage could take place." He'd been out of control. "I should have been there when you had our baby. Tell me what it was like."

"I was terrified!" Then a smile lit her face. "The pains started early on a Thursday morning and were unreal. After they'd grown five minutes apart, my grandmother drove me to the hospital. Dimitra was born at eight thirty-two in the evening. My grandfather came to the hospital two hours before the delivery."

Nico groaned. He reached for her hand as they walked. "You were in labor twelve hours?"

She nodded. "The doctor told me that was pretty normal. I could hear Dimitra cry while she was being delivered. It was like a gurgle at first. They put her across my chest and I'll never forget that feeling of holding her for the first time. She was beautiful, with olive skin and dark hair like yours. I wanted you there more than anything."

Nico could hardly breathe thinking about it. "How much did she weigh?"

"Seven pounds, two ounces and she was twenty inches long. Perfect. I stayed in the hospital two days so I could learn how to nurse her. She took to it fast. I have so many pictures and home movies. Dimitra will show all of them to you. The grandparents doted on her as much as I did."

"I can't wait to see everything." Hearing about the delivery made Nico hunger for every detail of her life from the time they'd been apart.

"What did you want to talk to me about?"

He stopped walking and let go of her hand. "I wondered what you would think about a weekend cruise on the yacht, just you, Dimitra, Gavril and me. We could leave on a Friday afternoon and come back Sunday. I thought we could visit the island of Samos."

Her eyes widened in surprise. "You used to tell me how much you loved going there with your friends."

Nico had the satisfaction of knowing she hadn't forgotten all the things they'd talked about. "Dimitra will love it too. At night you could get out all those pictures and home movies to entertain us. I only have one question. Do you think our daughter could stand to be away from Kristos for two nights?"

She darted him one of those impish smiles he remembered, almost giving him a heart attack. "I'm the wrong person to ask. During those three weeks years ago, I resented every second we weren't together. But Dimitra's case is different. She'll have the incentive of spending hours with her newly discovered *baba*. I can't imagine anything being more wonderful for her. You wouldn't need me with you."

He'd been afraid she'd say that, and he refused to let the fact that he hadn't loved Raisa as he should have get in the way now. He wanted to be with Alexa and needed to convince her. "You're wrong. This is still new to both of us and I want her to be comfortable. That can only happen if you and Gavril are there too. One of the stewards will be happy to help him with whatever he might need so please don't worry. If you're in agreement, would you broach the subject with her and let me know how she feels? I can arrange for any weekend."

"Spoken like the CEO who makes the rules," she teased.

"My only perk."

"Be honest. The best one." Talking with her like this made the lost years fade for a little while.

A smile lifted at the corner of her luscious mouth. "Do you know while we were together, I never realized what kind of life was waiting for you in your father's company. I'm embarrassed to think I didn't have a clue what responsibilities you would inherit one day."

Nico chuckled. "My problem was, I *did* know what was waiting for me, and it got in the way of my wanting to spend every second of my life with you."

She blushed. "I'm afraid I was oblivious to everything except just being with you. Monika's mother teased me mercilessly about being good for nothing while I waited for you to get off work. I helped clean and cook when Monika and I didn't go out, but my mind was constantly on you. Dimitra is just as bad when she's waiting for Kristos to come."

Her smile swept him away. "Do you think she'd like to be with the two of us for a few days?"

"I'll talk to her, Nico, and let you know."

"Do you think she might be home now?"

"I'm not sure. Let's find out and go back. My grandfather will be happy if I can watch the last of the match with him."

* * *

After Nico saw her to the door, Alexa watched him drive off. Once again, he took her heart with him. Nothing had changed. She would always hunger for him, but that hunger could never be assuaged if he didn't want her just as badly.

I should have been there when you had our baby. Those words Nico had said earlier reminded her how she'd kept him and their daughter apart. But as he'd said, it was over and there was no point in dwelling on it.

She closed the door and walked through to the study. If Dimitra showed excitement over the idea of an outing on the yacht with her parents, Alexa would go as a favor to Nico. But that would have to be the end of family trips. After all, the three of them weren't a family in the proverbial sense.

When broached the next morning, Dimitra acted overjoyed at the prospect. She phoned her father immediately. Alexa heard laughter from their daughter who said, "I can live without Kristos that long, Baba." The rapport between the two of them thrilled Alexa. Dimitra had been missing this all her life, but no longer.

By now it was July and the weather had grown hotter. The following Friday Nico came by for them and loaded his car with their bags. Before long they boarded the yacht and were shown to their staterooms. Even though Dimitra had already been on the yacht to meet his family, she walked around in a dazed condition. And she wasn't the only one—the opulence exceeded Alexa's expectations. Again she marveled that this had been Nico's life, but at seventeen she hadn't understood.

But Monika had known. Only too well.

Alexa needed to put all that away. In the car last week Nico had told her to stop ruminating. The past was over. So be it!

Friday night the four of them ate dinner and watched the home movies. Tears washed Gavril's face to see his beloved Iris holding the new baby. Before long Alexa and her daughter were also in tears. Nico watched the scenes at the hospital. At one point he turned to her. His dark eyes shone. "How incredible all this was filmed."

"Thank my grandfather. He insisted."

Gavril smiled. "There's much more to see."

They stayed up late watching movies of their home in Ottawa, Dimitra's different birthday parties. There were even films showing Alexa's parents when she'd been a little girl, and Gavril's investiture as ambassador in Ottawa, which Iris had taken.

No one wanted to stop, but Alexa eventually called a halt. Not only because her grandfather was tired and needed to go to bed, but because her heart couldn't handle any more memories that didn't include Nico. He'd missed out on his daughter's entire life until now.

By morning, the yacht had reached Samos in the Eastern Aegean. Nico told them it was the birthplace of the famous mathematician Pythagoras. Gavril insisted on staying next to the yacht swimming pool to read while the three of them went ashore. A small motorboat dropped them off and left them to explore the mountainous island.

They were a real family. All three of them wore shorts and T-shirts. Nico took them to his favorite places to see waterfalls, fields of wildflowers, a church on a summit and fantastic views. After a long hike, they reached the main village. Dimitra wanted to stop at an embroidery shop to buy a small gift for Irena and Nico's mother.

"While you do that, your mother and I will walk to that alfresco café jutting out in the water and order us an early dinner."

"I might be a while since I promised to phone Kristos."

Nico's smile took Alexa back nineteen years. "Understood." Dimitra took off, eager to talk to her beloved.

To Alexa's surprise, Nico took her arm as they walked along the beachfront. The action had been so natural, she realized he'd forgotten for a moment that they weren't a couple. But she'd forgotten nothing. His touch shot darts of desire through her body. The sensation caused her breath to catch. She wondered if he had any idea what the contact was doing to her.

Nico said, "Is there any doubt our daughter is wildly in love?"

"None at all. Did you notice she ambles over rocks and boulders exactly the way you do, Nico? Like father, like daughter."

When he chuckled, it reminded her of what Irena had told her at the engagement party about Nico. *I can tell you that your presence has brought about a miraculous healing.* Alexa wouldn't have known what he was like before he'd learned he had a daughter, but today even his eyes wore a smile.

He was so striking, every woman in sight, young or old, stared at him. What special female had caught his attention these days? Alexa shouldn't care or even want to know. But the possibility that he spent some of his nights with another woman who had to be crazy about him was consuming her.

They found a table overlooking the water and a waiter came right over. Nico eyed her. "The sautéed shrimp here is a specialty of the house. Would you like to try it?"

"I'd love it."

"I promise you will."

He ordered them wine. She felt like they'd gone back to the past. *But you're in the present now, Alexa. Remember that.* "How are your friends adjusting to the fact that you have a daughter who now claims some of your time?"

"Tio's gone, and I've never socialized much with my business associates. As for women, there's been no one recently." That particular piece of news shouldn't have pleased her. "Any rare free time has been spent with family and Irena. I enjoy scuba diving with Yanni and Kristos."

Alexa sipped her wine. "I never did learn."

"You're welcome to join us if you ever want to try it. If you remember, I promised to teach you one day."

As if she could forget anything he'd said or done. "Thank you, Nico. Maybe I'll take you up on it."

"When?"

She laughed out loud. "That sounds just like you. I'd say whenever we both have time."

"I'll make time."

"So will I. These days I'm working on a project that will keep me busy for another couple of months." Alexa wanted to do anything with him, but didn't want to sound too eager. All she could do was wait for more signs.

"That sounds intriguing," he murmured. "Tell me about it."

Their food came and they started to eat.

"After I got my BEd to teach, I went on to obtain a master's degree in classical mythology. Later on I compiled a series of myths I could water down for grade-school children. It took several years to find an agent. In time a publisher got interested. I worked with their art staff and eventually my collection came out in both English and Greek."

He stared as if he'd never seen her before. "Congratulations." His deep voice curled through her. "I remember how much you loved them."

"They fascinated me. The collection had enough success that I was encouraged to compile another series of myths for young adults."

"You amaze me you could do it at all."

"I believe the experience has been cathartic for me. I've worked on this collection with a different concept in mind by exploring a basic emotion and making it the title of each story."

"I'm impressed by your brilliance."

She smiled. "I didn't write those myths, Nico. All I've done is try to present them in an interesting way for teenagers."

His eyes narrowed. "Have you included Hera's myth?"

"No. I—I couldn't." Her voice faltered.

"I'm glad. That myth needs to be buried forever."

Oh, Nico...

Alexa took a deep breath. "If you want to read something creative and historic right out of my grandfather's incredible mind, you should sink your teeth into his first drafts of his ambassador memoirs on Cyprus. Then he'll start on his book about his experiences in Canada."

Nico finished the last of his wine. "I hope you mean that and make them available to me. More and more I'm realizing what an exceptional man Gavril is. He's had the job of being husband, father, grandfather, then starting again being a father to you and to Dimitra, all the while handling the difficult job of two ambassador-ships. Since you've inherited his genes, it's no wonder you're a star in your own right."

Heat filled her cheeks. "Hardly that."

"Do you write under your own name?"

"I've always gone by Alexa Soriano Remis. Soriano was my grandmother's maiden name."

"I noticed that on the birth certificate. Maybe we'll find a copy of one of your books in the bookstore here on the island."

She smiled. "No, but there are copies in the Aristotle University library in Salonica."

"How soon will your new collection be published?"

"I should have it finished by the end of this summer. Before the fall semester starts at the university, I plan to fly to Ottawa and work for a few days with the art-ists again. Then we'll see."

Nico ate the last two delicious shrimps she'd left on the platter. "Speaking of that timetable, Kristos called me at work yesterday. He and Dimitra want to get mar-ried before the end of the summer."

"I know, but that's only seven weeks from now."

He nodded. "Irena still wants them to wait a year."

"Oh, dear." She half moaned the words. "Another battle."

"Has Dimitra mentioned it to you?"

"Yes. Now that they're engaged, they don't want to wait and at this point I understand. Frankly I don't want to fight with her, not after this upheaval in our lives. I'm afraid to do anything to ruin the bit of peace I've achieved with her."

"I'll tell Irena what you said."

"How do you feel about it, Nico?" She looked into his dark eyes, worrying about him. "You've just discovered you have a daughter. Now she wants to get married. There's so little time for the two of you to enjoy each other."

He sat back in the chair. "I'm so overjoyed to have a daughter, I'm planning to take each day as it comes to the very end of my life. I hope you'll allow me to pay for their wedding whenever it occurs. I'm her father and it's time I did my part."

They'd been so engrossed in their conversation, Alexa hadn't noticed their daughter who'd approached carrying a bag of things she'd bought. Dimitra stood staring at the two of them with an expectant look on her face.

CHAPTER EIGHT

"I HEARD YOU talking about my wedding, Mama. Is it all right with you if Kristos and I get married at the end of the summer term at the university? It'll be the perfect time before classes start again. We've been talking about it on the phone."

"Honey, I'm fine with the idea, but you need to discuss it with his mother. She'd rather you waited a year."

"But we don't want to wait that long." Dimitra sat in a chair. "You talk to her, Baba. Kristos says she listens to you about everything."

Alexa exchanged a private glance with Nico before she said, "Do you know why she's asking you to wait?"

"Kristos just told me. His grandfather wants us to put off marriage until he turns twenty-five and knows what he's doing. That's why he didn't come to our engagement party."

"I see."

"His mother is worried he'll hold Kristos back in the company if he doesn't conform. But Kristos says he'll resign if necessary and find another job in order to marry me now."

Alexa and Nico exchanged a glance. Suddenly her

conversation with Irena in the bedroom about her elopement with Tio made perfect sense.

Nico covered his daughter's hand. "I'll talk to Irena and assure her that if Kristos needs another job, he can come to me."

"You mean it?" She jumped up and threw her arms around him. "I have to call him right now and tell him."

"Don't you want to eat first?"

"I couldn't. Excuse me. I'll be back in a minute."

The second she'd gone, Alexa looked at Nico. "Was Tio's father as controlling of him as he is of Kristos?"

His brows furrowed. "Worse. He's the antithesis of my father. If Irena hadn't been waiting for Tio when he returned from military service, he would have left Greece to find his own way."

"She told me they eloped. Nico, if you end up helping Kristos, won't you be making an enemy?"

His features tautened. "We became enemies the moment he found out I was Tio's best man at their secret wedding and helped them pay for their first apartment."

"You did that?" Nico had always been more generous than anyone she'd ever known. That quality in him had never changed, making her love him all the more.

He nodded. "His father cut off all his funds, but in time he had to make peace with Tio because Tio's mother threatened to divorce him if he didn't. It would have caused a scandal. The mansion Irena lives in now came from Kristos's grandmother on Irena's side."

"I can't believe he would threaten his son like that."

"It got ugly, but the good news is, Tio married Irena. They took vows at that church we visited earlier today on our hike."

A gasp escaped her lips. "What a beautiful place for a wedding! Why didn't you tell Dimitra while we were up there? It would have meant everything to her."

"That's Irena's story to tell. She walks a thin line when it comes to Tio's father. He wants to turn his grandson into the personification of himself, but it'll never happen."

"That's terribly sad, but how blessed she and her boys are to be able to turn to you. And Dimitra now too."

With her emotions spilling all over the place, she got up from the table and left the restaurant to catch up with her daughter, who was standing beneath a tree near the entrance.

Dimitra hung up, then hurried toward Alexa. "It's settled. Kristos is home and he's going to talk to his mother right now. Baba has made everything perfect. I'm so happy I can hardly stand it! I love him so much."

So do I, honey. So do I.

Nico walked over to them. "Do you want to do a little more shopping before we go?"

"Maybe another time, but I'd rather go back to the yacht. Kristos will be calling me soon. We have a lot to talk over."

The amused look in Nico's eyes told Alexa nothing was more important than that. She knew he was remembering how it was between the two of them years ago. To be together was all that had mattered. It lightened Alex's heart that Nico acted so happy about it. She wanted to protect him from any more hurt.

They followed Dimitra to the pier. He helped them climb in the motorboat that drove them out to the yacht.

She turned to him. "How come you never took us on board your family yacht years ago?" she whispered.

He studied her features. "I wanted you to myself with no staff around. Do you wish I had?"

"What do you think?"

Something flickered in his eyes. "I'll tell you later when we're alone."

Alexa hoped he meant it. Their arms brushed against each other, igniting her senses. He could probably tell how she trembled at his touch. If he only knew what was going on inside her.

Once aboard, Dimitra and Alexa went to their staterooms. The steward told her that her grandfather was in the club lounge enjoying his dinner while he watched TV. Alexa would join him in a little while, but right now she was hot and sticky. After changing into her swimming suit, she hurried to the pool and dove in the deep end. A good swim could help dampen the desire Nico had aroused in her.

Nico headed straight for the pool and was doing laps when he saw Alexa coming. His heart leaped and he swam underwater toward her. In her blue bikini, no woman would ever look as good to him as she did. He reached for her hips and turned her over before they broke water.

"Nico—" she gasped. Her hands clutched his shoulders.

"Kind of like old times isn't it." Unable to stop what was happening, he cupped her face and hungrily kissed the luscious mouth he'd been longing for. He'd never been able to get enough.

To his joy he was met with an equally hungry response from her. They clung to each other as if their lives depended on it, shaking him to the very core. He felt they'd gone back in time. The action took them under the water. He continued kissing her as he pulled her over to the side.

"You shouldn't have done that," she cried once they'd had a chance to catch their breath. After what had just transpired, he didn't think he'd get his back. How many years had he dreamed of being with her again like this? By now she was holding on to the side of the pool with both hands, refusing to look at him.

"It came naturally for both of us, so don't deny it."

"I'm not," she answered with honesty, but turned away.

Nico wasn't ready to let her go and held her so her back lay against his chest. Her whole beautiful body trembled. He moved her hair to kiss the side of her neck. "Don't you think it's time we talked about us?"

"I guess I'm a little afraid."

"Of what?" He refused to be put off by her despairing tone. "The fact that you're in my arms?"

"I didn't know you were in the pool. I suppose this was inevitable, but we're not the same people and can't pick up where we left off."

"Agreed, but we're still on fire for each other. So why don't we talk about our future."

"Be serious," she begged him.

Nico wrapped his arm around her waist, determined to make her listen. "I'm deadly serious."

"What are you saying?"

He held her tighter. "My wife and unborn baby died,

depriving me of the chance of becoming a father. Monika Gataki prevented me from raising our baby. You have no idea what it did to me to watch those videos of you in the hospital with Dimitra that I was no part of."

Tears filled her eyes. "I'm so sorry, Nico. I was afraid you might be hurt by watching them, and I was right."

He nestled her closer. "What it did was make me want to have another baby with you."

She trembled. "That's impossible, Nico."

"Of course it isn't. You're free. So am I. We're both still young enough to have another baby and raise it together. There's no Monika to interfere this time."

"That's true, but—"

"But nothing," he broke in on her. "That's past history. I want a baby and you're the only woman on earth who can give me what I want."

Alexa whirled around still locked in his arms. "There are other women out there who'd give anything to be your wife."

"But they can't give me another child as perfect as Dimitra. Only you can make that happen again. She needs a sibling. Don't you understand? I want to do what we'd planned long ago and get married, raise a family.

"Nothing has changed the chemistry between us. It's there, stronger than ever and you know it. We've missed the first nineteen years and aren't getting any younger. There's nothing to prevent our marriage now."

"Except that I killed something inside of you, Nico. I saw it in your eyes when I told you Dimitra was our daughter. Deny it all you want, but that pure love you felt for me before you left to go in the military isn't there anymore. It'll never come back."

"You don't know all that's going on inside of me."

"I know this much. I don't want anything to damage your relationship with Dimitra. Now that she's found you, she adores you. To ruin that would be the greatest tragedy of all."

He frowned. "What do you mean ruin?"

"Don't you see? If I started spending time with you, Dimitra would have to compete for your attention. She'd learn to resent me. I kept her to myself for eighteen years. But all that has changed now that she's found you." She broke into tears. "I refuse to stand in the way of the happiness you two bring to each other. I could never do that to either of you."

Alexa broke free of his arms and climbed out of the pool. Nico had no choice but to let her go for the moment. He did another ten laps to think about what she'd said. Her guilt was much worse than he'd imagined. Nico had his work cut out to free her of it.

A few minutes later Dimitra came out to the pool in her swimming suit, filled with excitement. Nico didn't imagine he'd ever get used to the joy of having a daughter, let alone one as satisfying in every way as Dimitra. She dropped a towel on a chair and dove in. When she emerged she said, "I'll never be able to thank you enough, Baba."

"What are you talking about?"

"You offered to help Kristos with a job if worse came to worse. Irena thought it over and has given him her blessing for our marriage to take place. We've tentatively settled on Saturday, the twenty-sixth of August. Mama says that date is fine for her. Will that work for you? I know how busy you are."

"Not too busy for anything as important as your wedding." Relief swept through Nico that Irena had capitulated. It fit in with a plan that had been forming in his mind. "That gives you seven weeks to arrange everything."

"After Papoú is in bed, let's find Mama and start planning. We might as well do it now while you're not at the office."

Contrary to what Alexa imagined in her mind, Dimitra showed no resentment of her mother and wanted both parents involved all the way. Nothing could have suited Nico better. The sooner Dimitra's wedding happened, the sooner Alexa wouldn't have an excuse.

"This is an opportune moment considering you need to put your intent to marry declaration in the newspaper before anything else."

"That's what Kristos said."

"Your aunt Giannina will take care of it once it's written."

"I'm so lucky."

"That works both ways."

Nico would do his part as father of the bride-to-be without making Alexa uncomfortable. Following through with plans for the big event would provide legitimate opportunities for him to be with her. She wouldn't be able to fight their need for each other indefinitely.

"How about a race before we go in, Baba?"

"You're on!"

Racing his daughter back and forth proved to be the stuff dreams were made of. He'd never had so much fun. A little while later Alexa came out to find them, saving them from having to find her, dressed in white shorts and a white top. She sat on one of the chairs. "I decided to find out if you two were still alive."

"Baba swims like a fish, Mama. No one could ever beat him."

Alexa chuckled. "I found that out years ago. It's how we met."

"Tell me."

The blood rushed into her cheeks. "Well, he was racing his friends off his cruiser and we bumped into each other, causing him to lose. It was probably the one and only time he went down in defeat."

Nico's gaze fused with hers. "That's because I met up with a mermaid whose superpowers rendered me helpless."

It pleased him when she averted her eyes. He knew bringing up that memory had slipped past her defenses.

Dimitra climbed out of the pool. She dried off before sitting by her mother. "Did Mama really look like a mermaid?"

Nico swam over to the side near them. "Her hair was long back then, and she knew moves in the water that blew me away. All that was missing was her tail."

Dimitra laughed. "Great-grandma Iris was a champion swimmer. She taught Mama from the time she was little. I can't wait to tell Kristos you thought Mama looked like a mermaid. Oh, just so you know, he's meeting us at the dock tomorrow at noon. We're going to see the priest at Saint Catherine's in Ano Poli. He wants to be married where their family has always worshipped."

"That's only natural," Alexa interjected. "It'll make Irena very happy."

Nico nodded. "I think it's the perfect choice, Dimitra.

If Kristos's father were alive, he'd want it there too." He couldn't be more pleased that his own daughter would be married there. Tio would have exchanged vows with Irena in that centuries-old Byzantine church if circumstances had been different for them.

"I'm so glad you both agree. Now we're trying to decide on a place for the reception. Do you have any ideas, Baba? Mama and I have been talking about it, but we think you're the one who would know the best spot."

Nico had already given it thought. "I'd pick the Macedonian Palace. Depending on the weather, you can hold the reception indoors or outside. The hotel is centrally located and easy to find for those coming from out of town."

"Kristos mentioned it, but it's expensive and—"

"But nothing," Nico broke in. "If that's his choice too, then we'll book it if that's all right with you, Alexa."

"I want what all of you want."

Good. "Then that will be one of my gifts to the bride. The other will be your wedding dress. I want you and your mother to shop your heads off for all the things you'll need."

"That's far too generous of you, Baba." Her eyes had teared up.

"You're my only child. A parent lives for a moment like this. Wouldn't you say, Alexa?"

"You know I would," she murmured in an emotional tone before getting up. "It looks like we've gotten the most important issues decided. Now if you'll excuse me, I need to check on your *papoú*, so I'll say good-night."

Dimitra jumped up. "I'll come with you. I promised

I'd phone Kristos after we'd had this talk. Good night, Baba. I love you so much."

"*Kalinikta, I kóri mou polytima.*"

Good night, my precious daughter.

The love in Nico's voice caused Alexa's eyes to close tightly for a moment. Nico would never know what those words had to mean to Dimitra, let alone to Alexa herself. He really did love his daughter! From the moment he'd known about her, he'd devoted himself to her. With the amount of time he gave her, you'd never know he was the famous Angelis CEO with huge responsibilities.

Dimitra lapped up that love like any child starving for a father's affection. There was a new glow about her that came from enjoying the security he gave her. Nico did something no one else could do.

Alexa realized he would have been just as attentive to Dimitra whether Alexa had contacted him the moment she'd known she was pregnant, or after she'd told him about Monika's revelation. It was too late to wish she hadn't kept them apart, but one thing she did know. Life was going to be wonderful from here on out for her daughter.

As for Nico, there was no doubt in her mind that whatever his circumstances—even marriage to another woman—he would have moved heaven and earth to have a relationship with Dimitra. Nico was a prince among men.

"Mama? Do you mind if I ask you something personal?" She'd come into Alexa's stateroom.

"Of course not. What is it?"

"Do you wish you could be with my father again? You know what I mean."

Alexa couldn't believe her daughter had asked her that question now, just after Alexa and Nico had shared that shattering kiss in the pool. "Oh, honey. That's all over with."

"I don't know. I've been watching the two of you and get the feeling you're both in a private world of your own half the time."

She bit her lip, pricked with guilt. "Has it worried you, because—"

"Worried me?" she cut in on her mother, sounding bewildered. "That's an odd thing to say. You should have been together and married as soon he'd returned from the military. That insane Monika wanted Baba for herself and did a monstrous thing to you."

"But that's old history, honey."

"You're right. Now that I know all the facts, how could I blame you for what you did? Your circumstances were horrendous at the time. Papoú agrees with me. So does Kristos's mother. She said she would have hidden the truth too if she'd been pregnant and had thought Kristos's father had only been having fun with her. But remember this: Monika hasn't won yet."

Those words staggered Alexa while Dimitra kept on talking.

"I hope you'll get back together with my father. Kristos wants the same thing for the two of you. Those other men who asked you to marry them were never good enough for you. And you couldn't have been interested in the man you went out with!"

"I'm not, honey. I said goodbye."

"Thank goodness. There's only one Baba. It's no wonder no other man ever came close." The words continued to pour out of her daughter's romantic soul. "You were right about him at seventeen. No other man is like him and never could be. Promise me you'll think about getting back with him."

Probably nothing could have shocked Alexa more. Not only had Dimitra forgiven her, she wanted her parents to get back together. It shook her to the foundations, leaving her speechless.

"I feel the same way about Kristos. He's my one and only. Good night, Mama." She gave her a hug and left the stateroom.

Besides Alexa's grandfather, Irena had a lot to do with Dimitra's ability to understand and forgive something so earth-shattering for her at the time. Alexa would have to find a way to thank her for what she'd done to help heal a wound she'd thought couldn't be healed.

She shivered after getting in bed, remembering what Nico had told her in the pool earlier. This evening he'd asked her to marry him. Dimitra's instincts hadn't been wrong about noticing the undercurrents between Alexa and Nico. But Alexa couldn't forget that this proposal had been prompted by a far different reason than the first one.

Nineteen-year-old Nico had been madly in love when they'd planned their marriage. Now everything was different. Since that time, Nico had lost his wife and unborn child. Furthermore, he'd be losing his newly found daughter to Kristos.

Tears poured from Alexa's eyes. She understood that

nothing could ever take the place of Nico raising his own child from birth. Alexa had deprived him of that experience. If she did agree to marry him to give him another child to love, maybe that could help make up for what had happened.

But even if the unimaginable happened and they did marry, there'd be no guarantee she'd get pregnant again. Worse, Alexa could never expect the kind of love he'd once showered on her. She doubted they could get back the pure magic they'd shared.

She could imagine the question her grandfather would ask her. *Can you survive in a marriage where you don't believe Nico will ever feel for you what he once did? Be careful before you say yes.*

Alexa wrestled with that question throughout the night, but never found an answer. Early the next morning she got up and put on her bikini. Her grandfather would sleep another hour. That would give her time to work off emotions in the pool before everyone awakened.

A gorgeous day, already getting hot, greeted her as she hurried along the deck carrying her beach towel. Her heart slammed into her ribs when she saw Nico already in the pool.

He must have seen her coming and lounged against the side at the deep end, his arms outstretched in a relaxed position. *Like a young Zeus who'd beguiled Io.*

"I'm glad to see you couldn't sleep either, and hoped you'd come out here early." His deep voice stirred her senses. "We'll be docking at noon and won't have a lot of time to talk alone."

Alexa sank down in one of the lounge chairs, knowing that if she dove in, he'd reach for her and there'd be no more talk. "I thought we discussed the important things about the upcoming wedding last night."

"Which one?"

Her heart thudded. "Nico—"

He swam to the side of the pool nearest her. "I've been thinking about it since you went to bed last night. When I first saw you at Irena's, I was incredulous that you'd had a baby with another man. But nothing has blotted out the image I've carried in my mind of the two of us all these years. That image intensified when you told me Dimitra was my daughter."

"I was so unfair to you." Her voice trembled.

"Then make it fair and marry me next Friday."

"What?"

He climbed out of the pool and walked over to her, dripping wet, and gave her a long, passionate kiss. "I told you last night I want another baby with you, and the idea hasn't left me alone. Maybe a son this time. Who knows how long it will take for you to get pregnant? We may not be as lucky we were that night on my cruiser and can't afford to waste any more time."

She shook her head. "You're not making sense, and certainly not with our daughter's wedding coming up."

"You're wrong. We'll fly to Sarti Friday morning while Dimitra is at school, and marry in the Church of the Assumption. The priest and I are good friends."

Her heart was running away with her. "But we can't do it that fast, not with all the regulations."

"We can because I have sources in high places who'll waive the rules for us."

"You're serious!"

"How can you doubt it? Except for telling Gavril our plans, our secret wedding will be private to the world. Afterward we'll spend several hours at the villa before we fly back to Salonica that evening without anyone being the wiser.

"Until Dimitra and Kristos are married, we'll slip away each evening before you have to get home to help your grandfather to bed. Once they're back from their honeymoon, we'll announce our marriage to the whole family. By then we might even be pregnant."

She got to her feet on unsteady legs. "Please don't say anything else. Y-You're not thinking clearly," she stammered, too alarmed, excited and terrified all at once to think.

"I've had five weeks to get my thoughts straight. Last night they became as crystal clear as the water on my private stretch of beach."

An almost primitive gleam entered his dark eyes. She knew what was going to happen before he swept her in his arms and they landed in the deep end of the pool. "I want another kiss from my mermaid who took a long swim away from me to the other side of the world. But she's back, and I'll make sure she never gets away from me again."

His mouth closed over hers, kissing her with a possessive intensity that overwhelmed her. Alexa could no more deny what she clamored for than she could stop breathing. It took her back to that time of pure rapture. But he hadn't said he loved her. Maybe she'd never hear those words.

Yet after losing his unborn baby, he wanted a baby so badly he'd asked her to marry him as soon as next

Friday. Deep down she had to admit she would love another baby with him. He'd be the greatest father on earth. But nothing was that simple. Even though Dimitra had forgiven her enough to want her parents to get together, there were other obstacles Alexa couldn't imagine overcoming.

"Let me go, Nico," she begged, struggling to separate herself from him. "I can hear voices."

"I'll let you swim away as long as you promise to fly to Sarti with me on Friday. Otherwise I'll tell Dimitra and your grandfather our plans right now while we're still on the yacht. The decision is yours."

"Nico, you can't!"

"They're coming."

She was desperate. "I'll think about it."

"You've got to do better than that." He had a ruthless side she'd never seen before. After what she'd done to him, it shouldn't surprise her.

"I promise." But it didn't mean she would marry him.

CHAPTER NINE

THE NEXT WEEK passed slowly for Nico and it wasn't until Thursday night that he finally went over to see Irena and told her his plans.

"I've never revealed something to you, but now I feel I must. When I married Raisa, I didn't love her the way I'd loved Alexa. I—"

"Say no more," Irena interrupted him with a smile. "I knew that Alexa had broken your heart, and I cheered the fact that you chose to get on with your life and marry Raisa. She knew it too, but she loved you so much, she married you anyway, knowing how you felt. She wanted any love you could give her, and I happen to know you made her very happy. She told me everything."

Nico shook her head. "I had no idea."

"I know, and I promised I'd never tell you. But now I can. So marry your Alexa knowing Raisa wanted you or no one else and the years you gave her were the happiest ones of her life. Now it's time to make Alexa happy again. She never married because you filled her heart so completely. That should tell you everything. I couldn't be happier for both of you."

Nico hugged her for a long time.

At nine o'clock Friday morning, he drove over to Alexa's on a burst of adrenaline. His daughter would already have left for class at the university. Other than a few phone calls discussing arrangements for their daughter's wedding, he'd given Alexa the space she needed. But today was the day he'd been living for.

The second he rang the bell, Alexa opened the door and came out on the porch looking anxious. She'd dressed in jeans and a sleeveless top, telling him what he'd feared, but it didn't surprise him.

"What happened to your promise?" he asked without preamble.

She rubbed her hands over womanly hips in a nervous gesture. "We can't do this, Nico. You know we can't."

"Did you tell your grandfather our plans?"

Alexa averted her eyes. "I haven't said anything yet."

"Then *I* will because the priest is expecting us in less than three hours, and I refuse to marry you without receiving Gavril's blessing."

"He won't give it, Nico."

"I think he will, Alexa. Admit it's what we both want."

"You know I do, but I'm nervous."

Nico waited until she turned and went inside. He followed her into the living room. "I'll wait here while you find him."

After one more worried glance at him, she disappeared. Nico walked around looking at framed pictures of her family. He caught sight of one taken of him and his daughter the night of the announcement dinner at his villa. He picked it up to study it. Nico had put his arm around Dimitra while they smiled at each other. His heart melted just looking at it.

"Well, Nico." Alexa had wheeled her grandfather into the room. He smiled at him. "I didn't know you were coming over this morning. Phyllis was just fixing me breakfast. You look like you're going to a wedding." Nico had come dressed for the occasion in a navy dress suit and tie.

He put the picture back on the table. "I am. Last week I asked Alexa to marry me and planned it for today. We'll be taking our vows at the church in Sarti at noon with Anna and Thanos for witnesses. But no marriage can take place until we have your blessing. I owe you more than you will ever know."

The older man looked at his granddaughter in surprise. When she didn't say anything Nico explained, "We didn't want to intrude on Dimitra's big day, so we've decided to marry in private. It's what we want and need. Only *you* and my friend Irena are privy to our news. I'll bring Alexa back here by the end of the day. Once our daughter and Kristos return from their honeymoon, we'll tell them and announce our marriage to the world."

He didn't have to wait long for Gavril to grasp Alexa's hand. The gesture shot relief through Nico. Gavril eyed his granddaughter. "Why aren't you ready, sweetheart?"

"You mean you're happy about it?" The fear and disbelief in her voice made Nico want to wrap her in his arms and never let her go. She'd suffered guilt for too long. Since Raisa's death no one understood what guilt could do to you more than Nico did. But now that Alexa had come back into his life, he'd made up his mind they both needed to rid themselves of those chains.

Gavril gave a gruff chuckle. "I've only prayed for it for nineteen years." By the look on her face, his remark had stunned her. "Go on. Wear that pretty dress you wore the night you went to meet Kristos's mother."

"You won't need anything else," Nico murmured.

"Hurry, sweetheart. You don't want to be late for your own wedding."

At her grandfather's admonition, she left the room.

Nico walked over to Gavril and clasped his hand. "I swear I'll love your granddaughter forever. I'm also making another promise to take care of you for the rest of your life."

The older man's eyes filled. He wiped away the moisture as Alexa came back in the living room and kissed her grandfather. She wore the blue-on-white-print dress and carried a handbag. "You're right. It's what I've always dreamed of."

Nico helped her out to the car and drove them to headquarters. En route he turned to her. "You look heavenly."

"Thank you. You look wonderful too. But Nico... there's something I haven't told you." Her voice shook.

"What? That you can't have any more children? Because if you can't, we'll adopt."

"No. I'm talking about my grandfather."

"While you were getting dressed, I told him I'd take care of him to the end of his days."

"But you don't understand. He needs me. Once Dimitra is married, he'll be too lonely. I could never leave him."

"You won't have to. I'll be your husband and plan to move in with you."

She stared at him in utter astonishment. "You have your own home."

"We'll have the villa in Sarti for a getaway and to entertain. You can be sure that Kristos and Dimitra will use it a lot. But now that we're getting married, my permanent home will be with you. I'll move in while the lovebirds are on their honeymoon. Gavril has taken care of you all these years. Now it's my turn to help him."

"I would never expect that of you, Nico."

"But I want to. Think what he did for me while I wasn't there. Naturally your grandfather is the most comfortable in his own home with Phyllis taking care of him. It's centrally located for friends who want to come by and visit. It's close to my work and the university where you teach. That's the way our life will be while I do all I can for you and your family."

Alexa broke down sobbing, the last reaction he'd expected.

"What have I said that has upset you so much?" By now they'd reached headquarters.

She wiped her eyes with the backs of her hands. "I'm not upset. I'm just overawed by your kindness to my grandfather."

"He's a remarkable man, and we're going to do everything right this time. A new chapter of life is starting, and we're not in our dotage yet. First we'll become man and wife as we'd planned ages ago."

"But I might not conceive." In desperation she cried, "If we do go through with this wedding, then I want you to give me your solemn promise about something."

"What's that?"

"If I haven't become pregnant within four months, then you'll move back to your villa. We'll get a quiet divorce so you can find a woman to marry who can give you a child. It's what you want and I refuse to stand in your way."

He turned off the engine and turned to her, giving her a penetrating glance. "Since I got you pregnant the first time we made love, I'm willing to bet the same thing will happen again, so I'll make you that promise."

Alexa couldn't believe it. "Y-you mean it?" she asked in a shaky voice.

"I always mean what I say, but four months doesn't give us much time. Just so you understand. If you are pregnant in four months' time, we'll stay together forever. I want your promise *you* won't back out."

"Of course I won't. You're teasing me again."

"You think?"

"I *know.*"

He laughed before opening the door. "Now that we've cleared the air, we need to go. My pilot is waiting to fly us to Sithonia."

The flight to Sithonia presented breathtaking images of the mountains and greenery. It gave a different perspective than driving there. Alexa sat behind the pilot while she marveled over the scenery from the helicopter.

"You've found paradise here, Nico. I can well understand why you settled here."

He looked over his shoulder at her. "Would you believe I had you in mind when I bought it? Though I never expected to see you again, the private beach seemed to have a certain mermaid's name written on it."

His words melted her heart. "Yet you're willing to live in my grandfather's home so we can be together."

"We'll get away on weekends. Perhaps the time will come when he'll want to live in the villa too. You never know what the future will bring."

Darling Nico. After he'd learned he had a daughter, he wanted another child to replace the one he'd lost when his wife had died. He'd suffered a great loss.

The fact that he was willing to go through all this with Alexa proved that he'd truly loved his wife and had looked forward to the birth of their child. Not knowing of Dimitra's existence, his need for that unfulfilled dream had gone much deeper than Alexa had realized. It explained why he was anxious to marry Alexa and have a baby.

Alexa couldn't promise she would be pregnant that soon. But she would try to give him what he wanted because she loved him heart and soul. If it gave Nico any hope, then she was willing because she realized his suffering had been infinite. No one had a stronger will than Nico, yet not even *his* will could guarantee such an outcome.

Thanos and Anna met them at the villa in an estate car. After she freshened up, they were driven to the charming Church of the Assumption in the village. The tan exterior with painted red facings featured a belfry with a cross. Nico helped her out and cupped her elbow. "Are you ready?"

Alexa didn't know what she was and couldn't answer.

"We're simply going to exchange vows. The ceremony will be short. The priest knows we fell in love as teenagers and he's happy to be officiating."

Anxious, she looked up. "Does he—"

"No," Nico cut her off, reading her mind. "He only knows Dimitra is our daughter, nothing else. Shall we go inside?"

It was too late to back out now, not that she wanted to. They walked up the few steps into the foyer. Beyond the inner doors the narrow nave extended to the icons of saints erected at the front of the chapel. The older priest in his robes stood smiling at them.

Nico led her up the aisle. Anna and Thanos sat on the chairs in front to witness the ceremony.

"Kyría Remis? It is my pleasure to meet the woman Kýrie Angelis has chosen to marry. If you'll join hands, we'll begin."

She glanced at Nico, who'd never looked more gorgeous wearing a navy dress suit to die for. It didn't seem possible that this was going to happen. Of course this was what she'd always wanted, but not quite in this way. So rushed and secretive.

He took hold of her hand and threaded his fingers through hers, giving them a squeeze as if he could read her mind.

The priest said a prayer, then looked at Nico. "Nicholas Timon Angelis, do you take this woman to be your lawfully wedded wife? To love her, provide for her in sickness and in health until death do you part?"

"I do," he answered in his deep voice.

That was so short, Alexa couldn't believe it. This ceremony was nothing like a normal Greek one. She swallowed hard as the priest stared at her. "Alexa Soriano

Remis, do you take this man to be your lawfully wedded husband? To love him, support him through sickness and health until death do you part?"

The priest didn't know about the four-month time limit she'd forced Nico to honor. "I do."

"Then in as much as the two of you have plighted your troth, I hereby pronounce you man and wife, in the name of the Father, the Son and the Holy Spirit. You may exchange rings now."

Nico reached in his breast pocket and brought out a ring with a dazzling green stone set in gold he slid on to her ring finger. Alexa hadn't bought him a ring because she'd never thought she'd marry him. But before she'd left the house, she'd grabbed the engaged-to-be-engaged gold ring he'd sent her in his first letter.

She removed it from the finger on her right hand and reached for his left hand. It only slid partway on to his pinky finger. He recognized it at once, flashing her an all-consuming glance she couldn't decipher.

"Congratulations. You may now kiss your bride, Kýrie Angelis."

The brief kiss Nico gave her was almost as surprising as the shortest marriage service performed in Greek history. Had this ceremony been such a painful reminder of his first marriage, he couldn't wait for it to be over?

Alexa didn't know what to think as he led her to the foyer where Thanos and Anna congratulated them. The priest followed and asked them to sign the marriage document.

With that over, Nico ushered her outside to the car. Thanos drove them back to the villa. When they entered the villa, Nico guided her to the patio.

"Anna is serving us lunch out here."

They sat beneath the umbrella. There was no sign of an eager young bridegroom so anxious to be with his new bride that food was the last thing on his mind.

He poured them wine while Anna brought the food. "Our ceremony had to be shortened. The priest texted me during the flight that he needed to leave on an emergency, and we arrived there later than planned."

That was the reason? "I didn't realize, but I didn't mind it being short."

"Believe me. Neither did I. It has given us more time to enjoy the rest of the day until we have to fly back."

Alexa had lost her appetite, but she didn't want to insult Anna, so she ate as much of the crab salad as she could handle and thanked her. Nico, on the other hand, ate two sandwiches along with salad.

She looked at her wedding ring. "This teardrop stone is dazzling. What kind is it?"

"A natural deep green diamond, very rare. It came from a mine in Africa. I bought it a week ago. It symbolizes harmony, freshness and fertility, the color of nature. The color of your eyes."

She looked away, unable to meet his piercing gaze.

"I didn't really believe you meant to marry me today. I'm sorry I didn't have a ring for you."

"But you did," he came back and held up his left hand. "I'm pleased to see you found this ring in that first letter."

"I was so moved when I read what was engraved on it, I fell apart. It's been sitting in my jewelry box."

"But no longer." He got up from the table. "Why don't we go to my bedroom so I can put it on you officially."

Alexa's heart thudded so violently, it was hard to breathe. She stood and followed Nico to another part of the villa, halting in the doorway of his spacious bedroom with its king-size bed.

The shutters had been closed to darken the room. She could smell the fragrance of orange blossoms. Candles had been lit and placed on the dresser and end tables. A huge plant of blue hydrangeas sat on a coffee table in front of two matching love seats.

"Nico—" she gasped and rested against the doorjamb. "I feel like I've entered the cabin on your cruiser and it's nineteen years ago."

"That was a night I'll never forget," he murmured. "If you'd like to freshen up first, the en suite bathroom is through that door. I've put a blue robe on a hook for you."

Her legs felt insubstantial as she thanked him and walked across the room to his private bathroom. With trembling hands she removed her clothes and took a shower, but all her actions seemed to be in slow motion. Alexa couldn't believe she was now a married woman. This was her wedding night, even if it was early afternoon.

How different from the first time when he'd carried her to the bed in his cabin below deck. Until they'd had to leave the cruiser, she hadn't thought about anything but loving him.

Alexa started to be afraid. She had been with other men and thoroughly kissed, but she hadn't made love since that night with Nico. What if he found her less than satisfactory, especially after his marriage to a young Raisa.

After leaving the shower, she used one of the fluffy

towels to dry off, then slipped on the blue toweling robe. Alexa glanced in the mirror, not thrilled with the sight of the thirty-six-year-old woman who looked back at her.

Last week Alexa had finally broken down and done a search of his deceased wife online. She'd been absolutely beautiful, a tall Athenian with flowing black hair and velvety brown eyes. Anyone would think she modeled for a living.

Alexa found photo after photo of the famous couple, including wedding pictures at the church in Athens. Nico had seemed so happy, but when information about the helicopter crash came up on the screen, she'd shut it off unable to go there. It hurt too much to imagine the pain he must have gone through.

"Alexa? Are you all right?"

She'd been so deep in thought, she hadn't heard the tap on the door.

"I'm fine, Nico. I'll be right out."

When she emerged, she found him waiting for her dressed in a black striped robe, looking the heart-stopping male she adored. He walked over and reached for her left hand. "This ring belongs with your wedding ring, Kyría Angelis." He slid the ring he'd been wearing on his pinky to her finger. "You're my wife now."

"I never thought this day would come."

He put his hands on her shoulders and looked into her eyes. "Another miracle. Now tell me what's wrong."

She looked everywhere except at him. "If you want to know the truth, I'm nervous."

"Why?" That wicked half smile of his was in evidence. "It isn't as if we haven't done this before."

"That's true, but it's been a long time."

"Then come over on the bed and we'll talk about it."

"I'm afraid."

"Of me?"

"Yes!"

"You've known me better than anyone else has ever known me."

"That's why I'm terrified!"

He laughed that deep, rich male laugh she loved before he picked her up in his arms and carried her to the bed. Then he rolled on his side next to her and kissed her mouth. "Even if the priest had an emergency, you need to know I didn't kiss you the way I wanted to at the church because I knew if I did, I'd never stop."

"Even if that's not the truth, thank you for saying it."

The sheen faded from his eyes. "What's going on with you?"

"Nothing. I'm sorry."

"You had a reason for saying that. Talk to me, Alexa."

She took a deep breath. "You've been married. Today probably reminded you of your wedding to Raisa. I could understand why it was hard for you to kiss me at the altar."

"You couldn't be more wrong." He sounded upset.

"Are you saying she's never on your mind?"

"I'm saying that when I do think about her, it's more to do with the crash I couldn't prevent."

"But it wasn't your fault."

"That's true, but the guilt lingers."

"Of course it does, and I'm sorry I brought her up. I guess I'm feeling terribly insecure. You have to understand this is all new to me."

Nico raised up on his elbow. "Are you saying you never slept with those two men you almost married?"

"No. After what happened to me, I vowed I'd never sleep with a man unless we were married first. No matter what, I couldn't risk the possibility of another pregnancy."

He looked down at her, cradling her head in his hand. His gaze wandered over every feature. "I know Dimitra has brought you joy, but you've suffered too. We need each other," he said against her mouth.

Suddenly this was the old Nico, kissing her as if it were life to him. They slowly gave each other kiss for kiss, savoring the taste and feel of each other. He might not be in love with her anymore and couldn't say the words, but their hunger said the powerful physical attraction they felt hadn't faded with time.

"I can't believe you're my wife and we're married at last." He kissed every part of her face and throat. "Our last night together on the cruiser was painful for me because I knew I'd be leaving you for a year. You don't know how close I came to kidnapping you."

"You don't mean it." She searched his eyes.

"I'm ashamed to say I had it all planned. Instead of going to work earlier that day, I loaded the cruiser with extra petrol and food for our getaway to Turkey. Once we arrived there I had contacts who would arrange for us to fly to South America undercover."

"You're kidding—" she cried. "Why didn't you? I would have gone anywhere with you."

"I know you would have. That's how much I believed in your love. But after making love to you, guilt and reason held me back. You weren't quite eighteen yet. If we'd been caught, I would have been sentenced in a court of law for disappearing with a minor and avoiding military service.

"Not even my family would have been able to protect me and I'd lose you forever while I went to prison. The thought of years of separation from you was anathema to me. At the last moment my sanity returned. I realized I would have to wait a year for you in order to get what I wanted, but I knew it would be worth it."

Tears filled her eyes. "Instead I'm the one who kept us apart for years."

He kissed away the moisture. "Hush. Right now all I want is to make love to you. Do you know you're even more beautiful than ever? I came close to a heart attack when you walked out on Irena's patio."

She buried her face in his neck. "I had one when I saw you on TV for the first time. You'll never know."

"But I do." He found her mouth and they began to devour each other. Every touch and caress created such rapture, she found herself in a world of ecstasy she never wanted to end. All the years she'd missed being with him like this no longer mattered. She was in his arms now, knowing a passion that had her spiraling.

Alexa clung to him, relishing the sheer joy of being alive and knowing his possession. How she'd lived this long without him, she couldn't comprehend. They were so hungry for each other, she lost cognizance of time. It was as if they were trying to make up for all the years of deprivation and couldn't stop.

She couldn't get enough of him. It was almost embarrassing how on fire she was, especially when she groaned aloud after his cell phone rang. The sound forced them to get unentangled enough for him to answer it, but their legs were still entwined. She lay back, trying to catch her breath.

The candles had burned down almost all the way. They had to have been making love for a long time for that to happen. She heard a short conversation before Nico leaned over and gave her a long, insatiable kiss. "That was Thanos. Would you believe it's after eight? The pilot was ready to take us back three hours ago."

"Oh, no. I need to get home. I promised my grand-father."

"Don't worry. He knows where we are and what we're doing."

"Nico—" A wave of heat engulfed her body. Inside she wanted to cry out in frustration. To have to leave her husband's arms was the greatest torture she could imagine.

His deep laughter was the final insult. "I'll phone him and let him know we're going to be late. I doubt he expects us at all."

"But Dimitra will wonder if I get home after she does."

"Would that be such a terrible thing?"

"I don't want her to know we're married yet." Some-how she managed to elude Nico's arms and reached for her robe lying on the floor. "I'll get showered and dressed."

"Don't plan to run away from me this fast again," he warned against her neck before letting her go. It sent delicious shivers through her.

CHAPTER TEN

WHEN ALEXA CAME out of the bathroom a few minutes later, she discovered Nico had already showered and dressed, this time in a sport shirt and chinos. His eyes were dark fires of desire before he extinguished the candles. "You must know the last thing I want to do is leave here."

"I feel the same way." But if she bared her soul completely, she'd blurt out her love for him, a love that had never died. Would he be able to say the same thing back? She didn't know, but prayed she was already pregnant. Alexa had conceived on the cruiser. Why not now, or in the next four months? She wanted to believe it.

Alexa wasn't the same woman who'd walked in his mountain villa after their wedding ceremony earlier in the day. Nico had made her his wife in every sense of the word. She had to be the envy of any woman who'd ever laid eyes on him and wanted a relationship with him.

Nico would never know how hard it was for her to leave this idyllic place. For a little while she'd been able to pretend that he loved her as he'd once done. Was she wrong and he did have those intense feelings for her even if he hadn't said the words?

The sound of whirring rotors broke into her thoughts before they approached the helicopter. Nico helped her inside, giving her hip a possessive squeeze before she found her seat and he strapped her in.

"We'll be there soon." Nico lowered his mouth to give her a heart-stopping kiss before he climbed in front and put on his headset. As they rose in the air, he looked over his broad shoulder at her. His dark eyes were alive with a light she hadn't seen in nineteen years.

He hoped he'd already made her pregnant. No one wanted that to happen more than she did.

A glint from her diamond caught her eye. Much as she hated to do it, she put both rings in her purse. That was all Dimitra would have to see. Even if she would be happy with the news. Deep down Alexa wanted their marriage more than anything, but didn't want their news to take away from their daughter's wedding day.

Once the helicopter touched down at Angelis headquarters, Nico helped her down and they rushed to his car for the drive home.

"Tomorrow let's meet for lunch at 7 Thalasses with Dimitra and Kristos. We'll eat outside. They have excellent seafood."

She shot him a glance. "Which you love."

"So do you."

Alexa smiled. "I admit it."

He reached over to clasp her hand. "Let's ask Gavril and Irena to join us so we can wrap up any details for the wedding."

His warmth crept through her body. "I'm glad you suggested it. Irena and I need to put our heads together."

"I'll call her. After we drive Gavril back to the house tomorrow, we'll slip away to my apartment above the office for a few hours. That's one time when no one will be around to notice."

"Let's hope." Just the thought of being in his arms again created so much excitement, her heart thumped too hard to be healthy.

When they drew up to the house, she saw no sign of Kristos's car. Nico walked her to the door and checked his watch. "It's ten to eleven. Our daughter probably isn't home yet."

"I'm not sure."

Nico pulled her in his arms and kissed her passionately before letting her go. "I'll be by for you at noon. I don't know about you, but it's going to be an endless night for me without you." On that note he walked back to the car and drove off.

You don't know the half of it, Nico Angelis.

Later Nico had only just entered his apartment when his phone rang. He grabbed it, thinking it had to be Alexa. Their wedding day had been cut short by having to leave the villa. To be forced to say good-night at her grandfather's door when he'd needed the rest of the night to make love to her had come close to killing him. If she felt the same way, maybe she'd changed her mind and wanted him to come and get her right now. With a pounding heart he checked the caller ID.

Disappointment flooded his system before he clicked

on. "Giannina? What's going on?" She'd never called him this late, and this was definitely not the time for a conversation.

"Can I drive over and talk to you in private?"

She sounded on the verge of panic. It was totally unlike her. "Can't we do this over the phone?"

"No. I have to show you something. It's an emergency."

He frowned. "All right. How soon can you get here?"

"Five minutes."

"I'll wait for you out in front and we can talk in your car."

"Thank heaven for you, Nico."

"Giannina, whatever is going on, it couldn't be that bad."

"You want to make a bet?" The line went dead.

Nico needed a glass of water, then he rode the elevator down to the lobby. He nodded to Gus and walked outside to wait for his sister. She drove her dark red Lexus LC overspeed most of the time. Tonight was no different as she screeched to a halt in front of the entrance.

He opened the door and got in. "Drive around the side where we won't be noticed."

Within a minute Giannina pulled to a stop and shut off the engine. She reached in the backseat and handed him a mock-up copy of the *Halkidiki News*. "This will be out in the morning. Read the headline. It has been attributed to me of course." She turned on the map light for him.

Lost Royal Heir of Hellenia Found Alive!

Nico's head reared. "*You* broke this story? With civil war close to breaking out in Hellenia, this has to be the biggest news to hit Europe in years."

"It's a lie of the worst kind, Nico. You know as well as I do Prince Alexandros disappeared a long time ago and has never been seen again. Since I'm the managing editor, I'll be blamed for spreading a story that has no proof. Someone on the inside wants me gone from the newspaper and caused it to be printed without my authority. I know who it is."

Nico was afraid he did too. "You're talking about Uncle Ari." The man held dual citizenship and spent a lot of his time in Hellenia. Who knew what was going on inside him?

"He has staffers who are loyal to him and would do something this monstrous behind my back."

"You're right. Where is Ari now?"

"Probably at the newspaper."

"Then I'll go over there now. After I get a confession out of him, I'll force him to print a disclaimer before I fire him. Our father should have done it years ago."

"Thank heaven for you, brother dear." She reached over to hug him hard. "I don't know what I'd do without you, Nico." Giannina wiped her eyes. "I'm sorry. I've only been talking about my problems. How's Dimitra?"

"Wonderful. I'll tell you about her later. Now I've got to go. If I don't find him at the office, I'll track him at home, then I'll call you to let you know what happened."

He got out of her car and walked around the building to reach his car. But before he did anything else, he needed to hear his wife's voice and know today wasn't a dream. Then he'd drive to the newspaper and confront their uncle.

Saturday after lunch, where more plans for the wedding were pinned down, Nico drove Alexa and Gavril back to the house. With Phyllis there, Alexa didn't need to worry about leaving her grandfather for a few hours.

Before they left for his apartment, she heard Nico ask her grandfather some questions about the political climate in Hellenia, of all things. She wondered why. Her two favorite men had admired each other from the beginning and were more alike than they knew, a fact that thrilled Alexa.

When Nico walked her out to the car and they drove to his apartment, she asked him about it.

"I wanted to pick his brains. That man knows more about what goes on than anyone in the government."

He kissed her senseless on the ride up in the elevator. But when they stepped into his luxurious apartment, she turned to him. "What aren't you telling me?"

Nico picked her up and carried her into the bedroom, following her down on the bed. "I promise to reveal all, but not yet. I've been living to be alone with you and don't want to waste a second of it."

After his late phone call last night to say good-night, Alexa had almost said she'd leave the house and come to him. Their wedding night had been cut short. She'd ached for him all through the rest of the night and had to suppress her feelings during lunch. But there was no holding back now.

They knew how to bring each other pleasure beyond

description. He swept her away on a new tide of passion that left both of them breathless. No woman wanting to conceive had ever had a lover like Nico.

Already she knew she'd been out of her mind to put a four-month limit on their marriage. She wanted to tell him she didn't mean it. She needed to tell him how deeply in love she was with him and always had been. Only one thing held her back.

There was no torrent of words about his love for her. She could wait, but he couldn't say them. While he lay there asleep with his arm hugging her hip possessively, she studied his striking male features, the lines of his compelling mouth. No other man had been created so divinely. It almost hurt to look at him he was so perfect to her.

"Alexa?" Nico had awakened and brushed the tears off her cheeks. "What's wrong?"

It was too late to hide emotions erupting inside her. "I've been reliving those early years when I didn't understand why I'd never heard from you. We'd been so happy, then suddenly it was all over."

"Tell me about it." He pulled her into his arms, crushing her against him. "But don't let it torture you. We're together now."

"We are!" She burrowed her face in his neck. More tears spilled out on his shoulder. "Do you remember that last Saturday years ago when we flew to Olympia?"

He kissed her hair. "How could I ever forget?"

"I told you how much I loved the Greek myths and you took me to the Olympia archaeological museum for a surprise. That was the first time I'd seen the statue of the life-size Hermes sculpted by the ancient sculptor Praxiteles. It had been done in that beautiful Paros marble. He was carrying the baby Dionysus to the Nysiades, the mythical nymphs of Mount Nysa."

Nico rolled her over so he could look into her eyes. "I said you bore a strong resemblance to the painting of the young, gorgeous nymph Erato who helped take care of him."

She nodded. Alexa never forgot anything he'd said to her. "Something happened to me when I saw that statue, but I didn't tell you at the time."

"What was that?" He kissed the end of her nose.

"We'd been talking about getting married and having a family. That statue reminded me of you. There was a look of such tenderness and fascination on his face as he held the baby in his arm. It was a brilliant work of art that stayed with me. I could imagine you carrying our baby like that one day, but I never dreamed that I'd be pregnant before you went away. You should have had the opportunity to raise our little Dimitra."

"Alexa..." He ran a hand through her hair. "Why are you still agonizing over that?"

"I can't help it. When I think of the years she missed out knowing your love and how fun you are. There's no one more exciting than you. Didn't you notice at lunch today how she wanted to talk to you the whole time? You light up her world. I've never seen her this happy in my life. I'm sure Kristos has seen a big difference in her. Irena remarked on it to me before they drove away from the restaurant."

"I've never been happier either."

"That's the problem, Nico."

"What do you mean?"

She couldn't look at him. "I know you want a baby so badly and are so excited about it."

"But you aren't?"

"You know I am, but I'm afraid I might not be able to get pregnant. I talked to my OB here in Salonica the other day. He said that from the ages of twenty-five to thirty-six you have an eighty-six percent chance of conception if you keep trying at the fertile time."

"I'll take those odds considering we won't miss any of your fertile days."

Oh, Nico. "But the odds aren't the same as they were when I was seventeen. He also reminded me that it's harder to stay pregnant if you do conceive."

"Let's take it one problem at a time. Right now we don't have any. In fact I don't believe we're in any hurry to get you home."

"Don't joke about this, Nico. Four months might not be long enough. I don't want you to have to wait another second beyond that time before you find another woman who can give you children."

His eyes wandered over her. "We've already had this conversation and have produced the perfect child together. You're young and I don't anticipate any problems. Now let's stop talking."

Within seconds he'd covered her mouth with his own and set her on fire as only he could do. She lost all sense of time while they found ways to bring each other pleasure. Nico created ecstasy beyond comprehension.

It was dark outside by the time she stirred and eased away from him.

"Where do you think you're going?"

"To the bathroom for a shower. I need to get back home."

He drew her back against him. "What if I ask you to stay the night with me?"

She wanted that more than he knew. "If we're trying to keep our marriage a secret, then it wouldn't be a good idea."

Nico pulled her closer. "The thing is, tomorrow I have to go out of town on important business. I might be gone several days and am not certain when I'll be back."

That shouldn't have upset her. "Where are you going?"

"Not far."

She frowned, sensing he was keeping something from her. "You can't tell your own wife?" she teased.

"I promise to tell you everything after I return."

Suddenly the idea that he was leaving Salonica for any reason at all frightened her. The last time he'd flown away from her, he'd never come back. It was silly of her to be this worried, but she couldn't help it. "I've a feeling this doesn't have anything to do with your work."

"My lips are sealed for now."

Alexa knew it, and didn't like the sound of it. But she didn't want to behave like a nagging wife. Instead, she slid out of his arms and hurried across the room to the bathroom.

Twenty minutes later he walked her to the door of her grandfather's home. She could tell he was preoccupied. "I'll text you when I can." After a hungry kiss, he walked swiftly to his car. Naturally there were no words of love from him.

How long are you going to wait for something that's

*never going to happen, Alexa? How long do you think
you can play house with him, knowing the most important ingredient for you is missing?*

It took all her self-control to keep from crying out
her love for him. If she did, she'd never stop.

Over the next two days, Alexa lost a lot of sleep. Until
she heard from Nico, she knew she wouldn't be able to
accomplish anything. On Wednesday morning she was
so anxious, she had no desire to go on her morning run.
It wouldn't help her.

Dimitra had just left the house for the university with
Kristos. Her daughter had no reason to be concerned
that her father was away on business. Alexa went into
the kitchen to make coffee, all the while waiting for her
husband's call. She could hear her grandfather talking
to Phyllis while he was getting dressed. It might be a
normal day, but it didn't feel like one.

While she was pouring coffee into a mug, her
phone rang, causing her to spill some on the counter.
She grabbed her cell without looking at the caller ID.
"Nico—" she cried.

"No. It's Giannina."

"Oh—" She gripped it tighter in disappointment.
"Hi. How are you?" They hadn't talked since Alexa
had gone to lunch with her.

"Alexa, it's obvious you haven't heard the news. Nico
left town for me on a secret mission."

What?

"In the middle of last night he was in a car on his way
home with some NIS agents when there was a collision."

Alexa's cry brought her grandfather and Phyllis into

the kitchen. She thought she was going to faint and sat on the nearest chair. "H-he isn't—"

"He's alive."

"Oh, thank heaven, thank heaven."

"Everyone survived, but Nico was brought to Saint Paul Hospital unconscious and still is. I don't know the extent of his injuries. My parents and I are here with him, waiting for news from the doctor about his condition."

Alexa tried to stifle a moan, but she wasn't successful. She feared for Nico's father with his heart problem.

"Is Dimitra there? I know this news is going to come as a horrible shock to her."

Dimitra... This was agony beyond bearing. "No. Kristos came by and they've gone to the university."

"Then he doesn't know either. I'll phone Irena. She'll want to be told and get in touch with her son. She adores my brother."

We all adore him.

A groan came out of Alexa. "I—I'll text Dimitra," she stammered. "She'll tell Kristos." It was a struggle for breath. "What floor are you on?"

"Six. We're in the lounge area, east wing."

"I'll be there soon." She hung up.

Her grandfather wheeled his chair next to her. "What terrible news has caused you to go white as a sheet?"

"Oh, Papoú—" She threw her arms around him. "It's Nico. He was in a car crash last night and hasn't gained consciousness yet. I've got to get to Saint Paul Hospital, and Dimitra has to be told."

"You leave that to me. I'll call her while you get

dressed. We'll all go and pick her up on our way to the hospital. He needs his family with him."

Alexa didn't remember getting dressed or driving to the hospital with her grandfather and Phyllis. Irena had already called Kristos. He was bringing Dimitra straight from the university.

Within a half hour, a congregation had gathered in the lounge area, everyone waiting to hear from the doctor. Alexa couldn't sit still and kept watching for any sign of someone to come and tell them what was going on.

How could this have happened after all the suffering Nico had been through in his life? It wasn't fair. He was the best man on earth. She looked around the room. Everyone loved and needed him. He held their world together.

Though they'd been separated all those years, Alexa had always known where she could find Nico. But if the worst happened to him now, there was no address on earth she could look up to find him.

The second she saw a nurse come in the lounge, Alexa ran up to her. "Do you have news about Kýrie Angelis?"

"The doctor will be in shortly to talk to everyone," she said before walking over to Nico's parents.

Dimitra ran over and put an arm around her waist. "What did she tell you?"

"Nothing. She said to wait for the doctor."

"I don't believe Baba is going to die. We just found each other."

Alexa hugged her around the shoulders. "I agree. He's going to pull out of this and walk you down the aisle. You'll see." Her daughter was trying valiantly not to break down. Alexa needed to be strong for her. "We have to have faith." More faith than Alexa had exhibited in her entire life.

A few minutes after the nurse left the lounge, the doctor came in and headed straight for Nico's parents. She clung to Dimitra while they waited to hear the news.

"The good news is Kýrie Angelis has awakened. He has cuts and bruises, but it's his head that was impacted by the crash." Dimitra broke down quietly, hugging Alexa. "We've run scans to know if there's been significant damage to the brain. We'll have the results soon."

"Can I go in?" his mother asked in a tear-filled voice.

"No one is allowed to see him yet. Since he came to, he has asked repeatedly for us to send in his wife."

Upon hearing that, Alexa's heart almost jumped out of her chest.

"It's an indication that he's lost some of his memory. Whether it's temporary or permanent, we won't know for a while."

Alexa took a deep breath. "He hasn't lost his memory, doctor."

Everyone looked at Alexa as if she'd lost her mind.

"I'm his wife."

A collective gasp resounded in the room. Dimitra looked at her in shock.

"We were married in a private ceremony at the church in Sarti Village the other day, and planned to tell all of you after Dimitra and Kristos were married. But circumstances have changed the timeline." He had to love her a bit to want to see her before anyone else, right? "May I see him now?"

"Of course," the doctor murmured. "Come with me."

"Go to him, Mama." With stars in her eyes, Dimitra gave her a hard hug before letting her go.

Nico prayed he wasn't hallucinating when Alexa came in the room and walked over to his bedside. She wore a filmy pale blue sundress with spaghetti straps. He had a royal headache, but there was nothing wrong with his vision. Her gorgeous face had a pallor that told him how she'd been suffering.

"Darling—" She finally said the word he'd been waiting for. Her sea-green eyes filled with liquid. "I had to tell them I was your wife, or they wouldn't have let me see you before anyone else. Everyone loves you so terribly and is clamoring to see that you are all right."

He lifted the hand that didn't have an IV so she would take hold of it. "Thank heaven our secret is out. I couldn't have lived with it another second. Don't you know I want to shout it to the world that we're together forever? *Agape mou.* I love you to the depth of my soul. Kiss me."

"Are you sure it's all right?" She sounded so frightened.

"Would you rather I expired while I wait for it?"

"Oh, Nico—I'm so in love with you, it hurts." She leaned over and gave him the kiss of life. Her shiny chestnut hair fell around them.

When she finally lifted her head he said, "As the car met head-on with the other car, I couldn't believe I had to say goodbye to my beloved again. I couldn't bear it and called on the powers that be to perform a miracle."

"It's more than a miracle," she cried softly. "You're

not only alive, you're completely yourself. I'm over-joyed. I love you, Nico."

"I've been dying to hear those words from you. I knew that if you said them, it meant you'd gotten over your guilt from the past."

"I have, and I'll keep telling you I love you till you're sick of it. You have no idea how much I love you. Are you really feeling all right?"

"Other than a headache, I've never felt this wonderful."

"That's the kind of news I like to hear," a male voice intruded. The doctor had come in the room and walked over to them. "Your tests are back. No permanent damage has been done. I'm keeping you here until tomorrow morning. If all is well, then you'll be released. And by the way, congratulations on your marriage."

"Thank you, Doctor."

"I'll give your families the good news, but I don't want you bombarded with visitors."

"I'll make sure he doesn't overdo it," Alexa assured him.

As the doctor left the room, Nico squeezed her hand. "The minute I'm released, we're going to fly to the villa and spend a few days alone. We need it in the worst way."

"Nico—" She laughed. "Now I know you're back to normal I need to tell our daughter she doesn't have to worry. Be good while I go get her."

"Don't leave me yet. I need another kiss."

"So do I, my love." She kissed him one more time before leaving his room.

Less than a minute passed before Dimitra appeared.

"Baba—" She leaned over to hug him carefully. "I'm so thankful you and Mama are married. I love you more than you will ever know."

"You took the words out of my mouth."

Life didn't get better than this.

CHAPTER ELEVEN

THOUGH THEY'D FLOWN to Sarti on Thursday, it was Nico who drove them down to his private beach in the estate car on Friday. Another glorious, hot July day greeted them.

Other than a few bruises on his right upper arm and thigh, you would never have known he'd escaped death in a car crash. There was a little cut at the corner of his right eyebrow, and another one on his right earlobe, but those would fade.

Nico was still Alexa's fantasy. In fact she would love to hire a sculptor who would create a statue of him, but no work of art could ever match the wonder of him in the flesh. She told him that as they ran out in the turquoise water. Farther on it turned a deeper blue.

"A statue of me?" He laughed his head off. Another wonderful quality of his was the fact that he wasn't in love with himself. No other man had more reason to think otherwise. Not Nico. He was perfect.

"Yes. I'll have it erected in the backyard and go out to look at you while you're at work."

He'd gone out deeper and was treading water while she swam to him. "How about we have a statue of you erected and put in the front yard. Everyone who comes to your grandfather's house will see the exotic mermaid and fall madly in love with her."

"I'm afraid I don't look like I did at seventeen and can't stand the scrutiny."

He flashed her a devilish smile. "I happen to think you're more breathtaking than ever and can't wait to see you pregnant. It's a sight I've been waiting for since you told me Dimitra was our daughter. Wouldn't it be something if the two of you ended up expecting babies at the same time?"

"I don't wish that on her yet. They're still young."

They circled each other. "I don't know, Alexa. After the way I've seen our lives turn out so far, I've stopped thinking about what we should or shouldn't do. Life is a gift and we need to welcome it."

"You're right, darling. She and Kristos have found each other, and their wedding day will be here soon enough. Imagine if you become a father and a grandfather at the same time."

"I *have* been thinking about it. Our *papoú* will be a great-great-grandfather."

For Nico to call her grandfather *our papoú* meant their world had come full circle and they were a family in every sense of the word. She loved Nico so much she did a somersault and wrapped her arms around his hips, pulling him under the water.

They played like children, relishing in the joy of being together. After a time Nico got serious. He carried her out of the water to the beach and lowered her to one of his big beach towels laid out on the fine sand.

His dark eyes burned with desire. "I'm going to make love to you, my wife, right under a blazing sun."

She smiled at him. "What took you so long? I've been waiting for you to fulfill the promise you made me before your accident."

"You mean about making up for the time we had to spend apart? I hope you're ready."

"Is there any question I'm not?" She rolled over on top of him and began kissing every feature of his handsome face. He kissed her back. For the next little while they forgot everything except loving each other into oblivion.

"I wanted to do this the first day we met nineteen years ago," she admitted later when the sun was in a different part of the sky. "I hated it that people were around so we couldn't swim back to the beach and kiss each other for as long as we wanted. It was all I could think about."

He pulled her next to him. "After we met, you were all I ever thought about. My father kept asking me what was wrong and accused me of wandering around in a daze at work. I was literally useless during those three weeks, waiting to get off work to be with you. I didn't know love could be like that."

"Neither did I," she cried. "It frightened me because I knew you were going to leave. There were nights after you left me at the Gatakis' when I wanted to die. That's how I felt last Sunday night when you told me you'd be gone for several days. It brought back the past and I didn't sleep. Can't you tell me about it now? How come Giannina knew about your accident before I did?"

"I'll tell you everything after we drive back up to the villa. We're going to look like lobsters if we don't get out of this sun. You could be pregnant already and don't need any complications because I was too selfish keeping you out here."

She got to her feet. "You haven't kept me out here. I've dreamed of being out here with you and am your willing slave."

Together they gathered their things and walked over to the car parked beneath some trees. On the drive up the road through the trees, Nico told her everything.

"So your uncle has disappeared?"

"I couldn't find him. He's now a wanted man in both countries."

"I can't believe he's caused so much pain to your family over the years. But after what Monika did to us, nothing should surprise me."

"My thoughts exactly."

"I hope your sister can now run the newspaper without any problems. She's such a lovely person."

"She feels the same about you. Now let's go inside for a drink. Then I'd like to spend some time in bed while we plan our honeymoon. We'll leave on ours as soon as Kristos and Dimitra take off."

"We'll only have a week."

"I've given it a lot of thought. Why don't we fly in the private jet to Ottawa to see your publisher. We'll spend a day there while you show me the sights. That will leave us a few more days. What would you like to do with them?" He pulled some drinks out of the fridge and they quenched their thirst.

"If you're asking me seriously, I'd love to go back to Olympia. We only had a day. This time we could stay at that hotel on the hill overlooking the ancient city. You'll never know how much I wanted to be married then and have weeks to spend time in your arms and explore the sites. It's our Greek history, Nico, and it sank deeply into my bones. I'll never get enough of it."

"What a relief, my darling. I was afraid you were going to say London or Paris."

"I'd like to travel to those places, but for our honeymoon I'd rather revisit the spot where I first laid eyes on the Hermes sculpture. It represents my feelings for the man I'd hoped to marry. *You.*" She looked into his eyes. "If you'd seen the look on everyone's face in the hospital lounge when I told them I was your wife... No one could doubt how I feel about you."

He pulled her in his arms. "I happen to know the news that we're married made everyone ecstatic. But no one more than me. For you to announce our marriage proved you've forgiven yourself and unlocked my prison door. It means I have my mermaid back."

"Forever."

They walked through the house to the bedroom. "I've never been this happy in my life. I'm married to the woman I've wanted from the moment I met her, and my beautiful daughter is getting married to a man I love like my own son. It's beyond wonderful."

She threw herself in his arms. "You talk about a prison. That's what I was in all these years, wanting to tell you the truth. I'm not that person any longer."

"We've entered a new phase of life. One exciting

aspect is that I get to take a shower with my wife." He
grabbed her before she knew what was happening.

"Nico—" she squealed.

"This is just the beginning."

EPILOGUE

DIMITRA'S AUGUST WEDDING DAY had arrived. Alexa drove her to the church early to help her dress in one of the anterooms off the foyer. The ceremony had been scheduled for ten in the morning and Phyllis wheeled their *papoú* to the front of the nave. He wore a new dark blue dress suit with a gardenia and looked splendid.

The well-known Papadakis and Angelis families who'd been in the news recently guaranteed a large crowd. Many of the guests had already arrived. Irena had told Alexa that this was going to be the biggest society wedding Salonica had witnessed in years complete with photographers and various news agencies covering the event.

Alexa had bought a pale peach chiffon knee-length dress with short sleeves and a scooped neckline. She wore a gardenia corsage on her shoulder. Nico liked her hair down so much, she didn't change it. Neither she or Dimitra needed blusher. Excitement had made them both feverish.

Dimitra looked exquisite in a white, A-line lace tulle wedding dress. It was sleeveless with an illusion neckline. The court train gave it a royal elegance. She wore a garland of flowers in her wavy brunette hair. No veil. She didn't want one.

Kristos had sent her a gift of pearls that were his grandmother's. Alexa fastened them around her neck and handed her the wedding bouquet of white roses and gardenias.

"It's almost time, honey. I'm going to find your *papoú.* Your father will be here in a minute to walk you down the aisle. God bless you, darling girl. You look a vision. Kristos is going to think so too."

"I can't believe I'm getting married."

"Are you sure it's what you want?"

"Mama—"

"Don't you know I'm teasing you?" Alexa's gift to her consisted of a pair of light green peridot earrings that matched her eyes. "You look like a princess."

"I feel like one."

She kissed her cheek. "I'll see you in a few minutes." Alexa left the room and hurried down the aisle to the front of the church. Her grandfather and Phyllis smiled when they saw her coming. Nico's family sat on the other side. Irena had joined them.

Alexa sat on the other side of her grandfather and reached for his hand. "You won't believe how beautiful Dimitra looks in her wedding dress."

"You look like a bride yourself," he whispered.

She gave him a kiss and looked around. The church was filling fast. "Are you really going to be all right while we're both off on our honeymoons?"

"Sweetheart, a week is nothing. I'll be able to keep working on my book, and I have Phyllis. I'm so happy for you and your baby girl, it's put a permanent smile on my face."

"I could never have made it through this life without you and Grandma Iris. I'm so sorry she isn't here."

"But she is."

She nodded. "I'm sure you're right."

Suddenly the organ music started and the priest walked in from a side door resplendent in his robes. Kristos and Yanni followed him, dressed in black tuxedos with gardenias in their lapels. Irena had to be in tears.

Everyone got to their feet as the "Wedding March" played. Alexa turned her head. A quiet gasp escaped her lips at the sight that met her eyes. She'd never forget her beaming daughter who came walking down the aisle with her father. Nico had to be the most magnificent, handsome man in existence.

He wore a black tuxedo, Kristos's choice, with a gardenia in his lapel. All eyes were on the two of them. They looked perfect together. There were no words to describe the feelings bursting inside her. When the two of them reached the front, Nico left his daughter in Kristos's care and walked toward Alexa.

Their eyes fused for a heart-stopping moment. He clasped her hand and never let it go during the nearly hour-long ceremony. The Dance of Isaiah where the husband and wife circled the table three times was particularly moving to Alexa. It was full of symbolism and tradition. By the time the priest gave the final blessing, she was fighting tears.

The married couple turned to the congregation. Dimitra looked at Alexa and Nico across the expanse. Her eyes glowed with happiness and joy. It was all there. Then Kristos looked over at them with the same expression. There were few moments in life more thrilling than this one.

Nico was so moved, he put his arm around Alexa and pulled her closer to him. She looked up at him. "I married you all over again during their ceremony."

He gave her that devastating smile. "I did the same thing. But if you want to know the truth, I felt we were married that night on my cruiser.

"I'm also thinking about the baby we're going to have, no matter how long it takes for us to get pregnant."

"You don't have to wonder any longer."

"Alexa—" His dark eyes blazed.

She flashed him an illuminating smile. "I did a home test today. We're going to have another baby. We can forget the four months."

"I hoped you didn't mean it, but I didn't want to argue with you at the time. I wanted to marry you so badly, I'm afraid I would have promised you anything. We're really pregnant?"

"Yes, darling, but we'll have to continue this conversation later. Everyone is leaving and we've a reception to attend. Dimitra and Kristos will wonder where we are. She let me know you and I seem to function in a world all our own all the time."

Forgetting everyone else, he bent his head and kissed her. "She got that right. Once our worlds collided, that was it."

"I'm so thankful you asked me to marry you while we were on the yacht. Now another baby is on the way. As it turns out, Hera didn't win. In the end Io, with all her journeys, was changed back to human form by Zeus and would bear his child, whose descendant would be a great hero.

"That's our story, darling."

* * * * *

THE MARINE
MAKES AMENDS

VICTORIA PADE

Chapter One

"Home again, home again…" Lexie Parker muttered to herself in relief as she headed for a restroom in the Billings, Montana, airport.

She wasn't quite home yet. Home was the small town of Merritt where she'd grown up. But this was the closest she'd been in over a decade.

"A little pit stop, get my luggage, rent a car and I'll be there, Gram," she said as if her grandmother could hear her.

It was the last Saturday in May and Lexie had been traveling since 3:00 a.m. If she'd waited for a direct flight, the trip from Anchorage, Alaska, would have taken approximately four and a half hours. Instead, she'd had to zigzag, enduring through two layovers, over the course of ten hours. But there was just no way she'd been willing to wait.

Her grandmother had had an accident yesterday that had badly broken the eighty-year-old's leg. Lexie had received a frantic call from their cousin Mary just as Gertie was being sent into surgery.

The surgery had gone well—so well that after spending the night in the hospital, Gertie had been released this morning. But still Lexie wanted to get to her grandmother. Ditching her original plan to move home from Anchorage ten days from now, Lexie had apologized to her boss for not finishing out her two-week notice, thrown everything she owned into two suitcases and rearranged her travel plans.

But the rush and the lengthy trip—not to mention the mess her life had been in for the last several months—showed on her face as she peered into the bathroom mirror.

"You look lousy," she told her reflection.

And not the way she wanted to look when she saw her very observant grandmother.

She decided it would be worth taking the time to spruce herself up before getting her bags and her rental car. Rushing to baggage claim wouldn't make her suitcases appear any faster.

Hair first, she decided, taking a hairbrush from

the floppy oversize purse she carried. She pulled her sloppy topknot free and flipped over to brush her hair from the bottom up.

It took a while to get the tangles out but she finally managed it, regathering the long thick strands into another topknot and tuck before replacing the hairpins.

Better, she judged when she glanced in the mirror again.

Being upside down had also helped put some color into her cheeks, though that was likely temporary. Since confronting Jason with her resolve to finally move back to Merritt—and the bombshell he'd dropped in response—Lexie had had friends and coworkers telling her she was pale. Normally, she didn't care, but it was something else she didn't want her grandmother to see.

So she fished around in her purse for some emergency makeup, digging out blotting papers, a well-used blush compact, a tube of mascara and an almost-used-up eyeliner pencil.

One of the blotting sheets went to work first, followed by just a hint of the blush on the apples of high cheekbones that were a bit more pronounced since stress had stolen her appetite.

Next she used the eyeliner, making a single thin line on the top of both lids, following that up with mascara to help bring out her silver-gray eyes and make her look less weary.

As she smoothed her ring fingertips over her dark eyebrows, her eyes were drawn to the lack of her wedding ring.

She'd taken the band off not long after filing for divorce five months ago and had stopped feeling naked without it—and yet right now, she felt so aware of the absence of it again. But she reminded herself that this was the beginning of her fresh start and that that was a good thing.

A fresh start, she repeated silently to remind herself of her goal.

Exhaling slowly, she shoved away thoughts of her past as she took a tinted lip gloss from her purse and applied it to lips that were just full enough and just rosy enough not to need more than gloss.

Better, was her decree when she moved her head from side to side to judge her handiwork.

From there she switched her focus to her clothes.

Her jeans were fine but the yellow turtleneck was making her too warm. Late May in Merritt meant warmer temperatures than she'd find in Anchorage, and she hadn't planned ahead.

But she didn't have a change of shirts in her purse so the best she could do now was smooth out the shirt's wrinkles and push the sleeves above her elbows.

"That's as good as it's going to get," she told

her reflection, slinging the strap of her purse over her shoulder to leave the restroom.

She wasn't far from baggage claim and went directly there, seeing that even with her restroom delay, no luggage had come onto the carousel yet.

She took a spot among the other passengers.

Any minute, folks, I want to get where I'm going...

"Lexie?"

The sound of her name startled her and she shot a glance to her left.

She locked eyes with the owner of the deep male voice, who then said, "Yep, that's you. I thought so. Gertie was right—you haven't changed..."

It took Lexie a moment to register that she recognized the man. And then came the sinking feeling when she noticed that he didn't have the air of a traveler about him—no luggage or carry-ons or reading materials.

Instead, he gave the impression that he might be there to pick someone up. The fact that his attention was on her and that he'd mentioned her grandmother's name made her instantly afraid that that someone might be her.

The man was Micah Camden and since the first week of their senior year in high school, she'd regretted ever having known him.

Old anger and resentment zoomed through her but she worked to keep it out of her voice when she said, "Odd to see you here..."

"I've been with Gertie and Mary since yester-day," he responded. "Mary said you were going to rent a car to drive to Merritt and Gertie didn't like that idea, so I came down to get you."

"She must be on a lot of drugs." *To send you, of all people*, Lexie thought.

The sound of the baggage carousel starting up drew his attention away from her. But Lexie continued to glare at him, frozen in disbelief that her grandmother would send Micah Camden.

A moment later, he turned his still-striking cobalt blue eyes back to her and said, "You don't have to take me up on the ride, if you don't want to. You can still rent a car and I can just follow you to town so Gertie knows I'm at least watching out for you."

That was an idea. Then she wouldn't have to be in an enclosed space with him for the hour it would take to get to Merritt. She wouldn't have to talk to him.

It was tempting.

But frugality was one of the things she'd learned well over the years and renting a car was not cheap. It even seemed a little frivolous, since once she got to town, she could drive her grandmother's car or truck until she could afford something of her own—but it had been the quickest way to get there.

Until now, when Micah Camden was giving her another option.

An option that irked her even though it was to her benefit.

She tried not to show too much of her irritation. "Renting a car if I don't have to would be a waste of money," she admitted reluctantly.

He nodded but didn't say anything else as she caught sight of the smaller of her suitcases.

Without saying anything else to him, she stepped over to scoop the duffel-like bag off and stayed where she was just to get some distance from Micah Camden as this situation sank in.

Until fifteen years ago, she'd considered him one of her three best friends. *The Four Musketeers*— that's what everyone had called them growing up. Lexie, Jason Lundy, Jill Gunner and *him*.

But fifteen years ago, Micah Camden had proven he was no friend at all. Not to her. Not to Jason. For the remaining two years Lexie had been in Merritt, she'd had nothing to do with him, and since leaving she'd put any thought of him out of her mind altogether.

And now here he was.

He'd said she looked the same and so did he. Only better, if that were possible, she thought begrudgingly as she secretly studied him.

The Camden brothers—all four of them—were known for a few things. Their good looks topped the list.

When it came to Micah, that meant coarse

brown-almost-black hair that he now wore crisply short over his very square forehead.

His undeniably handsome face was angular, with a straight, perfect nose poised between high cheekbones and a razor-sharp jawline that currently had a hint of five o'clock shadow that Lexie refused to admit was rugged and sexy.

His intensely masculine face was softened only by those blue eyes.

Those eyes…

Beneath a shelf of faintly unruly eyebrows, they were a little deep-set—just enough to somehow emphasize the color that was so remarkable and so distinctive to his family that there were actually articles written about *The Camden Blue Eyes*, focusing on his cousins, the higher-profiled Camdens in Denver who owned Camden Superstores.

Those eyes that were so blue, so bright, it was difficult not to stare at them. They hardly seemed real.

But real they were and Lexie forced herself to stop staring at them, moving on instead to his mouth in hopes of finding some fault there.

Nope, she couldn't find a flaw there, either. His lips were male-model impeccable, giving no evidence of the lies that could spew from them.

No, time hadn't diminished how drop-dead gorgeous he was. If anything, the added maturity had honed and added to his appeal.

And the body that went with the face and hair?

The last time she'd seen him it had been barely more than a boy's body. But over the years, he'd gained some height—at least three inches over the six feet he'd been. And now, barely contained by a military blue crewneck T-shirt, he had shoulders a mile wide, pecs that filled the knit impressively and wowza-biceps that stretched the short sleeves to their limits.

Below that were jeans that traced narrow hips and clung to sturdy tree-trunk thighs that made it seem as if nothing could make him fall.

Unlike the actual tree he'd crashed into her grandmother's house...

Lexie averted her eyes and concentrated on the bags coming out along the carousel.

Her main bag was approaching, and because she'd needed it to carry the lion's share of what she owned from one move to the other, it was trunk-sized. When she tried to grab it, Micah reached in front of her, saying, "Let me do that."

It was on the tip of her tongue to say *no* but too many times her recovery of that suitcase had been less than graceful, so she just let him. But as soon as he had it off the carousel she took over, pulling up the bar handle and tipping it onto its wheels.

"Sooo, the verdict is that you're going to let me take you to Merritt?" Micah asked.

His voice was lower than she remembered it.

And there was something strong and confident in his tone, too, as if her agreement was a foregone conclusion.

And, damn him, it was.

"I guess so," she answered with resignation.

He nodded agreeably—not victoriously—which was a good thing because Lexie might have accepted the ride but she wasn't conceding anything.

Fifteen years ago, he'd shown her his true colors.

And that was when she'd learned that he was an A-one jerk who couldn't be trusted.

After they loaded up Micah's big white pickup truck and finally got on the highway, Lexie tried to put her dislike of Micah Camden aside enough to get some answers about her grandmother and what had happened to cause Gertrude Parker's injury.

"*Is* Gram doing well enough not to be in the hospital or did she just refuse to stay?" she asked.

"She's doing great. By this morning when she asked if she could go home, the doctors didn't see any reason not to release her. She might have a lot of years under her belt, but you know how she is—she's a firecracker, she has spunk."

"I just don't want that to override anyone's better judgment about her health. She's *eighty* years old."

"I don't think she was fooling anybody. The surgeon and the orthopedist came over from North-bridge."

Lexie let out a sigh of relief. Northbridge was a fairly small town, but it had a bigger hospital than Merritt, making it able to sustain a few specialists. If Gram's doctor had called them in, then that meant they were taking the situation seriously.

"By this morning, they signed off on her leaving the hospital. Plus, her local doctor came in to talk to them and agreed. So Mary and I checked her out. And you know Merritt, it isn't like a big city—house calls aren't unusual. Joan—Gertie's regular doc—said she'd stop in every day for a while to check on her."

Lexie's worries weren't completely allayed—they wouldn't be until she saw for herself that her grandmother was all right—but she relaxed enough to ask the other question on her mind.

"What exactly happened?"

"You know I'm renting Gertie's barn as my brewery?"

Lexie knew, all right—and she considered it a deal with the devil.

"Yes, she told me she decided to rent you the barn the way she leases the fields to the neighbors now that she can't work the farm anymore."

"Right. Well, I'm using the space for a small craft brewery. Gertie is actually my adviser and my taste tester—not that that has anything to do with this. There wasn't any tasting going on when she got hurt," he added in a hurry.

Lexie knew Gertie well enough to know she only ever drank in moderation. And besides, after a lifetime of hobby brewing, she could handle what she did drink.

"Anyway," Micah continued, "I was having a new forklift delivered and it got away from the guy who was unloading it. It hit that tree that stands between Gertie's place and the little house—"

"*My* house—the house my dad built next door for him and Mom and me? The house where I'm going to live? It was involved in this, too?" Lexie demanded, alarmed.

"Yeah...well..." Micah said, clearly uncomfortable, "the forklift hit the tree and it went down. It took out the side wall of Gertie's house, and uh...a pretty good chunk of the little house..."

"*A pretty good chunk* of the little house? More than just a side wall?"

"There's damage all the way around," he answered reluctantly. Then, as if to avoid getting into more of that, he returned to her original question about her grandmother's injury.

"Luckily, Gertie was downstairs when the tree went down, on the opposite end of the living room—which was untouched, by the way. But she didn't know what had happened and she ran like a bat out of hell out the front door. She was in such a hurry that she tripped going down the porch steps and fell."

"Don't make it sound like it was her fault!"

"I didn't mean to," he assured her. "Of course, it wasn't her fault. She was scared—rightfully so—and ran out just like anybody would have. When she fell, her leg twisted out from under her, and the lower part of her femur caught the brunt of it."

He *was* just stating facts but Lexie was already upset about her grandmother. Learning that the house she'd expected to come home to was also a casualty pushed her unhappiness that much further.

Then, as she thought about her house and her grandmother's, something else occurred to her.

"How could Gram go home to a house without a side wall?"

"Actually it's the stairs that made returning to her house impossible," he informed. "The surgery put a plate and four screws in her femur—"

"Mary told me that."

"Well, the leg is in a cast and it has to be raised and stationary for a while. So they want her in a wheelchair for now. She can't be anywhere where she'd have to navigate stairs—"

"Or, I would assume, any house that's missing a wall."

"Well, yeah…"

"So where did Gram go home to?" Lexie demanded.

"Mary's apartment. It's tiny but there are two bedrooms and she really wanted Gertie to stay with her. She said she's bored and lonely and she'd be happy for the company. And she's a retired nurse, you know, so she's a good choice for taking care of Gertie. Plus, with the apartment in the heart of town, Gertie is closer to the hospital if anything goes wrong, and the apartment is easy for Joan to get to for house calls. So Gertie and Mary decided they're going to be roomies until Gertie's place is fixed and Gertie can handle that layout."

Mary had been in her apartment for as long as Lexie could remember so Lexie knew it wasn't big enough to house her, too, and she suddenly wondered if she was homeless.

Yet another unpleasant revelation from this guy...

She took a breath and focused on what was most important. "Okay, that sounds like a decent arrangement for them."

"I think it is," he said, sounding relieved that she wasn't kicking up more of a fuss.

"But," Lexie said then, "I was going to move into the little house—*my* house. Did the *pretty good chunk* taken out of it make that impossible?"

"It did," he confirmed, sounding guilty. "But," he added in a hurry and in a more positive tone, "I had both places inspected this morning by county inspectors. And while the little house can't be lived in yet, most of the damage to Gertie's house is really concentrated in that one spot. The rest of the big house is structurally sound, and has been cleared for occupancy. So you can move in there."

"With a gaping hole that could let anyone just walk in any time of the day or night," she said more to herself than to him.

"That's taken care of, too," he assured her.

"*How* is that taken care of, too?"

"I had the open side of the house tarped and I promised Gertie that I'll move into the sunroom downstairs and stay there so I can make sure there's no looting—and no kids trying to use it as a party spot..."

Was he honestly telling her what it seemed like he was telling her?

"*You* and *I* are going to be *housemates*?" she said, her voice louder than she'd intended it to be.

"You'll be upstairs, I'll be down—in the sunroom that's not really *in* the house. I'll use the bathroom downstairs. You'll have the one upstairs to yourself. I'll never even climb the stairs..."

"And we know how you like to take that kind of situation and spin it for your own benefit," she said, this time keeping none of her animosity toward him hidden.

That left a heavy silence for a moment before a

much more subdued Micah said in a somber voice, "I can never tell you how sorry—"

"As if that matters!" Lexie snapped, cutting him off. She was in no mood to hear apologies or re-hash the past with him.

Instead, as they approached the sign welcoming them to Merritt, she turned her head to glare at him again and added, "Don't forget that I *know* you. And don't think for one minute that I won't be watching your every move."

He nodded his head, accepting that with every indication of resignation.

Lexie went on glowering at him, furious with the situation but not seeing any way out. The one person on earth she didn't even want to know ex-isted was the person she was going to be cohabi-tating with. And worst of all, this was putting her in a position similar to the one he'd used to cause trouble for her fifteen years ago.

This was *not* what she'd wanted to come home to.

But, unlike the rental car, in this she didn't have any choice.

She couldn't afford a room at the bed-and-breakfast that was the only temporary option in town and she certainly couldn't pay for an apart-ment of her own. And while she could insist on him leaving her to stay by herself, she didn't like the idea of being alone in a house that anyone could walk into day or night. She had a feeling Gram wouldn't like the idea of that, either, and Lexie didn't feel as if she could add any more stress to her ailing grandmother by pitching a fit about it.

So she was going to have to put her own negative feelings about him on the back burner and make the best of a rotten situation.

But there would be no forgetting that even if Micah Camden had grown up to be as head-turningly handsome a man as she had ever seen, underneath that very impressive surface was nothing good.

Chapter Two

The drive from the airport in Billings to Merritt took until nearly four thirty Saturday afternoon. When Micah pulled up in front of the fourplex where Gertie was staying with her cousin, he asked Lexie if she wanted time alone with her grandmother and offered to wait in his truck if she did.

Lexie took him up on the offer so that left him with plenty of time to kill, sitting in the cab of his pickup truck and thinking that he must be getting soft. On active duty in the Marines, there had been more than one training mission that had cost him plenty of sleep. None of those had left him feeling as tired as he was now, even though all he'd done last night was sit in a chair in Gertie's hospital room.

Fighting his exhaustion didn't serve any purpose, though, so he closed his eyes and laid his head back against the seat.

He'd been told there was no need for him to stay last night but he'd still refused to leave. Gertie was eighty years old with a broken leg and had just undergone emergency surgery. She'd been groggy from the anesthesia and he'd been afraid she wouldn't have the wherewithal to ring for a nurse if she woke and needed care.

While he and Gertie might not literally be family, Gertie was still like family to him. Anything he would do for his brothers or his own grandfather, he would do for her. There was no question about it.

Add to that the fact that it was *his* runaway forklift that had caused this whole mess and there was all the more reason for him to make sure that whatever Gertie needed, Gertie got.

He hated that she'd been hurt at all, let alone over anything to do with him or his business.

"Damn it all to hell," he cursed for the hundredth time since it had happened, struggling under the weight of his guilt, wishing he were the one with the broken bone instead of Gertie.

Gertie, who had only ever been kind, generous, caring, compassionate and even sympathetic to him when he hadn't deserved it. When she'd had every reason to just write him off.

But somehow Gertie had found it in herself to forgive him.

Unlike Lexie, he thought ruefully.

The past hour had proven that her feelings for him, her opinion of him, definitely weren't any better now than all those years ago.

He understood that. He'd done something truly lousy that had caused a domino effect of problems. It hadn't been his intention to hurt anyone. But what he *had* intended had been purely self-serving and it had avalanched. Directly onto her.

He wasn't the same person he'd been then, the person his mother had raised him—and his three brothers—to be. The Marines had taken that raw material full of not altogether good values that his mother had given him and used it to make him into what he hoped was a better man.

But all Lexie knew was the person he'd been before the Marines taught him honor and integrity, loyalty, brotherhood and unity. All Lexie knew was the boy who'd had only a vague acquaintance with those things and so had brought disaster into her young life.

Disaster that had hurt her in particular, and cost him his friendship with her and with Jason. Friendships that had begun in preschool.

Hell, his singlemindedness was still costing

him, he thought. Most recently, he'd paid the price for it with Adrianna—even when he'd been sure he was doing everything right with his former significant other...

Tired or not, his racing mind wasn't letting him rest, so he lifted his head from the back of the seat and opened his eyes.

There was nothing he could do to rectify the current fallout with Adrianna. But he *was* going to make sure every inch of Gertie's and Lexie's property was fixed as good as new. And maybe in the meantime he could find a way to atone for the ugly part of his history with Lexie, too.

You didn't let me say it, but you can never know how sorry I am...

He'd just been so young and immature. And brainwashed.

And so damn head over heels, wildly and hopelessly crushing on Lexie for four years by that point—ever since the end of seventh grade—up until that day when it had stupidly seemed to him like an opportunity had finally presented itself.

Until the end of seventh grade, Jason, the boy next door; Lexie, the part tomboy, part sweetheart; Jill, the bookish, analytical mouse; and Micah, the push-the-limits smart-ass, had been inseparable best friends. They'd done everything together, and Micah hadn't felt anything but friendship for any one of them. It had been clear-cut.

And then little by little it had started to be confusing...

By the summer before eighth grade—about when his voice had cracked and he'd sprouted up five inches overnight—he'd begun to notice that he wanted to be with Lexie more than he wanted to be with Jill or even Jason. That he wanted to be alone with Lexie.

Little by little, he'd started to take note of things about Lexie that he didn't notice about Jason or Jill.

Lexie's hair. Lexie's eyes. Lexie's laugh—and how good it made him feel if he could *make* her laugh...

He hadn't understood what was going on at first—not until his brother Quinn figured it out and teased him about wanting Lexie to be his *girlfriend*.

He'd denied it, of course. Punched Quinn for laughing at him. And told himself that Quinn was wrong. But eventually he'd begun to realize that Quinn wasn't wrong.

The trouble was, about the time Micah had accepted that he might like Lexie as more than a friend, Jason had gotten on the same track.

At first it was as subtle as two thirteen-year-old boys could be—posturing, vying awkwardly for her attention, competing with each other, horsing around in order to entertain her.

They'd jockeyed for which of them could persuade her to study with him or do a school project with him. They'd both tried to be the first at her door in the morning to walk her to the bus stop. They'd wrestled to be the one to snag a seat next to her on the bus.

But over time, Jason had developed some game—he'd learned to flirt and his adolescent edges had smoothed out.

While Micah's hadn't.

Suddenly—or at least it had seemed sudden to Micah—Jason and Lexie started to have private jokes that neither Micah nor Jill had been privy to. Suddenly Jason was bold enough to whisper in Lexie's ear, sharing secrets just for them. Suddenly Jason was making her smile and giggle in a way Micah wasn't.

Before Micah knew it, there was something between Jason and Lexie that he couldn't quite seem to have with her.

And every time he watched Lexie with Jason, it tore his heart out.

You guys thought you were soul mates. What happened to that? Micah wondered, recalling how their young romance had developed while he'd watched from the sidelines, tortured by it...

It had taken years even after they'd all gone their separate ways for him to move on to the point where he could hope they were happy together.

But apparently that wasn't how things had played out. He knew now, through Gertie, that Lexie and Jason had just divorced. He was sorry for both of his former friends. Genuinely sorry.

And the fact that his first glimpse of Lexie at the airport this afternoon had given him a split-second flashback to his childhood crush?

That was only a memory, too. It didn't mean anything. He'd moved so far beyond those old days, those old longings for her, that a fleeting moment of recollection was all it *could* be.

The door to Mary's apartment opened just then and out came Mary and Lexie.

As they paused there to talk on the front porch, Micah watched them.

Well, not *them*—it wasn't white-haired Mary he was focused on. It was only Lexie.

In the two years between when he'd wrecked their friendship and when Lexie and Jason had left Merritt, Lexie had avoided him as much as possible. But he'd gone on stealing any glimpse of her he could get, so he knew that her looks hadn't altered any during that time.

But add another thirteen years?

He'd recognized her at baggage claim the minute he laid eyes on her, so when he'd told her she hadn't changed, he'd meant it.

But there *were* changes, he realized.

Changes that were all improvements.

And he couldn't help taking in every detail one by one.

Her hair was the same rich russet brown, shining reddish wherever the spring sunlight hit it. She'd cut it to chin length at the end of high school but now, judging by the scale of that knot wrangled at the crown of her head, he could tell that if she let it loose it would again be long and thick and luxurious. The way he'd liked it.

The years had refined and perfected her face. The pretty girl had become all-out beautiful.

Her skin was pure peaches and cream—flawless, without a hint of teenage blemishes, and so smooth and velvety that it couldn't possibly feel as soft as it looked.

She'd always had a refined bone structure—a straight delicate nose, high cheekbones, a patrician jaw that hammocked a perky chin. But now it was all more elegant-looking.

Her ears were still just right—small, close to her head and cute—with lobes he'd pictured himself tugging on with his teeth. And the neck that she'd always complained was gawky now just looked long and graceful. The neck that, in his obsessed youth, he'd fantasized about kissing.

Though not as much as he'd fantasized kissing those lips...

Plush petal pink lips that could expand into a smile warm enough to melt glaciers.

He didn't know if that had changed because nothing about their reunion today had brought it out.

And then there were her superhero-colored eyes, he thought with a laugh, recalling the moment she'd turned them to him at the airport.

He'd coined the phrase *superhero color* to describe them back when he'd first become infatuated with her—gray eyes that were streaked with so much luminous silver that they seemed something more than mortal.

The silver streaks only seemed to have brightened to make her eyes all the more sparkling, all the more mesmerizing...

Okay, yes, for maybe the span of one breath he'd felt mesmerized at his first sight of them again. But they were stunning eyes. Anybody would have been momentarily struck by an initial glimpse.

It had been only for an instant, though. Then he'd come out of it...and noticed the rest of her.

She was dressed in a turtleneck and jeans that were both just snug enough to accentuate a body that was even better than when he'd seen her last.

Curves that had filled out in a way that made it hard not to stare.

Oh, yeah, she'd definitely gotten better, he decided. Much better, really.

And you let her go? he mentally asked his childhood friend in disbelief.

It seemed hard to fathom—though not because he had any designs on her, he was quick to remind himself. No designs. No feelings. No nothing. Because when it came to Lexie, they were just…

Well, he didn't know what they were.

She hadn't seen him as anything except a friend when he was lovesick over her, and he'd long since lost her friendship. Whatever they were now, it wasn't anything good.

On the other hand, his relationship with her grandmother was important to him. So important to him that he didn't want to lose either the personal or the professional part of it under any circumstances.

So not only was it vital that he make peace with Lexie over what he'd done fifteen years ago just to right the wrong, he thought that it was also essential that he try to reach some sort of civility with her in order not to damage his friendship and association with Gertie.

If he didn't, Lexie's opinion of him might muddy the waters with Gertie.

"Honest to God, Lexie, I'm not the person I was then," he said quietly.

But he knew mere words weren't enough now. He was going to have to prove it to her.

He wasn't sure exactly how he was going to do that, but no matter what it took, he'd find a way.

Because even beyond his relationship with

Gertie, It would be nice if they could live in the small town together again without Lexie completely hating his guts.

Lexie had very little to say to Micah when she returned to his truck. In answer to his immediate question about how Gertie was doing, she told him that Gertie *said* she was doing well and that Mary had confirmed it.

But to Lexie, seeing her grandmother lying in bed, sleepy from the pain pill she'd taken just before Lexie's arrival, had been a painful blow. Gertie had looked so pale, so frail and so much older than she seemed when she was up and about, and being her usual feisty self. Lexie was left shaken and certainly not reassured that everything was as good as the two elderly women said it was.

Still, both her grandmother and their cousin had maintained that what Gertie needed most tonight was rest, and had insisted that Lexie go home, settle in and come back in the morning. Gertie had been especially intent on Lexie getting to the house to check out the damage so she could report back to her.

So after more of Mary's promises that everything really was fine and that she'd call should Gertie need Lexie in any way, Lexie was once again in Micah's passenger seat, not feeling any less worried than she had been before, and those worries continued to occupy her thoughts as they drove.

After a brief stop at the general store, where Micah ran in while Lexie stayed put so her luggage in the open truck bed in back wouldn't be left unattended, he took her home.

The property that had been in her family for generations, where she'd grown up, was just outside Merritt. She was braced for the damage that Micah had described, but it was still strange and awkward to arrive and see it looking like anything but the peaceful place she was familiar with.

Instead, the driveway was crowded with two other pickup trucks and a large wood-hauling truck, and a crew of six men were working on the downed tree between the houses.

The sounds of chain saws cutting through the tree, axes chopping what had already been cut and loud thunks as wood was thrown into the bed of the wood-hauling truck greeted them as they headed up the drive. And the huge oak tree that had towered above the houses—both the large two-story white farmhouse and the smaller version of it next door—was missing from the skyline Lexie had always known.

She hadn't really considered the mechanical details that cleanup and repair might entail. But seeing the size of the tree just made her dread all the more the moment when she'd finally see the damage to the houses.

"They're already demolishing the tree?" she said with some surprise, not having any idea what first step needed to be taken—or a second or third, for that matter—but somehow feeling as if it were too soon for so much to be going on.

"Yeah. I called this company in from Northbridge. They've been here since early this morning," Micah answered. "They got the limbs out of the houses first so I could put up tarps before I left for the airport—"

"There were tree limbs *inside* the houses..." she said, for some reason not having considered that before.

"Oh, yeah," Micah responded. "Once those were cut off and hauled out, they started to deal with the bigger part—most of the tree landed between the two houses. But from the looks of what they have loaded in that big truck, I'd say they're about done. Well, with this part. I'm having them move all the wood out behind the barn for now. When the repairs to the houses are finished and we're headed into winter, I'll bring it back to the woodpile so Gertie—and you—can use it for firewood."

Lexie nodded. She hadn't really thought that far ahead so it was good that someone was.

She was at the end of a very long day and hours

and hours of traveling. She'd just seen her ailing and weakened grandmother and nothing about that had eased her worries. And now this. It was a lot to contend with and she felt a little dazed by the magnitude of it all.

"How about we get you and your bags inside, and when you're ready, we can eat the dinner I got for us at the store?" Micah suggested then, speaking gently, as if he realized she'd reached her limit.

Lexie could only lift her chin slightly to agree.

She dragged her gaze from the work that was being done, gathered her purse and got out of the pickup at the same time as Micah. He took both of her suitcases from the truck bed and even Lexie's foggy brain couldn't help noticing how easily he wielded the weight of her heavy luggage and the way his enormous biceps stretched the short sleeves of his T-shirt as he hoisted the trunk over the sides of the truck.

When she realized what was going through her mind, she forced herself to look elsewhere and tamped down on the unwelcome appreciation of that view. Instead, she looked down at the ground as they approached the big house where he ushered her up the four porch steps and through the front door.

Once inside, the damage to the house became more evident even as Micah said, "I picked up all the tree rubble and swept, so it wouldn't be *too* dirty, but there's still some mess I didn't have a chance to get to…"

Straight ahead was the wide staircase with its stained wood steps that rose to the second floor. And although the stairs were clean, the family photos hung on the side wall were all askew.

In the big living room to the right were two overturned tables, lying on the floor next to fallen books and knickknacks. The two overstuffed easy chairs seemed to have jumped out of their usual positions, marked by indentations left in the tan carpeting inches away.

To the left of the entrance, though, was the kitchen. And that told an even harsher story.

Hazy light poured in through the tarp that covered a jagged edge around a great big hole where a wall used to be. The cupboards that had lined that wall were crushed and splintered where they'd fallen to the kitchen floor, their contents scattered and broken there, too.

"I know it looks bad," Micah said when he saw her stare in that direction. "But at least the appliances and the pipes and sink weren't affected. I had to turn off the electrical breaker to that outer wall but that's it," he downplayed.

Then, as if he didn't want her looking too closely at it, he hustled her upstairs where too much light was also coming from the door to her grandmother's bedroom, also to the left of the landing.

Lexie went as far as the doorway to peer inside and found the bedroom's hardwood floor had turned into a fragmented cliff up against the tarp there, while the bureau and the outer wall of the closet were missing. Clothes from both the closet and the bureau were piled near the side of the double bed, dusted with debris.

"Definitely a mess," she murmured.

Micah didn't say anything to that.

But just then there was a knock on the front door downstairs, immediately followed by the sound of it being opened as a male voice called, "Uh, do you want to show us where exactly to put the wood?"

"Be right there," Micah called back, looking to Lexie. "Unless you need me…"

"Does the shower in the guest room work?" she asked.

"It does. None of the plumbing was damaged," he reiterated.

"Then I'd like a shower. So do whatever you need to do—"

"And we'll meet downstairs when you're ready to eat," he concluded.

"Sure," she said unenthusiastically.

Micah bent over to pick up the luggage he'd set on the landing. Seeing that, she added, "You can leave those. I'll take them to the bedroom."

Micah nodded and stepped back, retracing his steps down the stairs.

Once he was gone, Lexie gave in to the urge to bend over and retrieve a framed photograph of her late grandfather from where it had crashed onto the floor.

It was a black-and-white picture of him smiling proudly as he stood beside a new tractor. The glass over the picture was cracked but still held in place by the frame. Lexie hooked the photograph back on the nail it had hung from for decades, making sure it was squarely in place.

Then she picked up the smaller of her bags, tipped the larger onto its wheels and headed for the guest room.

And with as many things as she *could* have been thinking about at that moment, somehow what came to mind suddenly was the image of Micah's bulging biceps.

She shoved the thought away and reminded herself that for the second time in her life, he was to blame for complications and hardships that she would have to deal with.

"I know this is a sore subject. But I'd like to talk about…fifteen years ago…"

Oh, this guy is pushing his luck with me today, Lexie thought.

A shower, a clean pair of yoga pants and a light-weight T-shirt had helped revitalize her somewhat.

While her hair had air-dried—and because her grandmother had told her to—she'd put clean sheets on the guest bed and then unpacked a few things.

When she'd come across her makeup bag, she'd been a little tempted to reapply at least some eye-liner and blush. But she'd resisted the urge. Why should she care what she looked like for *him*? And since she didn't, she'd left her face bare.

She had brushed out her hair, though. And for some reason, her rebellious side hadn't been strong enough to convince her to tie it back. Instead, she'd left it the way it looked best—falling the full six inches below her shoulders into the natural waves that air-drying gave it.

About that time, she'd heard the sounds of the workmen's trucks driving away from the farm, so she'd left the bedroom to come to the kitchen.

Micah had been standing at the unscathed round oak kitchen table unpacking the brown paper sack from the general store.

As he'd set out napkins and plastic forks, he explained that the general store now sold gourmet sandwiches along with their own macaroni and potato salads, and that that was what he'd bought for their dinner.

The sandwiches were grilled ciabatta bread

stacked high with pot roast, bacon, avocado, lettuce, tomato, cheddar and Monterey Jack cheese. Lexie had offered to pay for her share but he refused. She'd thanked him stiltedly and had just taken a bite when Micah had cut right to the chase with his sore-subject intro.

"I don't know what there is to talk about," Lexie responded flatly. "What you did, you did. It can't be undone so what's the point of going over it?"

Their senior year of high school had found them in the same science class. The first week, they'd partnered on a project that had sent them to an abandoned farm to collect vegetation samples.

Caught in a severe hailstorm, they'd had to run for the barn, crawling under a barbed wire fence in their hurry to get there. The loose blouse Lexie had had on had caught on the barbs and gotten ripped into wet shreds.

Micah had been dressed in a jean jacket over one of the many barely appropriate death metal band T-shirts he was known to wear, and since the T-shirt was moderately dry, thanks to the jacket's protection, he'd taken it off and given it to Lexie to change into in the barn's tack room.

The only thing that had transpired during their hour wait for the storm to end was a game to see which of them could throw the most rocks into an old tin can.

Then the rain and hail had stopped and they'd

emerged from the barn—Lexie dressed in Micah's T-shirt, and Micah with his chest exposed under his jean jacket.

At just that moment, one of the school buses had passed by carrying the gymnastics team. Windows had been lowered and heads had popped out to call out lewd questions about what the two of them had been up to.

By the next day, the story of them emerging from the barn had circulated and grown, with everyone believing that a whole lot more had gone on between them than merely waiting out a hailstorm.

And Micah hadn't denied it.

In fact, after a few times of merely smiling when he was asked about it, he'd begun to encourage the rumors, nodding as if to confirm the suspicions that he'd hooked up with Lexie in the barn.

Even if it had been just that, it would have been bad enough.

But gossip about them traveled through town like wildfire and while Jason had believed Lexie when she'd told him nothing happened—despite Micah only replying, *Wouldn't you like to know?* when Jason had confronted him—Lexie's extremely overprotective father had doubted her.

He'd torn her room apart, searched her computer, read her diary. And while he hadn't discovered evidence of more than a friendship with

Micah, he *had* discovered enough to reveal that she and Jason were having sex.

Lexie's father had hit the ceiling. He'd pulled her out of the local school and shipped her off to an all-girls religious academy for the rest of her senior year, putting her under house arrest when she was home on weekends.

"I need to tell you how sorry I am," Micah said.

"Too little, too late."

"I know. And I don't have any excuses—"

"Good, because there aren't any that can make what you did okay. You wrecked my senior year. I got stuck in a *boarding* school during the week, with girls who only saw me as an outsider. I didn't get to go to football games or homecoming or prom or anything else I was looking forward to. I didn't get to graduate with my friends, with the kids I'd been with since kindergarten. And when I was home, I was under constant watch by both my parents. My relationship with my father turned so..." She sighed angrily. "We fought so much. He was so disappointed in me. So..."

Lexie glared at Micah. "You know how he was—he was an altar boy as a kid. He considered being a priest. To him, it was a huge deal that I stay *pure* until marriage. Jason and I were sure we were getting married, so to us it was okay that we didn't wait for a wedding night... And we'd been so careful—my dad would never have known. But when he found out—" Lexie's voice cracked when she thought about her dad, her own regrets resurging that she hadn't maintained her virginity when it had been so important to him "—it changed *everything* between us. And it never went back to how it had been."

She fought tears over what had been so much more of a loss to her than football games or dances, focusing on her anger instead. "Jason and I *eloped* because my dad wouldn't walk me down the aisle of a church!" she shouted at Micah. "He *died* thinking of me as...not what he wanted his daughter to be. And all of it—*all* of it—was because of a misunderstanding that *you* wouldn't deny. That you *encouraged*! And why was that, Micah?" she demanded. "Because it made you feel like a big man? A stud?"

Micah closed his eyes and absorbed her rancor stoically. Then he opened them and shook his head. "There were so many reasons—but not one of them was reason enough to do that to you. To cost you all of that. And it's been the biggest regret of my life. The thing I'm most ashamed of," he admitted so quietly it was barely audible.

Lexie stared at him. His words, the tone of his voice, the expression on his handsome face, the look in his eyes didn't allow her to doubt that he genuinely meant what he said. And she knew that if she were an impartial third party in this moment, her heart would go out to him. That she would think, *How could anyone not forgive someone who's showing so much remorse?*

But she wasn't an impartial third party.

Until he'd done what he'd done, caused what he'd caused, she'd been the apple of her father's eye. A daddy's girl through and through.

Afterward, she couldn't remember her father even looking her *in* the eye again.

And then he and her mother had died in a car accident before their relationship had had a chance to heal, to evolve beyond it. With time, maybe her dad would have come to grips with the idea of her as a grown woman, an adult, a sexual being.

Instead, his life had ended and so had any chance for them to reconcile.

So Lexie wasn't an impartial third party. And the shame that *she'd* felt with her father was something she still carried with her. Something she was convinced she always *would* carry with her.

No matter how deep and sincere his regret, Micah had put into motion things that could never be set right again.

She didn't know what he expected her to say at that moment. It couldn't be that she forgave him, if that was what he was looking for. But she also discovered that she didn't have it in her to say more that might be hurtful, either.

Then, before she could come up with anything,

a crash sounded from upstairs that drew both their attention. They got up from the table and climbed the stairs to investigate.

The picture of her late grandfather and his tractor that she'd rehung had fallen again. Apparently, the frame had been too damaged to maintain its hold. And this time when it had fallen, it had broken completely apart, the slivers of shattered glass resting on top of the photo itself.

And there it was, a fresh reminder of what Micah had most recently wreaked on her life, on her family.

She bent over and lifted the picture, careful not to disturb the broken glass, and realized that this day had gotten the best of her, that there just wasn't any more she could take.

"I'm not really hungry. I think I'll just go to bed."

"Aw, Lexie...please..."

"Good night," she answered unwaveringly before she took the picture and left him standing on the landing.

He was still there when she reached the guest room.

She could feel his eyes on her, but she didn't let that stop her as she went into the room and nudged the door closed behind her.

Things were the way they were.
And nothing could change them.
Or the way she felt about Micah because of it.

Chapter Three

"Hey, Big Ben," Micah said affectionately to his grandfather early Sunday morning.

The Camden family farmhouse—a three-story sky blue structure with an elaborate wraparound porch—was where he'd been staying with his grandfather since he'd left the Marines.

He'd searched inside for his grandfather at first, but with no answer to his calls for the elderly man, he'd gone out the back door. The shed was the likeliest place for Ben Camden to be on the only day of the week that he didn't work. And that was where Micah found him.

"Mornin'," Ben greeted, glancing up from his worktable.

He was six feet tall and, at seventy-nine, had lost a lot of the bulk he'd had in his youth. He was now less muscular and more wiry, and all four of his grandsons were inches taller than him. But they still sometimes used the nickname they'd given him when they were kids, whenever they didn't call him Pops.

"Didn't expect to see you," Ben continued. "Would have waited to have breakfast if I'da known you were comin'. I could still whip you up some eggs, though. How 'bout it?"

"Nah, thanks. I came to ask a favor and then I have to get back—that tree removal service got everything done yesterday but left one hell of a mess on the ground between the two houses. I want to clean that up."

"Get more done with a good breakfast in your belly," his grandfather said, repeating the truism he'd said a million times before. Micah couldn't help but smile at the familiar words that—like his grandfather's other sayings—had formed such an irreplaceable part of his childhood.

Micah had only been three years old, the triplets barely two, when their father was killed and they'd moved with their mother to the farm. Ben had helped to raise his grandsons after that, and he'd actually been a better cook and more of a nurturer than their mother had been—and not just because he was the one who'd prepared most of their family meals. It was no surprise that he still wanted to feed Micah—and his brothers—whenever he had the chance.

And since Micah thought Ben might be missing his company, he decided to take the time to spend with him before getting back.

"Yeah, okay, maybe a couple of eggs," Micah conceded.

"And toast and the sausage I ground and made yesterday—it fried up great for my breakfast. You're gonna love it."

"No doubt," Micah said with a laugh as his grandfather led the way back to the house.

As they worked together to make the breakfast that Ben had decided to share in, he nodded toward the mangled picture frame that Micah had left on the counter when he'd come through looking for Ben. "That the favor?"

"Yeah," Micah confirmed. "Had a picture in it of Morey Parker with a new tractor. The tree crash knocked it off the wall—I saw it when I first went through the house and left it on the floor because it didn't look like it could stand hanging up again. But Lexie must have tried when she got there and last night it fell again and really broke. I was wondering if maybe you could fix it, repaint it? You're good at that stuff."

Ben left the sausages frying and took a closer look at the frame, then returned to the stove. "I think I can do that. Seems like a drop in the bucket of what's goin' on over there, though…"

"Yeah, it is," Micah confirmed. "But I kind of had the feeling it was the straw that broke the camel's back with Lexie last night and…I don't know… I'm hoping it might make a difference somehow…"

"Things not goin' well with her?"

Micah had never confessed his misdeed to his mother or grandfather. It had never come up. Lexie's father's discovery that she and Jason were up to no good had gotten a lot more attention in town, and Micah's part in what led to that discovery had not been widely discussed.

If his mother ever had any inkling, she hadn't said anything. But things with Ben had been different than things between Raina and her sons.

Ben had always been careful not to step on his daughter-in-law's toes, not to contradict her parenting and certainly not to question her authority over her sons.

But in his own way, he had tried to subtly impart lessons without ever overtly reprimanding them. He had given little talks about remembering other people had feelings. About thinking before acting. About making good choices.

He and Micah had never openly discussed what had happened with Lexie. But Micah *had* heard all those kindly-given lectures for the nth time after the incident, so he assumed his grandfather was at least partially aware that he'd played a role in what occurred.

At any rate, he knew that Micah's friendship with Lexie and Jason had ended then. And given that Ben also knew that Micah's forklift delivery had caused the damage to the Parker property now, it made sense that he'd assume there might be some bumps in the road of Lexie's return to Merritt.

"No, things are not going well with her," Micah admitted, seeing no reason to deny it.

"And you're hopin' a fixed picture frame is gonna help," Ben said, his tone making it clear that he thought Micah was barking up the wrong tree.

"Hell, I'm hoping *anything* will help, no matter how small. Plus, Morey was Gertie's husband. I don't want her coming home when she gets well and finding one of his pictures without a frame. And just in case the frame has some meaning... Well, I'm glad you can put it back together."

"I'll get right on it."

"Thanks."

"How's Gertie doin'?" Ben asked as they sat down to eat.

"Okay. Good. I just wish she hadn't gotten hurt at all."

The elderly man nodded his understanding. "Accidents happen, though. This one's not your fault."

Micah laughed slightly. "Maybe it's not my fault but I *am* accountable."

Another sage nod of the head. "Good that you recognize that. I'm proud of you. Of the man you are now."

Micah could acknowledge that only with a brief raise of his chin. The sentimentality embarrassed him. But he still liked hearing it and hoped that it was true.

"I think if you give little Lexie a chance, she'll come around," Ben said then. "Just give it some time."

Micah raised his chin in acknowledgment again, even though he wasn't convinced Ben was right about that.

But somehow his grandfather's words helped.

And he'd needed some help.

Because after last night, he'd been pretty discouraged and worried that maybe there was just no hope of reaching even civil ground with Lexie.

"Oh, you look so much better than you did yesterday!" Lexie exclaimed with relief when she first saw her grandmother on Sunday morning.

Gertrude Parker was dressed in a bright pink sweat suit. Her curly close-cropped, more-salt-than-pepper-colored hair was combed. And she was sitting in a wheelchair, her casted leg braced straight out in front of her.

"I thought you'd still be in bed," Lexie said, wondering if maybe that's where her grandmother *should* be.

"Hate lyin' around in a bed," the elderly woman said with her usual spirit.

Lexie knew better than to argue once Gertie had made up her mind about something, but she did look to Mary to ask, "Is it all right that she's up and dressed?"

"Doctor Joan says whatever she feels like she can do is all right for her to do—as long as she doesn't put any weight on the leg and keeps it elevated."

Glancing back to her grandmother, Lexie said, "How *do* you feel?"

"Good," Gertie answered unequivocally.

It was Mary who went on, "Doctor Joan and her nurse, Louise, were here early, and Louise is going to come every morning to help get Gertie up and dressed. And she's only had half a pain pill."

"Is that enough?"

"It is," Gertie insisted. "They were making me too woozy and the pain isn't that bad to start with." She had been raised by a no-nonsense German father amid four older brothers who had treated her like one of the boys. There was very little about the older woman that succumbed to weakness.

"Doctor Joan said she should judge her pain level and whether or not she needs the pills, and rest if she gets tired," Mary put in. "But Doctor Joan also says that she has forty-year-old patients who aren't doing as well as Gert is."

The color in Gertie's cheeks today helped Lexie actually believe the report of her grandmother doing well. It also helped her to believe that Gertie would be all right.

"I'm so relieved that you're okay," she said, relaxing enough to sit in the rocking chair near her grandmother's wheelchair.

"You look better than you did yesterday, too," Gertie said then.

Lexie laughed. "Did I look bad yesterday?"

"You looked tired and so on edge that I thought you might jump right out of your skin," her grandmother described.

"I *was* tired and on edge. It was a long trip that I started in the middle of the night and I was worried about you."

Gertie waved away her concern. "It'll take more than a broken bone to do me in, honey."

Lexie didn't want to think about anything ever *doing her in*.

"Are you ready for waffles yet, Gert? Maybe Lexie will have them with us…" Mary said then.

"You guys haven't had breakfast yet?" Lexie asked in some surprise. With all they'd accomplished already today, it seemed as if they must have been up for quite a while.

"We had coffee and toast," Mary answered. "Neither of us were up yet when Doctor Joan and Louise rang the doorbell this morning. I made the coffee for us all, Doctor Joan made Gert have a few bites of toast to make sure her stomach would accept food and they didn't leave until a few minutes ago."

"We'd just decided waffles might be a nice Sunday breakfast when you got here," Gertie added. "Will you eat with us?"

As tired as Lexie had been the night before, she'd still had some trouble falling asleep. She'd gone from being overwhelmed and aggravated by Micah and telling him off in her head, to picturing him in her mind and—for no reason she could fathom—recalling how handsome he'd grown up to be. The switch from aggravation to attraction was a phenomenon she'd found disturbing.

When she'd finally fallen asleep, though, she'd slept so soundly that at nine thirty, when she'd woken up, she hadn't even remembered the alarm on her phone sounding or her having turned it off—which she must have done because she was sure she'd set it.

At that point, she'd jumped out of bed, disgusted with herself for not getting to Gertie at the crack of dawn. With no thought other than seeing her grandmother as soon as possible, she'd thrown on the yoga pants and T-shirt she'd worn briefly after her shower the night before, swiped a brush through her hair and refused to add to the delay by applying any makeup.

Then she'd gone downstairs, thrilled to find only a note from Micah, snatched her grandmother's car keys from the hook near the front door and hurried out to the car—all without so much as a drink of water or a bite to eat.

And since she'd also forgone most of her dinner the night before, she was starving.

"Waffles sound great," she said.

"Then waffles it is," Mary responded enthusiastically.

"Can I help?" Lexie offered.

"You just sit and visit with Gertie," her cousin insisted, leaving them alone in the apartment's living room.

Her grandmother reached over the wheelchair's armrest and squeezed Lexie's knee. "I'm so glad you're home. And to stay!" the older woman rejoiced.

"I'm so glad you're glad," Lexie responded.

"But not glad yourself to be back in Merritt?" Gertie asked, obviously trying to interpret Lexie's uncertain tone. "I thought that was what you wanted."

"It was. It is. I *am* glad to be back. I don't ever want to leave again."

"But?" Gertie prompted.

But Lexie was having feelings that confused her.

"It's nothing really. Everything is all just so... not how I thought it would be," she said, trying to sort through her own emotions. "I thought I'd come back to find everything still the way it was—home, you know? I thought it would wrap around me like a big comfy blanket, and I'd be able to take a deep breath for the first time in a long time, and figure out my future. Instead—" she gave a humorless laugh "—I don't know what kind of shape the little house is in or how much work it'll need to get it to where I can live in it—"

"Micah is going to take care of it."

Lexie didn't comment on that. "Plus, this is the first time in my life I've been here without Jason." Lexie struggled for the words to explain what she was having trouble grasping herself. "I hadn't thought about it being weird, but for some reason it is. And on the flip side, there's *so much Micah*..."

"Do you want Jason back?" Gertie asked, probing while still clearly trying to keep her voice neutral.

Lexie answered with another humorless chuckle. "No. It isn't that. It *really* isn't. And this *is* where I want to be, where I've wanted to be for years now. But up until the last few months, whenever I've pictured coming home, I've also pictured coming home with Jason for a future that we could both dig into. Since the divorce, that picture changed and got sort of off-kilter, but I thought once I hit Merritt, I'd regain some balance—"

"Instead, you came home to chaos and commotion and upheaval. And that's the last thing you need right now," her grandmother summed up for her.

"Yeah," Lexie agreed wistfully before switching to a snarl and repeating, *"And there's so much Micah..."*

"But Micah is a good thing because he's going to get us out of the chaos and commotion and upheaval."

That didn't make Lexie laugh—humorlessly or otherwise. Especially after hearing the admiration with which her grandmother kept referring to Micah.

"How much of a mess are we in at the farm?" Gertie asked then.

"There's definitely a mess," Lexie said, hedging. She was unsure to what extent she should burden her ailing grandmother.

"How much?" Gertie demanded.

The older woman had never been a shrinking violet or the kind of person who liked being kept in the dark, so Lexie decided not to spare her. "I've only seen your house—I haven't been in the little house yet, though Micah left a note this morning asking me to meet him at the house later today so he could show me things there. But your house is… Well, I suppose it could have been worse…"

Lexie went on to tell her grandmother about that portion of the damage to the farm.

"The tree is already gone, though," she ended on a more positive note. "There was a crew there yesterday that took care of it."

"That was Micah's doing," Gertie said, again with clear affection for Lexie's former friend. "I heard him making arrangements before I went into surgery."

"It's *all* been Micah's doing," Lexie muttered, unwilling to forget that he bore responsibility for the situation in the first place.

"Don't blame Micah," Gertie said firmly.

"It's his fault."

"It's *not* his fault. This was an accident and he didn't have anything to do with it—"

"It was *his* forklift being delivered."

"But not him unloading it—it was the delivery-man who lost control," Gertie pointed out. "And accidents happen. I knew that old tree was unstable—the trunk was rotted out. I had it looked at in the fall and the tree man said a good wind could blow it over. But I didn't want to be bothered with it right then. I thought it could make it to this summer. I shouldn't have waited. It's as much—or more—my fault for putting off what I should have had done."

Lexie hadn't known that. But still she said, "The tree *didn't* just fall down, though. Micah's wayward forklift *knocked* it down."

"And now poor Micah is wracked with guilt."

Poor Micah...

Lexie couldn't say his name without scorn and her grandmother couldn't seem to say it without fondness. Why was that? she wondered.

"You've always been so easy on him—I never understood that," Lexie admitted.

When Micah had betrayed his friendship with her and Jason, Gertie couldn't have been more sympathetic to Lexie. Gertie had battled with her son over his punishments, fought against him exiling her to boarding school, fought against him ruining her senior year. She'd supported Lexie, championed her. She'd unwaveringly been in Lexie's corner.

But she also hadn't condemned Micah.

She hadn't defended him, she hadn't broached the subject of him with Lexie or advised forgiveness or even compassion, nor had she made any attempts to reconcile their friendship.

But it had seemed as if she felt protective of Micah, too—not just of Lexie.

And when Lexie had said outright that she didn't want her grandmother having anything to do with him, Gertie's response had been, *Oh, honey, I can't do that. But it doesn't mean that what he did was right. It wasn't.*

She *had* made sure to keep Micah far from Lexie. And given that Gertie had been her only advocate, Lexie hadn't been left with much choice but to ignore that Gertie hadn't shunned Micah.

"I never understood why you kept having anything to do with him—from years ago and right up until now," Lexie admitted.

"Well, it just wasn't so cut and dry, honey. He and Jason and Jill had been at the farm with you from when you were little bitty kids. I'd been baking the bunch of you cookies and putting Band-Aids on your boo-boos and helping you with your school projects and listening to your stories and your tall tales and your gripes—you were *all* like my grandkids."

Lexie begrudgingly conceded to that. Gertie *had* always grandmothered the four of them and Jason, Micah and Jill had frequently called her *Gram* the same way Lexie did.

"And if you'll recall," Gertie went on, "when everything happened with you years ago, Micah was a stock boy at the general store. He and I had been working together for months. You know taking a job at the store every now and then was how we got by during lean times, but when I signed up that time, they'd computerized everything and they told me I could only have the job if I could deal with that. Micah was my godsend. He helped me learn their whole system. If not for that, I wouldn't have been able to work there anymore."

"Okay, but then he kept coming around the house, too—the same way he had when he was hanging out with Jason and Jill and me—because you were letting him help you make your beer."

"He was so lost then... He was such a misguided boy..." Gertie said sympathetically. "And I knew why he did what he did to you—"

"Because he was a big jerk!"

"It was a rotten thing to do," Gertie agreed.

"And yet you still seemed to feel *sorry* for him."

"I felt sorrier for you," her grandmother reminded. "But I knew what was going on with him, too. I'd watched it for so long..." Gertie shook her head sadly.

"Watched what? All his competing with Jason?" Lexie asked. "Always trying to one-up him, to get under Jason's skin? Calling us *Mom and Dad* because we were a couple and he thought that was so stupid? I don't know what there was about any of that to feel sorry for."

"He was just so much a bull in a china shop," Gertie said. "But I knew he wasn't a bad boy— even when he caused all hell to break loose for you, it was only another blockhead move he made because he was stumbling around with no idea how to move toward what he really wanted. And he paid for it, too—he lost all his friends in one fell swoop because Jill was on your side of it all and wouldn't have anything to do with him, either. So yes, I did feel sorry for him, too, and yes, I did let him follow me around—and I gave him a job or two when I was making beer because he needed somewhere to go, something to do so he didn't get into more trouble. But he grew up, he went off, he served his country. He became the good man I thought he could be. So even though you might not have liked it then or understood it, I won't apologize for not shutting him out. It didn't make what he did any less wrong. I just thought he needed a little grace from somebody."

"Or maybe—when it comes to him—you were blind then and you're blind now," Lexie said with a sigh.

Gertie merely smiled a knowing smile. "I want you to play nice with him," her grandmother commanded.

"I'm not going to play with him at all."

Lexie didn't know why that had come out sounding salacious. She just hoped her grandmother hadn't noticed.

"I want you to *work* nice with him, then," Gertie amended. "Truth to tell, our insurance coverage on the houses isn't great, honey. I haven't been smart about keeping up on increasing it the way I should have—it's like the tree. I put it off. I know the insurance money won't cover everything. But Micah has promised to bring in help with the reconstruction and to do what he can of the job himself, too, to get it all done with as little burden on me as possible. So for your sake and for mine, you have to be nice. And thankful." Gertie sighed. "And maybe give him just a little benefit of the doubt?" she said hopefully.

"There's no doubt that he did what he did, or that what came out of it, came out of it," Lexie said flatly.

"But so much time has passed… Maybe you could work on letting go? I think it would do you a world of good—carrying a grudge is a heavy load. And especially now, with both of you living here again, and him with his business in the barn, right out our back doors… Maybe it's time to just bury the hatchet? It's important to me. It's two of my own at odds, and I want it to stop. I want things to be *okay*. I'm an old lady and I don't like fighting. I don't want to be in the middle of it anymore."

Lexie *could* understand that point of view.

"I'll try not to be unpleasant," she finally conceded.

"It isn't much but I'll take it!" Gertie said victoriously.

It may have seemed to Gertie like a small concession, but as Mary informed them that the waffles were ready, Lexie could only hope that she could pull it off. After all, she hadn't even been able to make it through dinner with him last night. And she couldn't really say she'd been pleasant at any point since he'd shown up at the airport in Billings yesterday.

Still, for her grandmother's sake, she vowed she would try harder.

And hope that before too long she could regain some distance from Micah Camden.

Lexie stayed at Mary's apartment until after three o'clock when the older women decided they needed naps.

On her way out, Lexie mentioned coming back later but Gertie nixed that idea. She let Lexie know that she didn't expect—or want—Lexie to play nursemaid. Mary and the visiting nurse had that covered. Instead, while she wanted Lexie to visit, she mostly wanted her to focus on dealing with the property damage and getting settled again in Merritt.

Besides, she'd been informed that the ladies' poker group that Gertie and Mary belonged to was bringing dinner over tonight, and if Gertie was up to it, they'd be playing a few hands.

So rather than making plans to return that evening, Lexie had said she'd be back in the morning.

The farmhouse was still empty when she got home. Micah had said in his note that he needed to be at the brewery this afternoon, but that he'd meet her at the big house at five o'clock. He'd warned her not to go to the little house without him because it was more unstable than Gertie's place and needed to be carefully navigated to avoid getting hurt.

Mary and Gertie had insisted on giving her portions of the over-abundance of casseroles they'd already been given by friends and neighbors, so the first thing Lexie did was take the paper bag full of food to unload into the refrigerator.

Then, with some time on her hands—and because it seemed as if she would be in the guest room indefinitely—Lexie went upstairs and unpacked her suitcases.

She finished that at about four o'clock, and decided to use the hour until Micah's return to do what she would have done if she hadn't been in such a rush to get out this morning—she took a long, leisurely shower and shampooed her hair.

When she was finished, she blow-dried her hair using a large round brush that left the long strands smooth and sleek. It was more trouble than she usually went to but she felt an unexplained urge to put more care into her appearance.

Then she went to choose what to wear and found herself wondering if it might be time for her to start wearing her post-divorce clothes.

Over the years, her personal style had continued in the vein of the tomboy-wear of her youth.

Given the bare-bones lifestyle she and Jason had lived, it had just made sense. Everything she'd owned—and there wasn't much of it—had been more practical and functional than fashionable, frilly or fancy. It all had to be easy to pack, easy to wash and dry, and sturdy enough not to need frequent replacement.

The fact that almost every job she'd had over the years had come with a uniform had helped keep her personal things minimalistic.

The post-divorce wardrobe was a different story.

It hadn't been her idea but Lily's—her boss in Alaska who had become a friend. Lily had decreed that while Jason had allotted himself a new life, Lexie should at least have some new clothes that didn't make her look so plain and *married*—something Lily had said with distaste.

Lexie hadn't realized that what she'd been wearing had done that, but on that particular day, when she'd been at a low point, she'd liked the idea of a new look. So she'd thrown caution to the wind with her first credit card as a single person and indulged in a shopping spree. A shopping spree with fun-loving Lily at the helm—Lily who had also given her a place to live when she'd left Jason, and let her stay that first month without contributing any money for rent or utilities since she'd spent all her money on her new look.

The shopping spree had netted Lexie three pairs

of better-fitting jeans, half a dozen new tops, two dresses and date slacks that went with three different date tops—despite her protests against the likelihood of dating anytime soon.

She'd also gone back to Lily's apartment that day with new shoes to replace her sneakers and loafers—some everyday Mary Janes, some ballet-style shoes, one pair of low heels and one pair of high.

She'd been the most uncomfortable buying the new underwear her friend had insisted on. But Lily had been even more adamant about the undies than anything. Nothing, she'd said, made a new woman more than new underwear. And so Lexie had ended up with a collection of less sensible and much lacier bras and panties.

The shopping had taken place months ago and Lexie had yet to wear any of it. Her waitress job had required a uniform supplied by the hotel restaurant that Lily managed, and on her off-hours Lexie had never felt like doing more than pulling on some sweats and hibernating until it was time for work again. And she certainly hadn't dated anyone.

But now?

Now she was in Merritt for her fresh start and the thought of those new clothes suddenly held some appeal.

As she opened her underwear drawer and looked

down at the old items on one side and the new on the other, the nearly-granny panties seemed like things only Gertie should wear. So she opted for a pair of bikini briefs.

And instead of choosing one of the old semi-sports bras she'd worn since college, she grabbed the much more feminine bra that Lily had talked her into because she'd said it didn't flatten her out so much.

She realized when she put on the underwear that it really did make her feel like a new woman, and that gave her a burst of confidence when she moved on to the closet.

It was the new things she was drawn to there, too, she discovered, telling herself that if the new underwear gave her a touch more self-assurance, why not let the new outerwear work toward that, too? Then maybe she wouldn't feel such dread over seeing Micah again. As far as she was concerned, she was facing a foe when she faced him, and it was always good to have any advantage in that situation.

So on went a pair of the new tightly fitted jeans.

With those in place, she turned her back to the full-length mirror on the inside of the closet door and craned around to look at the rear view.

Lily had said the better cut of jeans made her butt look great. Lexie had taken her word for it but now that she took her own assessment, she decided there *was* an improvement.

Next came a plain white tank top underneath a pale pink T-shirt with a wide square neckline. The double layer was a trend she'd always avoided, but now that she saw the effect, she liked it.

The fact that the T-shirts were tighter than she usually wore would take getting used to, but for some reason that snugger fit made her pull her shoulders back and let her new bra do its bit of added accentuation.

And sure enough, she felt a little surge of re-newed confidence shoot through her.

"Okay…" she said to her reflection by way of approval.

Then she returned to the bathroom where she'd put her makeup in the medicine cabinet.

During one of her many at-home nights after her split from Jason, Lily had also suggested a tu-torial on *not-married* makeup.

She'd been disinclined to do all Lily did—which required a full half hour of application. But after the tutorial, she had begun a routine of applying a tinted moisturizer to even out her skin tone, a powder blush, a darker eyeliner and mascara. So that was what she used now.

When she finished with that, she ran a brush through her hair one last time, returned to the closet to slip her feet into a pair of ballet shoes and allowed one more look at herself in the full-length mirror to take in the whole picture.

It *was* an improvement but mostly, she told herself, it meant she didn't look tired or stressed out.

And that made the new clothes and attention to makeup the right choices, she concluded. Tired and stressed out were not the impressions she wanted to give to anyone. Rested, healthy, strong, in control and ready, willing and able to take on the next chapter of her life—that was what she wanted anyone looking at her to think.

And if Micah was among those anyones?

She hadn't liked the way she'd ended the previous evening with him.

She'd come across as frazzled. Overwrought. Maybe even fragile. Fleeing from him.

And apparently looking tired on top of it.

That put her at a disadvantage.

If she had to again be face-to-face with him, then she at least wanted to look her best. She wanted to look as if she'd risen above all the blows in her life—the one he'd dealt and the ones Jason had. As if she was moving on. From them and from their actions. And even if Jason wasn't there to see the evidence of that, Micah was.

So go ahead and take a good look, she said silently. *You both may have knocked me down, but I'm getting back up!*

* * *

Micah still wasn't there when Lexie went downstairs even though it was past five o'clock.

She made her way through the smashed-up kitchen, glancing into the sunroom to the right—the room Micah had said he'd be living out of.

Sure enough, the foldout couch was made up with sheets, blanket and pillows, all in military precision neatness.

"Are you here?" she called out, just in case he was somewhere out of sight.

There was no answer and curiosity pushed her close enough to see more of the space.

There was a duffel bag peeking from behind a chair, but it was so meticulously placed there that it was barely visible. Other than that and the sheets on the bed, there were no signs that anyone was living here. It was as orderly as her grandmother kept it.

"So you're better at housekeeping than your old friend, my ex," she muttered as she retraced her steps to go to the kitchen sink and the window above it.

The barn was about a hundred feet from the rear of the house—easily visible from either Gertie's place or the kitchen of the little house.

The big barn doors were open wide and standing just inside of them was Micah and another man. Micah was facing out, as if he was about to make his exit, the other man was in profile and holding a clipboard he was referring to as he talked.

"Okay, it's almost five thirty..." Lexie said. "Will you live up to what Gram thinks of you or will you prove me right? Because I think you'll put yourself and your own interests before ours—like always..."

There was no possibility that he could have heard her utterance, but as if he had, he shot a glance at the big house.

So you know this is where you're supposed to be...

But then he continued talking to the other man.

And she continued watching him.

She wondered if he'd been clean-shaven earlier and his beard had grown back through the day, or if the scruff that shadowed that angular face was a holdover from the day before.

Either way, she wished he were clean-shaven.

If he were, maybe he would look more like he had when they were kids. When she'd recognized that he was boyishly cute but it hadn't done anything for her.

Not that the way he looked now did anything for her. Or to her.

She just kept *noticing* how hot he was now, and she didn't want to. His rugged masculinity almost made him seem like a different person and she didn't want to think of him as a different person. He was who he was and she didn't want any awareness of that fact to fade.

Micah had on what appeared to be military issue cargo pants and a gray hoodie emblazoned with United States Marines and the Marine insignia.

The hoodie didn't fit as tightly as the T-shirt he'd had on the previous day, and while Lexie didn't want to acknowledge it, she still had the image of that T-shirt's knit stretched tight across impressively well-developed pectorals, hugging a narrow waist and a perfectly flat stomach. The T-shirt had also better framed the equally well-developed neck that Lexie didn't recall him having when they'd known each other before. Plus, there was the T-shirt's short sleeves that had been stretched taut around massively muscled biceps.

Not that she *preferred* one view over the other, she told herself, but she did find herself mentally picturing what was under that sweatshirt.

And wondering if, once he was inside, he might take it off.

If he actually did leave the brewery...

"He's not going to come," she said with some derision to remind herself to keep her focus.

Micah did take a step more out the door but just then a third man rushed up to him to hand Micah a small vial that Micah drank out of.

Whatever he'd tasted made him recoil and shake his head as he handed the vial back to the third man.

He again glanced toward the house but he still stayed where he was as he spoke with the third man.

"You're gonna go back in there and leave me hanging," Lexie said. "Better listen to me, Gram, because when it comes to him you're—"

Not wrong?

Because just then Micah held up both hands to cut off the other men. From what Lexie could tell, Micah seemed to give them instructions—but then he left them behind to head for the house.

"Okay, maybe this time he's doing what he said he would. But just wait…" she muttered, convinced that like her ex-husband, like the Micah of old, ultimately his own interests would win out.

"I'm sorry I'm late," he said as he came in the back door. "Something went wrong with the flavoring of one of my tester batches of beer. We've been trying to figure out why but it'll wait. My hands are sticky. Let me wash up and we can get going."

So he'd left a problem in order to keep his word to her?

He really must be running on high-octane guilt, Lexie thought, certain this was a fluke.

She didn't say anything. She just moved to the side of the sink to free the way for him.

He pushed the sweatshirt's sleeves up, revealing massive wrists and forearms. Then he turned on the water and lathered hands that she didn't remember being so big, either. Big, strong, capable-looking hands that, for some reason, she couldn't stop looking at.

What could possibly be sexy about hands or washing them? she asked herself.

And yet it somehow struck her that way.

"How's Gertie today?" he asked as he rinsed the lather and took a sheet of paper towel to dry off.

Lexie forcibly snapped herself out of her reverie. "Gram is good—she said you called this morning to check on her so you should know that."

"Yeah, but she'll always say that. You have to have eyes on her to know for sure."

That was true. "She's well enough to try to play a little poker with the ladies tonight."

That made him smile and Lexie realized it was the first time she'd seen him do that since the old days.

His smile was still a little lopsided—the left corner of his mouth quirked up just a fraction higher than the right. It had always made his smile seem cocky but now that seemed sexy, too, and she wondered what was wrong with her to keep thinking of him that way.

"Ah, Gertie," he breathed with a small laugh. "She's one of kind."

There was no disputing that, either.

Finished with the paper towel, he tossed it in the trash. "So what do you say? Are you ready to see the little house?"

"Sure," she answered.

"I have to warn you, there's more damage there than here. And I spent what time I could yesterday cleaning up this house because I knew you and I would be using it. The little house hasn't been touched—except for the tarps I put up to keep out the elements. What I'm saying is that it might be harder on you to see—especially since you lived there with your folks. So brace yourself."

"I'm sure I'll be fine," she said, dismissing his concern.

In her mind, she could see her grandmother shaking a disapproving head at her for her curt tone, reminding her that she'd promised not to be unpleasant.

Mixed with that was her conscience reminding her that Micah's own attitude, even in the face of her snottiness, held no hostility or even impatience. Not even now, when he could easily have been out of sorts over abandoning a business problem to deal with her.

She wasn't forgiving him, but at this point, keeping up a bad attitude was beginning to seem petty. So not only to keep her promise to her grandmother but also for her own sake, Lexie took a deep breath and swore to do better.

"Shall we go?" Micah asked.

"Sure," she repeated, this time without the snark.

They went out the front door of the big house, crossed the yard and entered the front door of the little house.

Micah was right about there being more damage—so much more than Lexie had expected, despite his warning.

Almost half of the house where she'd grown up was rubble.

The floorplan of the little house was similar to Gertie's but in reverse. So, like the big house, the tree had taken out the side wall of the kitchen downstairs and the master bedroom upstairs, only it had destroyed more of both.

In the kitchen, no cupboards or appliances had survived, and neither had the kitchen table around which Lexie had had so many meals with her parents. The antique cupboard her mother had loved was just kindling. The kitchen sink had been ripped away, the pipes to it left poking out of the wall.

Micah explained that the plumbing exposure and the dangling electrical wires from the destroyed light fixture had caused the building inspector to order the water and power shut off.

There were also holes in the kitchen floor. A missed step could drop her into the root cellar.

Getting upstairs was more treacherous, too, because some of the stairs had been broken. Once they got to the second level, Lexie found that nearly the entire master bedroom and bath were gone, and that the bed and dressers her parents had used were demolished.

"The good news is that you'll get a remodel and an update," Micah said after the tour as they returned to Gertie's house.

It was on the tip of her tongue to lash out at him, to say that what had comforted her through her divorce was the thought of coming home to what was familiar, what was comfortable. She didn't want new and updated—she wanted her home back.

But she put conscious effort into *not* saying that, told herself firmly that moving forward was better than crying over spilt milk and replied, "Gram said something about you getting people to help do the work…"

"I belong to a Vets Helping Vets group in Billings. It's nothing formal, just some guys like me who got out in one piece. We do what we can for each other and for older or injured vets who might need a hand here and there."

That sounded commendable. In an attempt to be less caustic, she said, "That's really nice."

He didn't acknowledge the praise. He just went

on, "A lot of the guys in the group work construction, so I put out the word. I've already had a few callbacks—they're getting a crew together. Plus, there are a couple of guys who'll come on their own and do what they can in their off-hours. The biggest problem is time. They all have jobs and lives, so it won't be a matter of starting things here and working until they're done. It'll be a couple days work, then they'll be gone, then a couple more days work—"

"That could take forever," Lexie said, alarmed by the thought, the edge back in her tone.

"It won't be quick," Micah confirmed, still calm, not reacting to her cutting tenor. "Construction is a pain and I'm not going to lie to you—it'll be dragged out some. But I'll do everything I can to make it as easy as possible on you—and on Gertie when we can get her back here. And it'll be worth it in the end. The labor will all be free, we'll have a good-sized crew sometimes that'll make a big dent when they *are* here. Anybody who has a day they can spare even without the rest of the guys will come, and I'll do what I can... We'll get it all done," he assured her.

Lexie just sighed in frustration. She genuinely wanted to be wrong about him when it came to this, because she and her grandmother had no recourse but to count on him and his Vets Helping Vets. But it was clearly not going to be a picnic.

But because she thought she should give him a little credit for tearing himself away from his business to give her the tour, she said, "People have been bringing food to Mary and Gertie—more than they can fit in the fridge or freezer—so they sent a bunch of it home with me. If you want to fix something to eat and get back to work—"

They'd reached the front door of the big house by then and he held it open for her. "Why don't we both eat and then I'll go back?"

That shouldn't have been the answer she wanted to hear, and yet somehow it was.

Maybe she just hadn't been looking forward to eating alone...

"Okay," she agreed, having no clue why she was so all over the place when it came to him.

They decided to microwave bowls of shepherd's pie for dinner. As they sat together at the kitchen table for the second evening in a row, Micah said, "So the grand plan was for you and Jason to go to college to get teaching degrees. Then you were going to take a year to travel, come back here, settle down and teach. You figured you could save up during the school year and travel every summer during you time off," he said, surprising her with his clear memory of what she and Jason had talked about when they'd all been friends.

"Best laid plans..." she said under her breath.

"I heard through the grapevine—well, from my

brothers—that Jason got antsy and quit college during the first semester, and that after your folks were killed in that accident, you put off your second year. That surprised me."

"I was so scattered, so sad, I couldn't concentrate on school. And I just… I wanted to get away from it all. Escape. It was Jason's idea that I drop out, too, that we take off, and all of a sudden being practical appealed to me less than…just escaping…" she explained.

"Did you go to Europe the way you'd planned?"

"We did. Backpacking, camping or staying in hostels. We didn't have enough money saved to travel straight through, so instead we'd get whatever jobs we could, save and then move on to the next place when money allowed." She paused, then said, "But Gram must have told you—"

He cut her off with a shake of his head. "I've kept up with Gertie, she's kept up with me—we've talked beer until we're both blue in the face over the years—but we haven't talked about you. That's sort of been an off-limits subject since days of old. So I honestly don't know what you've been up to."

Lexie wondered if that was the truth, but ultimately decided to accept it. Gertie hadn't spoken one word to her about Micah, so it didn't seem far-fetched that her grandmother hadn't kept him informed about her, either.

"Okay," she allowed.

"Did you spend more than one year in Europe?"

"Thirteen months."

"And then? Did you get back to college and get your teaching degrees?"

"Oh, no. Neither of us had any more to do with college. There's no teaching degree for me to fall back on," she said with regret.

"Did you get into some other career?"

"Career?" she said with a disheartened laugh. "No. I've done a million different things, but nothing that felt like it was part of an actual career path."

"So how did it happen that you didn't follow the plan?" he asked.

"The *plan*..." Lexie said. "To get married but delay taking on responsibility... Jason said we'd spent our whole life here and would end up here, but we should take just a little break in between to see what else was out there. And I thought that sounded like fun. An adventure."

"Was it?"

"At first. For a while. The trouble was, once we were *out there*, Jason never reached a point where he wanted to come back and take on the responsibilities we'd postponed—a regular job that he couldn't quit on a whim, a mortgage that he claimed would mean something *owned us*... He just never got to where he wanted to settle down. So instead of traveling for a year, then coming home, it's been all about moving around, finding whatever jobs we could get, staying a while, then moving on and doing it all over again."

Micah didn't comment on that. "What all have you done for work?" he asked before he took a bite of the meat-and-vegetable-laden casserole.

"I've been a nanny. I've worked in day care. I've worked in nursing homes. I've waited tables. I've worked in restaurant kitchens and bakeries. I've cleaned hotel rooms and worked the front desk. I've worked retail and sold everything from surfboards to eyeglasses. I've checked out groceries and worked in factories. I've cleaned stadium seats... Just to name a few..."

"That's more than a few," Micah marveled.

"And now I don't know what I'm going to do," Lexie admitted.

She felt as if she'd revealed more than she'd intended. Then he said, "And even though that's how it's been for years—going someplace and just finding a job when you got there—it's bothering you that that's how it is coming home."

It wasn't a question. He was definitely seeing more than she wanted him to.

She took a bite of shepherd's pie to stall.

"You could go back to college now, get your teaching degree," he suggested.

"I thought about that but I've kind of come to

a point where I want to be in a position to start thinking about having kids of my own, not putting that off to teach other people's kids."

And why had she confessed *that* to him?

"I can understand that. That's part of why I left the Marines—to get started on the future I saw for myself. I put it off long enough to serve, but now I want to get to it."

"The brewery," she guessed.

"The brewery. And coming back here to live so I could start a family one day."

"You?" she said with a real laugh. "Mr. Too-Cool? You never wanted a steady girlfriend. You always gave Jason and me a hard time about being stuck with each other forever. You told us we should be playing the field. Now *you* want a *family?*"

He didn't seem willing to look her in the eye. "I was a kid," he protested. Then he did raise his striking blue eyes to hers to say, "Besides, *that's* more normal than sticking for life to the person you started dating when you were thirteen. *Now* I'm the right age to start thinking about finding a partner for life."

And now they were talking the way they had when they'd been friends—teasing, goading, debating, not walking on eggshells...

"Okay, yes, marrying my middle school boyfriend didn't go well—I can't argue with that," she conceded.

"I'm just saying that I can see why you don't want to go to college now," he backtracked. "So what *are* you thinking about doing?"

"I don't have the slightest idea," she said with a sigh. "But I'd like it not to be just answering an ad or a help-wanted sign in a window."

"So you have to figure out what you *want* to do."

She took a deep breath and breathed it out hard. "Yeah," she said without enthusiasm.

His smile then was compassionate but also tinged with devilishness as he quoted something she'd said frequently in the past, "Make a list."

"Of what I want to be when I grow up?" she said facetiously.

"How about of all the jobs you've had, which ones you liked the most, which you liked the least and what you might want to turn into a *career*."

That sounded so much like something she would have said to him years ago that it made her laugh again.

"Simple as that?" she said.

"Hey, it's a place to start," he countered as he finished his meal.

That was another thing she'd said to him in the past when giving similar advice.

"I'll spend tonight looking for paper and a pencil while you go to work," she said glibly, thinking it was time to let him get to that. Especially when she realized, somewhat guiltily, that she was actually beginning to enjoy talking to him.

"Over there—I saw paper and pencils when I put that drawer back yesterday," he responded as he stood to put his dishes in the dishwasher, obviously accepting her dismissal.

But he turned to her again when he'd finished with his dishes and said, "Do you need anything else?"

She shook her head. "Go!"

"I'm just out in the barn. Holler if you need anything."

"I won't need anything," she promised.

He nodded and exited without another word, leaving her to her own devices.

Lexie remained at the kitchen table, digesting the fact that she felt a little sorry to see him go, that for a few minutes it had actually felt good to talk to him the way they had when they were kids.

And more than that, she was actually considering following his advice about making a list.

She got up, went to the drawer he'd indicated and took out paper and a pencil.

But not without first glancing through the window over the sink to make sure he really was on his way to the barn so he wouldn't be able to see that she was taking his suggestion.

And in the process—before she reminded herself to look away—she got a gander of a backside that was almost as good as the front.

Chapter Four

Lexie was at Mary's apartment early enough on Monday morning to sit in on Gertie's visit with the local doctor.

To Lexie's relief, Doctor Joan was so pleased with how the older woman was fairing that she decided she could hand over daily visits to her nurse, Louise, and only do her own house calls once a week.

After the visit, Mary left to run errands and Lexie stayed with her grandmother until noon when Lexie had a lunch date scheduled with Jill Gunner—now Jill Harris—the fourth member of the friend foursome of Lexie's youth.

Lexie and Jill had always been best girlfriends and that had continued even after Lexie and Jason left Merritt. They'd kept in close contact by phone, emails and texts, and whenever Jill had been able to afford a trip, she'd either gone to stay with Lexie and Jason or met Lexie somewhere in the middle.

Jill had even planned her wedding at the hotel in Hawaii where Lexie and Jason were working at the time so they could help with all the arrangements and Lexie could be Jill's matron of honor.

But since then, they had only seen each other twice in person because in those seven years Jill had had four babies—two boys and two girls.

"I can't believe you're *finally* home—and home to *stay*," Jill said as they sat at the table in Jill's quaint country kitchen.

Jill's oldest son was in half-day kindergarten so had arrived home about the time Lexie got there. She'd helped Jill feed all four siblings lunch, then the kids had gone down for naps—though the kindergartner had insisted to Lexie that he didn't sleep, he only *rested.*

With the children tucked away, Jill had brought out tarragon chicken salad sandwiches for their lunch and settled in to chat. They covered Gertie's condition, Jill's life with her firefighter husband, Anthony, the latest on the kids and Jill's parents. Now, Jill was marveling for the third time on Lexie moving back to Merritt.

"That was waaay too long of a year," Jill added facetiously, referring to the fact that when Lexie and Jason left Merritt it was for what was meant to be a single gap year.

"Waaay too long," Lexie agreed.

"How're you doing with the divorce and everything?"

"Okay," Lexie answered, sharing with her friend much of what she'd told her grandmother about how odd it felt being back without Jason.

"It's all just kind of surreal... I thought we were a great love story. True soul mates..." she said sadly. "But somewhere along the way that changed. Well, actually I guess Jason changed. And I didn't. I don't know, maybe that was bad?"

"That you're stable and loyal? That after not putting down roots all this time, you came back to wanting stability in your life? Stability that Jason pretty obviously doesn't want? I don't think you're in the wrong here—but he really, really was."

Jill refilled their iced teas and took out a plate of cookies for their dessert. "But you didn't get to come home to much stability," she added. "How does your house look?"

Lexie filled her in on that subject, too. "Gram is convinced that *Micah* is going to fix everything," she said, once again unable to say his name without a sarcastic tone. "And all I can do is hope she's right."

"So now you and Micah are living together," her friend said.

"I wouldn't put it that way. We're under the same roof, but it's a big house and we stay out of each other's way."

"You know what I keep wondering?" Jill said mischievously.

"What?"

"If you had to marry one of them, do you ever think you would have been better off marrying Micah?"

"I think it would have been better if I hadn't gotten married a week after high school graduation at all. Plus, I should have stayed in college. Jason and I probably would have broken up like you and *your* high school sweetheart did, and then maybe I could have met and married somebody altogether new—like you did with Anthony."

"I can't argue with that," Jill said. "But if you *had* to marry one of our boys—"

Lexie laughed at the term they'd started using for Jason and Micah when they were small children.

"—would you have been better off with Micah?"

"I can't imagine how," Lexie concluded.

"He was the nicer of the two before he started being so determined to get what he wanted at any cost—so dog-eat-dog. Remember when he jumped over the church pew to walk with you behind your grandfather's casket? That was so sweet."

Her grandfather had died when they were in fourth grade. After the church service, her parents had walked on either side of Gertie to follow the coffin to the gravesite behind the church. Lexie had been left to walk alone behind them until Micah had forced his way to her side, where he'd stayed like a stoic little soldier through the burial. It had helped her more than any fourth grader could express.

Recalling that did touch a soft spot in Lexie. "Remember him looking all grown up in that suit and tie? We didn't even know he owned nice clothes," Lexie added in pure flashback to a time when she'd had only positive feelings for Micah.

"And remember how it was Micah and you who carried my books when I was on crutches with a broken foot in eighth grade?" Jill said. "You got mad at Jason for not helping out, and all he said was that he had his own books to carry."

Lexie nodded. There was no refuting the truth.

"I always liked talking to Micah better than Jason, too," Jill added. "He was by far the better listener."

Also true. And an experience that Lexie had revisited with Micah the evening before. Even though she didn't want to put any stock in it.

"And whenever you came to him with a problem, he'd always try to see if there was something he could do to help—I remember Jason saying more than once, *What do you expect me to do about it?*"

Lexie's laugh this time was wry. "Oh, yeah… When we first became a couple, he didn't say that kind of thing to me. But after we were married? That was like his mantra if I complained about anything. But don't forget that the one time I really needed Micah's help—to squash that rumor about the two of us in the barn—he just did more damage instead."

"Yeah, like I said, by that point, when he wanted something, look out! On the other hand, that's also what made him the star of the football team, the baseball team and the basketball team," Jill went on. "It was also Micah who always helped old Miss Jackson or mean Mr. Waters carry their groceries home from the store. Jason refused to do it because they were both so crotchety they never said thank-you, but that didn't stop Micah."

"It was why the manager eventually offered him a job—he said if Micah could put up with those two, he wanted him on the payroll." Still veering away from the positive column, though, Lexie added, "Maybe that was why he helped them. Maybe he figured there would ultimately be something in it for him."

"I don't think so. He never said that. And you

know he wasn't shy about bragging when he won something he'd set his sights on." Jill paused for a sip of tea. "But now it seems like he may have gone back to the way he was before he got so intense."

"I don't know about that," Lexie contended. "If I were you, I wouldn't risk running into a barn alone with him. It might cost you your marriage."

"No, seriously," Jill persisted. "It seems like he's turned into a pretty decent human being."

"Oh, no, not you!" Lexie exclaimed. "Gertie is definitely in the Micah Camden Fan Club, but I didn't think you would be, too."

"I wouldn't say that I'm a *fan*. Because of what he caused with the barn thing, you and I didn't get to have the senior year we'd planned. And my parents got worried about what I might be doing, so all of a sudden my curfew was *ten o'clock*! Not to mention that when Mark and I started dating, we were *never* allowed to be alone. You know I was as mad at Micah as you were. Well, almost."

Jill *had* completely cut him out, Lexie recalled.

Jill added, "And even before he pulled the barn stunt with you, Micah had gotten kind of full of himself. I haven't forgotten that."

"We tolerated it because we'd all been friends for so long," Lexie contributed.

"Until the barn thing. After that, I just wrote him off. When he left Merritt, I thought *good riddance*." Jill's tone went from heated to more quizzical. "But the thing is, he didn't come back as the same guy he was when he left. Now he's more like he was when we were kids. Now you just aren't going to find anyone who will say they're sorry he's around."

"Sure you will—me."

Jill laughed. "I know. But with everybody else? Not only did he come home a hero for serving his country but he's kind of become one around here, too. He actually saved the Mullen twins when they set fire to the basement playing with matches. Sara Mullen was out in the barn and he was just driving in from town and saw the smoke. He made her stay outside, ran in himself and got the kids out. Then he turned the hose on to keep the fire from spreading before the fire department could get there. He was so impressive that Anthony and the guys tried to recruit him. When they couldn't, they talked him into becoming a volunteer firefighter."

"So he did a good deed. But that doesn't mean he still wouldn't stab somebody in the back to get what he wanted," Lexie insisted.

"He just doesn't give that impression anymore, though. He's been right there with Anthony and the rest of the guys helping out with the hail damage that hit some people hard—even when it cost him time away from his brewery. I can't tell you how many things he's pitched in for when there's been a need—even at his own expense. And he's just..." Jill shrugged again. "I kept my distance when he first got back, but it's a small town and with both of us living here—"

"And with your husband and the whole fire department also apparently belonging to his fan club," Lexie put in.

"He and Anthony have definitely become friends," Jill admitted. "But anyway, I've had to sort of re-assess him. And the truth is, he's more like the boy in the suit at your grandfather's funeral than the barn guy. He's... I don't know... It's like he doesn't have anything to prove anymore. He definitely isn't full of himself like he was in high school. And I haven't seen any signs that he's only out for himself."

"Maybe there just hasn't been anything he wants badly enough to bring that side out in him yet," Lexie suggested.

"Oh, he wants that brewery to succeed," Jill said. "It's his baby and everybody knows it."

"Then that doesn't bode well for getting our houses fixed..."

"What have you seen from him so far? Would you say he's the same or different?" Jill asked.

Lexie thought about the evening before, about him leaving behind a problem at his brewery in order to keep his word to her. About him keeping her company through dinner before going back.

"Maybe he's just better at hiding things," she

said, unwilling to let down her guard any more than she already had.

"But I heard that he's been busting his butt taking care of everything over at your place since the tree…"

Lexie wanted to point out yet again that Micah was responsible for the damage—but she was tired of trying to argue that. Instead, all she said was, "But is he going to see it through to the end? Because there's a ton of work that needs to be done, and he said himself that it'll take a lot of time. That will mean a lot of time away from his own interests. Do you really think that when push comes to shove, he'll keep it up? Or do you think he'll prioritize his own stuff and leave us hanging?"

Jill shrugged, clearly not confident enough in Micah to be certain. "Maybe it's the optimist in me, but for your sake and Gertie's sake—and for his, too—I'm going to hope he really is the kind of man who won't let you down."

"I guess we'll see," Lexie said.

Something about that made Jill laugh a little wickedly. "And oh, boy, what there *is* to see now! Can you believe how that wiry kid we used to hang out with has buffed up? I mean, he always had a great face and those eyes…what I would have given to have eyes like those myself!" Jill rolled hers rapturously. "But there wasn't much muscle to him. But now… Whew, he's something to look at!"

Lexie laughed. And felt incredibly relieved. Every time her gaze got stuck on some spectacularly handsome detail of Micah, every time she discovered herself ogling him and appreciating the sight so much more than she wanted to, she'd start to worry that she might be developing some kind of involuntary attraction to him.

But hearing that her friend—who was devoted to her husband and who had only ever seen Micah as a brother—was aware of some of the same things?

That meant that anyone with eyes grasped that he'd become a fine-looking specimen of man. It wasn't only her. And it wasn't anything she had to be concerned about.

"Yeah, how unfair is it that he got better-looking with age? Drop-dead gorgeous—if we're being completely honest," she agreed with her friend.

"So you *have* noticed."

"I'd have to be blind not to," Lexie said matter-of-factly.

"Then it's probably a good thing you *aren't* a fan. Otherwise, with the two of you living in the same house, it might be asking for trouble."

"No chance of that," Lexie swore.

But considering the fact that she wasn't dreading the thought of going home to him? That she might even be looking forward to it a little?

Unfortunately, there was nothing in what Jill had said that could ease her mind about that...

* * *

"For dinner, I'm grilling bratwurst—my grand-father made it with my oat stout," Micah announced to Lexie when she arrived home a little after six o'clock.

He must have just showered because the clean scent of soap came with him and his hair was damp.

Altogether—smell plus the sight of him in jeans and a chest-hugging T-shirt—for a split second, it stopped her in her tracks as a purely primitive appreciation of him went to her head.

Or maybe she was just hungry since lunch had been hours ago.

She hung on to that thought because it made her feel better about her own reaction.

She'd stayed at Jill's long enough to say hello when Anthony got home from work, but she'd declined the invitation to spend the evening with them, telling herself that it was because she didn't want to intrude on their family time, and not because of Micah.

Standing there in her grandmother's kitchen with him, it did strike her that they seemed to have already fallen into a dinner routine. One that she should nip in the bud.

But then what? Start a new routine of trying to avoid him at mealtimes? Eat in her room so they didn't meet up in the kitchen?

That would only make this situation more awkward. The situation she'd promised her grandmother that she would attempt to make better, not worse.

She assured herself that it was not that she *wanted* to have dinner with him—she just wanted to live up to her promise to Gertie. That was the only reason she said, "Okay—I like bratwurst. But can I shower first? I'm coated in baby spit up and strained peas and melted Popsicle and some kind of fruit-in-a-pouch stuff. The mix of smells is kind of sickening. Plus, I think there's some finger paint in my hair."

He grinned.

And that just made it worse, because that grin was so disarming and lit up those damnable blue eyes of his.

"Jill's kids?" he guessed. When their paths had crossed earlier that day, Lexie had told him that she was seeing Gertie in the morning and their old friend in the afternoon.

"Four is a lot of them," she said in answer.

"Go ahead and shower. I'll get the coals nice and hot and won't put the brats on until you come down—so no hurry."

She took her time in the shower, relieved to note that Micah had left her plenty of hot water. Choosing what to wear afterward, she refused to let herself put too much effort into her clothes.

She bypassed the post-divorce things and put

on clean black yoga pants with a T-shirt. Admittedly, she'd only ever worn the T-shirt for casual-dressy occasions when she'd been married—it was a white knit crewneck with a crocheted inset across the top that raised it a notch above an everyday tee. But still, it was from the married side of the closet so she figured that gave it reduced status.

She also reapplied her makeup, reasoning again that that was merely for her own confidence.

As for her hair, she simply brushed it and left it down.

Micah was outside at the grill when she returned to the kitchen, his face still shadowed with stubble that was no thicker than it had been that morning, making her think he trimmed the stubble to keep it just the length he wanted it.

When he spotted her, he took a plate of raw bratwurst from the picnic table and put them on the grill.

While she was upstairs he'd also set the picnic table with plates, silverware and napkins, hot dog buns and spicy mustard for the brats, plus potato chips, dill pickle slices, cheese and crackers, and green olives to round out the meal.

"It's so nice today I thought we could eat outside," he told her as she went into the yard.

When the sunroom had been the patio, there had been nothing but topsoil from there to the barn. After enclosing the patio to make it the sunroom,

Gertie had laid a walkway of flagstones to the barn and planted a small patch of lawn. That was where the picnic table, bench seats and the barbecue grill were.

On the other side of the walkway, she'd installed a firepit with a small semi-circular wicker outdoor sofa that curved halfway around it.

That setup was more intimate than the picnic table so Lexie was happy to avoid it.

She offered to get drinks, and a moment later she retraced her steps into the tarped kitchen, filled two glasses with water and ice, and went out again.

"How's Gertie today?" Micah asked then.

Lexie gave him the update.

"And Jill?" he inquired afterward.

"She's good. And she's a *mom*…" Lexie mused, noting the thing she'd been marveling at all afternoon and the whole way home. "It seems so strange… Are we really old enough to have kids? And *four* of them?"

She had no idea why that made him frown for a minute before he said with some solemnity, "We're definitely old enough."

There seemed to be some underlying darkness about that subject for him, but Lexie decided to skirt around what was none of her business. "Well, anyway, she's taken to parenthood like a duck to water, and her kids are cute and funny, and I've liked Anthony since the first time I met him, so altogether I'd say they're a perfect little family."

"I don't think four kids counts as a *little* family, but perfect? Yeah, it seems that way to me, too," Micah agreed. "Good for them."

"I hope it always is," Lexie said quietly, hearing the solemnity in her own voice. The topic touched a divorce nerve with her.

Micah let the subject drop. Instead, they both breathed in some of the aromas of the cooking bratwurst. They agreed that the smell alone was great.

Then Lexie said, "I didn't know your grandfather made sausage. Does he grind his own meats and everything?"

"Oh, yeah. It's become a hobby for him. He makes all kinds but this is his first experiment adding my beer."

"How does he add beer to it? Does he inject it after it's in the casing? Or mix it with the spices? Or—"

"He won't tell me. He says he's keeping it a secret and hinting that I might not end up being the only one of us selling products through the Camden Superstores."

"So he wants to turn it into a side business?"

"Maybe."

Micah tested one of the brats and judged them cooked. He grabbed an empty plate from the picnic table, put two links on it and then moved the rest off the heat to the outer edge of the grill where they would still be kept warm. "Let's see how they are."

"Is there something unique I should taste from the beer being yours?" Lexie asked as they sat across from each other, assembled their sandwiches and filled their dishes with the other things on the table.

"I hope so," he said. "If my beers aren't unique, they won't make it. And that would be... I can't even think about it..." he said, his tone weighty for a second time.

"You have a lot riding on this," Lexie guessed.

"Nah, not a lot. Everything," he said simply.

"Everything?"

"Every penny of my own money—the money I've saved through all the years in the Marines. My grandfather turned over half his fields to me to grow hops—which means that if I fail, he'll be losing money on the land, cutting into a substantial part of his income this year. My Camden cousins in Colorado have invested in the brewery, along with putting a lot of money into an advertising campaign to launch selling Camden Microbrews exclusively in Camden Superstores. All three of my brothers have sunk money in the brewery. And Gertie has postponed charging me rent on the barn—or charging me for her advice and tasting expertise—as her investment."

"Wow. That's a lot of people depending on you to succeed," Lexie observed, feeling a twinge of guilt for taking him away from his work last night just to show her around the damage in the little house.

Micah merely inclined his head in acknowledgment as he tasted his bratwurst.

Then his eyebrows rose when that flavor registered. After swallowing his bite, he said, "But that's pretty good... What do you think?"

Lexie let her own eyebrows arch as she finished chewing and swallowing, too.

"I agree—that's *good*," she said emphatically. "There's an earthy, spicy, just-the-right-amount-of-bitter-with-a-little-tang-to-it taste. Is that from the beer?"

Micah laughed. "You have Gertie's sensitive taste buds?"

Lexie shrugged. "I don't know. Do I?"

"To pick out that much of what I'm going for in my hops and in my stout blend, even when it's mixed in as just one of the flavors in the bratwurst? I'd say so."

"Are your hops different than other hops?"

"I spent five years crossbreeding them until I came up with exactly what I wanted. They're my own hybrid. They're *my* secret."

"You did that *while* you were in the Marines?"

"Yeah. Experimenting with the hops and with

the brewing were a sideline. Something I did whenever I was stationary."

"I didn't know you were interested in botany."

"I was *interested* in making beer. The botany part just came from being the grandson of a farmer."

"In high school, you were into chemistry," she recalled. "We teased you about becoming a mad scientist. And I know you always liked to *drink* beer—when we could get our hands on it. Did those two things mix when you started hanging out with my grandmother?" It was another guess because brewing beer was not something he'd ever mentioned when they'd been friends.

"It did."

So this was an interest that had sparked after the barn incident.

He stood up from the picnic bench and took his plate with him. "I'm having a second brat—I think they're great. Want another one?"

"One is my limit. But they *are* great," she agreed. "I have a chocolate cupcake recipe that calls for stout in it—after tasting it in these, I think it might be good in those, too. If the stout is too bitter, it ruins them but yours isn't."

"You put beer in chocolate cupcakes?" he said, sounding doubtful about the combination.

"I spent a year working with a pastry chef in New Orleans. He was a horrible ogre but I came away with pretty much the same skills he had—or else my head would have rolled."

"So baker is one of the skills in your jack-of-all-trades arsenal?"

"It is."

"Why did you stay working with an ogre for a whole year?"

"I liked the job, just not the boss. Of course, that could be said of a lot of jobs I had. Or the reverse."

"But you like to bake and you know how to run a bakery?"

"I do," she confirmed, not sure why he seemed to find it important.

"Are you good at it?" he persisted.

"I've been told I am. The ogre was furious when I quit—he thought I was leaving to open my own shop to compete with him. When I said we were moving away, he softened up a little and said I'd been his best apprentice."

"Hmm..." Micah mused as he ate a few chips.

Lexie had one of those, too, giving him a curious look even as she drank in the sight of that sculpted face of his.

When he'd finished his chips, he said, "In that case, I heard something today that you might be interested in."

"What did you hear?" she played along.

"Nessa Bryant has decided to retire. She's selling the bakery in town. Maybe you should think about taking it over."

Lexie laughed at that notion. "I sent Gram a little money out of my paychecks now and then over the years—without Jason knowing—so we'd have a nest egg when we came back. It's all mine now but there isn't enough to *buy* a bakery."

"One of the things I've learned with the brewery is that you have to put some creative thinking into how to bankroll yourself. What if Nessa agreed to carry the loan? You could offer her a down payment and set up a payment plan with her—it would be like a retirement supplement that could give her income every month while you paid it off," he suggested, sounding very businesslike. And very unlike the boy she used to know.

"Or who knows," he went on, "the bank might take a risk on a business loan for you—you're a hometown girl, your family helped found Merritt way back when. Factor in that the bakery is a staple around here, a meeting place on top of supplying breads and rolls and goodies for everything that goes on, and that's more incentive to give you the backing to keep it going. Can you make wedding cakes?"

"I can and I have. I made Jill's..." And was this possibility really starting to gel?

"So here's an idea," Micah said as something

seemed to occur to him. "There's a food festival coming up—"

"I saw the signs on my way through town to Jill's."

"I'm renting a booth. It'll be the first public outing for my beers—well, not for the flavored stouts, they're not perfected yet and I need Gertie for that. But what if you make your beer cupcakes, sell them at the booth, too, and see how they go over?"

"Using your plain stout?"

"Cupcakes and beer," he said with a laugh. "It'll give the booth some novelty if nothing else."

Was that his motive?

It was just so difficult for Lexie not to be suspicious of Micah. Tonight—like last night—felt again like old times. Old times talking, supporting each other, problem solving together... But could she trust that?

"Let me think about it," she hedged.

"I have three different stouts—want to taste the one that's in the brats straight from the bottle and the other two, too? Then you can choose which one might work the best in your cupcakes—*if* you decide to make them? We can do a tasting right now."

They'd both cleaned their plates and were done eating. So were they going to just sit here and drink beer together?

That didn't seem wise.

But it *was* a good idea for her to taste all the options and choose…

"Okay," she said.

He again stood up from the picnic table, went into the house and returned with three bottles of beer that she'd seen in the fridge but not thought much about.

"We bottled these last week," he said as he opened each one and gave her samples of them all in the paper cups he'd also brought out.

She tried them, one by one. "Ooh, I think the second one would be even better in my cupcakes than the one that was in the brats. It's richer—I think it will bulk up the chocolate."

"I think you really do have Gertie's taste buds," he responded. "And her oven didn't get damaged so you could use it…"

"I'm still thinking about it," she insisted.

He offered her more beer. She refilled her small cup with the one she'd chosen as the best for her cupcakes and he took the third blend for himself, drinking it from the bottle.

"That was always your response," he said as they settled into enjoying his libations. *"Let me think about it,"* he mimicked her playfully. "You weighed the pros and cons, made your lists."

"And you were our daredevil," she countered, realizing only after she'd said it that it had come out fondly, unclouded by resentment.

But it felt kind of nice so she ran with it. "You were always determined to test every limit—"

"We had some fun," he reminded. "How about when the four of us sledded down Dead Man's Hill on that old door?"

"Oh, that *was* fun," she confirmed.

"And kayaking down the river when it was close to flooding?"

"Dangerous but also fun," she decreed. "Not to mention a lot of trouble afterward when we got caught sneaking the kayak we'd *borrowed* back…"

"Worth it," he judged.

"And there was our horse rescue…" she said.

"Hey, I was going to do that alone," he pointed out. "You guys wanted in."

"Because those sleazy people who had moved in outside of town had trapped that wild stallion and were abusing it."

"So we set it free," Micah concluded.

Another good—and heroic—deed that he was responsible for. Like the things Jill had told her about today.

Was it just that one incident with her where he'd gone wrong?

"Since I was only a kid, I didn't think the sheriff would believe me if I told him what I'd seen," Micah reminisced. "Seemed like the logical thing to do was just let the horse loose. Those creeps didn't have any right to him anyway—it wasn't like they'd paid for him."

"But four fourteen-year-olds skulking around private property at two in the morning? Not smart. *We* could have ended up their next captives and no one would have known where we were." She shivered with the memory. "I was glad when those people left town."

Micah seconded that by raising his beer to her and she instantly became much too aware of his big strong hand around the bottle.

When he took a swig then, she drank from her own cup, needing the beer to wash back whatever it was that had reared up in her in response to him.

But instead another memory cropped up. It made her laugh even before she said, "What about the night you talked us into climbing that tree to watch the seventh-grade history teacher and the school nurse parked up at Potter's Point?"

He grimaced. "Yeah, in hindsight all four of us on one branch was bad planning—I should have known the branch would break and dump us onto the hood of Mr. Snyder's car."

"And before we got to see anything but kissing even though you were sure they were *doing it*."

"But that was some steamy kissing," he defended with a devilish laugh.

It had been.

And why remembering it caused her to wonder about Micah's kissing skills, Lexie didn't know.

What's going on with you? she demanded of herself.

Hearing Gertie's and Jill's praise of Micah, combined with remembering some past good deeds, seemed to have opened up a soft spot in her.

She couldn't let that get too far, though. Especially not when her thoughts verged on sensual.

She sat up straighter, glanced around at the darkening sky, then at the remnants of their dinner on the table and said, "Since you cooked, if you need to go back to work, I can clean this up."

Her tone was aloof now, and she saw the way it made those full eyebrows of his pulse together in confusion.

What she didn't know was why she regretted it once she'd done it. Why she was sorry to conclude their evening together.

"You're sure?" he said, sounding tentative.

"I'm sure," she said too firmly.

He nodded, and she thought she glimpsed sad acceptance in it. Then he placed both big hands flat on the picnic table and pushed himself to his feet.

"Okay." He hoisted one leg over the bench seat and then the other. "How 'bout we bring dinner over to Gertie and Mary tomorrow night?" he suggested then.

"I'm sure they'd like that," Lexie said, knowing her grandmother would be thrilled and recognizing that the gesture was thoughtful of him. "I'll tell them when I go over in the morning. I'm babysitting for Jill in the afternoon while she goes to the dentist and then I'll be home."

"Gertie loves the burritos from a Mexican food place that's in town now. If that sounds good to her, we can bring those."

It was something Lexie didn't know about her grandmother that *he* did.

Something that said another good thing about him.

But she pushed that thought out of her head along with everything else that was confusing her tonight.

"I'll talk to her about it," she said, looking at his handsome face and trying not to appreciate just how striking it was.

"See you tomorrow, then," he said.

"See you tomorrow," Lexie echoed, beginning to gather the things on the table.

There was still plenty of beer in the bottle she'd been pouring from or she might have been able to blame the liquor for the fact that as Micah headed across the yard to the barn she couldn't keep from watching him.

Long thick legs. Glorious derriere. Narrow

waist. Broad powerful shoulders stretching his T-shirt as far as it would go...

Once upon a time, she'd liked him...

She didn't know where that thought had come from but there it was.

But yes, she *had* liked him, even if it had been only as a friend.

What if those fond feelings were cropping up again?

That might be risky, she warned herself as she forced her eyes away from his backside.

Risky and unwise after the lesson she'd learned.

And it seemed even less wise when, all on its own, her head raised so she could get one last glimpse of Micah.

Oh, definitely risky and unwise, she thought when she realized that just around the edges of those fonder feelings was a hint of something else.

Something that seemed like...

Attraction?

No...

That couldn't be...

She'd never been attracted to him before.

She certainly couldn't be now, post-barn-incident. And yet *something* was going on with her that she didn't understand. That she didn't *want* going on with her.

She might have agreed to be pleasant, she might have recalled—thanks to Jill and to their conversation tonight—that there had been good days with Micah along with the bad, but when it came to her thoughts about him?

Uh-uh.

She just wasn't going to let herself forget what he'd done.

Chapter Five

"You look like hell, boy. And what are you doin' here? First Tanner shows up at four thirty and now you at barely 6:00 a.m.? You boys have something going that takes two of you to tell me?"

"Tanner's here?" Micah asked his grandfather in surprise when he got out of his truck at the family home Tuesday morning.

It was common for Ben to have his first cup of coffee sitting in one of the white rocking chairs on the front porch. That was where he was when Micah drove up. Nothing unusual about that.

But the mention of Micah's brother Tanner?

"What are you talking about?" Micah asked. "Tanner is deployed overseas."

The elderly man shook his head, then nodded in the direction of the front door. "Four thirty this morning," he repeated. "The damn fool's lucky I didn't shoot him. Heard the porch creak and came downstairs with my shotgun."

"You didn't know he was coming?"

"Not a clue."

"Is he all right?"

"Says he is. Said it was a last-minute thing. But something's up."

"He isn't saying what he's doing here?"

Ben shrugged. "Says he has something he has to check out. Didn't look happy about it, whatever it is. Kind of like you—you look like you've been ridden hard and put away wet. What's up?"

"No crisis, I just pulled an all-nighter and haven't been to bed yet. I was in the brewery ruining fifteen gallons of stout." Not ideal, but hardly an emergency.

Tanner, on the other hand... Nothing short of a family emergency would be reason enough for him to get leave and a transport back to the States from a deployment.

But as far as Micah knew, there weren't any emergencies—family or otherwise. He'd spoken to both of the other triplets, Quinn and Dalton, yesterday and they were fine. Ben was sitting right there, also fine. Micah was fine, and that was their whole family. Well, except for the extended part of the Camdens, but Micah had also talked to their cousin Beau last night and there were no emergencies on that front, either.

His grandfather seemed less curious about it and more focused on Micah's early-morning visit. "When I called last night to tell you that picture frame was ready, I didn't mean for you to rush over at the crack of dawn."

"I know. I just want to get it back to Lexie."

"I could have brought it over. Especially if you're so busy you're workin' through the night. Things goin' bad with the beer?"

"No, not bad," Micah was quick to reassure him. "I'm just still working to get the flavored stouts right. Last night I guess maybe I overdid the add-ins? I'm not quite sure. But whatever I did wrong, I ended up with swill. The plain stouts are all still solid, though—in fact, Lexie and I both loved your bratwurst. You have a big hit with that one."

"I thought so, too. Want to make sausage-flavored beer?" Ben joked.

"Uh… I'll pass on that."

"Anything else I can do at the brewery to help out?"

"Nah, thanks. It's all trial and error. Eventually I'll get it right. I'm seeing Gertie tonight—I'll run a few things by her, see what she thinks, and that'll help."

"How is she?"

Micah told him what he knew.

Then Ben said, "Well, you still look like hell. Tanner's sleepin' up in his room—why don't you shower and catch a few hours in yours?"

A lack of sleep definitely wasn't helping anything. He'd left instructions for his staff on how to start the day so he knew they could—and would— go to work without him. And if he went back to the Parker place to rest, he'd have to stretch out in the sunroom—which was great when it was dark, not so great for sleeping after sunup. And a few hours nap in his own bed sounded pretty good right then.

"I might do that," he said.

"Go for it. I'm headed into town after a while. If I'm not here when you get up, there's food in the fridge. The frame is waiting for you on the entry table."

"Thanks for doing that for me."

"Just get some rest. And shower—you smell like a brewery," Ben said, amused by his own quip.

Micah reached down and squeezed his grandfather's bony shoulder as he went past him into the house. He trudged up the stairs to his room.

His grandfather was right—he *did* smell like a brewery, he realized as he stripped off his clothes to get in the shower in the connecting bathroom. He was so used to the smell—so overexposed to it from the endless hours of work—that he barely noticed it unless someone pointed it out.

The brewery that he had so much riding on and so many people pulling for. So many people who he didn't want to—and couldn't—disappoint.

But the previous night's fiascos were eating at him.

Failure was just not an option. Not even if it meant he had to lose some sleep, he thought as he stepped under the spray of water.

But he'd really thought he was closer to success with those flavored stouts. He'd thought the last batches were going to work.

And they'd ended up the worst yet.

He scrubbed hard and then washed his hair, too, fighting a heavy wave of discouragement.

Don't go there, he cautioned himself as he stood under the water to rinse the lather. *Take your lumps and keep at it...*

But damn if there hadn't been a lot of lumps to take...

The beer failures.

The tree damage.

The disaster with Adrianna...

He could make a solid argument for the disaster with Adrianna not being his fault but he refused to let himself off the hook. It *was* his fault that what Adrianna had seen from him—and heard from his mother—had led her to her decision.

And the mess with Adrianna was the toughest lump to take. The costliest. The one with the outcome that he couldn't fix...

Wow, he was carrying some heavy stuff with him today, he realized.

Lack of sleep, that's all it is, he told himself as he turned off the water.

But once he dried off and got into bed, hands behind his head on the pillow, sleep didn't come instantly the way he'd expected it to. The way he needed it to.

Instead, his mind kept chewing on that argument with Adrianna, especially the part where she'd used lack of sleep as her justification.

So what if a baby would have kept him up at night when he was home? He would have found a way to make it work. He would have found a way to make it *all* work.

Just like now, when he would find a way to fix Gertie's and Lexie's houses despite his other problems.

Not that Lexie believed him any more than Adrianna had...

Lexie...

Well, hey, it had been maybe fifteen or twenty minutes without thinking about her.

He should probably count that as a victory...

He sighed, pressing deeper into the pillow, hoping to drift off.

But still he was restless. Exhausted and restless.

It was starting again.

Thinking about Lexie almost every minute.

Noticing her hair, her eyes, her nose, her lips, her body...

Loving it when he made her laugh.

Wanting to be with her so much that he'd taken time he shouldn't have taken away from the brewery.

Looking over at the back of her grandmother's house a million times a day, hoping to catch a glimpse of her.

It was puberty all over again...

Not that he had a crush on her like he'd had then. He didn't. Of course not.

But he had this awareness of her that he just couldn't seem to shake. No matter how hard he tried to fight it, she was just there, in his mind. Day and night.

And it didn't help that things seemed to be getting better between them. For the past two nights, there had been moments almost like when they were friends. He'd always liked talking to her and it seemed like they might have found their way back to that.

He did want things between them to be amicable, he reminded himself. He didn't want animosity to tinge his relationship with her grandmother.

But it was going beyond amicable to crave the

scent of her when she first came downstairs after a shower. To long for the chance to run his hands through her hair. To want to bury his face in the side of her neck...

None of that had anything to do with Gertie.

Just keep the mission in mind, he told himself, trying to call upon his military training.

The primary mission was to make beer. To make the brewery succeed.

The secondary mission was to repair those houses.

The Marines had taught him focus and he needed to draw on that discipline now.

Lexie wasn't the enemy but there was bad blood between them and he definitely needed to resist this draw toward her.

He already had more than a full plate.

And if those weren't grounds enough, there was also the fact that she hadn't ever seen him as more than a friend. How dumb would he have to be to let himself fall for her again when his feelings would never be returned?

Pretty dumb, he concluded.

So block it!

That's what he was going to do, he resolved with conviction.

But as he finally began to drift off, the image of Lexie's face kept him company.

And so did that quiet urge to do whatever he could to be with her...

* * *

When Lexie went downstairs Tuesday morning, she found a note from Micah telling her that a vet work crew was coming the next day to frame the side wall of the bigger house. Then they were going to camp overnight in the backyard and frame the side of the little house on Thursday.

In response to that news, when she returned from visiting Gertie, she spent the day preparing her grandmother's house for construction—moving things out of the way, placing protective tarps over what needed to stay in place, and taping up clear plastic dividers to keep construction dust and debris out of the undamaged sections.

She planned to do the same in the little house the next day while the construction crew worked on her grandmother's house. Then she used the rest of Tuesday afternoon baking two large pans of brownies. She cut a few to bring to her grandmother and Mary—the rest she put away for the coming construction crew.

Just before five o'clock, she showered and changed into a clean pair of her new jeans and a previously unworn red top with small frills that formed cap sleeves—it was what Lily had called a casual date outfit. Not that she and Micah taking dinner to her grandmother and cousin was a date. Instead, she told herself that the red blouse was bright and cheery—the perfect outfit for visiting someone who was ailing.

She applied her makeup—adding a touch more eyeliner than usual, plus mascara and a hint of shadow—and left her hair loose around her shoulders.

Lastly came a pair of ballet shoes before she went downstairs and found Micah waiting for her.

He again had on a military-issue T-shirt—this one white and tight enough to make any normal, healthy woman's mouth water. He also wore a pair of jeans that highlighted thick thighs, a narrow waist and a derriere to die for.

His face was still stubbled but the short scruff was trimmed and neat, and he smelled freshly showered and unfairly wonderful.

But recalling her resolve of the night before not to lose sight of his treachery from the past, she worked to not let it affect her.

Micah drove and after a stop in town to pick up Gertie's new favorite Mexican food, they went to Mary's apartment.

It was an evening of burritos, green chili, a delicate rice flecked with red peppers, guacamole, chips and jovial conversation during which Lexie told her grandmother about Micah's idea that she consider buying the bakery.

Gertie was enthusiastically in favor of it and as

she took her third brownie, Mary chimed in with her support, too.

What Lexie found the most interesting through the evening, though, was what she witnessed between Gertie and Micah.

They really had become the best of buddies and an impressive team when it came to talking about their favorite subject—brewing beer.

Until witnessing it, Lexie hadn't realized just how much of a bond had formed between them. How much of a genuine connection they'd made. And she found herself having the oddest reaction to it.

It made her a little jealous.

Although she couldn't tell whether she was jealous that Micah seemed to feel every bit as close to Gertie as she was herself, or if she was jealous of what her grandmother shared with Micah...

"I don't know what I'd do without your Gram," he said as they got into his truck to return home.

"You two really love that whole beer-making thing..." Lexie responded.

"Sorry, did I monopolize Gertie?"

Anxious to cover up any hint of jealousy—no matter what was causing it—Lexie said, "No, I talked to her about the bakery idea. And she was in her glory talking beer with you—I wouldn't have taken that away from her."

Then she changed the subject. "I heard Gram

say that she thinks you need to add your flavor-ings in stages?" she said. "Add some when the wort is cooling, more later and then more at the cold crash—whatever wort and cold crashing are?"

"Wort is the liquid that comes out of mixing the malt grains and hops with hot water—that's the start of the process. Cold crashing is when we cool the stout to near-freezing temps, just before bottling it—the end of the line. Gertie thinks I should hold off on a fuller fruit infusion until the end, when the beer is cold and the yeast is dormant so the sugars in the fruits won't ferment. I think that was what I did wrong with my last batch." The excitement that had come to life in him while he and Gertie hashed through his problems was clear in his voice.

Lexie ran with it. "I had another thought—well, three, actually—when you guys were talking about flavorings," she said tentatively.

"Let's hear 'em."

"I was just thinking about adding flavors to things I bake. If I bake anything lemon or orange, I always add fresh peel into the batter and use it as a garnish, too. I wondered if putting a curl of orange and lemon peel in each bottle at the end might brighten your citrus stout and give you a last hint of sweet-tart flavor."

"I could try that," he allowed.

"For your sour cherry stout, I was thinking that

whenever I bake cherry-anything, I put in a touch of almond—you don't necessarily taste it but it boosts the cherry flavor. I wondered if the same might be true in beer."

"Hmm… Okay. I'll test it out. And number three?"

"I worked in a bakery in New Mexico for a stretch, too. They made a lot of breads with peppers in them. I heard you tell Gram that you're using habaneros but you don't think they're giving you enough flavor, so I was thinking you might want to mix in either roasted New Mexico green chilies or chipotles. The chilies would give you an earthier taste while the chipotles would add a smoky flavor."

He took his eyes off the road to glance at her. "Okay…" he said again, this time as if he were impressed. "Those are all good ideas. That's the sort of thing Gertie helps with but she mainly thinks in terms of the beer. Coming at it from a baker's perspective is a new twist."

He looked ahead again and then said, "So what did you think about Gertie's idea that you be my taster while she's on meds for her leg?"

What Lexie had thought was that her grandmother was trying to push them into spending more time together.

But when that hint of jealousy gave her another little jab and made her think of the warmth between her grandmother and Micah over their common interest, she found herself saying, "I'm not a beer expert, but I guess I could tell you when I think something tastes good or bad, when there's enough or too much of the other flavors."

"She said to taste at each stage," he reminded.

"So you're just going to keep me drunk?" Lexie joked.

He laughed. "Now there's a thought... But, no, you just need a swig to tell if I'm on the right track. You won't be drinking anywhere near enough to get drunk."

"I suppose I can do that," she agreed before she heard herself say out of nowhere, "It's kind of strange to see the way you and Gram are now."

"How so?"

She shrugged. "I know you were always close, but years ago it was more of an adult-child sort of thing—I mean, even though you were seventeen, you weren't really an adult so it wasn't like two equals. Two friends. But now—"

"Yeah, I guess it just evolved. I've seen her every time I've come home over the years. We wrote, emailed—beer was the main topic but she always asked what I was doing and kept tabs on me. I did the same with her. I guess along the way I grew up and yeah, we became friends."

"Friends with the same obsession," Lexie qualified. Maybe that was what made them seem so close. Anyone seeing the two of them together would think that Gertie was his grandmother, that he was her grandson.

"We *are* both obsessed with beer," he conceded.

"She always liked making her home brews—it was her hobby. But now it seems like it's given her a new lease on life." It was no wonder Gertie had let him put his brewery in her backyard so she could be an active part of it. But Lexie wasn't convinced that was what was best for her grandmother.

"You say that like it might be bad. Isn't a new lease on life a good thing?" Micah asked, apparently hearing the uncertainty in her voice.

"Sure, but…"

But it *did* concern Lexie that he might let Gertie down. "I just wouldn't want you to learn what you need to learn from her and then…you know, cast her aside or something…"

"Cast her aside?" he repeated. "Like I'm just using her?"

"I hope not," Lexie said.

Micah shot her another glance. "You have no idea how much your grandmother means to me," he said seriously. "Or how much I owe her."

"Because she taught you about beer?" Lexie said with some skepticism.

"It's more than that. A lot more. She stuck by me when she probably shouldn't have. And she was a better influence on me than my own mother was."

"Your mother was a bad influence on you?"

"In a lot of ways. Not that she was a bad mother," he added. "She just had some screwy ideas."

"Like what?"

"You know that my great-grandfather—Hector— was H.J. Camden's brother—"

"And H.J. Camden was the guy who made a gazillion dollars with Camden Superstores."

"Actually H.J. made a gazillion dollars even before there were superstores—he was the guy who built the whole empire *behind* the superstores. The two brothers—Hector and H.J.—started in the same place. They grew up in Northbridge on the family's farm that they inherited together. But while my great-grandfather was content as a simple farmer, H.J. had much bigger plans."

"Superstores?"

"That idea was actually Hector's," Micah said. "But that came later. At first, back on the farm, H.J. started his wheeling and dealing, buying up anything he could just to *own* as much as he could—"

"Whether it was on the up and up or not—isn't that what they say about him?"

"It is. But, anyway, my great-grandfather just wasn't as ambitious as H.J. was and he didn't like being around all the wheeling and dealing. Hector wanted a simple farm life. So he sold his half of the Northbridge place to H.J. and came to Merritt. But once H.J. had accumulated land and lumber mills and mines and factories and what have you, it was Hector's idea that H.J. open a general store—because general stores sell pretty much everything and H.J. had his fingers in so many different industries. One big general store would be a place for H.J. to sell all he was producing from his other holdings without a middleman cutting into his profits."

"So the superstores were your great-grandfather's idea? Doesn't that mean he should have had a cut or something?"

"Now you're thinking like my mom. That rubbed her wrong—even though Hector always said that H.J. offered him a partnership in the first store but that he turned it down. He still didn't want the pressure of H.J.'s ambitions."

"Or maybe he didn't want any part of H.J.'s dirty dealings?"

"Could be," Micah admitted with a shrug. "All I know is that no matter what else went on, Hector and H.J. were always close."

"Just not close enough for your family to end up with a share of the wealth—"

"The way my mom thought we should have," Micah finished for her. "It ate at her even before my dad was killed flying the Camden private plane—which poured fuel onto the flames."

"I knew your dad was a pilot in the air force— I thought that was how he died."

Micah shook his head. "He served in the air force, which is why my brothers and I were all sort of drawn to the military—following in his footsteps. But when Dad got out of the air force, he went to work piloting a private plane for H.J. and his family. We lived in Denver then, until I was three and Dad was killed in the plane crash along with H.J.'s son and both of his grandsons and their wives."

"But not H.J.?"

"H.J. was home laid up with a bad back, being taken care of by his daughter-in-law—we've always called her GiGi. She and H.J. ended up raising my ten Camden cousins who were orphaned by the crash."

"We've known each other since we were kids but I never knew all this," Lexie marveled.

"Family history—it's not like it's sandbox chit-chat."

Lexie conceded to that. But she returned to what he'd been saying about his father. "So your dad was flying the plane?"

"It wasn't pilot error. It was mechanical," Micah was quick to add. "That was the second thing that my Mom resented, the biggest thing was that she lost her husband because he was *working for* that rich side of the family. She held on to those two grudges the rest of her life. It made her kind of an angry, resentful, intense person."

"And that made her a bad influence on you?"

"Partly. Plus, somewhere in her head, as much as she blamed the other Camdens, she also blamed Hector and my grandfather and my dad," Micah explained. "Don't get me wrong—she loved them all, she was devoted to them. But she also fixated on the idea that if they'd been more ambitious, more aggressive—the way H.J. and his son and grandsons had been—then we would have had a share in the superstores and that would have changed everything. Maybe then my grandfather wouldn't have settled for just running a small family farm, and maybe my dad would have been something more than the hired hand of the rich Camdens."

They'd arrived home by then, but Lexie still didn't understand how his mother's perspective had made Gertie a better influence on him than his mother. And she honestly wanted to know.

So rather than saying good-night and going upstairs, she went with him into the kitchen and prompted him to go on by saying, "Okay, your mom had some baggage..."

Micah leaned his hip against the edge of the countertop and crossed his arms over his very flat stomach, extending his legs and crossing them at the ankles, too.

"That *baggage*," he went on, "translated into some strong ideas about the kind of men her sons needed to be."

"She didn't just want you to be good men?" Lexie said as she found a spot against the edge of the kitchen table, facing him.

"My mother wanted us to go after whatever we wanted with a vengeance. H.J.'s kind of vengeance. She was hell-bent on raising us to be men who were as hard-hitting and ambitious and unde-featable as the other side of the family had been."

"But the rumors were that they were ruthless, too."

"I don't ever remember her using that word…" he hedged. "But she did foster really extreme com-petitiveness. Anything we wanted, the question was always, *How bad do you want it?* If it was the last cookie, getting our driver's licenses, borrow-ing the car, you name it—that's what she said. Fol-lowed by, *Show me how bad you want it…* Usually, convincing her meant we had to do more chores, give up allowance, bite the bullet on something she knew we didn't want to do—whatever it took to let her see that we were willing to go to all lengths to overcome any obstacle."

"Didn't that just lead to kids who never took no for an answer?"

He chuckled at that. "Sometimes we *did* take no for an answer just because it was easier—but then she made it clear how disappointed she was, how worried it made her that we would settle. She'd lecture us about how no one who settled got anywhere in life. She'd praise whoever showed initiative and determination, and...I guess you could say she'd shame whoever didn't. So yeah, kids who took no for an answer were *not* what she wanted."

"And when it was something that more than one of you were competing for, didn't that cause a lot of fights?"

"With four boys? Oh, yeah," he confirmed with another laugh. "There were a *lot* of fights. And undercutting and backstabbing and wrangling and outmaneuvering and ratting each other out and—"

"Nothing came without that?"

"Christmas and birthday gifts were freebies. But other than those? Every privilege, every decision about where to go, what to eat, how the work around the farm was doled out, any extra money we asked for, a cool pair of boots or an unnecessary new jacket or shirt—"

"I had no idea that's how she brought you up," Lexie said. This cast new light on how competitive he'd been with Jason, how much more strong-willed he'd been all the way around than the rest of them. It seemed like such a strange—and subtly harsh—way of growing up. "What about your grandfather? Did he do that, too?"

"No. He softened the message some—it was Pops who would talk about us being good men. His expectations and example probably kept us all from going too far—most of the time, anyway."

Micah paused, gave her a regret-filled frown and said, "Not when it came to the barn thing, but other times…"

Another moment's silence followed that before he went on.

"But Big Ben was careful to stay on the side-lines—there was no question that we were raised by our mother. He never once crossed or contra-dicted her. Even if we went to him with a com-plaint about her, he supported her and refused to even mediate. *Your mom is the boss*—that's what he'd always say."

"So that's it—it was her way all the way, even if her way was sort of extreme?"

"Mom thought she was helping us, toughening us up so we'd be like H.J. So we'd be successful."

"It just sounds so severe," Lexie ventured.

"Maybe…" was as far as he would go to agree with that. "But I do know that it made us all good candidates for the military—although Mom was hoping more for business moguls or titans of in-dustry," Micah said. "But I think it was lucky that we all did go military—the military took the drive and discipline she'd cultivated and put a better spin on it. That's where we learned the kind of brotherhood that Pops had tried to encourage in us—"

"He didn't succeed?"

"His message that we were family, that we should stand up for each other, worked when it was one of us against an outsider—none of us were going to let the others get pushed around. But at home it just couldn't survive the mentality that Mom wanted us to have—we were fierce competitors there."

"Because you were pitted against each other to get what you wanted," Lexie noted. "It seems sad to me that you all had to join the service to learn to be brothers."

Micah shrugged that off. "The important thing is that we *did* learn it. Before that, we were kids and kids don't have the best judgment. Not using my determination productively was how I got into trouble that last year of high school—not only with you but with the law, too," he said. "I wanted to brew beer, so I brewed beer. I wanted to make money from it, so I sold it—even though I knew it was illegal as a minor to make and sell alcohol, especially to other minors."

"Which got you arrested," Lexie filled in. She'd heard about it through the grapevine at the time, despite all her efforts to avoid it.

"Which got me arrested," he confirmed. "But

not until after the sheriff had given me one warning, and then brought me in front of a judge for a lecture and a fine that took a chunk of my proceeds. When those two reprimands weren't strong enough noes for me, he finally arrested me. I was arraigned in juvenile court and given the choice—either the judge was going to try me as an adult because I was a week from turning eighteen, or I could go into the military..." He paused and said in an aside, "Gertie never knew about the warning or the fine."

"She won't hear it from me. But if you think she hasn't heard about it somewhere along the line, I think you're being naive."

"Probably," he said with another chuckle.

Only now Lexie was even more confused. "I hate to point this out, but it was my grandmother who taught you about brewing beer... Doesn't that make her as bad of an influence on you as your mother was?"

"No," he said, giving her a look as if she were missing something. "What Gertie taught me gave me a skill and a goal. What I turned around and did with it was all on me. Gertie was nothing but a good influence."

"Because she was loving and caring and—"

His laughter at that cut her words short.

"Sorry," he said when he stopped laughing. "I'll grant you that my mother's how-bad-do-you-want-it stuff was a little warped but other than that she was very loving and caring. That wasn't what I lacked. Gertie helped by being hard as nails on me."

"It didn't seem that way," Lexie refuted.

"Because you weren't there listening to her!"

The thought that Gertie might have been harder on him than Lexie had known gave her a little satisfaction. "So she wasn't just taking you under her wing and excusing what you'd done to me."

"Oh, hell no! Gertie read me the riot act over it and lectured me until she was blue in the face. She made no bones about the fact that I was a rotten friend to you and Jason both—which had never occurred to me," he confessed wryly.

"You kept coming around..." Lexie reminded.

"The lecturing didn't go on forever or I probably wouldn't have."

"She didn't dwell on it because she knew how your mom was and couldn't hold you completely responsible?"

"No, she didn't know what went on in my house."

"Then she just forgave you," Lexie tried again, attempting to understand her grandmother's motivation.

Micah was looking very intently at her and she had the sense that he thought she was playing some kind of game with him. But his expression lost all humor and after a moment he said, "Gertie cut me some slack because she understood why I'd done what I did with you."

"If she didn't know what went on in your house, how could she understand you pouncing on someone else's misfortune for your own benefit?"

"And again you're thinking that my own *benefit* was what? Looking like a big man or a stud?"

"Yes," Lexie said, standing her ground. "Or to stick it to Jason," she added.

He shook his head. "I told you, boosting my reputation at your expense was *not* what I wanted. And Gertie understood that."

"What did she understand? What *did* you want?" Lexie demanded.

"Come on, Lexie, you had to have known."

"I had to have known what?" she challenged. "That you were competitive? Sure, I knew that. I knew that you used me to needle Jason about being *soft* because he was with me, that you thought you were more of a man because you didn't let yourself get *stuck* with one girl. I knew that you always had to prove you were better than Jason at every sport, every game. What else am I supposed to know?"

"I did feel competitive with Jason—you're right about that," he acknowledged. "But I was competing with him because of how I felt about you…"

His deep voice had grown even deeper and so quiet it was barely audible.

"How you *felt* about me? What does that mean?

We were friends, and then you turned on me—what changed? Did I do something that aggravated you? Did you feel like I'd taken Jason away from you? Is that why you always called Jill by her first name but started calling me *Parker*—like we were barely friends anymore? Is that why you gave me such a hard time about everything? Why you made fun of Jason and me being together? Why you told him all the time that he was dumb to let himself be tied down with me?"

"It was all just a cover," Micah said, putting the brakes on her outpouring. "A cover for what Gertie had seen in me. For what she'd guessed was going on with me—"

"*What* was going on with you?" Lexie nearly shouted.

Micah hesitated, then spoke. "What Gertie knew and the reason she had mercy on me was that I liked you…"

Lexie could only stare in shock and disbelief.

"It's true. I liked you. Too much. I had for years—since we'd started middle school, about the same time Jason went after you. I did, too—I tried to impress you, to win you over, to make you see me as more than a friend, but he was better at it than I was." Micah shook his head as if at his own ineptness.

"But after that day in the barn," he went on, "when the rumors started flying, I thought I saw my chance. I thought if Jason believed we'd gotten together in the barn that he'd break up with you. And then maybe I could have you. So I took the opportunity. Because you were what I wanted and I went after you in any way I could think of."

Plain and simple.

She had honestly never considered this possibility and it wasn't easy now to adjust that thinking.

As if he knew the message needed reinforcing, he said, "The bottom line was that I had the biggest crush on you."

Was *that* what Gertie had been talking about seeing in him? Not his overly competitiveness with Jason?

It must have been...

"I fought it," Micah was saying. "I tried everything to squelch it. I tried going after other girls. I tried to ignore it. I wished it away. But whenever I saw you..." He sighed helplessly. "Then that day at the barn happened and the gossip started and I still wanted you so much I could taste it. I thought it was my opening. So no matter how ill-conceived it was, I went for it the way I was supposed to go for anything I wanted—full steam ahead..."

Wreaking havoc on her life in the process. Permanently hurting her relationship with her father.

In light of the consequences, how could she feel anything but anger and resentment for him?

But she did. She was starting to feel glimmers

of sympathy, of compassion, of understanding for the young Micah. The kind of sympathy and compassion and understanding her grandmother must have felt for him.

That made so much more sense...

"It was a stupid, desperate kid move," Micah was saying. "And Gertie recognized that. So after raking me over the coals for it, and making sure I was well aware of what a rotten thing it had been to do to you and Jason, she took pity on me." Micah paused and after another moment said, "And since then I've been so damn sorry..."

It was the explanation and apology he'd been trying to give since she'd returned to Merritt.

An apology that was genuine. Heartfelt. Raw and full of tangible remorse and regret.

She couldn't seem to stop it from deflating some of her righteous indignation.

Then he seemed to draw himself up out of the past, pull himself together and said, "Gertie's lectures, the things she made me see—coming on top of what my grandfather had tried to teach along the way—finally made me start to reevaluate what my mother had drummed into me and my brothers. The Marine Corps took care of the rest, teaching me how important it is to be loyal, to have loyalty from other people, to act honorably. That's when my mindset finally got channeled in a better direction. But if it hadn't been for Gertie," he said, "I might have ended up in jail instead."

Lexie didn't know what to say, torn between new sympathy and long-held pain.

Silence fell for a few moments.

Then Micah said, "So one more time—*I am sorry.*"

Lexie nodded, knowing—believing now—that that was true but still not quite able to grant forgiveness.

"And don't ever think," he continued, "that I will *cast your grandmother aside.* She's as much family to me as she is to you. Without her, I wouldn't be who I am—which, believe it or not, is very different from who you used to know."

Lexie still needed more evidence before she could truly accept that.

But for the first time, she could concede that he might actually have changed into the better man her grandmother contended that he was.

And what she knew now did alleviate her fear that he might let down her grandmother in some way—so that was good...

Lexie had the impression that he'd said all he was going to say. That seemed confirmed when he pushed off the edge of the countertop with his hips and headed in the direction of the sunroom. But then he spoke again.

"Before I forget, I have something for you."

He was full of surprises tonight…

He disappeared into the other room and returned carrying something wrapped loosely in tissue paper that he brought over to her.

"I asked my grandfather to see if he could fix this and he did…"

Lexie unwrapped the item.

It was the old picture frame that had held the photograph of her grandfather and his new tractor. The frame she'd tried to rehang only to have it fall a second time and break.

Ben Camden had made it good as new.

"I didn't even realize it was missing…" Lexie mused, turning it over and seeing that the repair had made the frame sturdy enough to hold the cherished picture again.

Then she looked up at Micah, at that face that had matured into such rugged glory, into those impossibly blue eyes, and she couldn't deny that it was something sweet and thoughtful for him to have done. It touched her that he had taken the trouble—especially since it wasn't his fault it had broken.

"Thank you," she said softly.

"No big deal. Just keep in mind that you shouldn't hang it back up until all the construction is finished."

Lexie nodded. As she went on looking into

those eyes, she wondered just what kind of man he really was.

If he wasn't the boy she'd known, then who was this guy?

This tall, muscular, gorgeous mountain of a man who was studying her face.

Whose eyes were peering into hers.

Whose gaze drifted to her mouth as if he might be taking aim...

To kiss her?

That couldn't be...

And why would her chin tilt up just a little at that thought?

Certainly, she wouldn't *let* him kiss her.

Would she?

She realized suddenly that she was looking at his lips—such perfect masculine lips.

That parted ever so slightly just then...

And had his handsome head moved a fraction forward, too?

For a moment, she held her breath. She just waited, knowing she should move. That she should deflect.

Only she didn't.

But a split second later, Micah stepped back and away from her.

Nodding at the frame in her hands, he said, "Pops did a good job, but don't forget that it's old. I don't think it can be fixed if it falls and breaks again." For some reason, his voice seemed more gravelly than it had been earlier.

"I'll keep that in mind," Lexie assured him.

"Better get some sleep," he suggested then. "My crew will be here bright and early and you won't be able to sleep through the noise."

"I'll just be glad to get things started."

The repairs to the houses.

Not whatever it was that had seemed on the verge of starting between them.

Unless she'd just imagined it.

Which she probably had.

Because Micah *liking her too much* might have been the case years ago.

But that was ancient history.

And no more welcome now than it would have been then even if she'd known about it.

So why, she asked herself once she got behind her closed bedroom door, was she still thinking about those lips of his?

And why was she just realizing that she'd been a little excited by the idea of him kissing her?

And feeling a hint of disappointment now that he hadn't...

Chapter Six

Wednesday and Thursday were busy days.

The sun was still rising on Wednesday when six burly marine veterans arrived in three pickup trucks and went to work.

As planned, once Lexie was dressed for the day, she went next door to prep the little house for Thursday's tasks. It was a bigger chore than her grandmother's house had been because there was more structural damage to sort through and work around. There was also more damage to possessions, so she had a greater number of things to evaluate as she decided whether to salvage and protect them or dispose of them.

Work was still going on when she finished but she showered the grime away in time to get to Mary's place for dinner.

On Tuesday night, Gertie had suggested that she should leave Micah and his friends to a boys' night and come spend the evening with her and Mary, and Lexie had agreed, staying until Gertie and Mary were ready for bed.

When she got back home, construction had stopped for the night, and Micah and his friends were in the backyard, nearer to the barn than the house. Sleeping bags were still rolled up but ready to use and they were grilling steaks on Gertie's barbecue. It did indeed look like a boys' night on a boisterous camping trip, beer bottles in hand.

The sounds of a whole lot of deep voices and laughter were still drifting up through the window from below when Lexie got into bed. She fell asleep listening hard for which voice, which laugh was Micah's, trying not to analyze why she cared…

She woke Thursday morning to the sound of more power saws and hammering, and spent the day cleaning up the debris the construction had left behind in Gertie's house. The kitchen and her grandmother's bedroom were powdered with sawdust that—despite the plastic sheeting—had also crept onto the stairs and into the living room.

Finished with that late in the afternoon, she

rushed to Mary's apartment to stay with her grand-mother while Mary went to the dentist.

"How's the work on the houses going today?" Gertie asked when Lexie brought them both iced teas.

"Good... I think..." Lexie answered uncer-tainly. "I told you yesterday when I got here that they hadn't really done anything except tear down what was left of the damaged wall. But when I got home last night, all the old stuff was gone and they'd framed the wall in—all nice and neat from the eaves to the ground—and nailed the tarps to it so the tarps don't flap around as much. Now it looks like it's ready for a whole new side wall, though."

"Plastic tarps still aren't locked doors so I'm glad Micah is there making sure nobody comes in," Gertie said.

Lexie nodded rather than agreeing or disagree-ing aloud, then went on with what she'd been say-ing. "Today they're working on my place. The demolition part was finished quicker. The old side was all gone and they'd already started to put up the new frame before I left."

"But they aren't cutting corners, they're doing it right, doing a good job," Gertie said, her tone implying that it was what she assumed to be true.

"It seems like it. Your house has a nice wooden skeleton for the new wall, and Micah said my place would be in the same shape by the time his crew goes home today."

"Poor Micah," Gertie said then. "He has so much to do to get his beer ready for the food festival this weekend—it was bad timing that this was when his friends could get here to work on the houses. But he wouldn't put them off, even though I told him it was all right if he did. Has he been breaking his back working the construction and at the brewery, too?"

It struck Lexie as strange, but in that moment she realized that, unlike before, she wasn't annoyed by Gertie's sympathy for Micah. She also had no inclination to vilify him in response.

Instead, she said, "I didn't know you told him he could put this work off."

"I did."

Okay, he got points for not accepting Gertie's permission to postpone so he could focus on his own interests.

But Lexie didn't tell her grandmother that as she went on to answer Gertie's question. "We haven't even had a full five minutes together since the marines landed, but from what I've seen, I'd say that yes, he is putting in a lot of hours keeping up with both things." And Lexie had seen quite a bit while watching him through every window.

Not to admire how he looked with the tool belt riding low on his hips, of course, but in order to keep tabs on him. To see if he was bailing on the construction to tend to his brewery while other people did the work he'd promised to do.

But that wasn't what she'd seen. He had seemed to check in at the brewery multiple times a day but he'd never stayed long before returning to work alongside the construction crew. If anything was suffering from inattention on his part, it was his brewery, not work on the houses.

"Poor thing," her grandmother repeated.

"He *is* doing a lot of running back and forth," Lexie conceded. "But from what he told me Tuesday night, I guess he was raised for hard work—I just never knew it. Did you?"

"I knew he was a hard worker from when we worked together at the store," Gertie said, obviously not understanding what Lexie was getting at.

"But did you know his mother kind of drove him and his brothers to be competitive and aggressive about every challenge?"

"Raina Camden?"

Lexie didn't think anything Micah had told her about his upbringing had been in confidence. Plus, she knew anything she told her grandmother would never go beyond the two of them. So she told Gertie how Micah was raised.

It came as a surprise to Gertie, too.

"I knew Raina had a bitter side to her," Gertie

said, describing the town's opinion of her as having a chip on her shoulder.

"So that was all she was really known for—her grudges," Lexie mused.

"It was all she ever talked about. She was a pretty woman, caught the eye of half a dozen men. But things never went past one or two dates because all she did on the dates was grouse about the bad hand she'd been dealt in life."

Micah hadn't said his mother was bitter, but the description seemed to fit.

And suddenly something gelled in Lexie's mind.

Micah's mom had been bitter because she'd held on to her grudges. Because she hadn't moved on.

And as much as Lexie recoiled from the thought, it struck her that maybe holding on to her grudge against Micah could be considered bitterness on her part...

Righteous indignation was one thing—and that was always what she'd thought she felt.

But to call it a grudge? To call what she felt bitterness? Those were things she didn't want in her life, coloring who she was and impacting her future.

And now that she had some understanding of what was behind what Micah had done?

As strange as it seemed to her, she found herself thinking that maybe it was time to let it go...

"I'm gonna get more tea—want a refill?" she

asked her grandmother, needing a moment alone with her thoughts.

"No, but if you're getting up I need my afternoon cheesy puffs," Gertie announced.

"I'll get them," Lexie promised, heading for the small apartment's kitchen, taking with her those two ugly words—*grudge* and *bitterness*—and the idea that they might be infecting her...

She definitely didn't want that.

But she also wasn't sure about *not* holding on to what the barn incident had taught her.

Micah *might* be what he claimed he was—changed and matured. But she wasn't absolutely convinced of it. And she still didn't think for a minute that she could trust him.

But what if she stayed cautious and alert while letting go of the resentment, the grudge, the bitterness?

Caution was okay, she decided. Caution wasn't a grudge. It was just learning that with some people she had to be careful. It was just learning a lesson.

On the other hand, she had come home wanting a fresh start. And how could she have a real fresh start if she didn't also work to put the barn incident behind her?

So she had to let go, she decided there and then. The same way she was working to let go of her divorce fallout, she had to let go of her resentments over what Micah had done.

"My cheesy puffs are in the cupboard next to the fridge if you can't find them," Gertie called from the living room.

"Got 'em," Lexie called back, taking the bag and her tea to return to Gertie, and feeling lighter somehow, as if a burden had been lifted from her shoulders.

"Are you getting along better with Micah?" her grandmother asked then.

"I guess you could say we're getting along better."

"*How much* better?" Gertie asked. "Because Tuesday night, Mary and I both thought—"

"We just aren't at each other's throats," Lexie insisted.

"Micah was never at your throat," Gertie pointed out.

"Okay, then I'm not at his throat anymore."

"So progress," Gertie said with satisfaction.

"Sure, I guess," Lexie conceded.

Maybe a little *too* much progress, given that Tuesday night had ended with her thinking he might be on the verge of kissing her...

And worse yet, she *might* have been feeling let down that he hadn't.

"Things are really mixed up for me right now, Gram. I just got divorced, remember?" she said to remind them both. "That throws everything off-kilter. And now I have to deal with Micah, I have to crawl out from under that divorce, I have to get my life restarted, get myself a way to make a living, get my house fixed—believe me, I've got my hands full. If you and Mary are concocting some fantasy that anything is happening between me and Micah, you should forget it because it just isn't possible. I'm in no shape for any kind of new relationship, let alone with *Micah Camden*!"

"Micah isn't a new relationship, he's an old one. And sometimes what was old can be new again..."

"Nope, not happening," Lexie said dismissively.

But secretly she had to admit that in some ways the good parts of their old relationship actually were resurfacing and bringing with them a new twist.

And what if letting go of the past and her grudge and any bitterness made way for more of that new twist? For what might have even started edging toward an attraction to Micah?

She just had to draw the line, she told herself firmly.

She could let go of the past and her grudge and any bitterness, but that was it.

A fresh start definitely didn't mean getting involved with someone from her past.

Especially not with someone from her past who she couldn't trust.

There was nothing—not one single thing—that could or would or should support or encourage an attraction. And so many reasons why an attraction had to be *dis*couraged.

Not the least of which, she told herself, was that his *crush* on her from years ago was history—proven by the fact that he *hadn't* kissed her.

Or even tried to.

So it was cut and dry—nothing was happening between them.

And nothing ever would.

Mary returned from the dentist just then, and she and Gertie tried to persuade Lexie to stay for dinner again.

But Lexie begged off, saying she needed to get home and shower and wash the sawdust out of her hair.

Which was the truth.

And the fact that the marines were leaving, that when she went home, she and Micah would once more have the place to themselves?

She assured herself that that was not a factor.

After all, she'd drawn that line between letting go and attraction.

And she wasn't going to cross it.

As expected, the marines were gone by the time Lexie got home. The side of the little house was framed and ready for a new wall.

She went in the main house's front door, expecting to find Micah inside. Instead, she found a note on the kitchen table telling her he had work to catch up on in the brewery and would be there until late.

Of course, he was behind on his work there, Lexie thought, trying to ignore the deflated feeling she had.

Then it occurred to her that working or not, he still needed to eat. And since it was the construction on her house and her grandmother's house that had put him behind at the brewery, she owed him.

Taking out her cell phone, she texted him that unless he had other plans, she would fix dinner and bring it to him.

He texted back that that sounded great and thanked her.

Lexie felt a small rush of excitement that she told herself was because she was excited to cook.

And she forced herself to believe it.

After showering and fixing her hair and makeup, she again dipped into her new wardrobe to dress, choosing a pair of white capri pants and a lacy white halter top that knotted at her left hip as well as behind her neck.

Sandals finished the look before she went downstairs.

Merritt's generosity had again left Mary and Gertie with more food than they could use so they'd sent her home on Wednesday night with plenty of groceries, including a package of raw chicken breasts, lemons and dry pasta.

Knowing there was cream in the fridge and that Gertie always kept some grated parmesan cheese on hand, too, Lexie set about making lemon chicken alfredo.

While the pasta was boiling and the chicken was sautéing, she put two salads together, made an Italian vinaigrette, baked a baguette of already half-baked bread, sliced it and then made the Alfredo sauce, too.

When everything was done, she took out two cookie sheets to use as trays, loaded them with the food and went out the back door.

She was halfway to the barn/brewery doors when it occurred to her that she could have—and should have—brought only Micah's dinner...

She hadn't said anything in her texts about eating with him. He'd probably planned only to have her bring him a sandwich or something and leave so he could eat *while* he went on working.

And instead, she'd dressed in date clothes, prepared a date-like meal and was on her way with two of everything...

She stopped in her tracks and asked herself what in the world she was doing! And why!

What had she been thinking...

She spun around to return to the house to leave behind her portion, but no sooner was her back to the barn than she heard his deep voice call to her, "Forget something?"

Her sanity? That line she wasn't going to cross?

She slowly pivoted to face the barn again, finding him standing in the open doors.

Standing there with his combat-booted feet apart, his wide shoulders and chest outlined in crisp white knit, she was struck by the undeniable proof of his masculinity. And a simmering sexiness that she did *not* want to be aware of.

Oh, yeah, she'd definitely crossed the line.

He didn't wait for her to answer his question, instead coming toward her, saying as he did, "Let me take those."

Lexie decided to opt for honesty so she said, "For some reason, I brought my dinner, too, and I just realized that I shouldn't have. I'm sure you weren't planning on company. You're probably going to eat while you work. So I was going to take my dinner back and just bring yours."

"No!" he said quickly, taking a tray in each of those big hands. "I don't want you to do that. I can take a break."

The fact that he showed no signs of annoyance did not make Lexie feel any less embarrassed.

"I don't want to bother you. I don't know what I was thinking. You have to be behind."

"But I can take a break," he repeated. "And you're not bothering me. I was glad to get your text. I've been looking forward—" He cut himself off and instead said, "Come on, I'd like you to see the brewery, anyway. Maybe have a taste of the citrus stout at this stage and see if I'm on the right track."

There didn't seem to be a graceful way to decline, so she followed him into the barn-turned-brewery.

Since all the food was covered to stay warm, Lexie opted to leave the trays on the picnic table in a rear corner of the barn, which Micah jokingly called his *break room*, and take the tour first.

The barn was original to the house, but about the only thing that remained from her recollection were the outer walls. The hay loft and stalls were gone, and the floor had been covered with concrete.

Electricity and plumbing had been added and the entire structure had been modernized and sanitized.

As Micah showed her around, he pointed out and explained the use for mash tanks, steam generators, lauter tuns, wort pumps, malt machines, heat exchangers, fermentation tanks, filter tanks, pumps, and cooling and refrigeration equipment.

He outlined his safety measures and the equipment and process for cleaning and sanitation, and told her about the gear used to both bottle and keg his finished products.

And all the while his passion for what he was doing, for the brewery itself was evident.

"Gram always made her home brew in the kitchen," Lexie said when they'd finished the tour. "I had no idea it was this involved to do it on a larger scale."

"Actually I'm a *micro*brewery so this is about as small a scale as it can be done commercially," he informed.

"Good thing it was a big barn," she joked. "And no wonder you had to take investments from your family—this is a really big endeavor."

Seeing it for herself gave Lexie a clearer picture of how serious he had to be about this. Which made it all the more noteworthy that he'd left it to work on the houses with the marines. She felt just a twinge of guilt that couldn't be diffused even by reminding herself that his forklift had done the damage in the first place.

"Before we eat…" he said then, going to one of his tanks and filling a small plastic cup from a spigot. "Taste this and tell me what you think— this is the citrus stout. I haven't done the infusion yet, so keep in mind there'll be more flavor added, but tell me if I have the right balance."

Lexie took a sip and then said, "I'm getting the orange but no tartness," she judged. "I'd say increase the lemon."

"Yeah, I thought it might be a little too sweet. Thanks for the input."

They sat across from each other at the picnic table then and settled in to eat.

He praised her cooking, and then Lexie finally had the chance to get to the news she'd been bursting to share with him.

"Yesterday, I went into the bakery and talked to Nessa Bryant," she announced.

"You did?" he said with just the amount of surprise and enthusiasm she'd hoped for.

"Your information was good—she *does* want to sell and retire." And almost the moment Lexie had stepped into the bakery, the thought of it being hers, of making a career out of it, had felt like the direction she should take. "Nessa said she's put the word out but so far no one has shown any interest—she said I was the first."

"Then there's no one to outbid you if you make an offer."

"We didn't talk price but I did ask her if she might consider carrying the loan. She was on the fence about that. She said she had to talk it over with her husband. But she also said that he still works at the bank and might be able to help me get a loan there if necessary."

"Okay, so you have two options—either she'll decide to carry the loan, or Frank will try extra hard to work it out at the bank for his wife's sake as much as yours," Micah said.

"And if your offer to let me test the market with cupcakes at the food festival is still good—"

"Absolutely," he confirmed.

"Then Nessa said I can use her pans and ovens tomorrow afternoon to make them so I get a feel for the place."

He laughed. "You've been busy. But that's great, too! It'll give you a chance to make sure everything there works the way it should. It'll give you more bargaining power on the price if you know you'll have a big equipment expense going in."

"Good point," Lexie said.

"And what about the rest of the place? I've been in there a few times since I came back but I never looked at it with an eye for making it my business. Did you have any thoughts about what you'd keep the same and what you'd change?"

That she had considered. And as they ate, she told him that the display cases were old but that she thought refinishing them would improve them while keeping their vintage coziness. That she would want to replace the tables and chairs, maybe expand the seating area by making the display windows into window seats because she didn't like Nessa's idea of putting baked goods there and exposing them to the sun and heat.

As for the menu, she'd studied what Nessa was

selling and thought about what she would want to continue to offer, what she might want to omit, what she might want to add.

She went on and on with the thoughts that had been racing through her mind since the day before and Micah listened to it all, making comments, suggestions, encouraging her and showing an interest she hadn't even garnered from Gertie.

"Okay, I'll stop," she said when she realized they'd both finished eating. "I've just gotten really excited about this since yesterday. When I walked in there, it felt meant to be for me."

"I get it. And I'm happy that something has you so inspired. Plus, you know I'm going to take the credit for telling you about Nessa wanting to sell out in the first place," he joked.

"You get full credit for it," she granted. "And thanks for paying enough attention to figure out I might like to own a bakery. And for taking me seriously."

"I didn't really do anything other than listen— to the gossip about Nessa selling and to you talking about enjoying baking. That's not such a big deal," he replied, balking at her gratitude. "Taking you seriously isn't something you need to thank me for, either," he said with a slight frown that showed some confusion.

"You'd be wrong—it is all a big deal. To me, at

least," she said, thinking about her marriage—and about her relationship with Jason overall.

Which led her to something she'd been wondering about since Micah's candor about his adolescent feelings for her. "Did Jason know about your crush all those years ago?" she asked.

"Well…" Micah hedged. "We didn't talk about it. I didn't confess to him or anything. But early on, we were racing to see who could get to you first to walk to the bus stop with you and he'd gloat whenever he won, so that seems like he knew I had the same intentions. In middle school and high school, we had a couple of tussles over you and I being partners in some school projects—he got in my face, said I'd better not forget that you were his. I don't know if he realized feelings were involved or not—he might have just seen it as us competing to be alpha dog…" Micah paused, then said, "But how did we get from being happy about you maybe buying the bakery to *that*?"

"Our talk on Tuesday night just got me to thinking… Jason and my relationship didn't stay the way it started out—the way it was for all those years we were here—"

"And you're wondering if I might have been a factor?"

"Yes. Would he have wanted me the way he did if he hadn't been determined to win out over you?"

"You think the only reason he wanted you was

because he suspected that I did? I don't believe that," Micah said dismissively.

"I don't know... Things between us changed so much after we left here."

"Did things change right away when you left?" Micah asked.

"It wasn't drastic at first, but yes, a little," she said, really thinking about the timeline. "Before we left Merritt, I basically always called the shots—"

"Yeah, I gave him a hard time about that—he followed you around like a puppy. Jill said he was just devoted to you."

"Well, that *definitely* changed," she muttered. "I guess the first time Jason did something that I wasn't on board with was when he dropped out of college six weeks in—he said he needed a break from school, that he'd rather work full-time, save more money for our year of travel, then get his degree when we came back, while I worked."

"That's what you weren't on board with?"

"I would have rather he stuck with our original plan, but his idea sounded reasonable so I went along with it."

"But then you didn't stick college out, either," Micah probed.

"No, I didn't. When my folks were killed, I was a wreck. I just... We were still living here while I commuted to Northbridge for freshman year and Jason worked at the lumbermill, and I wanted to get away from the memories. So when Jason suggested we leave, do our year of travel and then worry about college later—"

"I kind of thought losing your folks was why you took off," Micah contributed.

"It was, at least partially. But once we left," she continued, "what I wanted began to take a real back seat. At first it wasn't as obvious because Jason had already mapped out where we should go, so we just followed that plan—"

"But once you reached the end of that? Of your *year of travel*?"

"That was when we were supposed to come home and go back to college."

"And Jason wasn't ready to do that yet?" Micah said.

"He wasn't. But neither was I…" She sighed. "I still just couldn't deal with the thought of coming back to the memories. So the idea of another year of being footloose and fancy-free—as Jason presented it—of still living day to day and seeing some of the states the way we'd seen Europe… That had more appeal."

"So you went with what Jason wanted because it was basically what you wanted, too."

"Right. But the thing was, I thought I'd have more input on the plan for that."

"And you didn't?"

"He blew off pretty much everything I suggested."

"I can't imagine him blowing off anything with you."

"Like I said, things changed."

"And you didn't put up a fight?" Micah said as if he couldn't believe that.

"I know," Lexie agreed, "it seems strange. I never had any problem speaking up for myself before. But losing my parents left me...I don't know, really vulnerable-feeling, I guess. I had this overwhelming sense that Jason was going to be *it* for me when it came to family... That I'd better make things with him work—that I had to make him happy."

"So you let him call the shots."

It was something she regretted now. Something that had cost her too many years away from her grandmother, away from Merritt and Jill, traveling on an endless journey she wasn't even enjoying because by then Jason had completely stopped taking what she wanted into consideration, and had merely expected her to go on following forever.

"How long were you okay doing what he wanted?" Micah asked.

"Not long," she admitted. "When I could think of my parents again without being miserable, when I started wanting to come home, problems started between us."

"Because Jason still didn't want to come back."

"No. And by then he'd been *in charge* long enough that what I wanted didn't interest him."

"It didn't matter at all?" Micah asked with surprise.

"Things really had changed," she reiterated. "There was a lot of fighting, especially every time I'd say I wanted to come home and settle down—"

"And he never did."

"Nope. And every time I'd just cave," she confessed, feeling the frustrations and anger she'd felt each time.

"That doesn't sound like you, either."

"We were *married*. I kept telling myself that marriages have to have compromise, patience. Jason would swear that he only wanted a little more time away, I'd worry about what it might mean if I *did* push him—"

"And so you'd decide to just do what he wanted again."

Another shrug.

"But here you are without him…"

"Alaska," she said. "That's where we were last winter."

"Winter in Alaska? Don't people go to warmer climates for the winter?"

"Jason thought it would be an interesting experience and I couldn't persuade him otherwise. By that point, it felt as if he deliberately chose to do the opposite of whatever I wanted."

"To prove he had the power? The control?"

"Probably. I was getting too tired of everything—of him—to really care why," Lexie admitted quietly.

"But you went to Alaska."

"Maybe I really needed an extreme to finally get me to face what I needed to face. So we went to Alaska last October. By Christmas, I told Jason that was it for me. I missed Gram, I wasn't spending any more of the time I could be having with her away. I said that after the holidays I was moving back home, with or without him."

"I want to say *finally* but I don't want to make you mad," Micah said cautiously.

"*Finally* is actually fitting. The relationship had been too one-sided for too long and I was *finally* taking back what I'd given over to him."

Micah nodded knowingly, somberly. "One-sided decision-making doesn't work," he said as if he knew it firsthand. But rather than expand on that he encouraged her to go on. "But again, here you are alone…divorced…"

"When I told Jason, he thought he had a bargaining chip—we were both working at a hotel in Anchorage—me in the restaurant, him at the front desk. He told me he'd been having an affair with the concierge—"

"*That* was a bargaining chip?"

"He said he'd break it off and we could move again, but if he did that for me, I had to agree not to move back to Merritt."

"Oh, jeez," Micah said in disbelief.

"That was when I realized just how little I really had come to mean to him… And frankly, how little I cared about being with him anymore. No matter the place."

"Wow. I just can't picture it going so wrong…" Micah marveled.

"Because the relationship was so different before, when he wanted to beat you by being with me," she said, returning to what had begun this. "Now I have to wonder how much of a part the competition between the two of you played in our relationship—whether it would have happened at all if he hadn't been so intent on *winning*."

Micah's only response was a questioning arch of his eyebrows.

"I just have to wonder," she went on, "if the competition hadn't been at play, would he have tried so hard with me in middle school or high school, would he have put so much effort into pleasing me or would he have shown his true colors—because that's what I think really came out after we left town."

"I'm sorry if that was the case," Micah said, sounding genuinely contrite. "But one way or another, Jason didn't have the right to run you around the way he did, to cheat on you."

Micah reached across the table and covered her hand with his. "As far as I'm concerned, cheating is a lowlife move no matter what. But if it makes you feel better to blame me and the competition—"

That actually caused her to laugh. "You'll just be the catch-all for every lousy thing that's happened?"

He shrugged those glorious shoulders that did look broad and strong enough to bear the weight.

"No, you don't get the blame for Jason's bad behavior. He can carry that on his own," she said, trying not to nestle her hand even deeper into Micah's.

He squeezed and then let go, retrieving his hand as if he weren't sure if *he* might have crossed a line by touching her.

"So if that all happened at Christmas, why did you stay in Alaska through the rest of the winter?" he asked.

"I didn't want being in different states to complicate—or delay—the divorce. Because I stayed and did it there, and because we didn't have any property to divide, it only took thirty days. Once it was over, though, I still couldn't leave right away. I'd gotten to be friends with my boss, Lily. She'd helped me through the whole thing and had three waitresses going out on maternity leave, so I didn't want to jump ship when she needed me most. But I was set to come home two weeks from when Mary called about Gram."

"I'm sorry, Lexie, that it all went the way it did," Micah said then. "I'm sorry you got hurt—I never would have thought you were in line for that with Jason."

"I never would have thought that, either."

It struck Lexie then that she'd been talking for much longer than she'd intended.

"I didn't mean to keep you from your work so long!" she said, standing up and beginning to reload the cookie sheets with the remnants of their dinner.

"No complaints," he said. "As far as I'm concerned, you can stay all night—I'd be happy for the company..."

She was sure he was just being nice.

"No, I'll get out of here and let you go back to what you need to be doing."

But once the cookie sheets were reloaded, Micah reached for them before she could, picking up both of them. "I'll carry these over to the house, help you clean up."

"I cleaned as I cooked so there are only these few dishes. I'll take care of them. And I can carry—"

"Come on," was all he said as he headed out of the brewery.

On the way across the yard, he nodded in the direction of the newly framed wall. "You haven't told me what you think about the work on the houses."

"It looks good," she said, still fighting embarrassment for having overshared and eaten up his evening.

When they got to the house, she moved in front of him to open the door, holding it for him and then following him into the kitchen.

"Were we too rowdy last night?" he asked as he set the trays near the kitchen sink. "Did we keep you up?"

Why did it sound as if he were just searching for an excuse to linger? Surely he'd already lost more time than he should have and needed—wanted—to get back. Didn't he?

But he'd asked questions it would be rude to ignore, so she said, "No, you didn't bother me." And she could have left it at that. But since he propped a hip against the edge of the counter and seemed in no hurry to leave, she did the same thing, facing him, and said, "It seemed like you had a good time. Are you friends with all those guys?"

"Some of them. Some I just met when they got here."

"I would never have guessed that—I thought you were all buddies. It *looked* like you were..."

"We're all vets. Most of that crew were marines but the branch of service doesn't matter. The military is a brotherhood—there's a bond even among strangers who have served."

Seeing what she'd seen had left her curious. "You were so...one of the guys. So relaxed. Years ago, you were constantly horsing around, wrestling, playing keep-away, elbowing your way to the front of lines, vying for something or another—"

"That was the whole competing thing," he said.

"But from what I saw last night, you weren't anything like that," she observed, recalling the comradery she'd witnessed. "You're so much more calm now. Comfortable in your own skin—or at least that's how it seems..." Strong, confident, certain of his own power. It was all different from the Micah she remembered—but it was also potently attractive, especially for the way it made her consider more seriously the idea that he really might have changed.

"It's like you don't have anything to prove anymore," she said.

"I have to prove I can make good beer," he responded with a laugh, stretching his right arm out to lay his hand on the countertop not far from where she was. Then he returned to the subject of the repairs. "It looks like most of the crew will be able to come back for another two days next week to get the walls up. We'll be tarp-free when that happens."

So more days when he'd be otherwise occupied, when she would barely see him, when they wouldn't have evenings like this one...

Lexie nodded, reminding herself that she and Gertie needed the work done. That mattered much more than the ridiculous internal voice saying that she'd missed him...

"Can you spare more time away from the brewery?" she asked.

"Can or can't, I will," he said. "I promised you and Gertie I'd get this mess fixed as soon as possible. Besides, it's to my benefit to make sure everything is up to code so we don't have any problems with the inspections."

She nodded a second time and something else occurred to her suddenly—if the houses were securely walled again, there wouldn't be a need for him to stay in the sunroom...

And that thought didn't sit well, either.

Although it certainly *should* have.

"I suppose when the walls are up, you'll be able to go home..." she said, testing the waters.

He grinned a mischievous grin that made his blue eyes sparkle as they stayed raptly on her. "Will you be sorry to see me go?" he joked.

He was obviously kidding—but that didn't make it any less true. She didn't know how or when it had happened, but she didn't want him to go.

"I might be just a little sorry..." she heard herself admit before she realized she was going to. Then backtracking, she added, "I've never stayed out here—in the country, at the farm—alone."

"If it helps, I can stay," he offered. "It's easier for me to be closer to the brewery."

"Then you could make up a little of the time you lose working on the houses," she reasoned, even though she knew, knew, knew that she should be eager for him to go.

He seemed as surprised by her words as she was herself, looking at her so intently, so quizzically.

"Are we on better terms than we were?" he asked her flat out.

They'd been on horrible terms before. Admitting to a small improvement didn't seem too bad. It didn't mean she had to admit to the attraction that was becoming harder and harder for her to deny.

So she said, "Maybe. A little."

His well-sculpted face erupted in a smile that was pleased, relieved and oh-so-sexy.

Damn him...

"Are we friends again?" he asked.

"I don't know if I'd go that far."

He didn't seem to buy that phony aloofness because his smile turned into a devilish grin. "Okay..." he said, with mock confusion. "Then what are we?"

Good question...

"I don't know," Lexie answered.

She also didn't know why her voice had gone

quiet. Or why she kept looking up into those mesmerizing ultra-blue eyes.

"Maybe we're getting to be more than friends..." Micah suggested, his deep voice almost a whisper.

She knew she should stomp on that idea before it sprouted any roots.

But somewhere along the way he'd come closer and all she could think about was Tuesday night when she'd been half ready for him to kiss her.

Tuesday night when he hadn't, and she'd come away disappointed.

She'd been thinking about him kissing her almost every minute since then.

Wondering what it might have been like. What it might *be* like.

Wanting to know despite every argument she'd had with herself against it...

Now he was leaning in by infinitesimal increments. So slowly that there was lots of opportunity for her to call a halt to it or back up.

But there she was, holding her ground. Almost daring him to do it.

This guy who she knew never turned down a dare...

His mouth was so near hers. So near but not touching—yet.

And she couldn't take it anymore.

Without another thought, she kissed him.

A little laugh rumbled in his throat just before he took over, kissing her for the first time.

And whoa, what a kiss!

Never had she been kissed like that.

There was special talent in those amazingly adept lips. Lips that met hers with just the right amount of pressure and command, just the right amount of softness and allure, parted just enough to entice and tempt and promise more.

That big hand that had been resting on the counter rose to the back of her head. His long fingers combed through her hair, pulling her just slightly closer. It felt so good that there was just no way Lexie could keep from losing herself in it all.

She kissed him back with a kind of hunger she'd never experienced with her ex. A kind of hunger she hadn't known she was capable of feeling.

Which was a bit alarming.

And a little voice in the back of her mind suddenly shrieked, *What are you doing?*

This is Micah Camden!

This can't happen!

This has to stop!

And yet it went on for a few moments longer because she just couldn't bring herself to end a kiss that good.

Until she finally forced herself to, pulling out of it.

"We can't do this," she muttered, hating that she sounded so breathless.

"We can't?" he challenged.

"No," she said firmly, offering no reason but finally looking him in the eye again to meet his challenge.

His eyebrows rose once more as if he were tempted to argue. But he didn't.

"Okay," he said.

He took his hand from behind her head and stepped back. But he went on looking at her.

Then, as if hoping she would argue, he said, "I better get to work."

Lexie confirmed that with another nod.

Still, he studied her face for a moment more before what looked like marine discipline came over him and he was suddenly all business.

And for some reason she was sorry to see that.

"Text me how much stout you need for your cupcakes and I'll bring it over so you'll have it to take with you to the bakery tomorrow," he said.

She'd forgotten about that. "Oh...sure... I'll need to increase the recipe. Once I do the math, I'll let you know."

"It'll be in the fridge," he promised, his gaze staying with her another minute before he broke the connection, turned and went out the back door.

As she watched him go, Lexie told herself that

she hadn't just crossed the line, she'd leaped over it. Bounded over it. Left it far behind.

And she shouldn't have.

You can't let that ever happen again, she warned herself, going over in her mind all the reasons why—she was only months out of her marriage; this was *Micah* and even if she'd let go of old resentments for the barn incident, she still shouldn't trust him; she needed all of her focus and energy put into her fresh start before she even contemplated getting into a relationship again.

But no matter how much she tried, she couldn't wipe away the memory of that kiss.

And she also couldn't deny how very—very—much she'd liked it...

Chapter Seven

"Oh, man, that's good beer!"

"That's what I'm going for," Micah said, pleased with his brother Tanner's praise for the bottle of oat stout he'd offered when Tanner came to the brewery Friday afternoon.

Micah had shown his younger brother around and—like the night before with Lexie—they'd ended up sitting at the picnic table together.

"How did you do all this in just the six months since you resigned your commission?" Tanner asked with some amazement.

"Workin' day and night," Micah confirmed. "But you know I've been experimenting with the hops and the beer itself for years. This has all just been putting everything into play on a bigger scale."

"And you're launching at the food festival tomorrow night—I'm impressed," Tanner said.

"I don't know if the food festival can be called a launch, but it will be the first time the three plain stouts will be for sale. Once I get the flavored stouts right, the Denver cousins will give me a real launch with the plain stouts in the Camden Superstores."

"I had a layover in Denver on my way here, spent the night at GiGi's house. She had a big family dinner and everybody was talking about you and your beer. They're all excited about it."

"Nice," Micah said before solemnly adding, "I hope to God I don't disappoint them."

For years, their mother's resentment of the Denver Camdens had kept them away from their cousins. Their grandfather had never given up lobbying for a connection, though. Ben had finally struck pay dirt when he'd pointed out that if her sons had a relationship with their successful cousins, the drive for all that success might inspire them to work even harder. Raina had seen some logic in that and had finally conceded.

As a result, when Micah and the triplets were just entering their teens, they'd begun the ritual of long summer visits with the Denver cousins. During those annual trips, they'd forged strong family ties with all ten of their cousins, and had also grown fond of the cousins' grandmother, GiGi. In fact, they'd come to think of GiGi Camden as a surrogate grandmother.

Tanner took another drink of his beer, then said, "They won't be disappointed with this."

"I'll send a case home with you—Pops likes the rye stout better so I keep him stocked in that." Micah paused and then segued into what he and their grandfather were curious about. "Shall I send you with two cases? Will you be around long enough to drink more?"

Tanner stared at the label on the bottle in his hand. "I don't know," he said. His tone made it clear that something was weighing on him.

"How long is your leave?"

"I have thirty days coming, if I need to take them."

"If you *need* to take them…"

Tanner didn't say anything to that.

Micah decided to push his brother a little to see if he could get to the bottom of whatever was on Tanner's mind. "Are you okay?"

"I'm fine," Tanner assured him.

"But you *needed* to take a leave and come all the way here?"

To Micah's frustration, Tanner dodged the question, saying, "You've been home six months—what do you know about Della Markham?"

Micah hadn't expected that. "Your old high school sweetheart? I know she died two months ago in childbirth—even though I hadn't realized that still happened these days outside of third world countries."

The rarity of it had caused it to be widely talked about around town. That was the only reason he'd really been aware of it.

But why would that have brought Tanner home on sudden leave?

"I met your old buddy Nate McAdams in a bar a couple of weeks ago," Tanner said then.

Micah nodded his understanding. Nate had become an architect like his dad. He worked out of the office in Merritt, but Micah had heard that most of their business was somewhere else.

"He was in Iran building a house for a sheikh, if you can believe it," Tanner continued. "We had a drink. He was telling me all the news from Merritt. The news about Della was the biggest."

Big enough to bring Tanner home?

"Had you kept in contact with Della all these years? Even after..." After the enormous ruckus she'd caused that had almost derailed Tanner's whole future?

"No, but I did run into her when I was home last time. We had coffee," Tanner admitted. "What do you know about the baby? About the father of the baby?"

"Nothing much," Micah answered. "I've been deep into getting the brewery up and running. Della dying when she gave birth was the first time I'd heard anything about her since I got back. That was...I don't know, I guess two months ago? Part of the gossip was about how nobody knew who the father was. I guess she'd kept it under wraps the whole time she was pregnant. People were figuring the father was married."

"That *would* make sense..." Tanner said, sounding surprised. "But nobody stepped up—married or not—to claim the baby?"

"No. Actually that was what made folks believe it *was* a married man who was hiding the affair—and that he figured he could keep his wife from ever knowing what he'd done as long as he kept his mouth shut."

"McAdams said Della's sister took it?"

"If I'm remembering right, *it* was a girl, and yeah, I heard something about a sister taking her... I didn't even remember there *was* a sister," Micah said.

"Addie. She was a lot younger," Tanner informed. "I think she was like...eleven or twelve when Della and I graduated..."

"But grown up now so she could take on her niece," Micah concluded.

"McAdams said she's still in town. With the baby."

Micah shrugged. "I honestly don't know anything about that. The only thing I know for sure is that Della died. The rest is just what I recall hearing—but I can't claim I was listening all that closely," Micah said, his curiosity about Tanner's interest only getting bigger by the minute. "You want to tell me why any of it matters to you?" he ventured, finally being direct.

"No," his brother answered flatly.

Micah wondered if it was possible that Tanner had retained a soft spot for his old girlfriend. Maybe he'd come home to pay respects, maybe to make sure the infant she'd left behind was cared for.

Or maybe there was more going on than his brother was telling him.

Part of Micah wanted to force the information out of Tanner, the way he would have when they were kids.

But they were both grown men now.

And how could Micah fault his brother for not wanting to share when Micah also didn't want to talk about what was on his own mind today?

So all he said was, "I'm here for you, if there's anything I can do."

"Thanks," Tanner said. Then he changed the topic with a nod in the direction of Gertie's house.

"How about you? How are you doin' over here with Lexie after everything?"

The triplets had only been a year behind Micah in school so they'd known the whole barn story—including all the fallout.

"It started out bad," Micah answered honestly.

"I'm not surprised. She really had it in for you."

"Not without cause."

"Yeah, what you did was pretty uncool," Tanner said with a sympathetic laugh. "But you wanted her like nothing I've ever seen and you know how we were raised…"

"Definitely not cool." All the way around.

"And now Pops says you did that damage to the houses?"

"Not personally, but yeah, it happened because of me…"

"That couldn't have helped things."

"Nope."

"So she still wants your head on a platter?" The amusement Tanner found in that idea seemed to lighten his own concerns.

"I think things are smoothing out." Although he didn't know if that kiss the night before might have roughed them up again. Especially since she'd left this morning before he'd had the chance to see her or talk to her.

"How smooth are they getting?" his brother asked with a hint of innuendo.

"Not *that* smooth," Micah shot back. "We've had some good talks. She's pinch-hitting for Gertie while Gertie is laid up, helping me get the levels right in the flavored stouts. I steered her toward maybe buying the bakery from Nessa Bryant and offered to share my booth at the food festival with her—she's making cupcakes with my stout in them to see what kind of reception her stuff gets. I'd say that we're not doing too bad. But the past casts a shadow..."

To Micah that had all sounded neutral but it seemed to spark some instinct in Tanner because he said more solemnly, "You got over her, didn't you? I mean, there's been a steady stream of the female persuasion in your life—most recently Adrianna, right? That was even serious. It isn't as if you've been carrying a torch or something. Or have you been hiding it all this time?"

"You've just shown up here out of the blue because of your old girlfriend—I could ask you the same thing," Micah countered.

His brother got the message to let the subject drop. "Fair enough," he said with a slight laugh, backing off much the way Micah had with him. "If there's anything *I* can do..." he returned the offer.

"Thanks."

Tanner finished his stout and set the bottle on the table. Then he pushed himself to his feet. "Big Ben sent me with a list of errands to run in town.

You have any you need me to handle while I'm there?"

Micah didn't.

"Then I better get going. Thanks for the beer. And don't forget my case."

Micah got up, went to the cooler and returned with the promised supply of stout.

"I'll let you know if and when I need another," his brother said. "It's good stuff, might be sooner rather than later."

"Just holler."

He walked his brother to the barn door where they said goodbye.

Micah should have returned to work then. But instead, he leaned a shoulder against the door frame, staring at the back of Gertie's house long after Tanner had driven away.

Catching a glimpse of Lexie was usually the reason he looked over at the house, but he knew she was gone. Right now, it was just that she was on his mind. On top of the bigger issue that was dogging him today.

He *had* gotten over her—that was the answer to Tanner's question. He had *not* been carrying a torch for her.

It hadn't happened instantly, back in high school. But it *had* happened. Time, growing up, moving on to other things, other attractions, other relationships, had all taken care of it.

Sure, he'd thought about her here and there but it hadn't been to pine for her, but to grapple with his shame for what he'd done. Shame that, it turned out, was a fairly decent antidote for a crush.

What his brother hadn't guessed was that something new had begun since her return. Something more than a crush. Yes, he was back to thinking about her all the time, noticing every detail, wanting to be with her. All that was just the same as it had been when they were kids.

But there was also something that went beyond the schoolboy crush to something deeper in him. Something that was getting increasingly harder to fight. Something that was even defeating the marine discipline that had become fundamental to him.

It was why he'd nearly kissed her on Tuesday night. It was why he'd been on the verge of kissing her last night.

And the fact that it had actually been Lexie who had kissed him when he'd been trying to talk himself out of kissing her?

That sure as hell hadn't helped matters. In fact, the surprise of that had sapped all the fight out of him.

She'd kissed *him*...

And he couldn't stop wondering why. Could it be that something was coming to life in her, too?

If there might actually be something *mutual* happening this time…

That was a dangerous thought.

Especially when he knew what he was dealing with.

She was half a step out of a marriage. A marriage to her first love. The only person—as far as he knew—who she'd ever kissed before, who she'd ever been with.

To kiss him now, at her own instigation, shouted *rebound* to him. It seemed all too likely that she was experimenting just to see what it was like to kiss someone else—*anyone* else.

So she'd kissed him.

But probably only because he'd been there at the time. And because he'd been inviting it.

Rebounding, testing her wings, experimenting—that was basic and superficial. That was Lexie going backward to do what most everyone did in their teens, what she hadn't done because she'd coupled with Jason when they were both kids and hadn't uncoupled until just now. That was Lexie needing to try everything she should have tried long ago.

Yeah, that had to be what it was.

And as much as he would have liked to convince himself there was more to it, he couldn't let himself get carried away. Instead, he had to keep his wits about him. Keep from reading more into anything she did than was really there.

The bottom line, he decided, was that they were once again on different pages.

Years ago, he'd been obsessed with her and she'd seen him simply as a friend.

Now she saw him as someone to practice on to get her feet wet again, while he was afraid that one flip of a switch and he could be into more serious feelings for her.

But only a fool would let himself fall for a woman who had no intention of loving him back.

And he wasn't a fool.

But damn if it wouldn't have been a whole lot easier if she *hadn't* kissed him last night.

Because as much as he'd wanted to kiss her, he'd never expected kissing her to be like that.

Kissing her had been better than he'd ever imagined—and he'd imagined it a *lot*.

It had knocked him for a loop more than kissing anyone ever had.

But he needed to keep his feet firmly planted on the ground.

The last time he'd been knocked for a loop was painfully vivid in his mind, and the memory of it had been tormenting him since he'd opened his eyes to this particular day.

So he was going to take a giant step back from Lexie, he decided. Yes, they were living in the same house and he needed her to help with his flavored stouts, but mentally, emotionally, he was withdrawing.

Back to where he hadn't lost sight of the true nature of things between them.

Back to where he hadn't been thinking about her every minute—or at all.

Back to where he wasn't haunted by the image of her.

Back to where kissing her wasn't so much a thought, let alone an option.

Romance between them just wasn't meant to be. He'd accepted that once. He was accepting it again now.

Regardless of how incredible that kiss had been.

And never was there a better day than this to remind him that good did not come out of the shadows cast by his own self-absorption. Not with Lexie. Not with Adrianna.

"So open your eyes and keep them open," he muttered to himself, determined to stop playing with fire when it came to Lexie.

"Hi..."

It was after ten o'clock by the time Lexie got home Friday night. When she went in, she found Micah sitting at the kitchen table.

His elbows and forearms were on the oak top, both big hands wrapped around a bottle of beer, and he was staring at that bottle, so lost in his own thoughts that he didn't seem to have heard her entrance.

Her greeting was tentative, since she was uncertain about disturbing him.

His head yanked up in surprise at her voice, and he turned in her direction as he sat straighter in the chair. "Hi," he said in response. "You're just getting home?"

"I am," she answered.

"Long day or did you go to see Gertie tonight?" he asked, pivoting in the chair to face her.

"I saw Gram before I went to the bakery this morning."

"How's she doing?"

"She feels good, and she and Mary always have something going on—this afternoon it was quilting and tonight it was a potluck supper at the apartment."

Micah nodded but didn't say anything.

Something seemed off with him. Ordinarily he gave the impression of having the strength and energy of ten men.

But tonight, he seemed drained in a way she'd never seen before.

Maybe he was tired? Or sick? Or had gotten some bad news?

"Are you okay?" she asked.

"Sure," he answered listlessly. "Are you?"

"I am," she said a second time, determinedly

cheerful. But thinking about ill-health, she said, "Did you know that Nessa decided to retire and sell the bakery because she's not well?"

Micah shook his head.

"When I got there today, she was in bad shape—I guess she has arthritis in her hands and knees. Neither of the girls who work for her were scheduled or could come in on short notice so I offered to run things."

"Did she let you?"

"She did—I think she was so miserable she just wanted to go home."

"So you ran the bakery today?" he said with a faint hint of his usual excitement.

"I did. But since I was on my own that meant I couldn't really do anything but prep for my cupcakes between customers. I couldn't mix or bake until after closing so I had to stay late."

He chuckled half-heartedly. "Welcome to owning your own business. Did it change your mind about buying her out?"

"No. It was a good day, just a long one. And it let me know that business is booming."

"Great," he said as if he were trying—and failing—to rally.

Maybe he'd had a bad day?

"How was your day?" she asked, fishing.

"Fine. I did the citrus infusion…maybe tomorrow you can give it a taste?"

"I can taste it now if you want."

"Yeah, I was going to bring a sample but then I forgot and everything is closed up now... So tomorrow?"

"Sure," Lexie said, more certain than ever that something was on his mind if he'd been distracted from his beer making.

She held up the pink bakery box she'd brought in with her and said, "Nessa said I could leave my cupcakes there—it'll be easier to get them from the bakery to the festival tomorrow—but I brought a few home. I thought you might want to try one..."

"I do. But I worked until about half an hour ago, too. I should probably eat something else first. Did you have dinner?"

"No time. I was going to make a sandwich now. How about I make two?" she suggested.

"I should shower..." he said, sounding unenthused about moving.

"Okay, shower while I make sandwiches. And it's stuffy in here and I was cooped up all day and night—how about if we eat outside?"

"Yeah, sure, whatever you want..." Another lackluster response before he got up and left.

Instantly, Lexie began to worry that his dark mood was because of that kiss last night.

Had she misread the signs? Maybe he hadn't been about to kiss her. And if that were the case and she'd just jumped him...

Maybe he was struggling with the need to tell her she shouldn't have. To tell her that that wasn't something he wanted. To tell her never to do that again.

Oh, that would be awkward and so, so embarrassing...

That kiss had been on her mind all day.

It had been so incredibly good.

And bad...

Bad for her peace of mind, that is. The kiss itself had been so good she just wanted to do it again.

No, she didn't *just* want to do it again; she'd been itching to do it again. Craving it. Wondering desperately if there was any chance of doing it again.

But on the other hand, she knew she shouldn't be fixated on repeating something she'd already decided could *not* happen a second time. Something that never should have happened a first time.

And yet no matter how often she'd reminded herself *why* it shouldn't have happened and couldn't happen again, she'd kept circling around to that yearning for more.

Only now was she realizing that she might have made a huge faux pas. That Micah might not have wanted to kiss her. That she might have come home to find him struggling to find a way to tell her...

She wanted to slink away into the night.

But what good would that do? She would still have to face him eventually. And if he needed to talk to her about it, better to get it over with.

Maybe she should beat him to the punch. Tell him it should never have happened. Maybe apologize? Assure him it would never happen again. Would it be less awkward and uncomfortable if she said it than if he did?

Since she'd been the one to kiss him, she thought it should come from her. So as she gathered the ingredients and began to make two sandwiches, she started to rehearse in her mind what to say, how to say it.

She couldn't come up with any way that didn't seem humiliating.

What had she thought—that just because he'd had a crush on her when they were kids that he still wanted her now? Had she only imagined that he'd been moving in to kiss her? Was that just what she'd needed to think because she'd wanted so badly to kiss him?

Was she just completely clueless when it came to this whole being single thing?

There was no question about it—she was definitely clueless when it came to that.

But still...

Yes, she'd ended up initiating that kiss but the minute she had, he'd run with it—she hadn't imagined that! She hadn't imagined his hand in her hair, holding her to the kiss that *he* had escalated.

Then it occurred to her that just because she'd been immersed in thoughts of that kiss since it happened didn't mean it had been a big deal to him.

In fact, there was no reason to think it had meant anything to him at all...

But if he wasn't bothered by that kiss, then what was wrong with him tonight?

By the time she'd finished making the sandwiches, put them on plates with chips on the side and loaded a cookie sheet to use as a tray again, she didn't know what to do.

Once she'd carried everything outside, she had two options for where they should eat—at the picnic table again or at the more intimate firepit...

Picnic table, she told herself.

But the semi-circular sofa was so much more inviting and comfy...

Long day, she deserved comfy...

So to the firepit she went, leaving it covered so it could act as the table for their food.

With her mind still spinning, Lexie sat just off-center on the outdoor sofa, settling in place a moment before Micah came out.

"This is nice," he commented as he joined her, sitting close by because the small sofa only provided so much room.

She could smell the clean scent of his soap but she tried not to like it.

He was dressed in his gray sweats. His hair was still damp. And his scruff of beard was freshly trimmed. But there was still a solemn air about him even though he smiled and thanked her for making the sandwiches.

So when they'd both taken their plates on their laps and settled into eating, Lexie decided to do more probing and said, "Did something go wrong with your flavored stouts?"

"No, why?" he asked, sounding surprised.

She finally chose to just be blunt. "I'm trying to figure out what's going on tonight. Since I got back to Merritt, you've been...I don't know...gung ho, upbeat, full steam ahead. But tonight, you look like you lost your best friend..."

"Do I? I'm sorry, I didn't mean to be a drag."

"You don't have to be sorry. I'm just wondering what's wrong. Have you had bad news?"

"Nah," he said, taking a bite of his sandwich.

"I don't mean to pry. Is it something you don't want to talk about?" she asked because he didn't offer more than that.

He seemed to use the time it took to eat his bite to consider that, following it up with a swig of the beer he'd brought out with him.

Then, rather than setting the bottle down he raised it in what appeared to be a mock toast and said, "Today is the day I could have become a father. And I've been carrying that thought around with me since I woke up this morning. I guess it's got me down. That thought and the reason for why I'm not." He took another mouthful of beer.

Lexie was so stunned she nearly choked. Sputtering, she pressed a hand to her sternum and took a drink of water.

"Are you all right?" he asked.

She nodded but bought herself another moment by drinking more water.

As she did, she recalled a comment Micah had made several days ago that had seemed odd to her at the time.

After her day with Jill's family, she'd joked about it not seeming like they were all old enough to have kids. She remembered that there had been an unusual seriousness to his confirmation that they were. Was this part of that?

She was too startled to do anything more than repeat what he'd said. "Today is the day you could have become a *father*?"

"It was the due date."

Still stunned, it struck Lexie that since she'd returned to their home town her thoughts about Micah had revolved around their issues—the barn scandal of their past, her anger over the damage to the houses, even her jealousy over his closeness to Gertie.

Nowhere in any of it had she considered his personal life. The *women* in his life.

But, of course, there had been women in his life. Look at him—there were probably hordes of them clamoring after him. And for all she knew, there could be one special woman he was involved with right now. Someone she just hadn't crossed paths with yet...

Lexie drank more water as if it might wash away the weird feelings that were rising in her at the thought of Micah and another woman.

Weird feelings that seemed like jealousy...

It was all very confusing...

"Were you married? *Are* you married?" Lexie said, trying to sort through things. Given how little she'd kept up with his life, anything was possible.

"Am I *married*? Do you think if I was married that wouldn't have come up by now?"

"I don't know. It just this minute occurred to me that I haven't thought about you and...*women*..."

A bemused frown came across his handsome face.

"I know, it doesn't make sense," Lexie said in response. "I know there have to have been women in your life. I just...haven't thought about it..."

"There *have* been women in my life."

"A lot of them?" she heard herself ask.

"My fair share."

"Women you were serious about?"

He didn't answer that in any hurry. Then he said, "I have only been serious about the Marines and getting my brewery built."

"Were there women who were serious about you?" she asked, taking a different tack.

"I was always up-front with anybody I started to see more than a time or two. I made it clear that as long as I was a marine and until I had my brewery up and running, I wasn't interested in anything long-term. I didn't want to mislead anyone."

Lexie knew that was his way of saying he'd learned his lesson with the barn incident and changed his ways.

"But yeah, there were a couple of women who started thinking they could change my mind."

"Was the woman who got pregnant one of them?"

"I'm not sure," he said with another frown, this one dark. "I didn't think so but... I don't know..." He sighed. "Her name is Adrianna. She's a nurse I met when a buddy got hurt in a training maneuver. She worked in the veterans hospital in San Diego, so she understood what it was like to get hooked up with somebody in the military. She was patient about deployments, missions, assignments. And she had her career to concentrate on, so she didn't want anything serious, either."

"How long were you together?"

"*Together...*" he parroted. "Kind of hard to call it that when one person is stationary and the other is just in and out... We started seeing each other about...I don't know, I guess about two years ago."

"Exclusively?"

"I never juggled women," he said resolutely. "That's something you can take credit for—I heard what you had to say about guys in school who did that, and those words stuck with me. But yes, we had that conversation about a year ago and agreed to be exclusive."

"But there still wasn't talk of the *long-term*?"

"No," he said.

Lexie merely nodded, wondering if the woman truly hadn't wanted more—or had just known better than to ask for it.

"And then this woman got pregnant?" Lexie asked.

"First, she came here to take care of Mom at the end."

"From San Diego?"

"She was looking to make a job change, thinking that she might like to become a hospice nurse. She had a lot of vacation time coming, Mom was in a big decline and hospice had been recommended, so Adrianna offered to come here and stay. She said it would be a trial run to see if it was a change she really wanted to make—two birds with one stone. And my brothers and I paid her what we would have paid any private nurse."

"So it didn't seem like she was doing it because

she was more invested than you in the relationship—
it seemed career-motivated," Lexie said.

"Right. I came home on leave about the same
time Adrianna got here to help get her settled in,
and to introduce her to Mom and Big Ben. I had a
three-day leave, then I had to go back on duty, so
we had three days together—"

"And you found a way to get some privacy..."
Lexie filled in.

"And six weeks later, Adrianna called, told me
the doctor didn't think Mom had more than a few
days left, that I should put in for emergency leave.
And that she—Adrianna—was pregnant..."

"That was a double whammy."

"At that point, I was talking to Adrianna almost
every day on the phone for an update on Mom,
so I knew she was failing—that didn't come as
a shock. But the pregnancy news... I wasn't expecting that..."

"I imagine it was like a bomb dropping," Lexie
suggested.

"Oh, yeah..." he muttered as if experiencing the
shock all over again. "I had to get my bearings. In
the moment, all I said was that we'd talk when I
got home. That was where we left it."

He'd finished his sandwich and chips and set
his plate on the firepit. When he sat back again,
he was more angled toward her.

"I put in for emergency leave," he went on. "And

while I was waiting for that, I did a lot of thinking. Marriage wasn't in my plans, but if there was going to be a baby... I decided I was going to propose as soon as I got home—"

"Even though you didn't love her?"

Micah sighed. "You're right that I didn't love her. But I had feelings for her. I cared about her. And there was going to be a kid. *My* kid. I knew Adrianna was a decent person. I was going to make the best of it. I *would* have made the best of it."

He said that with so much conviction that Lexie didn't doubt him. He would have done his best to make the marriage work.

"Mom died before I could get back," he continued. "I got in the morning of the funeral. You can't propose at a funeral. I figured I'd wait for the dust to settle, then ask Adrianna to marry me."

His expression went dark. "Before I had the chance, Adrianna had her bags packed. She got me alone and said that she'd had the pregnancy terminated—and that she and I were done."

"Oh," Lexie said in surprise. "I was thinking that you might have been wrong about her, that maybe she did want something long-term, and was playing a waiting game until you got on the same page."

"You're not wrong. There was a waiting game— but it was one that my mother had changed. Adrianna said that when I didn't seem thrilled with the news, she started thinking back to what Mom had said while she'd been taking care of her. I guess Mom had talked about how proud she was of her sons for how we'd turned out, for how much we'd taken to heart what she'd tried to teach us about not letting anything or anyone stand in our way. Adrianna said she'd looked at our relationship, and how my priorities had been Marines first, the beer making and brewery plans second, and her a distant third."

"But that was how you'd laid it out from the beginning," Lexie said in his defense.

He nodded his agreement but it didn't seem to console him. "Adrianna said she'd been kidding herself, thinking things might be different with her and that I might change my mind about commitment. But after listening to what Mom had to say and reevaluating how things had been between us, she'd decided she'd never be my priority—and she didn't believe a baby would be, either. I was just too into my own stuff…" he finished, his voice filled with sorrow.

"That seems a little premature, though," Lexie felt compelled to say in his defense again. "It was a surprise when you got the news. A shock. Didn't she think she should give you a minute to let it sink in and *then* judge your reaction?"

"She said she didn't think she should bother," he said as if repeating his ex's argument.

"But it seems like she should have at least talked to you about ending a pregnancy before she did it," Lexie said quietly. "She should have given you the chance…a say…in the decision."

"Yeah, I did a lot of yelling about that, believe me. But it was too late. She said it had been about her body, her future, so it had been her decision. And part of that decision was to walk away from a relationship where she felt like an afterthought— and to decide against bringing a baby into the situation."

Lexie didn't know how much credence to give to the other woman's thinking. She hadn't known Micah as a marine, but she couldn't picture him as anything except dedicated—probably to the exclusion of all else. She'd seen his ambition for his brewery and knew it was strong. She *had* experienced the consequences of his self-interest of years ago. So she had to allow that the other woman might have had a point about him not making room in his life for anything else. It left Lexie not sure what to say.

Then Micah took a breath, exhaled with a humorless chuckle full of self-disgust and said, "The joke is, I'd been going along thinking I'd made so many strides since you. That I wasn't self-involved anymore…"

Lexie, having eaten enough herself, set her plate on the firepit with his, angling slightly more to face him then. "You hadn't misled her," she pointed out. "This time it was being honest about your plans and what you wanted that caused the problem."

"Yeah, I was riding my high horse thinking that as long as I was clear about what I wanted, what I was working for, I was covered. But I'd missed the second piece of the puzzle—mainly because I *was* so wrapped up in myself. I'd missed that going after what I wanted *without* ever taking anyone else into consideration was as big an issue as not being honest. Adrianna saw it, even if I didn't."

And he seemed to be beating himself up for it.

"I still hadn't learned," he said, "that what my Mom had pushed us to do could translate into just plain selfishness. And because of that, my baby didn't get to be born…"

"A baby you wanted?" Lexie asked softly.

He looked so sad it nearly broke her heart.

"I can't explain it," he said quietly, "but that baby was real to me. And yeah, I wanted it. Once the news sank in, I actually got excited about becoming a dad. Taking that away hit me harder than I ever would have thought it could…"

It wasn't something she would have predicted of him, either. She could hear in his voice that he felt responsible for that baby not being born and was carrying a heavy load of guilt. But once more she wasn't sure what to say.

Treading carefully she chose to say, "Having ambition and focus aren't *bad* things..." She'd often wished Jason had had more of both so he'd want to settle down and build a stable life for them.

"They aren't bad things until you take them to the extreme and they hurt people—like you. They aren't bad things until you can't see beyond them and they cost you your kid," Micah countered.

Lexie wondered if this new realization was a factor in why he was so diligent about helping with the house repairs. But all she said was, "Not getting to become a dad when you discovered that you wanted to was a pricey lesson... I'm sorry."

"Yeah, me, too," he answered. Then, as if he were trying to put a stop to the melancholy atmosphere, he concluded in a lighter vein. "It's just messing with me today."

Lexie wanted to move the subject away from topics that were obviously hurting him, so she smiled and said, "I thought it was my fault so I guess that shows that sometimes none of us can see beyond ourselves."

"Why would you think my lousy mood was your fault?"

Oh. Yeah, that was a reasonable question...

That she didn't want to answer.

Hoping to distract him, she reached for the bakery box, opened it to offer him a cupcake and said, "Chocolate is comfort food..."

He took one out of the box and so did she.

Once it was eaten, Micah gave a rave review of the blend of his stout with the best cupcake he claimed to have ever eaten.

But as glad as she was to hear more enthusiasm in his voice now, it still didn't keep him from going back to that question when they'd finished the cupcakes.

"How could my mood have been your fault?" he reiterated.

Lexie made a face, still hoping to avoid answering.

"Come on—did you do something?" he cajoled. "I'm always the bad guy who has to admit it. If it's your turn, man up," he challenged, relaxing back into the sofa's cushions and stretching an arm along the top edge.

Lexie realized he wasn't going to let her off the hook.

Hating herself for having gotten into this, she sighed before she said, "It was about last night... I shouldn't have...done what I did—"

"Kissed me?" he said, relishing it.

"Yes. And I thought you were stressed out trying to find a way to tell me not to do it again..."

He laughed. Which was a positive change even if she wasn't thrilled that it was at her expense.

Especially since she found herself thinking that he was a man of the world now, while her experience was far more limited. Maybe the kiss that had seemed incredible to her had been barely mediocre to him.

"No, you shouldn't have kissed me," he confirmed when his laughter calmed. "I was close to kissing you and trying to stop myself and you blew that. And then you rocked my world with that kiss and that wasn't fair."

Rocked his world?

So not barely mediocre, after all.

That boosted her confidence.

"*I* rocked your world?" she repeated.

"You were there, right? That was *some* kiss..."

"I thought so..." That had slipped out. "But why wasn't it fair?"

He was serious again but he wasn't brooding any longer, instead he just sounded like he was being sensible. "For me, a kiss like that is the start of something, Lexie," he said. "But for you... What was it?"

"Something I wanted to do and I *couldn't* stop myself..." she confessed.

"It wasn't just you launching yourself out of the marriage gate onto somebody familiar and safe?"

"*Safe?* You? The bad boy of the group? The guy who—"

"Somebody you're safe from any risk of having feelings for," he clarified.

Safe from having feelings for?

That surprised her but it shouldn't have. Until recently she might have said that herself.

But now?

"Actually, *not* being safe from that is on the list of reasons why the kiss was...unwise..." she said softly. "And I wasn't *using* you," she added more firmly since it seemed as if that was part of his concerns, too.

He studied her for a long moment before he said, "So you're *not* safe from having feelings for me?"

She shook her head no but that was as far as she was willing to go.

He went on studying her as if to convince himself that was possible. Then he said, "I guess I had some of my own flashback cautions..."

"I'm not sure what a flashback caution is..."

"The old days make it hard for me to believe that that kiss meant as much to you as it *could* mean to me if I let it..."

"So you didn't let it mean anything to you?" she asked, challenging him this time.

"I've been trying not to..." he answered with a half smile, lifting his hand from the back of the seat to run the side of his index finger along her cheek.

It was so nice that she had to fight the urge to nuzzle into it.

"We do have that history..." he went on quietly. "Plus, you're pretty fresh from being locked into the same guy since we were kids... Seems kind of *unsafe* for me to be on the other side of both of those things..."

"Oooh, so kissing me is dangerous for you... For the big, tough, worldly marine," she joked.

"Sooo dangerous," he said without any levity at all.

Lexie curbed the teasing.

"I don't know what's going on here," she admitted. "And it's strange for me, too. You were one of my best friends. Then you were someone I *hated* for years. Now...you're something else... I keep looking for that shallow, selfish, superficial guy you've been in my head for all these years and instead I just find a guy who isn't any of those things anymore. A guy who's grown up. Who's—"

"Getting to you?" He asked that as if he liked the possibility.

She only conceded to it by raising her eyebrows before she went on. "As for me being fresh out of marriage... I've still been around the block, you know? And my marriage should have broken up a long time ago when I started being unhappy with it. I'm a little ashamed to admit it, but I'm more relieved to have it over with than grieving the end of it…"

She paused, sighed again, then forged on, "The one thing I know for sure is that whatever is happening with you and me doesn't have *anything* to do with the past, and it definitely doesn't have anything to do with Jason."

She wasn't sure why she'd been as candid with Micah as she had been.

Except maybe because it was all true—and his honesty with her about the baby seemed to call for some honesty of her own.

She tried to lighten things again and said, "But if you want to run and hide, I'll understand."

"If I had any sense at all…" he said in a too-sexy voice, his eyes delving deeply into hers.

He stopped stroking her cheek and instead slid his hand to the base of her neck, under hair she'd set free in the car from the bun it had been in all day, bringing her slightly toward him as he leaned in and kissed her.

A kiss that kicked off with an instant bang.

His lips were parted and there was something so innately sensual in them that her own lips had to part, too, had to meet and welcome his tongue when it came.

His hand rose into her hair, cradling her in place as that all-consuming kiss swept her away.

Giving as good as she was getting, she laid her

hands on his pectorals, reveling in that first feel of the muscles she'd been admiring for days.

But rather than soothing her craving, it only whetted her appetite, and when his other arm went around her, pulling her nearer, she took the opportunity to put her arms around him and slide in closer.

The kiss became a plundering of mouths that was arousing feverish things in her. Her back seemed to arch on its own, her breasts yearning for him, for contact with him, straining for it.

And with a mind of their own, too, her hands slipped under his sweatshirt.

Warm and oh-so-sleek over oh-so-many muscles, she reveled in the feel of that solid wall of strength, in the breadth of those shoulders that seemed to go on forever.

But as good as it was to have her hands on his bare skin, it only made her want his hands on hers.

Her front was already plastered against his, her nipples pressed into him, sending their own signal through the thin white blouse she had on. But he didn't seem to be reading the signs.

Or was he still lost in those flashback cautions?

She took a deep breath to expand her chest into his at the same time she opened her mouth a little wider, let her tongue be a little braver and upped the sex quotient of that kiss.

He answered by showing her how it was really

done—almost making her melt—but still he didn't take his hands from those safe spots behind her head and on her back.

Maybe he'd learned some lessons too well...

But he was driving her to distraction, raising a need in her so fierce and overwhelming that she was nearly out of her mind. She started considering physically grabbing his hand and repositioning it on her breast if that was what it took to give him the go-ahead...

A sound rumbled in his throat that made her think he was giving in to something. While the hand on her back stayed in place, the one in her hair took a slow descent down to the outer curve of her breast.

More, more, more!

Lexie inhaled again, expanding into that testing hand on her side.

He appeared to take that as the permission he'd been waiting for, because he brought his hand the rest of the way around to cup her breast. And when she breathed out again it ended up sounding like satisfaction.

But that seemed to unleash him because he stayed only briefly on the outside of her shirt before he had the buttons unfastened and his hand not only deliciously inside her blouse, but under the cups of her bra, too.

And oh, what an adept hand it was...

Big and strong and gentle, he kneaded that tender flesh, circling and tugging and teasing her nipples, turning her to mush, making it impossible for her to think about anything but what he was doing to her.

It was the lower half of her body that went into motion then. One of her jean-clad legs went over his thick thigh and her hips arched in his direction in response to even more hungers coming to life in her.

His hand left her back then to clasp her leg and pull her closer still, not fully on his lap but not far off before giving the same attention to her rump that the other hand was giving to her breasts.

But just when Lexie was pondering tearing off his sweatshirt, he began to slow things down.

He let go of her derriere.

He eased her leg off his.

He repositioned her bra and refastened her blouse even as he cooled off that kiss until it was more sweet than passionate.

And then he stopped even that.

He blew out a long deep breath that somehow sounded as if he were conceding to something really difficult to accept, dropped his forehead to the top of her head and said, "So one of the things I've learned the hard way is that I can't just give in to everything I want when someone else is involved, too…"

He sat up straight. Lexie had the impression that he was shoring up his resolves.

Then he went on, "Right now, what I want is you. In the worst way... And it's not that I don't believe all you said a few minutes ago, but I can't let this go any further until I know you've had time to make sure it's what you want, too. Absolutely, without a doubt, and for no reason other than the fact that you want me as much as I want you..."

"What if I say—"

"Uh-uh," he vetoed before she could say more. "I mean it, Lexie. I have to know that I'm not stacking the deck in any way. That what *I* want is second to what you want."

His hands were loosely around her waist, but he took them away and deflated back against the sofa, putting even more space between them.

"Now do me a favor and go the hell up to bed so I can have a few minutes to pull myself together..."

Lexie tugged at her bottom lip with her teeth, wanting to kiss him again, wanting his hands on her again, wanting him.

But not wanting to ignore what he'd said, because she knew he was right—she *did* need to consider what she was doing.

So she steeled herself against the urges of her body and stood up to go.

Before she could, though, those urges got the

better of her—just a little—and she paused, bent over and kissed the tip of his shoulder.

Then without looking to see if that had even registered with him, she went inside, through the kitchen and upstairs to her room.

All the while wondering how exactly she had come from being friends with Micah and then hating Micah to wanting Micah so much she ached...

Chapter Eight

"Are you afraid he's going to sneak a free cupcake?"

"What?" Lexie asked Jill late on Saturday afternoon.

Lexie and Micah had been together running Micah's booth at the food festival all day. Periodically they'd given each other a break. Lexie was taking one then, sitting on a bench under a tree in Merritt's town square with her friend while Jill's husband was off somewhere else at the festival with the kids.

"You're watching that booth like a hawk," Jill explained. "Or is it Micah you're watching? Last time we talked, you told me you were not a *fan* of Micah Camden and you were sure that nothing would change that. But look at you now, getting an eyeful…"

"I was just watching the booth to see if my cupcakes are selling and if there are more people than he can handle," Lexie claimed.

"Bull," Jill countered, clearly not fooled. "Has he started *handling* you?"

Oh, boy, has he…

And Jill was right, she *had* been staring at Micah. All day long. Every chance she had. She was definitely having trouble taking her eyes off him.

But rather than admit anything she glanced over her shoulder to make sure no one had overheard her friend's lascivious question. "Jill! Shhh…"

"Nobody's listening. But come on, what's going on with you two?"

"We're just working the booth together."

Jill laughed. "Uh-uh. You've joined the fan club," she concluded. "How'd that happen?"

Denial wasn't working so Lexie gave up on it. "I don't know," she said. "But I wouldn't say I'm a *fan*, just that… I don't know… I guess maybe I'm coming to better grips with the past…"

"By *gripping* him?"

"No!" Not that she wasn't thinking about it.

And thinking about it, and thinking about it, and thinking about it…

"It would make such a nice story," her friend suggested. "Childhood best friends hit a rocky road in their teens, go their separate ways, take some hard knocks, then come together again and find true, everlasting love with each other."

"We're just hanging out—admittedly more amicably—and selling beer and cupcakes out of the same booth," Lexie contended.

"Sure you are," Jill said sarcastically. Then, glancing at Micah herself, she said, "Do you like the way he looks better with scruff or without scruff?"

Micah was clean-shaven today—the first time Lexie had seen him that way since she'd been back. It had been a surprise this morning and yes, that had been part of her study of him as the day had gone on—trying to decide which look she preferred.

"I don't think it matters," she said, giving her final verdict. He was hella-handsome with and without—more rugged-looking with, more businesslike without, but equally as hot either way. "He did it so he'd look more professional," she explained, sharing the reason he'd given to her.

"Did you watch?"

"Watch him shave? No!" Although it was an interesting idea that Lexie hadn't thought of before.

"I like to watch Anthony shave," Jill said. "It always gets me going."

Lexie laughed and shook her head at her friend's outrageousness.

"How about you," Jill asked then. "Did you like to watch Jason shave?"

"No," Lexie said honestly. "He always had that smooth baby face, you know? His beard never came in in more than thin patches and even if he missed a day, you could feel it but you couldn't really see it."

But thinking about that, about her ex, Lexie thought about how little sex appeal he'd actually had in comparison to Micah—Micah, who seemed to exude it from every pore.

Jason's build had stayed boyish, skinny even. His biceps hadn't looked much different than Lexie's.

But still she'd found him appealing because she'd loved him.

Now, with Micah, the physical attraction was monumental, but her feelings were more confusing.

"With Anthony, what came first for you?" she asked her friend. "Sex or love?"

Jill laughed again. "Sex," she said without hesitation. "Are you kidding? He's a big, brawny, beautiful fireman."

"You didn't have any feelings for him before you went to bed with him?"

"I did. I think I was on the brink of loving him and sex was what pushed it over the edge. Why? Are you thinking about sleeping with Micah?" Jill's voice was full of delight and titillation. Until, with shock, she said, "Or are you thinking you might be falling for him? Because that's more than just being a fan…"

"There's just a lot of stuff going on…"

"*Have* you slept together?"

"No."

"But you want to!" her friend said, sounding absolutely certain.

Lexie didn't answer that. But she was staring at Micah again because no, she couldn't take her eyes off him.

Not only was he clean-shaven today, but he had on dress slacks and a crisp pale blue shirt with the sleeves rolled to his elbows. The dressier style smoothed some of his edges and gave him a dashing look that was irresistible.

And yes, she did want to finish what they'd started the night before.

She just didn't know if she should…

"Want my two cents' worth?" Jill said.

Lexie laughed. "Like I could stop you."

"If you even *think* you might be falling for him and if you're even *entertaining* the idea of sleeping with him, you have *got* to do it, Lex."

Lexie laughed at her friend's forceful declaration. "Not a question in your mind, huh?"

"And if Micah wants to, too, that makes three reasons why you'd better do it."

"How do you figure?"

"It's the only way to give you both the whole *present-day* picture and a reality check," Jill decreed authoritatively.

"Still not sure what you're getting at," Lexie said.

"I'd say look at him, but you're already doing that," her friend began, "but first of all, he's just one great big tower of sexy, gorgeous guy now. So it's no wonder he's got you all churned up. You have to get that out of your system before you can know how much simple attraction might be coloring things for you. And only when you've done that will you be able to judge what it is you're really feeling for him—are you genuinely falling for him or do you just need some close-order drill with him. That's what solved it for me with Anthony— I just wanted him so much I couldn't be sure if it was because he was such a hunk or because he was such a hunk *and* I loved him."

"Okay, that's one," Lexie said, seeing some sense in that.

"Two, it isn't only your current feelings that could be clouded by the churned-up thing," Jill contended. "There's senior year and what Micah did, too. The only way you're going to be able to judge if you've really forgiven him for that or if the churned-up thing has just thrown a tarp over it, is to get the churned-up thing calmed down. Once it is, the tarp will get pulled away and you'll see if you still resent Micah underneath it."

Also reasonable.

"And three?"

"There's Micah's side. His feelings for you when we were kids had to have been *extreme* for him to do what he did. There could be some flicker of that old flame and he could be carrying around a teenage fantasy of what finally having you would be like. You want—and need—that worked out of *his* system so he's only left with present-day reality, too."

Also reasonable.

But none of it romantic.

"You definitely know how to make a clinical case for doing it," Lexie said.

And how to cool her off in the process.

"I'm just saying there's a lot to sift through between the two of you and I think sex might be the tool for the job."

"Still clinical, Jill," Lexie judged.

But she had to admit that her friend had made some decent points.

And had given her more to think about...

* * *

"Oh! Hey…"

When Micah appeared from inside the house at the back door late Saturday night, Lexie was sitting where they'd had dinner the night before—on the curved wicker sofa at the fire pit.

"Hi," she returned. "I heard fireworks going off when I got out of the shower," she said, pointing at the sky to explain what she was doing out there.

"Yesterday was the last day of school for seniors around here. I heard the Cartwright twins had a big party planned—fireworks included," Micah informed.

"They're putting on a good show. Come watch."

"I'll be right there," he promised, disappearing in the direction of the sunroom.

The food festival had gone on until ten o'clock. They'd both needed to arrive separately in the morning and also had to go their own ways when it was over—Micah loading kegs and equipment into his truck to return to the brewery, Lexie needing to take borrowed display towers, trays and racks back to the bakery and wash them before she could drive home in her own car.

It had been a long day and with Micah still in the brewery when she got home, Lexie had headed upstairs to take the shower she had been dying for after so many hours outdoors.

She could have just gotten into bed when she'd

finished that but instead she'd blow-dried her hair, applied a hint of color to her cheekbones and a thin line of eyeliner to her lids.

Then, rather than putting on pajamas, she'd opted for something between those and street clothes—a lounging set made up of a charcoal colored V-neck T-shirt over a pair of lighter gray shorts—both of them loose-fitting and not at all sexy.

It was the lace demi-cup bra and matching bikinis underneath that provided the sex appeal. Just in case...

And it *was* just in case because after spending the entire day with Micah, there was no indication that last night had ever happened. There hadn't been a single mention of anything. There hadn't been any meaningful glances. Any fleeting touches or brushes against each other. There hadn't even been any bantering between them.

And not just because there were other people around. Even in the lulls between customers when they'd been alone, things had been purely cool and detached. If anything, Micah had deliberately busied himself as far away from her as he could get.

Things had been so impersonal that she'd begun to wonder if *he'd* thought about last night with a cooler head and talked himself out of taking it any further.

So a very casual, very loose T-shirt and shorts made up her outfit of choice.

With some underwear that could be a potential surprise or remain her secret forever.

Besides, what Jill had said *had* cooled *her* off some.

The idea that Micah could be working out an old fantasy was haunting her. Especially if that meant the fantasy might be put to rest for him once and for all as soon as it was fulfilled.

So all the way around she thought it was better to be cautious tonight.

Micah was gone only a few minutes before he reappeared at the back door and came outside to join her.

Sneaking a peek at him from the corner of her eyes, Lexie saw that his hair was shower damp, and he'd shaved again so his face was still completely clear of scruff.

He wasn't in pajamas, either—instead, wearing his well-worn jeans and yet another navy blue crewneck T-shirt with the Marine insignia. Unlike what Lexie had changed into, though, his T-shirt fitted him like a second skin and nearly made her mouth water.

Which was why she determinedly directed her view back to the fireworks.

Only comments about those fireworks passed between them until the lights in the sky ended in several overlapping bursts, and the far-off sound of clapping and whistling came from the neighboring farm.

"That was a nice end to today," Micah noted, angling toward Lexie and again laying one arm across the top of the sofa's back.

"So," Micah said then. "We emptied every keg, sold every case of beer and every cupcake, and still had folks wanting more when we were closing up at the end. I'd say that means we did pretty well today."

"I think we did great," Lexie chimed in.

"Did it convince you to buy the bakery?"

"I was pretty convinced before, but it definitely helped—along with all the enthusiasm for my baking... I forgot how news travels here. I didn't think anyone knew and instead everyone did."

"Small towns," Micah said. "But having everyone hoping you *do* buy the bakery is better than having everyone telling you not to."

"True. I think I'll talk to Nessa on Monday about the financing. Either way, after working there yesterday, and today's festival, I'm sure it's what I want to do."

"Good for you!"

"And today was good for you," she pointed out. "You even got interviewed by a network news crew!"

"The marketing people for Camden Superstores

arranged that. It was the first in a bunch of things they have set up to get the word out for the launch of the stouts in the stores."

"Are you going to be ready for that soon?"

He let out a worried sounding laugh. "I hope so. We're working hard to be."

"But you're still experimenting with the flavored stouts. And we never got to the tasting you wanted me to do last night."

"That's okay. The first launch is just for the plain ones, anyway. The flavored ones will be a second wave so they can get highlighted on their own. And you can do the tasting tomorrow." He raised the index finger that was near her shoulder and tapped her. "That reporter loved your cupcakes, too," he reminded.

"She bought a whole dozen," Lexie said, having been pleased by that. The food festival had been one big reunion, bringing out a constant stream of familiar faces. And while Lexie hoped those familiar faces had purchased the cupcakes because they wanted to, and given compliments they meant, it was a little hard to know for sure. Friends and acquaintances of hers, of Micah's, of her parents', of Gertie's might have just been buying and complimenting out of kindness. But she could rely on the opinion of a network news reporter who was a complete stranger.

"And her photographer bought another dozen, didn't he?" Micah added.

"Along with *two* cases of beer," Lexie pointed out.

Micah's grin showed how happy that had made him. "I think we both did okay," he concluded.

Since he seemed ready for a change of subject Lexie nodded at his clean-shaven face and then at his chest stretching the knit of his T-shirt. "And then there was you… No beard and all dressed up in clothes that weren't military issue?"

His grin this time showed some humility. "I told you I shaved so I'd look more businesslike. And I sank every penny I have into the brewery when I got out of the Marines. I couldn't spare much for civvies so my closet is all military issue until I'm making some money. Those pants and that shirt were an investment for me."

"Well, it payed off—you looked great all business-manned-up."

His eyes dropped for a mere second to what she was wearing and he said somewhat under his breath, "And you look great right now…"

"Did I look bad all day?" she asked in mock offense.

"No, you looked good then, too. And every other day…"

So maybe he was starting things again?

If he was, Lexie wasn't sure she was ready for

it. Instead, she said, "So your plain stouts are ready to go, your flavored stouts aren't far behind, your brewery is up and running and now you've had your soft launch with publicity already started for the formal launch... You're on your way. What does your life look like in five years?"

He laughed wryly. "I haven't thought much beyond any of that."

But he looked off into the distance and seemed to give some thought to it now in order to answer her question.

After a moment, he said, "I'm in Merritt to stay. I like the brewery being out Gertie's back door and having her input, so as long as she'll have me and I can meet the demands of the superstores with this setup, I'd like to stay here."

He paused and seemed to be thinking more before he went on. "And I want to get married, have a family, build the kind of life I've seen people around here have."

After seeing his sorrow over almost becoming a father, that made sense. Plus, now that he'd left the Marines and had his life's goal underway, he was at that point in his timetable that allowed for it.

He looked back at her then. "What about you? What's your five-year plan?"

She laughed. "I have the plan for next week that I told you about—right now I'm just proud of that!"

He smiled but didn't push her for more. Instead,

he changed the subject again. "I couldn't believe Gertie came out today."

"With poor Mary pushing that wheelchair! I don't know if that was a good idea. I was glad when you offered to push it back to the apartment."

"After Mary had made the rounds to all the other booths and scored enough samples and tasters for two days," he said with another laugh. "Gertie said on the way back that they thought the wheelchair was actually going to be a help, making it easier to transport things home so they could really load up."

"I told them when I was there this morning before the festival started that I'd bring them whatever they wanted."

"They were afraid the elk chili would all be gone before you could score some. And they also wanted to get out and have a little while at the festival," Micah said.

"Against doctor's orders."

"Gertie didn't seem the worse for wear when I got her back."

Lexie could confirm that that was true because she had spent one of her early evening breaks at the apartment.

"Nobody's gonna keep her down, not even you," Micah warned.

"Or broken bones," Lexie said wryly.

"You gotta love her," was Micah's amused comment on that.

"I do. I just worry about her, too."

He nodded his understanding. "And how's Jill? The two of you were deep into talking about something…"

You…

Lexie decided to tell him, wanting to gauge his reaction. "She's wondering about you and me… wondering if you're playing out a teenage fantasy…"

He made an unpleasant face. "That's a revolting idea. And just FYI—the fantasies I'm having about you now are all brand spanking new." Then he seemed to think twice and said, "Is that why you're giving me a little of the cold shoulder tonight?"

"I'm not," she protested.

"A little," he persisted.

Because she hadn't flirted back with him a few minutes earlier? Or *had* something changed in her behavior toward him?

"You know," Micah said then, "puberty hormones are a funny thing. For me, they cropped up, aimed in one direction—at you—and after that… Will it piss you off if I say after that nothing mattered, not even you as a person?"

"Are you saying that I became a piece of meat to you?"

"That sounds bad! And no, that's not exactly what I'm saying. I'm saying that you became something I just *had* to have and it wouldn't have mattered if you robbed banks or kicked dogs or took candy from babies because it was an obsession. Like those weird red boots you wanted when we were sophomores—remember those?"

Lexie grimaced. "They were so horrible!"

"No argument here," he agreed. "They were some kind of cross between a cowboy boot and a combat boot—shiny red leather, pointy steal-tipped toes, studs up the sides, those soles—"

"Patent leather platforms," she named them for him.

"I always thought they should have come with a whip," he said, laughing.

Lexie made another face.

"But nothing any of us said about them changed your mind—you *had* to have them. You worked yourself to the bone flipping burgers, you nearly flunked biology because you were working too many hours to get homework done or study for tests. You spent a *fortune* on those damn things..."

All true. And yes, she remembered her obsession with them.

"You told us more than once how you saw yourself in those boots, walking down the halls of school in them—your Power Boots, you called them... You had some kind of fantasy about those boots, about yourself when you wore them, didn't you?"

She had, but she only acknowledged it with a raise of her chin.

"That was a teenage obsession, right?"

Another raise of her chin.

"And now? Are any of those fantasies about those red boots still alive and thriving in you?"

She didn't even like remembering those awful boots. "No," she admitted.

"So why would any fantasies I had then be any more long-lived than that? Believe me, I didn't set eyes on you at the airport and think, *Maybe now's my chance*," he said facetiously. "At first, when you got back to Merritt, you were just a bad page out of my past. If not for Gertie and what had happened here with the damage to the houses, I would have given you a wide berth."

Lexie recalled that he'd been more patient and friendly toward her than she'd been toward him at the start but she had to admit that there hadn't been anything that made her think he was angling for a second chance.

"Things just...*developed* from there," he went on. "You're different than who you were growing up, too. We're both whole human beings now—"

"As opposed to?"

"As opposed to two teenagers who were still

figuring themselves out. What's on my mind about you now has nothing to do with anything then."

"What *is* on your mind about me now?"

His smile was lopsided and sweet. "What I liked about you when we were kids is still there—your sense of humor, your boldness, that you never shrink from giving me a hard time. But now, I also see that you've suffered your own wounds and risen out of them. That you know your own mind. That you've circled back around to find a new place in Merritt the same way I have. That the things that are important to me are important to you, too."

She hadn't expected such a long list.

Then he paused, a flicker of wickedness coming into his eyes as he added. "And you're so damn beautiful I can't get enough of looking at you, and my hands are literally itching to run all over that body…"

And yet rather than reach for her he actually leaned slightly farther back, putting a few inches of distance from where his hand had been near enough to her shoulder to tap it earlier.

Then, without any guile or flirtation or insinuation at all, he said, "But…"

"But?" Lexie prompted when he didn't elaborate.

"Everything I said at the end of last night stands."

She knew what he meant. Last night he'd said

he wouldn't go any further until she was certain that it was what she wanted, too. And unless she convinced him of that, she knew he wouldn't make another move.

Since talking to Jill, she *had* thought more clearly. But as she took a long look at him, she went over it in her mind again just to be sure.

She thought about his first response to the suggestion that he might be acting on some long-ago fantasies—that it was *revolting*—and realized that that response had had the ring of truth to it.

She thought about those horrible red boots of hers, how much they'd dominated her image of herself and how far she'd come from what had definitely been a teenage obsession.

She thought about the fact that she was no longer the girl who young Micah had had a crush on—the girl who had been more outlandish, more outrageous just for the sake of getting noticed, of showing off.

None of that was a part of her now and she had to think that that teenage bravado in her had likely had a role in what the push-the-limits Micah had found appealing.

Of course, she couldn't know without a doubt what was in Micah's mind. She could only trust him—and herself. And when she analyzed what her instincts were telling her, she had her answer.

"What *were* your teenage fantasies about me?" she asked, letting a hint of flirtation seep into her tone.

He raised an eyebrow at her as if asking if she really wanted to know that. When she held her ground he said, "Actually they were almost more about me than you—I was pure ego then, you know? They were about me being your hero, rushing in to save you from peril, and you not being able to resist me from that minute on. Me strolling in in a new jacket that made me look like a tough guy and you getting turned on because I had so much more edge than nice-guy Jason..." He smiled at what he seemed to be recalling. "Me beating up some jerk for making fun of you in those red boots, you trading up to the stud who could take down guys like that for you. That kind of thing."

Lexie doubted those examples covered everything but she only said, "I think the red boots are still in Gram's attic—you want me to put them on, see if we can get someone to make fun of me so you can beat them up?"

He made two fists. "These are lethal weapons— I'd end up in jail," he joked.

But looking at the size of those fists, Lexie thought they probably could be lethal weapons.

And still all she really wanted was to have his hands doing more of what they'd done the night before. She snaked her fingers into his fists, between his fingers, and pressed her palms to his.

"Before I talked to Jill, I still wasn't thinking with a cool head," Lexie confessed quietly.

"But after?" he asked, tightening his grip on her hands.

"A whole lot cooler."

He nodded in a reserved way that told her that if she was telling him no, he would accept it.

"How about you?" she asked then. "Your head seemed pretty cool all day."

"Don't be fooled—things are still sizzling inside of me."

"That sounds painful," she joked with a smile she hoped was as wicked as his had been a moment earlier. Wicked and alluring...

"If you're not feeling the pain, too, I'm not budging," he challenged.

Knowing what she was starting here sent a shiver of anticipation through her. "I wouldn't call it pain exactly..." she mused. "But I do need something done about it..."

"Is that so?" he said with a deep chuckle.

"Any ideas?"

"A few," he tempted, using their entangled hands to pull her toward him.

Lexie thought he'd done it to kiss her but instead, with her face close to his, he looked intently into her eyes.

He must have been reassured by what he saw because his own eyelids lowered to half-mast and the smile that came along was happy and full of the promise of delight.

Then his supple lips parted, his head tilted and he kissed her. Chastely, tentatively, invitingly, but as if he were giving her the opportunity to still step away.

Which Lexie had no intention of doing.

She proved that by escalating their kiss, sending her tongue to do a little audacious flirting of its own.

She felt him smile at that. He let go of her hands and cupped both sides of her face as the kiss became open-mouthed and very, very steamy.

Her hands dropped to his thighs where she felt the massive muscles she'd only ogled in the past, working them just a little and thinking about that other part of him not so much farther up, raising her own desire another notch.

They went on kissing, mouths opening wider, tongues going from cat-and-mouse to thrust-and-parry. But hands stayed where they were, even though Lexie's need to feel those hands of his everywhere else grew and grew.

Micah ended the kiss and looked into her eyes again.

"You're sure about this?" he asked in a gravelly voice.

"I am. Are you?"

He laughed. "Yeah, pretty sure..." he understated, taking one of her hands in his and pulling her with him off the sofa.

"Upstairs or down?" he said.

"Upstairs but... I don't have any..."

"I put a few in my pocket earlier."

A few?

Oh...

"Then upstairs," she said with some laughter in her voice.

That's where he took her, leading her into her bedroom with moonlight's glow to brighten the space with a milky illumination.

It was enough to glisten off his dark hair and highlight that sculpted face when he spun her around into another kiss—this one sensual enough to keep her mouth captive and his hands free.

Hers went to his chest and his clamped around her upper arms, giving a massage similar to what she'd done to his thighs.

Then it was her shoulders he cupped and squeezed, her shoulder blades, lower on her back, lower still to her derriere...

His big hands were doing such wonderful things but as good as they felt right where they were, she wished he were doing those same things to breasts that were straining for him.

But in the meantime, she decided to satisfy another hunger and slipped her hands under his T-shirt to again lay her palms to his sleek skin, this time caressing the pectorals that had fed her own fantasies.

The problem with those tightly fitting T-shirts was that they were too constrictive and Lexie wanted him freed from that particular one.

So she raised her hands up to his broad shoulders, taking the shirt with them—breaking away from that kiss to pull it over his head.

She kissed him again, but not on the mouth. Instead, she pressed her lips to one of those pectorals before she veered back just enough to finally see his bare chest.

His oh-so-grand bare chest...

Micah used that opportunity to reach for the hem of her T-shirt and roll it upward, taking it off to drop to the floor with his.

With that gone, his hands came to her sides, the heels of them just barely riding the outer swells of her breasts. But tonight, it wasn't about needing encouragement. Instead, it was as if he were savoring every step, every moment on the way to the next.

And in the next moment, both of his hands cupped her breasts.

She wished she'd gone braless. Even the demicups felt like too much in the way of nipples that were screaming for the feel of his palms, for his fingers working her pliable flesh.

Then he abandoned her breasts altogether to unhook her bra and she got her wish.

Leaving one hand splayed against her back, his other returned to her breasts until her knees were weak.

He stopped then, scooped her up and laid her on the bed, leaning over to kiss her again while he slipped her shorts off and unfastened his jeans.

But he didn't remove them and Lexie wasn't letting *that* go on. She sat up enough to grasp his waistband.

Micah stopped her long enough to take protection from his jeans pocket and toss the packets on the bed before he let her dispose of the only thing he was wearing on the bottom.

Lexie couldn't help laughing to herself at the thought that he'd come prepared with a surprise of his own. Then she put an end to that kiss and fell back, allowing herself the opportunity to look at him in all his glory. To see if he was as magnificent everywhere as she'd imagined him to be.

There was no disappointment. He was even better than she'd guessed and that sight of him took her desire for him up to an entirely new level.

He removed her bikini panties, too, and indulged in just enough of a look at her naked body to bring a smile to his handsome face before he joined her on the bed and pure, primitive need was let loose.

His mouth found hers again and then deserted it for a breast that he engulfed in wet warmth while his hand kept the other one engaged.

Tugging at her nipple with careful teeth, flicking the tip with a pointed tongue, teasing and tormenting her. She tried to keep from writhing but couldn't.

Especially not when his other hand began to travel.

There was something extraordinary about how he touched her and kissed her, about everything he did—even in the muscular thigh that curved over one of hers and nestled up into the V of her legs.

Inhibition was gone but everything he did was slow and tender and alert to even the slightest response so he knew just how hard or soft, how long or short, how rough or how gentle to make every caress to maximize her enjoyment.

He wasn't lost in himself and his gratification, and instead was so in tune with her that he seemed to know what she wanted, what she needed, almost before she did. That was a first for her. A first that made everything so much more intense. So much better...

Not wanting to be the only one of them in the throes of such pleasure, though, she explored his body, reveling in all that smooth-silk-over-steel musculature before she reached for the long hard proof that he was as worked up about her as she was about him. She stroked him, hoping to drive him wild, too.

And if the guttural moan that rumbled in his throat was any indication, she succeeded.

His hand glided it down her stomach then and his knee freed the way for it to slip between her legs in its place. Her spine arched in reflex and her grip around him tightened just enough to elicit a flex in him as one finger found a path inside her.

The intensity of it stole her breath for a moment and made her writhe a little more with all he was arousing.

But as she approached a near frenzy of wanting him, he rolled over to find one of the condoms he'd thrown onto the mattress and use it. When he rolled back, he spread her thighs with his knee and repositioned himself between them, slipping something so much more substantial than his fingers into her instead.

A soft moan echoed in her throat as her hips angled upward into his. She clamped around him to hold him there in order to prolong how amazing it felt.

But there was only a momentary pause before the strength of his hips pulled out of that hold. Just far enough, just briefly enough to build her anticipation, only to delve back in even deeper.

Out again and then in deeper still, in and out,

every retreat, every return increasing the urgency in her.

Faster, harder, speed grew and Lexie kept up, clinging to his back, matching him until their bodies raced together to a peak that exploded in her like nothing she'd ever known, robbing her of every thought and leaving her held in exquisite suspension from time or place, where nothing existed but Micah and what he'd awakened in her.

Just as that started to decline, his climax hit. When he plunged all the way into her in his own explosion, she curled her legs around him to bring him as far into the core of her as he could go. At that moment, something that hadn't ever happened before struck her and she was carried away to a second pinnacle even better, stronger, longer lasting than the first.

A second pinnacle that—when it began to ebb—left her drained just as Micah's big body was settling atop hers.

For a while, neither of them moved, replete and speechless in the aftermath.

Then Lexie heard herself say in nothing more than a faint whisper of revelation, "Oh…"

"What? Did I hurt you?" Micah asked in alarm, raising to his forearms and lifting some of his weight off her.

"No," she assured him in a hurry. "I just didn't

know it could be like that…" Because it never had been before.

In response, he gave her a profound, meaningful kiss. Then he slid out of her, got off the bed and disappeared into her bathroom.

When he came back, he lay beside her, insinuated an arm underneath her back and brought her close to his side.

"Don't scare me like that," he said as if there hadn't been an interruption. "I thought I did something wrong."

Lexie could only laugh at that notion. "Mmm… according to the textbook *I* read, you did everything right. Really, really, *really* right…"

"Does that mean I get to do it again?"

Oh, definitely… she thought, hoping that his enthusiasm meant that her one-partner training hadn't disappointed him.

But what she said was a saucy, "Maybe. If you give me a minute to regroup."

"I'll need a little more than a minute but…not too much more," he answered tantalizingly.

His arm tightened around her while the rest of him relaxed, and her own body sank against his side, fused so perfectly there that it was as if she'd found her match.

That was also something new. Something unique. And so was the sense that she'd somehow landed exactly where she was supposed to be…

But even as that thought went through her mind exhaustion overcame her and she had to surrender to it.

Chapter Nine

"Where would Lexie have gone so early in the morning?"

Gertie's question was a good one. Micah had asked it himself, too—about a hundred times since waking up. Since waking up alone in Lexie's bed to the sound of her cell phone ringing on her night-stand after a night full of lovemaking and falling asleep with her beautiful body tucked safely in his arms.

Ordinarily, he was a light sleeper. But after the fourth time they'd made love, he'd conked out so soundly that somewhere between then—around 5:00 a.m.—and eight o'clock when Gertie had called, Lexie had slipped out of his arms, out of bed and out of the house without him having any inkling.

"And then there's you," Gertie said as if she was doggedly on the trail of a solution to a mystery. "Your stouts had their maiden voyage at the food festival and were a big hit. Your brewery is on its way. But instead of riding high today, you look like hell. I haven't seen you this down in the mouth since everything hit the fan when you were in high school."

Micah studied the television's remote control as if it held the solution to all the world's problems and didn't respond to the elderly woman's rant.

Gertie went on, anyway. "I thought you and Lexie were friends again. She's been so happy to be helping out with the flavored stouts until I can do it. She gives you credit for the bakery idea—it's all sounded good and it looked like you were getting along just fine yesterday. Did you have a fight or something last night?"

"No, we didn't have a fight." *Not in the slightest.* "We've been doing great." *Sooo great...*

Last night had been like no night, no day, no time he'd ever had with any woman anywhere. So great he'd never wanted it to end. So great he'd fallen asleep thinking he'd do anything to make it last.

Only to wake up and find Lexie gone.

But he was trying to keep Gertie from knowing he'd slept with her granddaughter so he said, "Maybe she went for a walk—"

"It's ten o'clock and you said she wasn't back when you left—she could have walked to Kansas by now!"

"Maybe she went to have breakfast with Jill. Maybe she needed to do something at the bakery—she used all of Nessa's stuff for her cupcakes, maybe she had cleanup she needed to go back to do—"

"Did she take the car or the truck?"

"I didn't notice," Micah lied. He knew Lexie had taken Gertie's sedan but he didn't want Gertie to realize he'd been paying attention to that. "Whatever she left to do, she just forgot her phone," he concluded. "I was in the kitchen when you called, I hollered for her but there was no answer, and I was afraid something might have happened with you, so I picked up…"

All but the locations of that account of events were true. Then, when he'd found out what Gertie needed and hung up, he'd searched everywhere for Lexie until he'd had to admit that she'd bolted.

"You didn't have to be so Johnny-on-the-spot for this. It wasn't that important," Gertie was saying. "We just needed somebody to fix our TV so it wouldn't be in Spanish—neither one of us could figure out how we did that…"

"I didn't want you sitting here alone, watching TV in Spanish while Mary went to church," Micah said just as he resolved the issue. Besides, once he'd known Lexie was nowhere to be found, he hadn't been able to calm down enough to sit still, so he had decided he might as well do what he could for Gertie.

"I don't like that Lexie doesn't at least have her phone," Gertie said, starting up again.

"Like I said, I'm sure she just forgot it and I'm also sure she's fine."

"I don't think you're sure about anything," the elderly woman said. "I think the two of you got into it and you don't want to admit it."

Got into it meaning that they'd fought, not the way they really *had* gotten into it, Micah thought.

"We didn't fight, Gert," he repeated honestly.

And apparently something about the way he said it tweaked something in Gertie because her eyes got very big before she said, "Ohhh…" as if light was dawning on something interesting and scandalous.

He thought he'd better get out of there before this got any worse.

"Your TV is fixed so I'm gonna take off. Unless you need me to do something else." He set the remote on the TV tray beside Gertie's wheelchair.

Her shock seemed to have passed because she was sitting there with a Cheshire cat grin on her lined face. "The two of you are *more* than friends," she deduced.

I guess not if Lexie ran out this morning...

"Is my granddaughter home in bed and you're letting her sleep off a big night?" the elderly woman said.

I wish...

The fallout he was suffering from Lexie leaving him high and dry must have shown on his face because Gertie sobered instantly with another far more ominous, "Ohhh..." Followed by, "Did she have morning-after remorse and run out on you?"

"Jeez, Gertie!"

But Lexie had definitely run out on him and morning-after remorse was exactly what he was worried about.

Along with the fear that the night they'd spent together hadn't meant to her what it had to him.

Along with wondering why the hell it *had* meant so much to him.

Along with so many whys...

"I don't know what's going on, Gert," he said then. "I don't know what's going on with Lexie. I don't know what's going on with me—"

"So something *is* going on between the two of you!"

"Gertie, you have to leave this alone. Please... We did *not* have a fight and whatever is going on we'll have to work out."

Unless they couldn't...

But he didn't want to think about that. He *couldn't* think about that.

"Patience, Micah," Gertie advised then. "With beer and with Lexie..."

Because the ink was barely dry on her divorce papers. He'd been kicking himself all morning, thinking that maybe he should have bided his time. That maybe he *had* just been a rebound for her, a testing of her wings, a practice run to get her feet wet.

But then he was also remembering what he'd done that had hurt her when they were teenagers, what he'd done that had caused so much damage that she'd hated him for over a decade, and worrying that something about that had resurfaced and that she might not be able to forgive him for it.

And if that wasn't enough, he was remembering as well that she'd been fretting over the idea that he wanted her as a way of acting on that old crush—which had him wondering if he'd done something to make her think that last night *had* been about that.

He was just in a bad spiral, a bad headspace, and he didn't know what to do about it...

"I gotta go, Gert," he said. "I really do..."

He went to the apartment door.

"Micah!" Gertie said with the bark of a drill sergeant.

He stopped with his hand on the knob and looked over his shoulder at the woman he considered his friend and mentor, the woman he considered family.

"It'll work out," she said in a softer, more comforting voice.

He could only answer with a raise of his chin that pretended to believe her.

"When I see her, I'll tell her to call you," he promised.

"I know," the elderly woman said with the kind of confidence she'd always shown in him, even when he hadn't deserved it.

Appreciating that as much now as he had then, he left the apartment and got in his truck. But he didn't start the engine, he just sat there, looking around for any sign of Lexie, of the car she'd taken.

He didn't find a single one.

He thought about going to Jill's house. He thought about driving up and down every street of Merritt. He thought about going anywhere Lexie might have gone—about every pond, every lake, every field, every barn, every hangout they'd frequented as kids that she might revisit for who-knew-what reason.

And again he thought why, why, why hadn't she just stayed in bed with him...

Then Gertie's advice to have patience echoed in his mind and he decided not to do anything but go back to the house, hoping she might be there now, deciding to wait there for her if she wasn't. Regardless of how hard it would be for him to do that.

He turned the key in the ignition and pulled out of the parking spot, thinking that this was *not* how he'd pictured this morning when he'd fallen asleep a few hours ago.

But how could he have guessed this would happen after the night they'd had? When Lexie had been as into everything as he'd been? When she'd enjoyed it as much as he had—enough to instigate that fourth time herself. How could he have guessed this would happen when she'd curled up against him afterward as if it were where she'd been sleeping forever?

He *couldn't* have guessed this would happen—and he certainly *wouldn't* have guessed it when he'd been thinking that having her curled up against him was where he *wanted* her to sleep.

Every night from last night on…

No, this wasn't a twist he'd seen coming.

And it was like taking a battering ram to the gut…

"Okay, pull it together," he ordered himself as he turned onto the road that led out of town and toward the Parker farm.

It took him a few miles, a few deep breaths, a few reminders that he was a marine trained to handle anything, before he gained any kind of control over himself.

But when he'd managed that, it helped.

And he started to sort through his own thoughts. And feelings.

He hadn't been lying when he'd told Lexie that his old crush was long gone, long dead. It was.

But in its place was something else, he realized now. Something new. Something that had started the way the crush had but had become so much more.

He'd been determined *not* to flip that switch, not to let his feelings become more, become something potent and deep-rooted.

The trouble was he hadn't been able to keep that switch from flipping.

And now that it had, he knew that those feelings for her were *not* a schoolboy crush.

They weren't centered around him or his ego, they weren't superficial or fleeting.

They were definitely deep-rooted, they were intense, they were unshakable.

And they were very, very real.

"Oh, my God, Gertie, I'm in love with her..."

He pulled over to the side of the country road he was on and stared into space, lost in that recognition that rippled through him.

He was in love with someone who could have woken up this morning hating his guts again.

He was in love with someone who he suddenly knew without a doubt he wanted to spend the rest of his life with, who might want to never set eyes on him again…

Was this the universe doling out the ultimate punishment to him?

"It'd be a good one," he said. Because what could hurt him more?

He stayed there on the side of that road for a long time, torturing himself by mentally exploring what he now knew he wanted—in the same moment, he was sure he'd never have it…

First and foremost, he wanted Lexie. And not like he'd wanted her as a kid—not as a trophy, not as a victory over a competitor, not as the answer to his own self-centered fantasies.

He wanted her as his wife. The person he could build a life with, raise a family with.

He wanted her as his sounding board, his advisor—because even though their businesses were separate, they still made a good team when it came to hashing out problems, brainstorming, helping each other.

He wanted to always have that feeling he had every time she walked into a room—that feeling that there wasn't light or warmth until she was there with him.

He wanted to always have her hand to hold.

He wanted to always have her by his side to face whatever life threw at them.

And there was a really good chance that he

might never have any of that because, once again, he might be the only one of them to feel this way...

"Oh, Gertie, what the hell am I gonna do?" he whispered.

But as much as the drive to do something—*anything*—urged him to pull out all the stops, to go to any lengths, to hatch plots and ploys and strategies to get Lexie to be his, he sighed a deep sigh and resigned himself to doing nothing. To having that patience Gertie had told him to have. To hoping—and God help him, praying—for the best.

And to accepting her decision, whatever it might be—even if she decided she didn't want those same things with him.

There was that battering ram to the gut again...

Because never had he reached a harder decision.

But one way or another he was determined that, should he need to, he would see it through.

And that if Lexie hated him again, if Lexie didn't have the same kind of feelings for him that he had for her, if he could never have her, that's the way it would have to be.

He just didn't know how he would survive it...

Going home to face Micah was not easy.

Lexie had hoped that he might still be asleep, that he might not know she'd ever left. She'd hoped that she could sneak in the way she'd sneaked out, play it cool and that he'd never know the difference.

Instead, when she pulled up in front of her grandmother's farmhouse, he was standing on the front porch, leaning one wide shoulder against the porch post.

He was dressed again in camo pants, combat boots and a tan Marine-issue T-shirt, his biceps stretching the short sleeves taut, his muscular forearms crossed over his flat stomach. His striking face was once more stubbled with dark beard and he couldn't have looked more somber as he watched her approach. And still, to her, just that initial sight of him fed a craving in her.

"Hi," he greeted her, his tone full of questions.

"Hi," Lexie responded with some guilt in hers.

"Are you okay?"

It was nice that her well-being was the first thing he addressed. He didn't even sound angry, despite the fact that she'd so stealthily gathered jeans, a T-shirt and a pair of flip-flops to sneak out of the room like a thief in the night. She'd dressed downstairs and slipped away without leaving him any explanation. And after all their hours together before that, he'd earned better treatment.

"I'm okay…" she said without much certainty.

As she climbed the stairs to join him on the porch, he pivoted out of her way, his stance the same, just facing her rather than looking out at the road she'd driven in on.

"I just...uh...freaked out," she confessed when he left it up to her to make the next move.

"Okay," he said as if he were bracing himself. "You had regrets—"

"Regrets? No!" She'd been so lost in her own issues that it hadn't occurred to her that he might have thought she was sorry for last night.

"You *didn't* have regrets but you still took off?" he said as if that didn't make sense.

How much should she tell him? Should she tell him that by the time he'd fallen asleep this morning, in her mind they were a power couple—successful small-town business owners, married with two kids and a dog—and that she was mentally remodeling the little house to accommodate baby number three?

And that when she'd realized that's where her thoughts were going, she'd panicked?

That she'd panicked because she *hadn't* been able to convince herself that the idea was silly? Because it had struck her that that was all something she suddenly might actually want with him?

That she'd panicked because as irrational as part of her brain had told her it was, she still hadn't been able to *believe* it was irrational and instead had seriously considered waking him up and telling him?

That she'd only hesitated when it had occurred

to her that he might think she'd lost her mind to be leaping ahead that far after one night together?

She'd wanted so much, and feared his rejection so deeply, that she hadn't been able to stay with him.

That seemed like too much to say.

So she said, "I was thinking about the future. As if us having a whole future together was just the next step—after one night—and I was afraid I was getting carried away."

Micah nodded slowly, calmly. "And that freaked you out."

"Because, for all I knew, last night was a one-night stand—"

"Not if it's up to me it wasn't."

That was music to her ears but Lexie went on without saying that. "I was fast-forwarding too far and I needed the voice of reason from Jill to push Stop."

Another simple nod of acceptance. "And Jill said what?"

"A lot."

"A lot that was good or bad?" he asked.

It was beginning to sink in that he wasn't upset with her, that he just didn't understand what had happened. But he was trying to, even though it seemed as if she might have hurt him a little by running away. That made her more inclined to try to explain herself.

"Jill said a lot that was good *and* bad. A while ago, Gram made a comment about what was old being new again with us. Jill kind of said the same thing. She said that there was still the old relationship as a sort of foundation between us, so already thinking about the future after one night together didn't sound strange to her. And she said a lot of things about feelings, destiny…"

Jill had said that maybe reconnecting and finding their way back to being friends and then moving from that into what had developed now, into the feelings Lexie had for Micah, into feelings Jill was convinced Micah had for Lexie, was a sign that they were meant to be together. That Jason and the rift over the barn incident was just destiny's way of sending them each in different directions to learn what they'd needed to learn, to grow in ways they'd needed to grow so that they could come together at last as the people they were meant to be. She'd said that regardless of how they'd gotten here, regardless of how long it had taken, regardless of how bumpy the road had been, when it was right, it was right.

It had been what Lexie had wanted to hear, what she hoped was true.

"And the bad?" Micah prompted.

"She asked me if I really could put everything behind me. If I could trust you—" *and happily spend my life with you* "—or would it all come back when the bloom was off this new rose. She wondered if we might have a fight and there it would all be again…"

"Would it?" he asked in a quiet voice.

"I hated you so much, for so long…"

"I know. I deserved it."

"And I still hate that you did what you did. But now that I understand it…and now that so much time has passed…it's like a balloon that's lost all its air. And you're so different… You've changed so much…" In all the ways she'd taken note of since coming home. "Getting to know the man you are now just makes it more clear that you were a big dumb, misguided kid then. And since I don't see any of that kid in you now, I'm sure that when you make me mad, I'll be mad at you, not at that boy—unless you revert to being that boy…"

"I can guarantee the Marines left him in the dust."

She thought so, too, because from what she'd seen—from what she could see standing there in front of her at that moment—the cockiness was gone and in its place was a genuine strength, someone confident enough in himself not to have to prove anything.

He was a man whose hotheadedness had been replaced by tolerance.

A man who had gone from self-centered to caring and insightful and thoughtful enough to have had that picture frame fixed for her.

He was a man who had put aside himself and everything he was working so hard for to help with the house repairs because he'd given his word that he would.

A man who had listened to her and put his mind to the task of helping her find her way.

"I can believe that the boy you were is long gone," she said. "I expected the worst from you and waited and watched for it to show itself, but it just isn't there anymore."

And little by little, the man he'd become had won her over.

"What about the trust part of it?" he asked.

"I wouldn't have thought it was possible but somehow that's come along with it all," she said, having realized the previous evening that trusting him was what had allowed her to let down her guard enough to spend the night with him. That she never could have if she *didn't* trust him.

"Did Jill have more to say on the bad side?" he asked.

"She said, *what about kids,*" Lexie informed him. "She wondered if I had kids with you, would I look at you being a father to them and remember that what you did changed my relationship with my own dad."

Micah's handsome face sobered even more. "God, I never thought of that..."

"The voice of reason—that's why I needed to talk to Jill," Lexie said.

"Would it be bad?" he asked with dread in his tone, in his expression.

Lexie hadn't thought about the possibility, either. She'd only been thinking about how much it had impacted Micah to *not* have his baby born, and how touched she'd been by the story of it, how much she'd liked the idea of being the person to give him that family he knew he wanted now.

But when their friend had brought it up, she'd had to give it serious thought.

"What you did set the wheels into motion for what played out our senior year," Lexie said. "But when I really looked at it… All these years, it's been so much more neat and tidy to just wrap the rift with my dad into the package of blame I laid at your feet because what you did led to him finding out about Jason and me."

Micah nodded, accepting that blame yet again.

"But that's as far as your responsibility goes," she said then. "What really broke my dad and me apart was what I was doing…what Jason and I were doing. It was my own actions that disappointed my father, that made him look at me differently. I think I've taken the easy way out all this time by framing it as your fault. In all honesty, he probably would have found out sooner or later without you having anything to do with it. And he'd have felt the same way. Reacted the same way."

"So I get a little bit of absolution there?"

"You do. And I'm taking responsibility for what really set my dad off."

"And say you and I have kids…" Micah ventured cautiously.

The image of that, of Micah with a daughter she'd given him, brought some moisture to her eyes. "I'd try to make sure that you accepted it when your little girl grew up and wasn't just a little girl anymore," she said, sad that her father hadn't ever gotten to that point.

"Ah, Lexie…" Micah said, seeing the tears in her eyes. He pushed off the post with his shoulder and stepped closer, taking her into his arms to comfort her.

Again, he put her comfort first when he could have maintained his distance, could have agreed it was about time she let him off at least one hook and took some accountability herself, he could have been miffed at her for sneaking out on him.

No wonder she loved him. Now, today and from here on despite their history, despite the fact that this new chapter of their relationship had only just begun and she was relatively fresh from her marriage.

And even if it wasn't the same for him…

Because ultimately that had been what had really

sent her panic over the edge this morning—when she'd accepted that just because she'd developed feelings for him, it didn't mean he'd developed those same kind of feelings for her...

After a moment, Micah's arms around her loosened and he leaned back enough to look down at her again.

"Did Jill have any more bad things to say?"

"No." But even though their friend had bet her that Micah had fallen back in love with her, Lexie had been afraid to count on it.

Then he said, "It really shook me up when I found you gone this morning. But now that I know that it isn't because you went back to hating me—"

"No, not that..." she said wryly.

"It opened my eyes to some things, too... What if I said that as far as I'm concerned, you can go ahead and fast-forward for us all you want?"

Lexie merely raised her eyebrows at him, thinking it was time he did some of the talking, wanting to hear what he had to say before she revealed any more.

He went on to tell her about seeing Gertie this morning, about the fright he'd felt over finding Lexie gone. He told her it had led him to realize how he felt about her and all he wanted, too. It all sounded so much like what had sent Lexie into her tizzy that it almost made her smile.

"The crush I had on you passed and I've never

had another one—it really was a teenage thing. But I've also never felt before what I feel for you now—not about anyone," he said. "And something inside me just *knows* I'm only completely what I'm supposed to be when I'm with you…"

He sighed, dropped his head to the top of hers and seemed to gather strength before he said in a deep voice for her alone, "I'm in love with you, Lexie. I want to be your husband. I want to have kids with you. I want the rest of my life with you. But I want you any way you'll have me… If you need more time, I'll give you that. If you need space, I'll give you that." He paused and when he finished, his voice was even quieter, heavier. "But if you just don't feel the same way and you want me to step back and never bother you again…it'll kill me but that's what I'll do…"

Because he didn't know how she felt about him because she hadn't had the courage to be the first of them to say it.

"All the years with Jason, the divorce, feel surprisingly far away for me," she told him. "So I *sooo* don't want time or space," she said with a hint of a laugh, because even just the fact that his arms were loose around her put more distance between them than she wanted right now. "And I definitely don't want you to step back because I think that might kill me, too…"

He raised his head from hers and grinned down at her.

"Oh, thank God..." he muttered. And as if he'd been set free to say it with even more conviction, he said, "I love you, Lexie. Will you marry me?"

Relief washed over her. "I love you, too, Micah. And I will marry you."

His grin grew wide enough to put creases at the corners of those stellar blue eyes. "And promise me you will *never* make me wake up and wonder where you are again."

"Scared you, huh?"

"Terrified me. I was worried you really might be just using me."

"Well..." she teased as if that were even a possibility. The truth was that making love with him had been so tremendous she couldn't imagine never doing it again.

"Okay," he played along. "Use me all you want."

"Oh, I intend to," she assured him. His grin went even wider just before he gave her a kiss that seemed to claim her finally, once and for all, as his own.

It ended far too soon.

"But right now you need to call Gertie and let her know you're home and everything with us has smoothed out," he said.

"Tell me the truth—you just want me in order to get to my grandmother," Lexie joked again.

"Well…" he answered in the same teasing tone she'd used before. Then he said, "I'm all for the package deal."

But he delayed that call just a little longer by kissing her again.

And as Lexie indulged in it, in no hurry to do anything else, she marveled at where she was and who she was with—and how much she honestly did love this man.

This man who had somehow gone from the boy who had done her wrong to the person she couldn't imagine herself ever living without.

* * * * *

MILLS & BOON

Coming next month

ITALIAN ESCAPE WITH THE CEO
Nina Milne

'What's wrong?'

'Nothing. Just keep talking. But I think we've been spotted.' Out of the corner of her peripheral vision, she saw someone point at their pod, camera in hand. 'We *have* been spotted.' Her mind went into overdrive, on automatic she appraised the scene. Champagne, private pod, the whole thing shrieked of date night. This was the perfect set up for a launch of their relationship, discovered by accident, it would reek of authenticity.

Instinct took over; and leaning over she kissed him; her intent had been a simple quick featherlight brush of the lips but she hadn't bargained for her body's reaction. Or his. Because it wasn't enough, the sheer giddy sensation whirled her head. After a first startled second where he froze, he turned his body, raised his hands and cupped her face in his hands, the firm cool grasp made her catch her breath.

Then he deepened the kiss, slowly languorously as if they had all the time in the world and Ava forgot where she was; forgot everything except this heady moment in time where nothing mattered except the sweet sensations that glided through her whole body. Then all too soon it was over, the wheel literally stopped turning and Ava realised they were near the top.

As she pulled away she caught sight of his expression, knew it mirrored her own. Shell shock, surprise. All wrong screamed the one bit of her brain that was still in gear. Pull this together. Seamlessly she pulled a smile to her lips and whispered. 'Don't look surprised.' Knew that a photo like that splashed on social media would give away too much.

To her relief Liam got it instantly, leant forward to hide his expression, looked as though he were whispering sweet nothings in her ear and then he moved away to pick up the champagne bottle to top up their glasses, a smile of sorts on his lips.

Ava focused on breathing, sipped the champagne, wished it were the bubbles that were swirling her head rather than the aftermath of the kiss. 'Sorry. I reacted on instinct – I saw an opportunity to make this look real and I took it without thinking.'

'There's no need to apologise – you took me by surprise that's all.' With an obvious effort he cleared his throat, brought his voice to a normal tone. 'What do you think will happen now?'

Continue reading
ITALIAN ESCAPE WITH THE CEO
Nina Milne

Available next month
www.millsandboon.co.uk

COMING SOON!

We really hope you enjoyed reading this book.
If you're looking for more romance, be sure to
head to the shops when new books are
available on

Thursday 21st January

To see which titles are coming soon, please visit
millsandboon.co.uk/nextmonth